BETHLEHEM PUBLIC LIBRARY
3 3150 002325
P9-DYY-379

Inspired Sleep

A NOVEL

Robert Cohen

SCRIBNER
New York London Toronto Sydney Singapore

SCRIBNER
1230 Avenue of the Americas
New York, NY 10020

This book is a work of fiction. Names, characters, places, and incidents either are products of the author's imagination or are used fictitiously. Any resemblance to actual events or locales or persons, living or dead, is entirely coincidental.

DESIGNED BY ERICH HOBBING

Set in Garamond No. 3

Manufactured in the United States of America

3 5 7 9 10 8 6 4 2

Library of Congress Cataloging-in-Publication Data

Cohen, Robert [date],
Inspired sleep: a novel/ Robert Cohen.
p. cm.
1. Sleep disorders—Fiction. 2. Women—Fiction. I. Title.
PS3553.O4273 I57 2001
813'.54—dc21
00-057337

ISBN 0-684-85079-6

The Old Mistakes and *The Fickle Gods* were previously published in slightly altered form in *Ploughshares* and *New England Review* respectively.

"Neither thought nor emotion can occur without some chemical change. The cruelty of the tyrant, the compassion of the saint, the ardor of lovers, the hatred of foes, all are based on chemical processes. However hard we may try, however earnestly we may wish to do so, we cannot separate mind from matter or isolate what we call man's soul from his body."

DR. ROBERT DE ROPP, *Drugs and the Mind*

"If a man could pass thro' Paradise in a Dream & have a flower presented to him as a pledge that his Soul had really been there, & found that flower in his hand when he awoke—Aye! and what then?"

COLERIDGE

I

The Old Mistakes

ALL AFTERNOON there had been a chilly, puttering rain. Now, though the clouds had torn open with the onset of dusk, Bonnie could feel the dampness lingering in her sinuses, smudging the lines of the road ahead. Perhaps she was coming down with the flu. She hoped so. Stuck in rush-hour traffic, daylight failing, the tinny and diminutive roar of the heater her only comfort, she conceived an alternate vision of herself dozing in bed, sipping fatty soups, and acting generally like the pampered creature she was destined, but for circumstance, to be. Oh God, she hoped to hell it was the flu. But she did not really think it was.

On the radio, a voice was pleasantly droning out the closing prices of shares. Some were up, some down. For all her education she could not have said why.

It had been her intention to take a shortcut to the meeting, avoiding the traffic on Massachusetts Avenue by routing through the flatlands of Somerville, but due to some new phase of construction or demolition on the roads, this had turned out to be an error. And now she was stuck. On Beacon Street the cars were inching forward. Brake lights glowed like embers in the mist. They might have been spelling out a code, a dimly luminous fragment of instruction, but whatever it was she failed to read it through the fog-smothered windshield.

Slowly the city ebbed past. A black statue, an idling milk truck, a dry fountain in a vacant square. A dog lay facedown in the stiffening grass, limbs twitching spasmodically from some febrile dream.

Bonnie yawned. She herself had lost the talent for sleep, the nocturnal equipment. Lately four hours in a row was a signal event. More often it was three. Her friend Suzette, an ardent interventionist in these matters, had recommended Ativan, but Bonnie, for reasons that were not entirely clear, had to this point resisted. Now for all she knew it was too late. The long blue nights had torched her nerves. Her head felt fried, its gray matter calcifying; her eyes, scooped and raw, rattled around irritably in their sockets. These days even when she didn't have an actual headache she felt as if she had one. And today she actually had one. Which meant, she thought crabbily, that she was currently entertaining *two* headaches: the usual one, plus this other one, which was not in truth so unusual either. Plus a third that came from performing all this pointless math on the other two. Or was it just one enormous ache?

However you added it up, the pain was debilitating, so she tried as she drove to affect some relief. She massaged her temples with the balls of her thumbs. She listened to a tape of light, noodling piano jazz. She performed several deep-breathing exercises. When it became clear that none of these remedies would make, would ever make the slightest bit of difference, she began to fish around in her shoulder bag for the echinacea and zinc tablets Suzette, who had moved to Vermont with the man of her dreams—the absence twitched inside her like a phantom limb—had also counseled her to carry, but which as yet, it seemed, she did not. Just as well. Her stomach wouldn't have been able to handle them anyway.

Her stomach, as it happened, was in arguably the least presentable shape of all her essential organs. Queasy and capricious, it was running through its full repertoire of post–red meat convulsions, attempting to cope with the enormous trapezoidal hamburger Alex, her eleven-year-old, had—as he did every second Tuesday of the month—overcooked for her, and which Bonnie, standing at the sink with her coat on, staring dolorously into the charred, soapy skillet, had bolted down in record time. Alex's hamburger, truth be told, had tasted pretty good. She regretted it now, of course, on her way to the meeting. But it appeared that was her character, if not her fate: to do and to regret.

"When's Cress coming?" Alex had asked, watching her eat.

Bonnie checked her watch. "Ten minutes ago. As usual."

"It's not fair. Why can't we stay alone?"

"Because you can't."

"Why not?"

Bonnie allowed her eyes to close just for a moment, savoring the delicious, timeless witticism that was her life.

"Because," she sighed, "you can't. It's against the law."

"It's not fair," Alex repeated, failing to hear her, or perhaps himself, above the music playing on his Walkman, which he had neglected as usual to take off. "I can put Petey to bed, you know. I've done it lots of times."

"I thought you liked Cress. I thought you had fun with her."

"She's weird. All she does is eat and space out in front of the TV."

"She's a baby-sitter," Bonnie said. "They're paid to do that. Someday if you play your cards right, people will pay you to eat and watch TV all night too."

"Yeah, right."

She looked at him, this bony, crew-cut creature in his Red Sox cap and oversized T-shirt, hunched like a gargoyle over his plate, his vast complement of aggressions swathed in twenty-five milligrams of Prozac and some syrupy overproduced top-forty dream. A poor thing but my own, she thought. How had they arrived at this windy station? Who was driving the train? For a moment she thought she glimpsed in the boy, furled up like a flag, some of the coiled, recalcitrant DNA of his father. But perhaps that was only her imagination. The yearning of a vacancy for the shape that once filled it.

"Baby, please," she said. "It's been a rotten day. Give me a break, okay?"

Alex made a grudging frown. Giving his mother a break had become something of a domestic catechism by this point, a fervent daily appeal. Possibly, after all that repetition, even he had begun to see the justice in it.

"Anything left in the fridge for Cress?"

"Couple of apples. Mustard. We're out of Dr Pepper again."

"Good," she said.

"Hey, you're the one who said it was good for you. Some kind of medicine. You and Suzette."

"That was in the old days, we said. A hundred years ago. Now, of course, it's full of junk."

"You say that about everything," Alex pointed out.

"I'm late." She pulled on her gloves. "All right, so I'll leave my credit card. If Cress's hungry she can order a pizza."

"Large or small?"

Bonnie, yawning, waved her hand in exasperation. "Whichever she wants."

"I thought we were so *broke,*" Alex reminded her, in his own helpful way.

Half an hour later, sitting on the floor of the preschool's gym, Bonnie tasted the hamburger again, and while she was at it, everything else she had eaten that day too. Things were backing up on her. Closing in. Her gaze swept over the padded room—the pale, perforated ceiling, the dangling ropes, the blue wrestling mats against which she seemed forever pinned. Life is containment, she thought. Its most vivid events were only a play of mind, nervous and persistent, like the flutter of a starling, or the fitful industries of a magpie adorning its cage. No wonder she craved transport. But where to? Her life was a sunken temple. The doors were swamped in sand, the windows of sleep were shuttered tight. It was not just some rogue mood that had overtaken her but an absence of mood: a crusted ring left around the body when the waters of dreams were drained.

How long since she had slept with a man, really slept? Surely what she had done with Stanley Gottfried back in December could not be counted as sleeping. For that matter it probably could not be counted as fucking, either.

The image of Stanley Gottfried, and the familiar mix of guilt, longing, and distaste he evoked, led inexorably to thoughts of her unfinished dissertation, the pages flung messily across her desk like so much urban sprawl. The desk was solid pine; it had been fashioned from an old door by Leon, her ex-husband, during one of his brief though conscientious nesting phases, and mounted sturdily onto sawhorses for the express purpose of bearing up her thesis. Once, she remembered, that door had opened to a burgeoning closet, full of shoes, cross-country skis, long, tumbling dresses. . . .

"Hey, Bon."

Larry Albeit, Caitlin's father, sat down beside her on the wrestling mat and officiously unbuttoned his suit jacket. "Better get comfortable," he said, crossing his legs. "We're in for a long one."

"Oh no. Not tonight."

"Oh yes." He loosened his tie in the casual, distracted way of someone long accustomed to dealing with knots. "Next year's budget. Remember last time? It'll go on for hours."

"But I told the sitter I'd be home by nine."

Larry Albeit shrugged and offered her a wide-angle view of his high white teeth. What did he care? He was a lawyer in a litigious culture; meetings were the connective tissue of his life. Besides, at home he had his cheery, blond, and incredibly narrow-waisted wife, Kip, reading *Madeline* to the girls, free of charge.

"Well," he said, rising to his knees, "I think I'll get some coffee. Want any?"

"Yeah, okay."

"Caf or decaf?"

She hesitated. One would have thought from the amount of time it required that the choice was a profound one. "Make it decaf," she said, more to herself, as it turned out, than to Larry, who had already sprung up and bounced gallantly away to fetch it.

"Okay, guys," said Geoff Dahlberg, brandishing his clipboard. "I move that we get started. Lots of business tonight."

First the secretary, Bill Lake, went over the minutes from the previous month, which had to be accepted by voice vote and put into the record. Then Bethany Freitag ran down the membership report,

Eileen Smith reviewed the new curriculum committee proposals, and Dennis whatever-his-name-was gave an update on the physical plant renovations, which were as usual ongoing and expensive. Finally the treasurer, Alice Orkin, was called upon to report on fiscal matters. The preschool was actually in the black for a change, she conceded soberly, though not by much, and of course that wasn't taking into account the rent increase and the inevitable spike in staff salaries and benefits that would come like mud in the spring. To cover all these expenditures, tuition would have to go up. But then tuition went up every year. The only question was how high.

The other question—Bonnie's question—was how on earth she was going to swing it. For a moment she contemplated the slim, well-toned figure of Alice Orkin, standing at the front of the gym in black jeans, a high-necked velvet blouse, and amber earrings, brandishing one of her CPI charts and speaking with the genial and inquisitive stammer of the well-bred. A decade and a half ago, Alice had won a Rhodes scholarship in medieval poetry, but gave it up to marry Steve Orkin and his whole fabulous Brattle Street gene pool. Now she had three children, the youngest of whom was borderline autistic, and passed the time monitoring investments in their huge, turreted, daffodil-yellow Colonial, from whence she emerged on the second Tuesday of every month with her terrific jewelry and laser-printed graphs to command, in her hesitant, soft-toned way, everyone's fiscal attention. Not that Bonnie begrudged her. She too longed to step out from her high tower and address the crowd. But armed with what?

"Thank you," Geoff said, bobbing over his clipboard. "Those are fine reports. We all appreciate the work you guys put in."

Alice, Dennis, Bethany, Eileen, and Bill nodded modestly in acknowledgment.

"Okay, if there's no other old business, I move we proceed to the memo you received in your boxes last week, concerning the benefits package. Now, those of you who survived last year's meetings may recall these budget issues can get kind of delicate at times; they tend to generate some pretty strong emo—"

"Excuse me: Geoff?"

A hand was in the air, bunched into a fist. It belonged to Ginny Stern, whose son Jason was the precocious darling of Petey's class. Why shouldn't he be? He had a principled and outspoken mother who taught Comp Lit at Wellesley, and who took him to museums every weekend, and to France in the summer so he'd grow up bilingual, and the presence of whose hand in the air just now did not bode too well, Bonnie thought, for the pace of the evening.

"I'm confused," Ginny said, frowning. It was her standard opening line, and as usual not even remotely true. "Why are we using Styrofoam again, exactly? I thought we settled this months ago."

She pointed accusingly to the nearest coffee cup, which happened to be Bonnie's, and was in fact comprised of materials that would outlive them all. Guiltily Bonnie snuck a look into the bottom of the contraband cup, where the letters .ꟼ.H.Ↄ were laid out in small, puzzling indentations.

"She's right," said Bill Lake, checking his notes. "Nine/seventeen: Unanimous vote."

Geoff, his brow furrowed, looked around for help.

"I have an issue with the procedure here," Ginny said. "What happened to the mugs my committee went out and bought for replacements? I gave them to Mia myself."

All eyes turned to Mia Montague, the waifish, ponytailed assistant director. She sat propped against the back wall of the gym, the same spot she always occupied at meetings, blank-faced and serene, stitching their fates, in the form of clustered violets, onto a macramé tablecloth. It was Mia's job to stock the kitchen. Several times in the past this had brought her into direct engagement with Ginny Stern, often on the losing side. But now her mouth had a coy little twist, as if she were sucking on a piece of butterscotch candy. "Mugs?" Mia asked faintly, after a moment.

"There were three dozen. They had dancing cows on one side."

"Oh," Mia said, "those." She shook her head, wistful. "Those were no good. I had them inspected."

"Inspected?" Ginny looked dubious.

"By a ceramicist. She said they were improperly fired, and anyway there's too much lead in the glaze."

"But they're from *Conran's.*"

"Well, they're a health hazard."

"So's Styrofoam," Ginny shot back.

"Yes, but that's environmental. It's completely different."

All this time Bonnie was sleepily contemplating the decaffeinated dregs at the bottom of her cup, wondering: Her mugs at home—weren't a couple of those from Conran's too? Was she poisoning the kids? Wait, but the kids didn't drink coffee. Thank God, she was only poisoning herself.

"Listen, people," Geoff said, "I don't mean to suggest this isn't an important issue, well worth discussing, but we've got a helluva long agenda to get through. So I move that in the interests of time we go ahead and use the Styrofoam tonight, and meanwhile let's ask the food committee to purchase new mugs, safe ones, for next time. Anyone care to second?"

In deference to Geoff's long service on the board and his eminent if semi-maddening reasonableness, several people rushed to second the motion. Bonnie, sipping surreptitiously from her contraband cup, would have liked to second it too, but she did not trust herself to open her mouth. Already she'd acquired a reputation as something of a loose cannon in these meetings: fickle in her loyalties, wanting in seriousness, slow to volunteer. Doubtless it was all true. She did not feel like a good citizen these days. She lacked the energy, the time, the patience; ultimately, she supposed she lacked the will. It was a shameful thing to admit at this stage in global culture, but she'd about had it with participatory democracy. She'd have been happier writing out a check every month and letting paid professionals make all the decisions. Or better, to give herself over, just for a while, to some stern and commanding fascist dictator. To have at least a few of the trains in her life running on time.

Leon, she thought. At times the name yawned inside her reflexively, a bad flower aching toward light.

It had been Leon's idea—one of the last in a series of charming coercions—that they enroll the boys in a cooperative preschool in the first place. Parental involvement, he'd argued, was the progressive, responsible choice: better for the children, statistically persuasive, and cheaper in the end for all concerned. Which was approximately the same line of reasoning he'd applied some months later to getting divorced.

But that wasn't altogether fair. Strictly speaking, Leon had been no more to blame in the matter than Bonnie herself, who had after all done no one any good by sleeping with Stanley Gottfried at the MLA in San Francisco, for reasons that remained shrouded in fog even now. She'd been five months pregnant with Petey at the time; she remembered thinking, rather magically, in retrospect, that the extra layer of flesh around her belly would somehow insulate her from consequence. But it hadn't, of course. And now here she was. As for Stanley, he still made an occasional appearance, flying in to attend a conference at one of the local universities and, as if incidentally, to screw up her life; but Leon, that dear, sweet, narcissistic mess, was gone—decamped to Santiago, Chile, where the winters were warm, the psychoanalysts were cheap, and at least one of the local theaters was sufficiently desperate for material to produce the artless and didactic neo-Brechtian plays that were his specialty. Yes, Leon appeared to be flourishing down there, across all those borders. Lately his child support checks had even begun to arrive roughly the same month they were due. Also, he no longer called her collect in the middle of the night to haggle over money or visitations. In fact he no longer called her at all.

". . . and so," Geoff was saying, "if you'll turn to page three, you'll see the charts drawn up by the personnel committee, detailing the various benefit packages available to the staff."

Bonnie dutifully studied the charts. The fact that they were incomprehensible to her, though discouraging, was predictable enough—like most humanists, she had never done well in statistics—and after the first few seconds her eyes began skating giddily over the numbers, making elaborate figure eights and pirouettes in the margins, fanciful little doodles that seemed to illustrate perfectly the chaotic, trivial nature of her thoughts. The mind, she'd once read, is just a piece of paper, tossed by wind. But the nice thing about these meetings was that she could sit here and let it blow around, and all the competent, initiative-seizing people—the *grown-ups,* she caught herself thinking—would bear her along in their wake. She could coast. Under the circumstances this was a rare pleasure, the kind of minor indulgence, like getting high in the bathtub or devouring a crumb cake from Entenmann's, in which single people often seek consolation for their grievances, and Bonnie would have been perfectly capable of enjoying it if not for the dull, formless ache behind her eye sockets, and the calamitous way Alex's hamburger had settled in her stomach, and the small test she would have to perform upon herself the next morning, of which the hamburger, in its heavy and dyspeptic way, was a reminder.

"Can I say something?" asked Lucia Todd-Frazen, meekly interrupting a discussion of the dental plan.

Geoff, sitting in a yoga position at the front of the room, nodded beneficently.

"I just want you all to know that Harvey and I, and I think I speak for both of us even though he's not here tonight? Because we really love you guys on staff, the work you do, you're like part of our family, your patience, your involvement, your overall . . . and we believe in labor, we do, we support it. Even though we're not technically working class ourselves, of course, and sometimes, like with the Teamsters, or the restaurant workers downtown, a couple years ago, those indictments? We had an issue with that. Harvey especially, it sort of shook his faith for a while. But this measure we're talking about addresses some important issues. And so I want to say we support it, we really . . . both of us . . . we really . . . thank you."

The tremulousness of Lucia's voice and the circuity of her phrasing were of a nature so profound that a kind of tender collective prayer went up at the end of her speech, that any additional pain might be spared her. Such is the tyranny of the shy. But her message had touched a nerve. Parents of both genders now began to let fly with a quarter-century's worth of repressed pro-labor sentiments and McGovernish endorsements. What kind of lousy package were we *offering* our staff, anyway? Dental was one small part of an intricate puzzle. What about, for instance, workman's comp?

"Work*person's,*" grumbled Thea Doyle.

What about mental health? Job security? Paternity leave for the men on staff, never mind that half were gay? A flurry of amendments were proposed; each had to be discussed at some length before being tabled and referred to the appropriate committee chairperson, that it might be studied and further discussed at the next meeting. Several voice votes were taken anyway. Bonnie tried to participate, but her mouth had apparently lost the talent for shaping sounds. One by one, her powers were deserting her. Pretty soon it was nine-thirty, and she had to go to the bathroom again, and even Larry Albeit in his five-hundred-dollar suit was beginning to look a little rumpled.

Then Lucia cleared her throat again, and everyone froze.

"I just want to say this issue, the one we're discussing? I've had it for a long time. Because my life, it used to be a different . . . a different . . . like that proposition for the farmworkers, back in ninety-two? I worked on that. Harvey didn't want me to, not at first, he thought it took too much time away, I guess, I don't really remember what he thought. But I said, Harvey? I have a real issue with the fact that people who work hard in this country should make as much as we make, and have benefits that are just as good. This is something I think we should wake up to. I have a real issu—"

Jesus, thought Bonnie. Give me a fucking break.

And then an odd thing happened. Lucia froze; her face went white; one hand flew to her mouth to stifle a sob. It was as if the walls of Bonnie's head had been made transparent, and her whole stark infrastructure of anger and cynicism was revealed to all. There Lucia stood, damp-eyed and immobile on the wrestling mat. From the clench of her hands, she might have been grappling with an angel.

Now, under normal circumstances, the sight of Lucia Todd-Frazen getting emotional at a meeting was no more surprising or upsetting a phenomenon than the buzzing of the sodium lights in the parking lot outside. But to Bonnie it seemed the evening's very skin had been punctured. Horrified, she tried to remember: *Had* she said the words aloud? Oh God, she'd done everything else wrong that day, why not this too? Here we go, she thought: her nature, her *true* nature, had finally revealed itself. She'd said something bitchy and awful, severed the thin, precarious cord that bound civilized, progressive, cooperative people together, and now they'd all feel perfectly justified in hating her, if they hadn't already. And meanwhile it would be Petey, poor Petey, who was tormented nightly by dreams, who could not even count past twelve, whose skinny nose, a small parody of her own, could not be persuaded to stop running—it would be Petey who'd suffer the consequences.

Abruptly, she stood, muttering something about the bathroom, hoping no one would notice the tremble in her voice, or the mottled and inflamed condition of her cheeks, or the tears that were now blurring her eyes too. Tears! There was no accounting for them; they'd simply arrived on her face, dumbly, brutishly, like strange orphan children toward whom she felt no family feeling but for whom she understood herself somehow responsible. Room would have to be made, but where? There was no room left.

Only when she was alone in the bright-tiled shelter of the bathroom did the anxiety begin to subside. Standing at the sink, she rinsed her trembling hands with antibacterial soap and splashed cold water on her face, sensing that some personal crisis—she could not have said what—had been narrowly avoided. Nonetheless she was left feeling more than a little depleted. Lucia's speech, in the momentary stillness, continued to galumph indignantly through her head. *I have a real issue with this.* When had issues become possessions, Bonnie wondered, and why didn't she own more of them herself? But then she did, didn't she? She owned plenty. What would it matter if she added one more to the pile?

Though she had not lost her looks, increasingly she had to hunt for them awhile in the mirror before they showed up. The nights were doing their work. Her cheeks were shadowed and pale. Beneath the skin, like red ink bleeding through a page, she could make out tiny flailing capillaries of desire. Her wide, generous mouth, her flashing brown gaze: Where had they gone? More makeup was needed. The bags under her eyes had begun to take on some of the depth and capacity of marsupial pouches. The skin over them was lumpy, erratic, as colorful and intricately scalloped as a rainbow trout.

There were no paper towels in the dispenser, so she wiped her hands on her jeans, which she intended to throw out soon anyway, because they were threadbare and shapeless, like so much of what passed for her wardrobe, from when she was pregnant with Petey.

Out in the hallway she stopped to call home. The line was busy, of course. Cress, her baby-sitter, was a popular girl. Though plain to look at, to say nothing of her rather limited child-care skills, Cress had something, an aura or energy or low-frequency signal, that endeared her to other people, particularly children and men. Or were these two separate categories? Standing at the phone, the busy signal pounding away angrily at the protective insulation of her heart—what now? what now?—Bonnie looked over the construction-paper lions and monkeys the Green Room kids had done that week (Petey's, she was relieved to discover, was no more crude or haphazard than any of the others), and two of the tears she had worked so hard to suppress back in the gym finally worked their way free.

"Hey, Bon?" Larry Albeit was approaching her with a concerned look on his high pink rectangular face. "You okay?"

Bonnie touched a finger to her cheek, where it was warm and wet. "Okay?" she said.

"You're kind of crying."

"So?"

"So I just thought maybe you could use a shoulder to lean on."

Bonnie shook her head. The offer was not promising. "You should probably get back," she said. "The meeting."

"Ah . . ." Larry waved his wrist cavalierly and, unless she was out of her mind, actually blushed. "Fuck the meeting."

Despite herself, Bonnie tittered. The sound it made in the hallway was so loud, so awful and garish, that it might have issued from the wall of paper jungle animals behind her. "I better go," she said. "I've got a lot to do at home."

"Who doesn't? Listen, come on out to my car. We can talk there."

"Your car?"

"It's nice in there. You'll see. Besides, I believe I've got some opiated hash in the glove compartment with your name on it."

Bonnie hesitated. Lately all the junctions in her life's road seemed to be marked by this same sign: WHERE NOW? But she was lonely and tired and felt vaguely inclined to please, if not herself, then someone else; and too, she was almost forty, and for all her previous experience in minor drug use had never in fact seen opiated hash with her name on it before. So she followed Larry Albeit through the double doors that led to the parking lot.

Outside the wind was being its dumb, arrogant night self, banging at doors and windows, tossing around the phone wires that dangled between the poles. The temperature had fallen. The day's puddled rain had turned to ice. Coatless—she remembered it now, too late, back in the gym—Bonnie skidded reluctantly across the asphalt in the direction of Larry's black Saab. There it gleamed under the yellow halo of the sodium lights, enormous and sleek, a vehicle for all the soul's burdensome dreams.

At the last moment, however, she veered off abruptly toward her own car.

"Better not," she said, giving Larry a quick wave over her shoulder at the same time, lest he too think her unbearably rude. "I should stay straight for the ride home."

"You sure?" His forehead crowded over his eyes. For all his surface congeniality there was about him a tenacity, a bullishness. "I could drive you."

"Maybe some other time."

She needed to go back for her coat, no question about it, but she knew that would appear strange and awkward to Larry Albeit, so instead she strode to her car, jangling her keys in a purposeful and businesslike manner. Her haste to get to the meeting had made her park in such a way, she observed now, as to occupy two spaces at once. It was not a surprise. Everything she did of late seemed faintly transgressive, contained this small, glowing trace element of waste.

The lock was frozen. Shivering, she bent down to breathe on the mechanism, a technique that had worked for her occasionally in the past.

"A problem?" Larry buzzed down his window to observe her better. He had just started his car.

"Just . . . this . . . *door,*" she said, pushing against it with her full, her swelling weight. But it refused to give. She began to look around for something to hit it with. "On cold nights it gets jammed."

"Leave it," he said. "C'mon, get in for a minute and warm up. We'll figure something out."

Her gloves, of course, were in the pocket of her missing coat. As if to remind her of this, a crack had opened on the back of her hand, a sliver of blood at the knuckle where the skin was dry and chafed.

You have to keep the body lubricated, she thought. It will turn on itself.

Quickly, so as not to change her mind, she crossed over the white lines that separated her car from his and climbed in on the passenger's side. The position gave her an odd sensation of backwardness, of the self inverted by mirrors—she was accustomed to being the driver, not the driven—but in the end she decided that it was no stranger, in fact, than anything else.

"Now . . ." Larry, bent over, was fumbling in the glove compartment with his right hand, creating in the process no small amount of incidental contact with Bonnie's right knee. "Where'd I put that hash?"

"Oh," she said, "it doesn't matter. I'm happy just to get out of there. You don't have any hand lotion by any chance?"

Larry, face pressed sideways to the wheel, mumbled inaudibly.

Bonnie leaned back and closed her eyes. "It would be nice to really freak out sometime," she sighed. "To just blow it all off. But I don't think I remember how."

"A lost art," Larry agreed.

"One thing became perfectly clear to me tonight, anyway. I'm living the wrong life."

"Mmm . . ."

"I mean, these college towns, really, how do you stand it? All these earnest, overeducated people with their careers and their issues and their meetings that go on forever, their perfect kids who just happen to go to private schools, their potluck dinners with pad thai and tabouli, all those stale wedges of pita laid out in a basket—"

"Actually," Larry admitted, "I like pad thai and tabouli."

"Oh," she said bitterly, "so do I. At least I think I used to. That's what's so awful. All these things I used to really like, and now I can't stand them anymore. Do you think something's terribly wrong with me?"

"Oh no, I wouldn't say *wrong*. . . ."

"I don't care if there is," she asserted. "I mean, good Lord, she was crying over dental benefits in there."

"Lucia," Larry allowed mildly, "has strong convictions."

"Well, so do I. And one of them is she's wacko."

"Now, now," Larry said, "she's not so bad as all that." He bestowed on her a tall man's gaze of laconic tolerance. "Around here everyone's in pretty much the same boat, I think. You want to do things the right way for the kids. Avoid the old mistakes. Sometimes it makes people clumsy. But all in all they're doing their best."

"Yeah, yeah. I know."

Bonnie leaned wearily against the door, too sleepy all of a sudden to be properly ashamed of her own small-mindedness. The door itself was so much more substantial a piece of metal than the door of her shitty little Subaru that she found it hard to believe both could be accurately described by the same word. "Can you turn up the heater?" she asked. "I've been cold all day."

Larry adjusted a dial on the illuminated dashboard. Warm air purred noiselessly out the vents.

"I want to go south," she said, thinking wistfully of Leon. "Somewhere loose and fun, where they play loud music. Where they eat honeydew and mango and take naps after lunch."

"It *has* been a long winter," Larry agreed.

"I need to speak a different language for a while. I've got this weird craving for vowels."

"I've always wanted to live in the desert," Larry confessed. "I have an ascetic streak, and I retain water pretty well. Kippy says I'd make a good camel."

She watched him rummage around in the glove compartment for the wayward hash pipe, tossing aside documents of insurance and registration, maps, receipts, bookmarks, school notices, and scraps of notebook paper, hastily torn, full of directions to other people's houses. The plenitude and casualness of it all, the intricate rustle of pages in the car's interior breeze, gave rise in her to a small, rolling wave of anger. "What is it with lawyers, anyway?" she demanded. "How come you're the only people who smoke dope anymore?"

"Our work," he said, "is very taxing."

"Psh. Whose isn't?"

"It's a question of degree. People are unsympathetic to lawyers, which is understandable but unfair. They only see the surface symptoms. The behavioral tics and rashes. What they don't see is the pressure, all the money that rides on our ability to make fine discriminations. Draw little lines between their side and our side."

"I know what discriminations are, thank you."

"Of course you do," he said. "It's just these little lines—how do I say this? They can be *very* little. Practically metaphysical. Take this napalm case I've got now."

"Napalm? I didn't know they still made that stuff."

"They don't," Larry said. "This is left over from Vietnam. It's been sitting around a storage facility up in Maine all these years, but there's some kind of leakage problem, evidently. Some groundwater thing. So now they want to ship it to Virginia. They've got a technology down there that breaks the stuff down into its chemical constituents and recycles it into clean, cheap fuel. Elegant solution, right?"

"I guess."

"The only problem is the transport issue. You can imagine how the environmentalists and citizen action groups feel about this. Six states, sixteen lawsuits. No one wants this stuff rolling through their cities at night, when they're asleep."

"I wouldn't either."

"Of course not. Though the fact is it's probably the best thing for everyone. The collective good. It's already out there, right? It won't go away. You have to do *something* with it. It may as well be something useful."

"Who's to say what's useful?"

"There you go," he said, "this is what we're up against. Semantics. You hear the word *napalm* and what do you see? That little naked peasant girl running half-dead down the street. But suppose I say there's twenty thousand gallons of gasoline mixed with a compound of benzene and styrene being stored in heavy metal isocontainers over a foot thick. That's a different story, right? I mean, people are *used* to that. Check out Charlestown, seven days a week."

"Whatever you call it," she said, "the vibes are still bad. Some things get tainted forever. Even if they're only words."

"My point is it's a gray area. There are a lot of gray areas in the law. That's all I'm trying to establish. You asked about the dope, I'm trying to tell you. It's because of the gray areas. The stress."

She nodded sympathetically, though in fact she felt only scornful and irritated. Stress. Another bad, tainted word. It was so inexact, so overused, so meaningless, she found even the casual, sibilant hiss of it objectionable. Still, she did not wish to sound as though she objected to everything, so she held her tongue.

"Hence," Larry went on, "the lawyer's lifestyle. The long hours. The early heart attacks. The dope, the booze, the kill-or-be-killed, thirty-five-and-over basketball leagues. Coping strategies. It's hard to sleep after you've been up late doing intellectual work. You need something to make those lines start to blur. Get a little loose, you know?"

Oh, thought Bonnie grimly, I know.

"Plus we can generally afford the good shit."

"Oh yeah? So where is it, big shot?"

"Funny. I stuck one in here the other day. I wonder if Kippy might have—"

"Kip smokes?"

"Like a chimney. Ever since the chemo. Though she promised me she was going to stop," he said. "'Cause we're trying to have another, um, bambino, hopefully a boy this time, and it probably isn't such a great idea just on the biogenetic end to be toking up every night when you're—"

"Jesus, Larry, I didn't even know Kip was ill."

"Oh, that was two, three years ago. We had a little scare, but it's in remission now. We've got it on the run. There's this mushroom extract, Maitaki? Wonderful stuff. Then there's Noni Juice, and Essiac tea, once in a while a tiny bit of shark cartilage. . . ."

"Noni Juice?"

"I know, I know. I'm as skeptical of alternative remedies as the next person. But I have to admit it's all been very . . . very . . . ah—" He extracted, at last, the hash pipe. When he'd got the thing lit, he blew out a jet of smoke and handed it across to Bonnie, who had fallen silent.

"Very what?" she asked.

"Hopeful. Very hopeful."

He waited for her to pass the pipe back to him before he spoke again.

"It's terrible what we're doing, isn't it?"

"I don't know about terrible. Irresponsible, maybe."

"No, I mean talking about Kippy's illness. Married people aren't supposed to talk about their spouses in a revealing way, especially to members of the opposite sex. It's a subtle form of betrayal. It violates any number of unwritten conjugal codes."

"What should married people do? Walk around feeling bottled up and lonely instead?"

Larry considered the question.

"That's what's so irritating about marriage," she announced, the blunt needle of her rage slipping into a well-worn groove. "The unspoken laws. They're so tyrannical and unnatural."

"Institutional insecurity," he said. "You have this great, dying empire. It's obsolete, true. But nothing's ready to replace it. So you pass new laws to prop up the *ancien régime*."

"Well," she said, "one thing I know about people is they're countersuggestive. They don't do well with laws."

"True. But they do even worse without them."

"Exactly," she cried, grabbing his arm with both hands. It was as if he had put words to something terribly elusive.

Larry, for his part, nodded vaguely. He appeared to have lost the flow of their conversation. Then, after a moment, he began to laugh.

It really was good shit. It must have been that, or the late hour, the nice car, the vast reservoir of boredom inside her, or simply the promiscuous way that laughter and empathy, like some canny hybrid virus, travels between people—it must have been something along these lines that caused Bonnie to begin laughing now herself. At least she assumed it was laughter. It had been a while. Was laughter supposed to make her stomach so sour, her cheeks so streaky and hot?

"Bon?" Larry was leaning forward again, his eyes small reddish stones on the placid pond of his forehead. "You okay?"

"I think I'm pregnant."

It was in the nature of an experiment, saying it aloud, and once the words were out, part of her continued to listen carefully for some kind of explosion. But nothing happened.

Larry nodded soberly. "I thought so."

"You thought so? What kind of crazy thing is that to say?"

"Just a feeling," he said. "I saw you back there when I first sat down. Very haughty and impatient. I remember that look from the hospital." He laid down the pipe and closed the ashtray with a snap. "I figured either someone died, or else you were pregnant."

"Actually, Larry, you may be right on both counts."

Both of them sat there digesting this information for a moment.

Larry cleared his throat. "Forgive me for prying, but I take it the father's not in the picture?"

"The *father*!" she snorted. "The *father* is a hot young turk poststructuralist. The *father* won't even concede an author is responsible for his own *book.* What's he going to make of this?

"Also," she added wearily, "he lives in Toronto. With a woman. Maybe two women. It's not entirely clear."

"Well," Larry said, rubbing his smooth jaw, "that's a tough situation."

"Yep."

"Anything I can do?"

"Do?" She tried to look out the window, but the glass had begun to fog over. She lacked the energy to wipe it clean.

"Sure. You know. To help."

She wheeled around to face him. "What are you talking about, *do*? I hardly know you. Our kids happen to go to the same preschool. What could you possibly do—adopt us?"

"Okay, okay. Take it easy. I'm just trying to help."

"What *is* it with you people anyway? Where do you get your confidence? Tell me the truth: Was it Mom? Did she love you so much you think you can just go around *do*ing things?" Her stomach was flopping over like a salmon. "Oh, shit," she wailed, "oh filthy mother of God—"

"Sometimes just talking," Larry said gently, inching toward her across the leather seat, "just letting it out . . ."

Though she did not herself subscribe to this theory, in truth something did begin to happen to Bonnie as the tears fell: her head became very heavy and at the same time, on the inside, remarkably light. She could feel it zooming off on its own, circling dizzily for a while and then slowing, easing itself toward the broad, solid topography of Larry's shoulder—the surface to which all earthly gravity would consign her. All right, okay: she allowed her eyes to close. And it *did* feel luxurious, damn it, like falling into a wide, silken net. And she deserved it too. She deserved it for all the meetings, all the parent conferences, the open houses and holiday programs, all the bills she'd paid or avoided, all the baths, the Band-Aids, the vitamin supplements and antibiotics, all the piles of laundry that never seemed to diminish no matter how often she ran the machine, all the omelettes and sauces from which she'd obligingly left out the herbs and the onions, all the aimless hours she'd passed in the middle of the night staring vacantly at the crack in the wall above the toaster, wondering how not to fall in. Yes, she had worked hard, very goddamned hard, and now she was due . . . well, *some*thing, she was certainly due *some*thing. . . .

How long her head rested that way on Larry's shoulder she didn't know. Not long enough to sleep. And then much too soon there it was again, in its stubborn, corklike fashion, bobbing right up. "I have to get back," she said, reaching for the door handle.

"Are you sure? The meeting, they'll still be at it, you know."

"No, no," she said, "I mean *home*."

But once she had extricated herself from the car, the wind caught her by both arms, whipping around like a shroud, as if to expose—or was it enfold?—her. Overhead, through the skeletal branches, she could see the cold clear eye of the moon. It was getting late. Lights were on in the Victorians across the road. Parents and children floated through the chambered rooms, silent and sure, like skaters in a dream.

And now the double doors were swinging open. People began to emerge from the meeting in clusters and pairs, making their way carefully across the parking grid in search of their cars. She could not make out their faces in the darkness, but she recognized them by their good bulky winter coats: Geoff Dahlberg, Lucia Todd-Frazen, Dennis (all at once, she remembered his last name) Peeler. Alice Orkin and Thea Doyle were hugging good-bye; Bethany Freitag was leaning into Ginny Stern's car, hammering out some detail of carpooling; Ron Kubikowsky was talking into his cellular phone, informing his wife to stick his dinner in the oven, he was on his way.

Shivering, she remembered her coat, still back in the gym. She had bought that coat on sale at Filene's several years back; a musk of obscure disappointment had clung to it ever since. Somehow it had never fit quite right. She was tempted to leave it behind, to cut herself free of it, of all her old mistakes, but the coat, made of the finest cashmere substitute of its day, was warm, and had another year or two left in it, and she could not afford another right now. So she turned and headed back through the double doors.

The hallway was deserted. Of the forty-odd people who'd attended the meeting, only Mia Montague, locking up the kitchen for the night, remained. Mia looked tired but content; apparently the Styrofoam debate had been resolved to her satisfaction. She stuffed her sewing into her shoulder bag and began to wind her scarf loosely around her neck. "Forget something?" she asked brightly.

"Just my coat."

"I think Geoff locked the gym when he left. He usually does."

"Oh. Oh well—"

"I think I can open it for you, though."

But when they got the gym door unlocked and flicked on the lights, Bonnie looked around with a dry mouth and a sinking heart. No coat was in evidence.

"Let's try the lost-and-found box," Mia suggested brightly.

The coat was not there either, though she did find one of Petey's T-shirts, mislaid since early October. She clutched it with both hands as she followed Mia out. *This,* she thought, was what had been due her, not escape, but a deepening of her hole. After all, she had been digging it for years; it would take more than a little hanky-panky with Larry Albeit at this point to vault herself free.

"Hello," Mia said. "Is this the one?"

Bonnie blinked. There, just outside the door of Petey's room, was her coat. It had been folded and draped, with what seemed an almost unnatural delicacy, across one of the tiny plastic chairs the children sat in. There was a rise to the shoulders she hadn't noticed before. She was reminded of wings. When she unfolded the coat a slip of paper fluttered off and fell to the floor. She looked down at it for a second, aware of being a little bit stoned, and of Mia Montague, keys in hand, holding the door that led to the foyer, watching.

The note, written in a mother's careful hand, read: *Does this belong to Bonnie Saks, Petey's mom? Please make sure she gets it.*

Suddenly a gate rose in Bonnie's heart, and all its channels flooded at once. She was here, she was known, she was being looked after. Things would be delivered unto her.

Outside the stars were tossing around like blossoms, swaying amid the tree limbs. This time the lock on her car door sprang open at once. Perhaps Larry, or someone, or the moonlight itself had breathed on it while she was gone.

Driving home through an infinity of green lights—they dangled in the mist like Chinese lanterns—Bonnie reflected upon the many people in her life who had been irritating her so. She thought of the kids, of Cress, of Lucia and Ginny and Larry, and Kip, poor Kip. She thought of Leon, and even Stanley, that careless, wretched bastard. They were, after all, to be pitied, not hated, for their estrangement from what they had wrought. And she thought of the writer of that unsigned note. It could have been any one of the parents at the meeting, tired, harried, laughably earnest, squeezing good works without recompense from their busy schedules. Larry was right: everyone was trying so hard to avoid the old mistakes—of course it made them clumsy, it makes all of us clumsy, she thought, all of us but not all the time.

When she got home she found Cress at the kitchen table, thoughtfully smoking a cigarette.

"How were they?" Bonnie asked.

"Monsters."

"Sorry. I tried to call."

"That's okay." Cress waved her wrist, dispelling the smoke. Above their heads, a bouquet of dried roses twirled indolently on a string, a petrified souvenir from Stanley's last visit. "I guess the meeting ran long, huh?"

"Yeah." Bonnie glanced over at the dishes piled in the sink. Was any pizza left? She was famished.

"Well . . . I gotta get me some sleep."

Cress stubbed out her cigarette and reached for her bag.

"Let me just sit for a minute, okay? Then I'll call you a cab."

"Okay, cool."

So they sat there awhile. Cress put down her bag and lit another cigarette, pausing every so often to tap the ashes into a teacup, and whatever obsessions were running through her head she chose to retain there. Bonnie, too tired to shrug out of her coat, allowed her eyes to fall closed. She was not thinking about the long evening she had just passed. She was not thinking about the dishes to be done, the lunches to be made, the sleep to be approached like some wary jungle cat, with stillness, reverence, and guile. No, she thought only of this moment right now, this space that did not demand to be filled because it was not in fact vacant, but only suspended—like the tiny unformed being in her womb, or the dried garland that dangled overhead—caught in time's web, between past and future, in a state of pure potentiality. And it occurred to Bonnie that in the final analysis she was a very capable person, capable of more, oh, much more than she could possibly envision, perhaps even capable of being happy. . . .

Then Cress yawned. "Can I go now?"

And Bonnie, her eyes still closed, purse clutched to her stomach, thought clearly and without bitterness, *This is going to cost me too.*

2

The Anxiety Team

THE PHONE was ringing in the outer office. Ian thought about getting up to answer it, but his left leg, tucked beneath his buttocks, appeared to have fallen asleep. Anyway, why should he bother? Surely in a major department of a major metropolitan hospital, some lonely salaried peon in the vicinity of the reception desk, some night nurse or suborderly or skulking, insomniacal intern could be relied upon to venture forth and answer the damned phone.

As for Ian Ogelvie, he had his hands full. There was Molloy to observe. There was his grant proposal to complete, his lab notes to write up. The latest in a series of administrative memos was piled atop the messy northwest corner of his desk, waiting to be reviewed. Normally Ian was a clean-desk person; it was a source of anxiety to find that the items left unattended to outnumbered those completed. Frowning, he gripped his pen tighter. The wind was sweeping off the river, moaning and scrabbling at the windows like a man dispossessed. It was halfway to dawn. And the phone was still ringing.

From: Howard Heflin, Director of Experimental Psychology
To: Relevant staff, sixteenth floor
Re: Advertising campaign

As you've all heard by now, our new owner, the Northern Services Corporation, has deemed us one of six "flagship" facilities in the New England area. In order to ease our transition in the months ahead from one division of a large multicare provider to a more streamlined and efficient "category healer" in mental health, we have been asked to comment on a draft of the advertisement copy (see page 2) which Northern Services has proposed to run in coming issues of the *Globe,* the *Herald,* the *Phoenix,* and *Boston Magazine,* in conjunction with their new promotional campaign throughout Eastern Massachusetts. Please take the time to review it, then fax or e-mail your comments to Joanie, who will pass them along to me. Thank you.

Radio and television spots are also in the works. We will be seeking your input on these as well.—HH

Before him on the lab table, toiling silently, was a shamrock spider named Molloy. He was not, as spiders go, a very interesting specimen. His size was average, his markings undistinguished. His circadian rhythms were utterly predictable. No, there was little about Molloy to reward the eye, especially now, when he was engaged in his nightly routine—the assembly of a large bowl-shaped web—an activity, to the casual observer, of only meager dramatic interest. But Ian was not a casual observer. He was watching very closely, noting the balletic poise of the dangling creature, the mathematical precision of the web joints, the collaborations of muscle, spatial memory, and sheer focused industry that made such an enormous and sophisticated construction project possible. It was pretty mind-blowing, really. But you had to be patient. You had to *attend.* You had to view the work as a privilege, the gift of bearing witness to a system of timeless, intricate species behavior. Otherwise he supposed it could all seem very trivial.

Methodically, the spider soldiered on. Perhaps his pace of construction was, thanks to the compound Ian had administered, a shade slower than normal. It was hard to tell. Time was, of course, a highly subjective business, colored in this case by Ian's concern over all the unfinished tasks on his desk. His research proposal to the

National Institute of Mental Health, for example, was due in three weeks. He would make it, naturally; he always made his deadlines. He'd been working against deadlines his entire life. Or was it the other way around? In any case, the whole deadline concept had begun to take on, in recent weeks, a certain literalness for Ian. Somewhere out there he sensed a fateful, longitudinal line, transparent as a spider's thread, which could be apprehended but not seen, and his life—that is, his professional life; at the moment he had no other—depended on his position in relation to it.

Below lay the Fens, swabbed in night's black paint.

He fingered his ballpoint, made some notes. It was necessary to stay focused, focused and awake, like Molloy himself. Block out the phone ringing down the hall, the ambulance wailing down the street. The colleagues—or were they the janitors?—laughing conspiratorially in an adjoining office. The ceiling tiles pulsing in dumb, plodding rhythm to the bass line of whatever reggae CD was playing this week up in Sukey Witherspoon's lab.

Working late did something to you, Ian thought. Flung open the doors and windows, punched holes in the walls. Let the world's B-side, its alternate, night music, come whistling through.

He sat there under his small nimbus of light, waiting for Molloy to finish his web, so phase two of the substudy could be concluded, and he could devote his full attention to phase three. A sleep researcher by training, Ian was used to this sort of thing, to the watery pace and meandering obscurity of dream time. He was a bit of a dreamer, he supposed, himself. Fame, love, a life of purpose and discovery . . . all the brilliant reveries of youth and ambition had in the course of one night or another tossed down their hair for him. Take away dreams, he thought, and what was left? Psychic disturbance. This had been conclusively documented by leading minds in the field. Granted, there were *other* leading minds in the field who'd conclusively documented just the opposite: pathologies that popped up *only* in REM, heightened blood pressure, greater risk of heart attacks, Freud's *Via Regia* potholed with threats and dangers, the night a sort of stupid, sadistic hazing session for the ego. But that was research for you, a tangle of oppositions. Sometimes it took all one's powers of concentration to sort them through.

Fortunately Ian was gifted that way. Bent over his desk, he had the methodical stillness, the tunneled and devotionary attention of a chess player, a fly fisherman. Even among his peers at the lab it set him apart. Americans distrusted fineness, self-containment; it was a culture of collage, he thought, of heterodox groupings, hybrid forms. Socially he fit in better with the Asians on staff. Stoic reserve, somber rituals and ceremonies. He'd have liked to see Japan; he'd heard wonderful things about the place from Howard Heflin, his chair and supervisor, who had been there several times, and had even gone so far as to let drop the possibility of Ian attending the next meeting of the Asian/American Receptors Conference with him—presuming, of course, his grant application met with success. Which, empirically speaking, he had every reason to expect it would.

For Ian Ogelvie was a comer, a hot young thing. Over the years all the fat, shiny plums of precocity—the internships, the fellowships, the awards, the publications—had fallen off the tree for him right on schedule, sun-ripened and sweet. That was why Boston General had wooed him from his sterling post-doc in New Haven; why they'd buttered and coaxed him from his shell like that thirty-dollar lobster they'd fed him at Hamersley's Bistro, and bade him join their anxiety team. Because they knew he'd fit in. He knew the language, the currency, of advancement. He knew how to work the conferences, how to talk at the dinners, how to navigate a rental car through the constellated lights of some prosperous city, where the glass towers leered and swayed and the limousines, whisking soundlessly to and from the airport, doled out cool, immaculate reflections. When you are on the outside, every window looks like a mirror. But Ian Ogelvie was not on the outside.

Hence, of course, he would make his deadline for the NIMH. Then he'd wrap up his next two papers ("The Effects of Methylenedioxy-Substituted Phenylalkylamines on the Structure of Arachnid Locomotor Activity" and "Sleep Cycles and Expectancy Theory: A Case

Study"), the outlines of which were already saved in rough draft on his hard drive. The previous month, no less significant a personage than Charlie Blaha, executive editor at *Neuropsychopharmacology Now,* had given Ian his business card at the New York Sheraton and expressed—albeit in casual, commitment-free, alcoholically enhanced terms—a gratifying quantity of palpable enthusiasm. *Placebos're hot, I can feel it. Those little babies're storming the gates. You give me a ring the second you've got something, hear?* And he would too. Because that was who he was. A valuable contributor. Someone whose opinions were solicited at senior staff meetings, whose research was copublished in the best journals. To this point his rewards had been for the most part the easy ones, the minor ones: tickets to the Bruins, conferences in San Diego and Hawaii, occasional junkets down at Hilton Head with executives from Merck and Upjohn and Schering-Plough and *their* hot young things. But there was time. He was still new; the winged promise of his career was just unfolding. All he needed was a lab, a computer, a desk from which to operate. *Give me but a place to stand, and I will move the world.*

On the other hand, he supposed it was possible to get *too* close to heat. He knew what that was like too, unfortunately, having watched his apartment in Coolidge Corner go up in flames the week before Thanksgiving, thanks, it turned out, to a wayward chemistry experiment by Avi Feinberg, the nine-year-old Orthodox Jewish boy who lived downstairs. At least his parents had the solid consolations of their faith to lean against that night. Ian had only the nightshirt he was wearing, his laptop, and his mountain bike. He remembered the ticking spokes revolving aimlessly in the frozen moonlight, as if trying to go somewhere, anywhere. . . .

"Hey." Marisa Chu had stuck her head in the doorway. "Get that new memo? I left it on your desk."

"I read the first page. I was going to read the rest later," he said. "After I was through."

"Well, don't wait too long. Howard's meeting with the honchos tomorrow. He says he wants our feedback before then."

"Why? He never pays attention to it."

"Sure he does. He's very into process," she said. "Up to a point. When he isn't too incredibly busy."

"I have it here somewhere," Ian said, making a halfhearted effort to find it.

Marisa yawned. "Any luck finding a new place?"

"I've got some leads," he said. "There's a group house in Belmont I'm checking out."

"Belmont? Ugh."

"There's also a couple of places in Davis Square," he added. Actually, come to think of it, he had forgotten to call them. How could he with these spiders and fish to observe, this grant proposal to complete, these graduate students being dumped on him to supervise? Also there was the issue of the security deposit, which would require an advance on his salary, which would require the intervention of *his* supervisor, the incredibly busy Howard Heflin, whom Ian rarely even glimpsed in the hallways of late and hence hated to bother with such trifling questions as where in the world at the end of the day he should lay his head.

"You should look out in J.P." Marisa lived, whether alone or not he wasn't sure, in Jamaica Plain. "It's a hot market."

"I've heard that." Why was his face all flushed? It was only real estate.

"You'd like it there. Maybe something by the pond. It's a great area. A lot's happening there right now."

"It sounds nice," he said. In reward for which tepid remark he saw her smile absently and look at her watch.

"I'll check it out right away," he added, too late. A phone had begun to ring down the hall, and Marisa's eyes had lost their playful, attentive light.

"That's for me," she said. "See you later. I'll keep my ears open."

He watched her go, made abruptly wistful for no reason he could identify by the low black fringe of hair ticking against the white shoulders of her lab coat as it receded down the corridor. Marisa too was incredibly busy. They all were. To be incredibly busy on the sixteenth floor at this point was something of a tautology; in questionable taste even to complain about it. And who would want to? The addictive properties of overwork were—Ian had read the studies—not simply psychological, but also physiological in nature. Work anxiety stimulated the adrenal glands, which in turn tapped into the brain's pleasure circuits, flooding the subject with dopamine. Thus to be incredibly busy was, for mind and body both, its own reward. Though no matter how incredibly busy you were, you could never dream of holding a candle in that department to the Grand Vizier of Incredible Busyness, Howard Heflin.

Certainly Howard Heflin had a lot on his plate. Chief of experimental psychiatry, captain of the anxiety team, chair of the teaching faculty, head of the sleep lab, senior consultant to a vast, far-flung empire of foundations, subcommittees, and corporations—it was difficult to say at this point where the Drug Czar's domain left off and God Himself's began. This, Ian thought, was merely a small, distressing fact of life. In light of several concurrent facts—the man's demanding home life, his formidable travel schedule, his various ongoing research projects, and the humming force field of obliviousness he generated around himself, either unconsciously or by design, when confronted by the basic, often tiresome human needs of his many subordinates—there was reason to be cautious if your advancement in the field was dependent, as Ian's was, upon Howard Heflin's good favor. And yet one could not complain about this either. Howard Heflin was not a bad fellow, merely a limited one. And even if he *were* a bad fellow, academia and other mental institutions were full of people just like him. They were the ones who kept the place running. They were the ones, these driven, curiously remote personalities in their blazers and vests, who wound up chairing departments, introducing speakers, taking job candidates to lunch. If there was an order or reason behind it, some obscure formula that dictated where you wound up in the hierarchy, Ian had not yet grasped it. He did remember how, one furtive summer night when Malcolm Perle, giddy from beer and sleeplessness, had snuck Heflin's CV out of the file cabinet in Joanie's office and passed it around the lounge for inspection, he had scanned the pages eagerly, his gaze skating past the second-tier education, the third-tier post-doc, the padded and derivative journal articles, and the long, undistinguished record as a clinician, and coming to rest in the cool blankness of the margins to ponder how a man of such lackluster credentials had come to accrue so much power over so many people, not least among them Ian Ogelvie. Who'd graduated summa cum laude from Cornell. Who'd doc'd at Yale. Who'd had drinks—well, one white wine spritzer anyway—just last month at the New York Sheraton, with a senior editor—or was he the only editor?—from *Neuropsychopharmacology Now.*

Ah, thought Ian, but Howard Heflin had drinks too. A lot of drinks, with a lot of people. So many people were lined up to have drinks with Howard Heflin at this point that he'd been forced to hire an additional secretary and overspend on his administrative budget just to deal with the invitations, the lecture offers from Montreal and Chicago and Beijing, the conferences, symposia, and black-tie benefits with the trustees who were now competing for a few short, highly remunerative hours of his time.

Then too it had to be acknowledged that the man had not let success go to his head. From what Ian had heard, Heflin was no different now than he was twenty years before—that is, shameless. Also disingenuous, name-dropping, petulant, and exploitative. And the terrible thing was it *worked.* Filtered through the golden valves and screens of success, each of Heflin's many irritating character flaws had magically alchemized, first into harmless quirks, then into lauded public virtues. It was a biochemical process Ian was forced to respect, as he did all of nature's mysterious and whimsical little power plays, even those he found mordant and twisted and dismaying, because it passed the critical empirical test: it worked. One did get the feeling, in the presence of Howard Heflin, that the world was a small, cheerfully efficient place, full of people he knew personally and went out to lunch with.

Dear Dr. Heflin,

Hello! I was a graduate student of Kyoto University. Can't you remember me? Your lecture to us especially for me made me good impression that I will never forget. You've told me that my research very excellent. You've correct me some French pronounciation when we had lunch or supper during that day. Though it past a long time, I remember it like yesterday. Now, christmas will come, I am representative of Eli Lilly, travel every week, paid vacation, excellent benefits for my family and self. And so I will give you the best wishes.

Good luck all the year!
William

He'd discovered the card, attached to a bottle of sake, in a bulging carton in Heflin's office closet, amid a trove of Viennese chocolates, Cuban cigars, French wine, Swiss watches, Jamaican rums, and Spanish sherries. Offerings from friends and admirers in distant lands, many of whom, judging from the attached notes, were currently enjoying the excellent benefits of one magnanimous pharmaceutical firm or another. Ian could still taste, like some foul pollutant on his tongue, a sea-green Czech liqueur that smelled remarkably like cough syrup, which Heflin had passed around the same night last August that they received notification of the grant from Furst. Ian had had to go along with everyone else and pretend to like the stuff. Team player.

Later, at home, it had taken three swigs of mouthwash to get the taste out of his mouth. He had watched himself carefully in the mirror above the sink, looking for signs. Where were his borders, his outer limits, the boundaries of what he would and would not do to achieve? It would be good to know for certain where his career was headed. But then maybe living, like sleeping, was best performed in the dark.

Anyway, that was months ago. Now he had other concerns, like his deadline. And Molloy. Enough of the web had been completed by now that the results had become obvious. Perfect. This one too. It would have been completely mystifying and unprecedented had he not achieved the same findings with Butch, Harry, and Felix earlier that week. A clear pattern of increased regularity in the angles. Spiderwebs, like snowflakes, were never as symmetrically proportionate as people thought; there were always exaggerations, imperfections, and distortions to be seen up close. But not this one. This one was perfect, the result of a .05 dose of Dodabulax, tinier than a drop of dew.

Ian's logbook was open beside him; in it he scribbled the following note:

> *. . . one may assume that the response variability is the manifestation of a spontaneous endogenous fluctuation in the excitability of the various synaptic sites interposed in the afferent sensory pathways . . . (cf. Watt 1991, Korella, Wells 1989) . . . one may go further and postulate that this variability is of critical compensatory importance to the well-being of the organism; thus the ability shown by the D compound group to decrease this variability suggests . . .*

Suggests what? A number of things. It was late. He was tired. Or was he? Actually he wasn't tired in the least; he merely felt, because of the late hour—a conventional response to a conventional stimulus—that he should be. Predictable. There were times he did not so much inhabit his life as observe it through glass, finding his every movement obvious and reactive, significant not of itself but of some larger, unknowable force that lay beyond the frame of his will.

Marisa Chu walked back in with her usual fine timing just as he was in the process of blowing his nose. "Here," she said. "I brought you that memo, in case you lost yours."

"Thanks. Just lay it on the desk."

"Did you hear? They think they may have an encephalitis lethargica downstairs."

"Sleeping sickness?"

"Do you have any idea how rare those are? It could be Parkinson's in disguise, though. They're calling Neurology to take a look."

"Why not us?"

"They said they tried, but nobody answered the phone." She set the memo face-up on his desk and peered over his shoulder. "Ugh. Spiders."

"You should see what they're up to," he said. "It's really amazing."

She gave him one of her little Mona Lisa half-smiles, which he received like a blow. *Really amazing* was one of those exclamations that seemed to issue from his mouth at regular intervals as if to ensure that no adult woman ever be required to take him seriously.

"That's what you said about the cats too," Marisa said.

"Did I? Well, it was true."

Marisa Chu regarded him for a moment, her expression impassive as ever though also, he thought, subtly bored. It occurred to Ian that he did not particularly like Marisa Chu. He had never particularly liked Marisa Chu. So why should it bother him then that Marisa Chu, from all appearances, did not particularly like him? Or that if his intuition was reliable in such matters, she was working late tonight only because she was carrying on some kind of covert extramarital affair with Malcolm Perle? Malcolm, whose wife taught second grade at the Cambridge Montessori School, a girl so generous of spirit she could be relied upon at least once a month to send along a tray of walnut brownies for the staff lounge, brownies which Ian adored and which Marisa Chu, who seemed to live on a diet of yogurt and Evian water, shamelessly wolfed down over the sink and then complained that they were "a bit gooey." Why should he find that so irritating?

"Go home, Ian," Marisa said, not unkindly.

"I can't. I have to do the Polaroids. And the fish. What about you?" He tried to keep suspicion out of his voice.

"I like to work at night," Marisa said coolly. "I'm an owl. It's the only time I can think."

"Me too."

"That's not what I heard. I heard you cut back your hours in the sleep lab because you couldn't handle the nights." Her tone, though seemingly neutral, was, he thought, layered with condescension; it was a point of pride to be the last on any particular night to leave.

"That was Boris, the techie. He caught me sleeping once and started this rumor." He went over to the filing cabinet and rattled the bottom drawer. "Damn."

"Here, I've got a key." She inserted the metal spine smoothly into the lock, and turned. Nothing resisted her. "Let me do it. I never get to."

"It's my area."

"Don't be possessive. We're a team, remember? Come on, just this once; I'll never ask again."

Ian frowned. Marisa Chu was a manipulative person, he thought, ruthless in her way. But she too passed nature's test. She too made it work.

"Well," he said, "just a few. And try not to scare him. He's had a busy night."

In the end, of course, he allowed her to shoot as many photographs as she liked. It took about ten minutes. All the while the bulbous, speckled shamrock sat there posing for her, showing off his perfectly realized web. Female power: it was so elemental, so persuasive. A perfect specific.

For a moment Ian cast his gaze around the office, wondering what *he* might show off. Himself? He eyed his reflection in the window. He was not such a bad specimen, when you factored in the neglect and bad light, the haphazard meals in the cafeteria, the inattention to routine maintenance. He was slender and fair, nearly pretty. His hair was long and thick, inky black; it fell into a neat, inturned wave at his temple, affording the paleness of his cheeks, he'd been told, a pleasant contrast. His Adam's apple, though, was more prominent than he'd have liked, and behind the wire-rimmed glasses his eyes bulged out just a bit from a thyroid condition in his youth, and together these gave him an impression of forward-tilting eagerness and receptivity that he had, he hoped, long since outgrown. At twenty-nine, he could have passed for twenty. Was this a good thing? His sister, Barbara, upon whose generosity and sofa bed he was currently dependent, liked to say that he'd won all the best family genes in nature's unfair lottery, but it was Barbara's role as a slightly overweight, cheerfully depressed elder sibling to be both overly deprecating about herself and overly generous toward him. No, he was more inclined to take the word of his former girlfriend and lab partner, Wendy Lesher, who had run off to Nairobi with the Peace Corps two years earlier lest she make what she referred to, in the last letter he ever received from her, as "a big, long-range mistake." Marrying him, he supposed she meant, though she had chosen not to explain herself. It never worked to explain these things anyway. Human relations were not scientific; there was no hard core of truth that lay concealed at the heart of things, waiting to be discovered. Only more concealments. And the crushed pulp of the heart.

Sometimes in quiet hours like these he'd picture Wendy Lesher's life across the ocean—it seemed no less dimensional or immediate than his own—supervising vaccinations in a sun-baked field tent, striding around in khaki shorts and work boots and a Giants cap, sunglasses riding high over the aggressive topography of her nose. Polio, diphtheria, bacterial meningitis: they were all big, long-range mistakes waiting to happen. Wendy Lesher would do something to prevent them.

"Ah," Marisa said. "Here we go."

Now the photos began to come into focus, the forms gaining light and definition through the chemical haze, emerging by degrees from the black matte like a sculpture rising out of its stone. Marisa blew on them softly, then tacked them onto the bulletin board to dry. Hanging up there, surrounded by the fish, the cats, the mice, the monkeys, and the rabbits, the spider looked rather glossy and sleek, pleased with himself and his labors. Ian was pleased too. His research often had this effect on him, gave him the sense of being at once part of and larger than his species, a member of a vast, far-flung clan. For some reason the proximity of Marisa Chu had this effect on him as well.

"Boy," she said with a sigh, gazing out the window, "you've got a great view."

"Thank you." Why was he thanking her? What had he done to create it?

"I should come hang out over here more often. Mine doesn't even have a window. It doesn't even have an *airshaft.* I get to look at filing cabinets all day."

"You should," Ian said.

"Should what?"

Come hang out over here more often, he meant to say. The words did not emerge in quite that order from his larynx, however, his brain having passed into some strange new beta state where the usual laws governing language function no longer applied. What came out instead was a rather cryptic, dyslexic-sounding exclamation, one that would have required a great deal of wearying exegesis had his voice been even vaguely audible to Marisa Chu, which, thank God, from the way she continued to regard him with the blankest, most impassive expression imaginable, it probably wasn't.

"Look at that," she said, diverted by something on the other side of the window.

"What?"

"Down there."

He leaned across her, trying in vain to identify whatever it was that engaged her so. It *was* a nice view. You could see the whole messy musculature of the city—the flexed joints and streaming arteries, the glass towers like so many aspiring limbs; the Common's shadowed torso, the bright blinking eyes of Back Bay, the lurid rouge of the Combat Zone, the bridges strung like pearls of light across the black neck of the Charles. At times like this, standing before his high window, it all looked to Ian like one enormous, pulse-driven organism, twitching with nerves and busy circulatory flows, consciousness and instinct, ego and id . . . a kind of self. Not complete, not autonomous, in no way perfected. But a self nonetheless.

"Forget it," she said. "It's gone."

"What was it?"

"Nothing. Nothing important."

She shook her head. Her black hair was short and spiky, accentuating the softness of her features and the round, flat-nosed, planetary nature of her face. Ian recalled something he had read about film stars, how big their heads were in proportion to their bodies. Marisa Chu was like that. Her head with its low monkish ridge of hair was heavy, substantial; it seemed to contain multitudes. A tiny ruby bestrode one nostril, severe as a drop of blood. Her life lay concealed inside it, he thought, at once reflecting and eluding light.

"I'm starved," she said. "I get so hungry at night."

"Amine surge," he said. "I read a paper on it. It's incredibly common."

Nodding, Marisa relapsed into silence. He had said the wrong thing again. There was, it seemed, too much paper in his life.

Recklessly his gaze skated down the sleeve of her lab coat, which had been pushed over her elbow, revealing the wan, ivory slope of her biceps. An inoculation mark from childhood—it looked like a moon crater—made him think again, achingly, of Wendy Lesher. Was she inoculating all the women in the world against him? He could have gone after her. But there seemed no basis for it, no precedent. To fly across the globe like that; it would have been a callow, desperate, hopelessly theatrical gesture. And he was just settling into the new job. . . .

Marisa's forearm, perhaps accidentally, brushed against his own. At once the short hairs above his elbow sprang to attention. He waited. A thin waft of scent rose off her scalp. It rippled the air like heat, messed around with the density of things. He wondered what would happen if he were to, say, invite her out for coffee. She was an Asian-American of some kind, perhaps she preferred tea. It didn't sound quite right, inviting someone out for tea. And even if he did, what in the world would they talk about?

"How's Malcolm doing?" he asked, stupidly, to break the silence. "I haven't seen him around these past few weeks."

"He's been out in California. Gillian's mother is sick."

"I'm sorry."

"Why? Did you know her?"

"I mean I'm sorry for him and Gillian."

"Oh." She sighed. "Well, he's quitting the project. Did you know that?"

This was such odd, unexpected news that Ian didn't trust himself to reply right away.

"They might stay in California. That's what Gillian wants. And he has an offer from Stanford."

"I didn't know they had a position open."

"They're offering to make one."

"Ah."

"He says he may go to India instead." Marisa had her nose pressed against the window. "They're going to inherit a lot of money when Gillian's mother dies. They can go wherever they want."

"Why India?"

"You don't know? I figured he would have told you."

"Told me what?"

"Malcolm's gotten into this whole Ayurvedic medicine thing lately. Purges, bleedings, evacuation of body fluids, God only knows what else. He's read a lot of books. It's not just the oldest form of medicine on the planet, he says, but the most effective as well. Half a billion Hindus can't be wrong, is basically the argument."

"Never heard of it."

"Me neither." She made an expression of controlled distaste. "I don't understand," she said, "how a person can just throw everything over so fast."

Ian had been thinking the same thing. "That expectancy conference last week in Palo Alto. Did Malcolm go?"

"Yeah. Gerstein presented. Lockhardt. Frantz. Sheinberg. The whole gang."

"I read Frantz's last paper," Ian said. "He claims he's found the endocrine molecules that carry out placebo responses. He's getting a seventy-percent success rate. Amazing stuff."

"Mumbo jumbo," Marisa said promptly, dismissing them all—Frantz, Ian, Gerstein, Malcolm, the entire population of northern California—with a wave of her hand. "Those expectancy types are so bogus. Someone should run a longitudinal study on why men get so mystical and softheaded about these things. Some hormonal reflex, I bet, that kicks in after thirty."

Ian considered reminding her that he himself was still in his twenties and thus exempt from that charge, at least. But lately he did not take quite so much pride as he once did in being younger than other people. Besides, it was no longer true; about a third of the project staff were his age or younger at this point. One or two were still graduate students. They were very hardworking and cost almost nothing. It was his job, in fact, to recruit more.

". . . he speaks a whole other language these days."

"Who?"

"Malcolm. It's like he's standing on his head—he keeps yelling how everyone else is upside down. Our whole approach, our whole methodology, everything we've worked so hard to . . . to *achieve,*" her voice almost broke on this word, "it's all wrong. Just like that. Too narrow, too cautious, too mechanistic, too East Coast, too Ivy Lea—"

Her voice broke off. She had begun to cry. When had *that* started? Could the moon cry?

In a tentative and experimental way he touched a hand to the back of her shoulder. She made no move to brush it off. Neither did she acknowledge it. It seemed possible to Ian, given how little force he'd invested in the gesture, that she did not so much as feel it. She merely stood there rigid in her low-wattage radiance, her breath fogging the window, as if waiting for something—or someone—to wipe the whole thing clear.

"Maybe some tea you want?"

Not only had the words tumbled out in the wrong pattern again, but they were also a good deal louder than he'd intended. Nonetheless he refused to disavow them, even as Marisa turned and stared at him in that infuriatingly stolid and impassive way.

"What about the fish?" Her voice was distant, preoccupied, as if she'd left something on the stove.

"Sure, if you're hungry. I mean, why not?"

"I mean the ones downstairs," Marisa said, blowing her nose. "The ones you're responsible for."

He flushed; he had forgotten about the damn fish.

"Listen," she said, "it's okay. I have to go anyway."

"Why?"

She was looking down at her shoes. They were low black slipper-like things. Sensible. That was the thing about Marisa Chu. Nose-ruby or no nose-ruby, she was terrifically sensible.

"I'm expecting a call," she said.

After she left, Ian continued to stare out the window, trying to read in the profusion of winking lights just what it was he should have said next, as opposed to what he did say: i.e., nothing. You'd have almost thought he *wanted* her to leave. Which, let's face it, he did. He was relieved to have her gone, and with her the tension, the unreality, the shadow of fateful repetition she evoked in him. He was not a cold, mechanical person, but there were times he almost wished he were. Cold, mechanical people got a lot of work done.

For a moment he considered going home—that is, Barbara's home—to practice his French horn, or take a spin along the river on his mountain bike. Something that came easily. From one point of view, he reflected, all human progress could be seen as a response to some species deficiency, some incompleteness. That was how nature drew you into its machinations, by leaving blanks and gaps, small organic vacancies to drive you forward, like carrots dangling on a stick. Of course, some people found a way to *eat* their carrots. Some people got married, had children, bought houses. But it seemed the goals he was chasing were not the usual ones.

Restless, he picked up another memo off his desk, read it over twice, and headed down to check on the fish.

Chewing on a stick of sugarless gum, he hummed mindlessly as he descended, some aspirin jingle from the radio. Around him the stairwell had that heady, toxic chemical odor of fresh paint. It was an idiosyncratic tenet of hospital policy that the physical plant was forever being worked on—repainting, rewiring, resurfacing, tearing down walls and erecting new ones—even as the administration were forever swearing poverty. But no doubt they knew what they were doing up there. Like the ad copy they had sent around the floor for review. At the top someone had thought to put an outline of Rodin's "Thinker." A shrewd graphics choice, Ian decided: witty but familiar, arresting in a timeless way.

LOSING YOUR MIND?

We can help you find it.

A growing body of scientific evidence indicates that what we call "mental" illnesses are really physical diseases of the brain. Conditions such as anxiety, insomnia, schizophrenia, bipolar disorder, and major depression are biologically based brain disorders with chemical and genetic components. At Boston Psychopathic, we treat mental illness in a caring, knowledgeable way. Our staff of world-renowned physicians and our advanced facilities will ensure that you get the treatment you deserve. So take your head out of your hands and put it in ours. Call for a free interview.

BOSTON PSYCHOPATHIC
Honoring most health insurance plans

It was, he thought, a very strong ad. Of course, there were people who disagreed, like Malcolm Perle, who claimed no hospital should ever stoop to advertising in the first place. Ian recalled a heated discussion among the staff, at the end of which he'd been left as he'd begun, undecided. In some ways the direct approach made sense to him. If you didn't advertise your virtues, how would anyone know what they were?

Maybe *he* should take out an ad, he thought.

The fish, for reasons of space and climate control, were housed in the basement, a converted storage closet off the laundry room that trembled from the massive, sluggish vibrations of the washers and dryers nearby. Ian closed the door behind him. He liked it down here. The warm hum of the generators, the fish swimming complacently in their violet fluorescence, the pumps belching away at regular intervals, keeping things going—it gave him a sense of continuity and grace, of an order beneath the surface of things. Making his way past tanks one through six, he felt the cool, crisp satisfactions that result when will and intelligence are conjoined with design. And then he came to tank seven.

In tank seven, the Siamese fighting fish, instead of nosing sullenly around the bottom as millions of years of evolution had determined they should do, glided blithely just below the water's surface, no less quiescent than the angel fish in tank three. Ian checked the indicators. The aquarium temperature was normal, the tank lights operating perfectly. And yet the fighting fish had stopped fighting. Moreover, they appeared to meet all the behavioral criteria of paradoxical sleep. Moreover, they appeared to be actually dreaming.

In truth, he pitied Malcolm for leaving the project, right now, in the middle of it all. To just up and go that way, with the data flooding in . . . he could not see the value. He thought of Wendy Lesher. Of Marisa standing rigid at his high window. *How can a person throw everything over so fast . . .*

The pumps gave off their low noises, their hollow percussion. Like a heart murmuring ceaselessly, through all the days and nights, even when no one was around to hear it. A heart or a mind. He stood there, Ian did, longer than he meant to or was even entirely conscious of, watching the Siamese fish traverse the tank in slow, graceful undulations, the languid fleck of their tail fins in the artificial light.

3

The Gestalt, If You Will

SHE WOKE, obscurely frantic, at 3:29. Here she was again. It had begun to take on the predictability, the solemn, impersonal intensity of a ritual. The darkness her shrine, the tangled sheets her vestments. And her prayer?

The night's sleep, such as it was, had been marked by unidentifiable signs, urgent ruined half-dreams she was powerless to reconstruct. They remained buried under her even now, jagged and mysterious, several layers deep, like fragments of pottery in an archaeological site. Her muscles were sore. It was as though she had fought a battle with the bed and lost. Flailing, seeking purchase against the springs, kneading the pillows like great white clumps of dough, she'd woken to find the sheets tangled around her legs. It took a ridiculous amount of effort to work herself free.

She went and peed and then came back to wait stubbornly for morning.

Her stomach, she noted along the way, was still stuck in its wash cycle: churning, foamy, with oscillating interludes of drift and collision she remembered all too well from last time. Last time, with Petey, had been difficult. But then so had the time before that, with Alex. Difficulty, it seemed, was just her thing: her medium, her message, her métier. Difficulty, in Bonnie's experience, was no problem at all. Difficulty was easy. It was everything else that was hard.

She propped herself against the headboard, trying to get comfortable. Fortunately she had grown accustomed to passing the dark hours this way. Nurturing her grievances, cataloguing her worries, scribbling fretful lists upon night's enormous blackboard while the red glow of the alarm clock burned its dull, irregular math into her head: 3:56. 4:39. 5:03. Her neighbors' windows were dark. The vacant streets were silent. She could feel the city bobbing along on slow, invisible tides, sailing wistfully through the millennium. What purpose was served, she wondered, in keeping her apart? What skittish night bird wished to reveal itself? What hard pea of revelation lay under the mattress, waiting for the princess to find it?

Reflexively she reached for a cigarette, but the pack was empty, and the vagrant butts that loitered broken in the ashtray had, she knew without having to examine them, long since coughed up their goods. It was time to quit again anyway. To shape up. A cold wind had insinuated itself in the night, slipping through warps in the baseboards and cracks in the storm windows, under the afghan and down comforter, past the oversized flannel nightgown that comprised her final, budget-busting layer of defense, and holing up where she was most vulnerable, most corrupt: in the lungs. She could feel it there now, waging its cold war, contracting into a fist around her heart.

5:53. Light was seeping under the drapes like a stain. Gradually patterns began to emerge in the faded wallpaper. She yawned and stretched. Her hands, in the ghostly dawn, were pale and pocked as moons. Overnight it seemed they had turned into her mother's.

A line from the Buddha drifted into view, as if her mind were a Magic 8-Ball: *Suffering is inherent in all compound things.* Not a hell of a lot of opium there, she thought, for the masses.

At 6:07 there came the slow, tumbling music of the recycling truck. Its tinkly glass, its metallic cymbals, its thumping percussion of newsprint, the hydraulic horn-wheeze of its brakes. She had forgotten to put out the bin. There was still time if she hurried. But no, hurrying would create its own mess. She'd leave a trail of cans and bottles behind her on the steps; the newspapers, unbound, would go skittering off down the street; and the guys in the truck would look up from the weighty business of saving the planet to see her flying toward them in bare feet and billowy kimono, lugging her overfull blue bin behind her, and then they would fix her with that hooded, lizardlike gaze of derisive boredom common to members of municipal employees unions everywhere; and things would escalate, or degenerate, or somehow get even uglier and more frustrating than they already were, from there. Forget the planet, she thought: it's you that needs saving.

Easing off the mattress, she sighed, pulled on her robe, and padded down the hallway in her thick wool sleeping socks toward the kitchen. It was a beginning. When she passed the boys' bedroom she closed her eyes, a sort of Zen calisthenic she'd mastered early in parenthood. She refused to look at the clutter; instead she syncopated her footsteps to the faint, breathy music of their sleep. She loved them fiercely, perhaps too much. Her ferocity was exhausting them all. She saw it in their sleep. A seeking of refuge. Asleep they had no need of her; like Theo, the box turtle they had generously abducted from Cape Cod the summer before, they drew up their limbs, disappearing into the foliage of their own natural homes, their thickened selves. It was a condition to which she aspired.

She thought of her parents down in Jersey, lying side by side in their twin beds under the earth. They had been turbulent and contentious people, particularly with each other. Even the pills they'd kept on their kitchen counter—nitroglycerin for her father's heart—were explosive. But now they were quiet. Now they slept their interminable sleep. At times her own life and that of her children seemed only an effusion of theirs, a pale bloom. A dream not yet enacted.

Today would be a work day, she thought.

For some years now she had been writing about Thoreau. It had begun, like so many of her unfinished projects, as a romance, a graduate school intoxication, roughly on the order of her affair with that tall, swivel-eyed TA in her Modernism seminar which had come to such grief after what, three months? Thoreau had lasted a good deal longer, had carried her through her master's and well into her doctoral studies. But after four or five years of her fitful, querulous scrutiny he too had wilted under pressure, failed to hold up. Somewhere along the way her love for the man had soured. Like a feckless but domineering boyfriend, he began to oppress her. His peevish opinions and self-righteous boasting grew stale over time, predictable, until even his great masterwork became reduced in her eyes to a slick transparency of his failings—an elaborate but ultimately rather half-assed gesture, a pup tent pitched in a suburban yard, a run-of-the-mill American dream.

Where had he gone, after all? *One short mile from home.* A thirteenth-century Japanese sage had gone off to the woods for thirty years and recorded it in a journal. Thoreau had lasted less than two. *With* frequent visitors, *with* daily trips to his mother's house to raid the cookie jar. Self-reliant? Transcendental? One might as well call Rip Van Winkle transcendental. And then there was the mirror. The man claimed to be roughing it, going native, letting his beard, like his thoughts, grow untended. So why bring a mirror into the hut? It made no sense. And yet it was this mirror, this paradoxical frame, she came to believe, that held the artist's true portrait—showed a man who, living one kind of life, imagined he was living another, more important one, all the while watching himself live it in a way that was not quite living at all. And if so, then his heroic adventure was only a form of retreat, under philosophy's smoke and camouflage, to a restful little condo by the lake. The mirror would tell her, she thought. She would step through the looking glass, burrow down to the heart of that utopian play world, and expose Thoreau as the preening, narcissistic mama's boy he was.

And so her dissertation had evolved, from love to contempt, from homage to scorn. By this point she could no longer remember what had made this inquiry of hers once seem so urgent and worthwhile, even to herself. She had chased a dead man through a looking glass, and had not yet found her way back.

In the kitchen, the phone rang once and stopped. It seemed only another tile in the night's blue mosaic.

Waiting for the water to boil, she discovered clouds of her own expired breath rising around her, gray and dissolute as dawn itself. Frost had inlaid the window with white forking scars. She tried to erase them with her finger, but they were on the far side of the glass, intricate and obscuring, perhaps even beautiful in a lacy, mocking way. Well, she thought, beauty's in short enough supply. Let them be.

When the coffee was ready—she'd allow herself one last day of caffeine—she poured it into her favorite, lead-bleeding mug from Conran's, added, in a gesture of concession, a bit more milk than she liked, and sat down at the table with the previous day's *Globe,* mindlessly blowing away the steam. She had ten minutes, maybe fifteen, before it would be necessary to wake the boys. The room began to take on light. Squirrels were jumping in the trees. Car doors banged open and shut, engines roared madly to life. On the table before her three clementines, ripened and immaculate, sat cradled in a wooden bowl. They cost seven bucks a crate and were so beautiful she could scarcely bear to eat them. Sometimes she felt content just to hold one, to pick it up and inhale the tart fragrance just below the skin.

Oh, she thought, let it be a girl. A poet, a dancer, a lithe, long-haired creature in tights and Capezios and extravagant scarves, a Sonya, a Nina, a Natasha. A moody but affectionate little Russian girl, one who'd speak French with her moody Russian friends, who'd sit curled in the window seat on rainy days sketching portraits of *ma mère* in pen and ink, and who with any luck at all would turn out to be a committed lesbian . . . was that too much to ask?

She reminded herself to call Dr. Siraj this morning.

The radiator was clanking merrily. Her socks were snug and warm. The coffee was strong; the clementine, its peel torn open by her thumbnail, miraculously sweet. Yes, a girl, she thought, a soft-armed child with a shining face. Why not? As she sat there scanning the time-lagged headlines, all at once she had a rather jaunty and omniscient perspective on things. Yesterday had been a terrible day. People had behaved badly; the world was a riot of transgression. And yet here it was tomorrow and they were all still around. And the day after that. And the day after that. She could feel her spirits just beginning to rise, to stand up and peek over the high hedges of her despair. Something was growing inside her. Taking hold. A few more minutes of quiet, another mug of coffee, maybe, oh God, a cigarette, and she might even be able to do some work today.

She reached up for the phone again without quite knowing why. "Good morning," someone said.

The voice was male, tentative, half lost in static. She had no idea who it was, but a hissing flare of confirmation went up in her head, some fateful quirk of dream-logic coming true. The phone, she now realized, had been ringing on and off for some time in the back bedroom; the fact that it had not been ringing here in the kitchen indicated, along with the static, that the extension was on the fritz again, a predictable result of Petey dropping the receiver about a hundred and fifty times onto the linoleum.

It would require yet another trip to Radio Shack. Which was next door to Burger King and Friendly's, so naturally Petey would demand a bribe to go along. Her life seemed bound by just these chains. Trapped like a fly in late capitalism's web.

"Hey, it's me." The voice struggled gamely through the wire's electrical storm. "I was a little worried about you, you know, last night . . . after you left . . . just wanted to make sure you got home, you know, okay . . ."

"Who *is* this?"

"Larry. Larry Albeit."

Bonnie tittered nervously. Apparently that was how her body responded to this man. There was some fickle but dynamic chemistry between them, good or bad, she wasn't sure. Was there such a thing as neutral chemistry?

"Look," he said, "I'm sorry to be calling so early. It's just I had this really weird dream about you, and I can't get it out of my head."

She said nothing. The idea made her feel at once flattered and envious and bitterly resentful. It wasn't clear to her which emotion would leap out of her mouth first.

"I was in an airport," he said, "about to take a night flight to somewhere, only I couldn't find my luggage, and then I saw you standing at the counter with these big blue tickets in your hand, and all these heavy bags. You were alone. Just completely alone. And then, I don't know, it was like you'd been waiting for me, you just opened up your arms. But then I suddenly remembered I'd left Kippy and the girls back in the parking lot with the luggage, and I . . . I . . ."

"Larry," she said, "get a grip. We didn't do anything."

"In a technical sense it was perfectly innocent, no question. And I want to emphasize that at no point was your conduct last night in any way reproachable, from a moral perspective I mean. Even in the dream. Which is something I can't tell you, looking back, how much I appreciate."

"Gee, thanks."

"It's just I was moved by your, you know, situation. I found it terribly provocative. I don't mean in the erotic sense necessarily, though to be perfectly honest it seems to have teetered over a little into that too. But just the whole thing. The gestalt, if you will."

"Where are you calling from, Larry? You sound fuzzy."

"Memorial Drive. I'm about to turn onto the BU Bridge."

"You're in your *car*?"

"I like to beat the traffic. Besides, it's nice from the car. There's this rush you get when you're zipping along talking on the cell phone. You feel like an alpha. A pilot."

"And your copilot?" Bonnie asked. "What about her?"

"Kippy? She's home making breakfast. Wednesday it's waffles. The girls," he added thoughtfully, "are really into waffles."

"You shouldn't be calling, Larry. It would be weird even if you weren't in your car."

"You're right. No question. It's just I kind of *had* to, for some reason. This dream, I can't seem to shake it out of my head. Of course it may just be from taking too many p—" There was a loud honk. "Bastard. And then there was that thing you said last night."

"What thing?"

"You meant it as a joke, I think. At least I'm pretty sure that's how you meant it. The truth is it's hard to tell with you. You have this kind of ironical sensibility, I guess you'd have to call it . . ." His voice faded out a moment, lost in the static.

Bonnie yawned. Stretching, her elbow made contact with some soft weight on the back of her chair. A shoulder bag.

". . . but I was thinking, maybe it isn't such a bad idea after all. I mean, given the particulars here, me and Kippy and so forth, and the whole ongoing bambino issue, and then you with all your . . . well, *needs.* And I do think we had a connection back there. A rapport. So I was thinking, what the hell, it might be exciting to get together and explore the idea and see where we wind up."

The shoulder bag, she realized, belonged to Cress. It dangled from fraying straps at a droopy, precipitous angle, poised to abandon its contents to the floor. A Kleenex, crumpled and pale, peeked out from its depths like an iceberg. The sight made Bonnie wistful.

"Of course I'd handle most of the practical difficulties on my end. These things can get unbelievably messy, just the interpersonal dynamics alone. Not that I've ever gone through one of them personally, but a colleague of mine, my squash partner, actually, has a lot of experience with this sort of—"

"The dynamics?" Bonnie asked, half listening. Larry's voice, perhaps due to the river, or some oscillation in the phone signal, had a washy, intermittent quality; it did not feel fully there. Or perhaps she was the one not fully there. Her gaze, unstuck, drifted over Cress's shoulder bag and down through the years, recalling a bag of her own, circa 1977, purchased from a combination head shop/used-clothing store on State Street . . . a Guatemalan rucksack, hand-stitched by rural artisans (a synonym, according to Leon, for ruthlessly exploited Third World labor), featuring an assortment of luminous blue birds and yellow suns wheeling deliriously across a black sky, in what might have been a vision of the apocalypse. She wondered what had become of it. Good Lord, State Street: What had become of that? And then there was the matter of Bonnie Saks: What in the world, since those light, trippy college days, had become of *her*?

". . . but only if you're interested, naturally," Larry Albeit was saying, his high thin voice ebbing and flowing. "I wouldn't want you to resent yourself for doing it later. Or me either. Or feel any more pressured about it than you already feel, which I got the impression last night was quite a bit. Not that anyone could blame you under the circumstances. . . ." His voice trailed off again.

"Which circumstances are you talking about?"

"Sorry, you have to speak up. I'm under an overpass and it's hard to hear."

"I'm confused, Larry. What is it you want, in five words or less?"

"Haven't I said? To buy you lunch."

"Where?" she asked impulsively. It was not the only question that came to her, but for some reason it was the first. This seemed a mildly bad sign.

"Well, let's see. Where do you like to go?"

She liked to go to a lot of places. Unfortunately she never seemed to get there. "How about Cafe Bacchae?" she asked. "I hear it's fantastic."

"Love it. Let's go."

"You know," she could not help reflecting, in a small, plaintive voice, "I've never been to Cafe Bacchae."

"That's a shame," Larry said. "I find it's generally better to do things than not do them, if you have a choice."

"I'll have to get back to you on that."

"Good. Call you later, okay?"

What for? she wanted to ask. But he had already clicked off.

The mug of coffee was now, officially, cold. Crescents of frost lay glazed over the windows like a second skin. She could just make out, on the other side, the flat lemon lozenge of the sun. Wasn't it time to wake the boys? All at once she felt unaccountably needful. It occurred to her that if she was going to allow herself a one-day reprieve on the caffeine-during-pregnancy issue, it would only be right and consistent to apply the same standard to cigarettes.

Possession being nine-tenths of the law, she ID'd Cress's shoulder bag as an obvious source. Of course, like most teenagers, Cress smoked Marlboros, which was a little disgusting, though forgivable, she supposed, under the circumstances. But where were they? Impatiently she ran her fingers through gum; TicTac dispensers; Mardi Gras beads; Motrins, presumably for her period; lipstick canisters (color: Delirious Vamp); tiny tubes of Vaseline; scraps of bad, semipornographic poetry; crumpled sketches of Brendan, her boyfriend, also bad and semipornographic; the petrified remains of at least one candy bar; a three-pack of blue-wrapped Trojans with extra spermicide, stolen, unless she was mistaken, from Bonnie's own nightstand (the lone withdrawal, sad to say, from that particular account in months) . . . and wasn't this, Bonnie reflected, the teenager's fate? To be a clumsy sieve for all life's most random, trivial, and transient phenomena while the really helpful, necessary items, the crucial ones, slipped right through your fing—

Ah, here was one, down at the bottom. A little crushed, but salvageable.

Hey, a motto, she thought wryly, lighting up. A mantra.

Smoking the purloined cigarette—and recording, with each inhalation, not just the usual admixture of shame, guilt, and worry, but also a kind of singular awe toward herself for doing so—she continued to work her way through the contents of Cress's shoulder bag, taking inventory so to speak, and it was in this mindlessly proprietary manner which was, she told herself, a mother's special province that she extracted the unsealed envelope from the bottom of the bag and discovered inside it the four baby-blue tablets.

What were they? They weren't aspirin. They weren't birth control pills. They weren't Quaaludes. They weren't speed. They weren't hallucinogens. They weren't any of the usual varieties of allergesics, antihistamines, or decongestants. Years of life and sinus trouble had given Bonnie a pretty thorough grounding in the pharmaceuticals area, and in all that time she had never run across these tablets before. Which meant they were probably something new.

She sighed. Now she was faced with a dreary decision: confront Cress about her drug-taking habits and thereby admit to spying, theft, and other ethically questionable behavior, or shut up and mind her own business, figuring that the baby-blue capsules, whatever they were, were as benign as they looked. Even if they weren't, she reasoned, they'd be likely to hurt no one but Cress, toward whom she felt a vague if not irrational attachment, but for whose health and welfare she was in no way responsible. Cress was her baby-sitter, not her daughter; her own children were still sleeping amid the lumpy detritus of their bedroom, perfectly safe. Still sleeping—

Oh God.

She ran down the hallway and into their darkened, sock-smelling bedroom. Alex lay curled on his side in the upper bunk, breathing noisily through half-clogged nostrils, his face tremoring just perceptibly from the effort as if from rage or grief. Below him Petey looked to be in the process of falling from a great height—his arms outflung over his head, his legs madly askew under the sheets. She stood there in the pale, scalloped glow of the night-light, watching. Tiny bubbles were gathered at the corners of his mouth, the tumid by-products of dreams. It was all she could do to restrain herself from popping them. But she knew that would be wrong. Selfish, grasping, intrusive, even cruel. When she was okay, when she was at the top of her game, it required only a modest effort to control herself.

Unfortunately she was not at the top of her game. Unfortunately she was nowhere near the top of her game.

So she set about yanking them out of their beds. They did not go willingly. Lest they slip back into sleep, she kept up a loud, nervous commentary as she extricated them from their linens, predicting the day's weather and sports highlights and reminding them how grieved their teachers would be should they arrive late, as they so often did, to their respective schools.

Alex, cursing loudly, picked himself up off the floor. "Why'd you wake us up?" he yelled.

Because I am lonely and frightened, she wanted to say, and don't know what to do. But all she said was "It's time."

"It's ten minutes early!" Alex insisted. His voice drew volume and authority from the sheer fact of being in the right for a change.

"You need to shower this morning, honey. It's been days and days."

"It's ten minutes early!" he repeated, perhaps because he hadn't heard her, perhaps because he had. But he went stumbling down the hallway toward the bathroom.

This left Petey, dazed and fighting tears, behind.

"You okay, pal?" Bonnie asked him. "Did you have another bad dream?"

Big-eyed and somber, the child nodded vaguely yes, though whether to one question or both—or neither—it wasn't clear.

The bad dreams, he'd once explained to her, came after the bad thoughts. If he had a bad thought before he fell asleep, then the dreams would be bad too. Often they involved coming into Bonnie's room to find a leering, emaciated skull where her head should be. Occasionally they were worse than that. It appeared that something along these lines was going on at naptime as well, for Petey's preschool teacher had called Bonnie aside one drear November day and handed her, in an excess of sympathy, the name of what turned out to be the world's most expensive child therapist.

Happily, the therapist, after ten minutes, had concluded there was nothing to worry about. A transient symptom. Though if it lasts, he said, there was, yes, a condition that might apply. *Shadow panic disorder.* He'd pronounced the words in a low, thrilled voice. An exciting new entry in the *DSM,* difficult to diagnose, origins unclear. Studies were being done, however, at the major universities. Symptomatic clusters being charted, curves and descents in the brain's chemical rivers. For the moment it was treatable with BuSpar. Call me, he'd said, tearing off a prescription, if it doesn't work.

It hadn't, of course. Though to be fair she hadn't really given it much of a chance. Two or three nights before the bathroom sink, watching Petey struggle to swallow the enormous pills, had been all she could take. In the end, she'd opted for a simpler, cheaper, more organic alternative: magic. Like many of her parenting strategies, it was conceived in panic, a shot in the dark. *Lumma-yumma-rumma-zah!* she'd whispered in the boy's ear. *You are hereby protected from bad dreams.* And yet, ridiculously lame as it sounded, it had somehow worked to keep the bad dreams away that first night, and then the next, and the next one too, and now whenever she tucked Petey into bed she felt obliged to recite the same words again and again, in the same low crouch, the same basso, stentorian whisper, until, by some invisible process she had no desire to understand, that stupid, random string of onomatopoeic incantations had begun to take on for her too a kind of gravity and sense, a fuzzy nimbus of reflexive logic. Though sometimes she forgot, or went out, as she had the night before, and left the boy unprotected.

"Look," he said, pointing to the turtle box. "We forgot to turn on Theo's light."

"And now he's asleep."

"He's always asleep," the boy complained. A suggestion of ontological betrayal was in his voice, anger at some lazy, careless god who did or did not arrange things. "That's all he ever does."

"I know."

She hugged him to her chest then, tightly, even violently, and closed her eyes. He was still her baby, her youngest; none of that had changed, not yet. How much time went by in this position she didn't know. Enough for Petey to begin to squirm in her arms, to complain, as he sometimes did, that her face was too cold. Enough for her stomach to send out another round of distress signals. Enough for Alex to finish up in the bathroom, forget to flush as usual, and stomp around the place bemoaning the dearth of clean clothes in his drawers. Enough for Bonnie to answer him a bit too sharply, and for the first of several tedious, protracted arguments to commence, and for the revelation, by means of a subtle pooling warmth against her chest, that in the terror and confusion of the morning Petey had wet himself again. And so the day was launched.

4

The Interpretation of Dreams: An Introduction

THE PROFESSOR, wearing a crisp blue blazer, a mustard-yellow shirt, and the red-checkered bow tie he seemed determined to make his trademark, strode into the lecture hall promptly at ten. Clicking open his briefcase, he withdrew the legal pad on which he kept his notes and set it on the lectern. He unfolded his reading glasses, examined each lens for smudges and dust, and pushed them up to their customary position on the wide, sturdy bridge of his nose. He took off his watch and laid it face-up on the lectern. He rolled back his sleeves. He fiddled with the microphone. He unwrapped a Life Saver and popped it, with studied casualness, in his mouth. Finally, he craned his neck to scrutinize the blackboard behind him, making sure that it had been washed clean by the often indolent though aggressively unionized maintenance staff, and wasn't strewn, as it frequently was, with dubious, illegible hieroglyphs from Irv Markson's Readings in Advanced Neurocognition seminar, which met the night before. It had. So he blew his nose again.

All this activity, though not in any way necessary, was, as he'd once explained to Ian, pedagogically useful for Howard Heflin, in that it helped to pass the two or three minutes he liked to allow for his students to straggle in late with their coats and backpacks, their complicated coffees and enormous fruit-studded muffins, and that sleep-soured look of defensive belligerence, or belligerent defensiveness—or was it open hostility?—which graduate students always seemed to bring with them in the morning, in Howard Heflin's experience, anyway.

"Let us suppose," the professor began smoothly, "that we're having a dream."

And indeed, they did look a little dreamy, Ian thought, now that they were in their seats, now that the lecture was getting started.

"It's two o'clock. We've just survived another lunch in the cafeteria, and our circadian rhythms have gone into their midafternoon trough. If we lived in Mexico or Panama we would go home, kick off our shoes, and take a siesta. But we live in Boston, busy and productive Boston, where we're enrolled in an expensive graduate program at the university. So we buy ourselves a jumbo latte and hope the caffeine does what it's supposed to do—block the adenosine action in the area of our brain adjacent to the suprachiasmatic nucleus.

"Today, for the sake of discussion, let's say the latte has failed us. Let's say we've fallen asleep in our library carrel instead. We've already passed through stages one and two, through the third phase of slow-wave sleep, and into an alternating cycle between stage two and the REM or paradoxical phase—a cycle that will last, on average, ninety minutes. As they say, we're dead to the world. Our prefrontal cortex has gone off-line. Our capacity to process external data—the fact that we're in danger of missing an important class, or might fall out of our chairs and bang our heads on the floor—has slipped to nothing. Our engine is running but the clutch, we might say, is out.

"To compensate, we experience a rise of motion and data in the unconscious. This creates imagery, which we call hallucination, and narrative, which we call confabulation. A wave of acetylcholine washes in, flooding the neuropathways with peptides, hormonal messengers. Suddenly we're not dead at all. No, we're alive, wonderfully alive, lying on a beach somewhere in the Bahamas, a beautiful place we may once have visited a long time ago. And we have company too—on the towel next to ours is that gorgeous person of the opposite gender who served us coffee this morning at the diner down the street. Or perhaps, for some of us" (he allowed, as if spontaneously, a cool smile) "the same gender.

"Of course, nice as the dream is, there are constraints. We lack control over events. We have no volition to pause, rewind, or fast-forward the scene. We may wish to reach out and caress the soft cheek of our companion, but find this simple motor command blocked by the brain stem. It's frustrating, isn't it, to be so energized and paralyzed at the same time? If the paralysis becomes extended, a by-no-means-uncommon phenomenon, we experience what the West Indians call *kokma*—a ghost baby who jumps on the sleeper and attacks his throat. A grisly image, you'll agree."

Now let's hear it, ladies and gentlemen, for our old friends Homer and Freud. . . .

"Now let us suppose, just for a moment, that we could travel back in time," the professor continued, "and tell the story of our dream to the epic poet Homer. What would he say? He would tell us it's a message from the gods. Freud would agree. Yes, it's a message, Freud would say—but a message from *his* god: the unconscious. Our dream, Freud would say, has provided a channel for the discharge of our repressed instinctual impulses—i.e., our wish for erotic companionship. It so happens he would be wrong, miserably wrong. We'll come to that in a moment.

"But let's return to the dream, shall we? There we are at the beach, sunning ourselves, having a marvelous time, when suddenly, unbeknownst to our sleeping self, a friend of ours, Bob, wanders into the library. Bob, it seems, has had a poor night's rest. Maybe Bob harbors some acute resentment of us he has not worked out in therapy, or maybe he has fought with his wife and is feeling unsettled, or it could be that Bob's just a nastier, more sadistic fellow than we gave him credit for—whatever the explanation, when he sees us napping peacefully in our carrel, Bob stops. He forms a voluntary response to the situation which he flatters himself is a witty idea. What he does is, he sneaks up very quietly behind us, and then he claps his hands loudly, like *so*—"

The microphone amplified the clap, to the point where Ian was nearly blasted out of his seat. Idiot. He had the syllabus in his notebook; he should have known better than to sit so near the speakers today.

"What's happened? Our beach is gone. Our beautiful companion has vanished. Why? Because the external input—Bob's clap—has overridden the internal one, and our amines, jolted by the shock, now leap into action and thrust us awake. We're awake enough to feel sad, sad and angry, as we begin to realize that we're no longer on a beach in the Bahamas, that we were never on a beach in the Bahamas, that in fact if we don't buckle down in our studies and the economy doesn't stay strong, we may never *get* to be on a beach in the Bahamas."

The professor pauses for laughter but none is forthcoming. That "economy" line is either too obscure or too close to home. Ian watches him scribble a note to revise it next term.

"No, we're still at our same old study table, in our same old library, in our same old earthbound life. We look up and discover our friend Bob, beaming down at us affectionately. Bob, we think to ourselves, is a nice, high-spirited fellow. Impossible not to like. So now that our muscles are no longer paralyzed, we reach up with both hands and we . . . *strangle that son of a bitch!*"

Finally he's got them laughing, though not half so loudly or convincingly, Ian observes, as the students did last fall. Odd, how variable these classroom dynamics are, how empirically unstable. No matter how good you are—and Howard Heflin can be *very* good—each class contains its own complex, mysterious patterns, its own unseen levels, encapsulated perfectly inside the others like a Russian doll. Observable behavior on the outside, then the Byzantine inner circuit of brain sites, then, flowing subversively below, a third strata of molecules, transmitters, proteins, and receptors, reacting to invisible factors and vibrations. Beneath that there's only what? The coiled strands of information that underlie all human events—the DNA itself.

Maybe, when you get down that far, Ian thinks, it's all been coded already. Like those troublesome nerve twins he's been working with, the agonist/antagonist. Each fits into its receptor like a key into a lock, but only the agonist can trick it open. The antagonist, on the other hand, just sits there taking up space, all cell function unchanged. Why? There's no *reason.* Or if there is, it lies latent in its cryptic, inscrutable codes, waiting for someone to read it.

Yes, it's an enervating and annoying realization, all right: the classroom too is a brain, and a rather crude one at that.

"Dreaming, ladies and gentlemen, is not *like* a delirium. It *is* a delirium—a delirium that occupies, let me remind you, roughly ten percent of our lives. We experience our beach dream as 'real' only because our brain lacks the serotonin and norepinephrine it needs for proper judgment. This same chemical shortfall accounts for why we forget it so promptly, of course, and why so much of it is lost to us. Which is fortunate. Because good dreams like ours are the exception. Two out of every three are highly unpleasant—draining, disorienting, anxiety-producing. And that's not the bad news. The bad news is, they aren't even *worth* it. Because the bad news, people, Freudian theory to the contrary, is that *dreams have no meaning at all.*"

Let me emphasize this point. . . .

"Allow me to repeat this point. The dream is not a wish fulfillment. The dream is not, in any important sense of the word, meaningful. The relevant stimuli are not psychological but organic, arising not from the cognitive areas of the cerebral cortex but directly from the brain stem. Think of your computer at home, how it reorganizes the information it has received that day. To keep it working properly the files must be continually moved, updated, erased. The brain does this too. The brain's far too busy to keep all these messy, tiresome dreams around. They must be thrown out with the rest of the clutter, the mental trash. Simple epiphenomena spun off when the brain tests itself during the night, performing its own inventory, so to speak."

Annoyingly enough, a hand went up.

"You there. Yes?"

"But what about anxiety dreams? Like running late for a train? Don't they manifest what we'd call meaning?"

"From a formal point of view," the professor explained, "the dream you describe is a typical REM sleep production. The anxiety arises from automatic activation of the amygdala. It is then aggravated by the inability of the impaired memory system to situate the dreamer in a manageable context. *After* the fact," he went on sternly, "we may attach any number of meanings that are pertinent to our own experience as educated urban people. Just as we may find correspondences with a tarot deck, say, or the constellations of the stars."

The young woman who had asked the question stood there forming a reply, her slender wrist with its silver bangles not yet retracted from the air. Her face, Ian observed, was small, ardent, and bony, pinched toward the center like a bird's. Even narrowed in concentration her eyes seemed to flash.

"Now, most of us," the professor went on, more quickly than usual, "make this strenuous round-trip, from waking to sleeping and back, every day, without ever going off course. Why then, we may well ask, do some of us suffer these same flights of delirium not when we're asleep but when we're awake?"

There's no easy answer. . . .

"Of course, there's no easy answer."

But we are exploring . . .

"But we are exploring these issues in clinical trials. For example, in animal experiments . . ." Ian's eyes rose from his notebook, in the margin of which he'd been idly doodling triangles and trapezoids, and leaned forward on the chance that some reference or acknowledgment of his own considerable contributions in this sphere might be forthcoming. ". . . we've found we are able to induce dreams in cats when they're awake. One small injection of carbachol is all that's required. Obviously we can't go around shooting carbachol into the human brain, but we *can* give a similar compound in tablet form to insomniacs, and find they slip more rapidly into REM sleep, stay there longer, and emerge more fully rested than before."

He began to wonder, idly, what it would be like to fall out of favor with Howard Heflin. It would be a long fall. Was that what had happened to Malcolm Perle?

"Suppose I tell you, ladies and gentlemen, that we have it in our power, right now, to improve the quantity and quality of sleep. Give it a chemical push. What do you think? Should we, as they say on television, *just do it*?"

Ian let out a quiet, involuntary groan, which was drowned out by a number of loud, cheerful, voluntary groans from the students, delighted to learn that their T-shirts and recreational equipment might prove relevant in some way for the final exam.

"Think of all the nights, people, that we fret away unproductively. All the mornings we wake up stale, unrested, and then trudge through the day like a sleepwalker, irritable and scattered. Think of the airline pilots, the truck drivers, the night-shift workers. The insomniacs and narcoleptics and early awakeners. The lost productivity. The staggering social costs. The road and workplace accidents, the pandemic depression. Why not put our finger on the other side of the scale? Through PET scans and supercomputers, we are now able to map out every one of the brain's receptors. We can increase cellular activity in one region of the brain and suppress it in another, make subtle readjustments in the circadian clock. Already we have compounds in clinical trials that make our current SSRI's as antiquated as the Edsel. In ten years—*five*—we'll be living in a world, people, where the biology of sleep and wakefulness is regularly manipulated through chemical means, with effects as revolutionary in the spheres of work and leisure as was the introduction of electric light."

He paused to wipe his brow with a handkerchief.

"Well? Say all this is in our power. What should we do?"

Nobody, it seemed, thought we should do anything. They may have assumed the questions to be, like so many of the professor's questions, rhetorical; or they might have lost track of the lecture at this point, wandering internal labyrinths of memory and desire; or they may have been scared off by his flinty response earlier to their fellow student. Was class over? Were they free to go? Or were they now in one of Professor Heflin's fatherly post-lecture "mentoring" sessions of "give-and-take" with his "young protégés"—a category that roughly included Ian himself?

Ian scribbled a note: *Call M & D tonight. Be in good mood!*

His father, his real one, taught philosophy at DeKalb. His mother was assistant dean of the law school. Ian had grown up with the Socratic method, had been subjected to it at the breakfast and dinner table throughout his long, seemingly endless childhood, and so he was able to say with some authority at this point that he really, truly hated the whole format. Of course his parents, to be fair, were also doting, intelligent, only moderately obsessive-compulsive people whose hopes for him and Barbara were by and large no different than their hopes for themselves: good health, careers of high achievement, intelligent heterosexual partners with pleasant dispositions, and a moderate number of affectionate but not overly demanding progeny. To ascertain how Ian was faring in pursuit of these goals, however—or rather, to ascertain why he had not as yet successfully achieved them—they could not stop tormenting him with questions. *Going out tonight? Anything fun on this weekend? Get that grant application in? Find an apartment yet? Anyone special in your life we should maybe know about?* By this point their weekly phone calls had devolved into a series of protracted, highly roundabout, infinitely meaningful solicitations (theirs) and short, guarded, inexpressive answers (his). Now that he was sleeping on Barbara's sofa bed the situation had gotten worse. He was forced to talk to his parents roughly twice as much as he was used to, and consequently the information he revealed each time was roughly half. It was something of a vicious cycle and he blamed himself for it, not them. Though he blamed them too. People who have welded the structures of their lives into place could not resist poking into all the weak foundations around them. It was human nature. In any case, it appeared to be the human nature of his parents.

"Dr. Heflin?"

A hand, he was distressed to see, had gone up in the third row. The same willful hand, at the same determined angle, as the one earlier. The professor nodded reluctantly. "Yes, Ms.—"

"Firestone. Emily Firestone. I'm just wondering about side effects," she said. "Like the SSRI's, they tend to cause insomnia, right? Inhibit REM? Also diarrhea, nausea, sexual dys—"

"True enough, Ms. Firestone. But the next generation of compounds show marked improvements in these areas. I would cite, for example, a substance we are testing in this very hospital, which has shown impressive results in extending REM."

"Excuse me," she said sharply, even resentfully, either of which qualities would have endeared her to Ian at once had he not been so eager to have the class over, "but won't it just turn out to be something else with those? Don't these changes you're talking about always destabilize the cognition system, and then you just have to *re*stabilize it with other drugs, the way you do with heroin and methadone? And doesn't that lead to subcellular habituation, which sets up sort of a vicious cycle?"

"Only with opiates," Heflin said. "Which the next generation of brain drugs are not."

"But aren't some people saying now that it's addiction *itself* that's addictive? That it doesn't matter so much what's in it? Besides, if these compounds are so new, couldn't there be properties we don't know abou—"

"These are excellent questions, Ms. Firestone. It so happens they're the very questions we're attempting to answer in clinical tests at the moment. Perhaps you'd care to help us?"

"Actually," she murmured, "I'm kind of swamped this—"

"One of my research assistants, Dr. Ogelvie, is in the back of the lecture hall this morning," Heflin said. "Feel free to stop by and speak with him. That goes for the rest of you too. We are, as many of you know, engaged in several research projects this term, exciting ones. An excellent time to step forward and volunteer. Other questions?"

As everyone else was kind of swamped this semester too, there were no other questions. So, without further ado, the professor launched into the second part of his lecture, which proved to be a good deal longer, drier, and more technical than the first; Ian Ogelvie returned to his doodling; and the students, released for the moment from the burden of engagement, slipped back into the state of gentle, precholinergic passivity they had traversed so often in previous lectures—wandering the borders, testing the fence posts for sway, gazing off into the distance toward sleep's shrouded summit, and the green, placid lowland that lay beyond.

5

The Fickle Gods

SHE'D HAD a therapist once, back when the state was flush and her health coverage generous, who believed that all human difficulties were "multiply determined." Divorce, insomnia, the '78 Red Sox, the Hundred Years War—so many random, hidden variables were attached to these disasters, in his view, that any retrospective assignment of causality was both a folly and a lie. Best to put them behind you and get on with your life. That was his message, the fruit of ten years' advanced education. Not surprisingly their sessions often ran short. His had not been the most orthodox analytic approach, nor was it, in her case, particularly successful; still, his pet phrase had stuck to her over the years, like a bandage on a wound. It almost seemed to insulate her somehow. And it had begun to take on a faint ring of divination.

Thus in the matter of her appointment with Dr. Siraj. There was the fact that her watch was set fifteen minutes ahead of those of everyone else in the time zone. There was the fact that Storrow Drive at that interim hour was uncharacteristically traffic-free. There was the fact that she'd cruised right into a parking space upon entering the garage, thereby avoiding the usual slow, hopeless, spiraling ascent up the ramps. Finally, there was the fact that she'd dismissed her Expository Writing class a half hour early—having, as she informed them, not yet finished grading their essays from the week before, which was perfectly understandable, she might well have added, given that she had not yet started. Though none of these factors alone seemed more determining than any other, taken together, they resulted in her arrival at the hospital some forty-five minutes early.

She pushed her way officiously through the revolving doors and into the bright, clattering lobby. She could if she chose go up to the fifth floor at once, get the insurance paperwork out of the way, and still have time to relax for a while amid the creamy mauves and grays of the waiting lounge, leafing through back issues of *Vogue* (their glossy covers webbed and torn, their fashions and celebrities no longer in currency, quite) and registering, if only half consciously, the flow of women in and out of the room: the teenagers trooping sullenly behind their mothers, the nervous young wives attended by nervous young husbands, the gals her own age with good haircuts and Chanel suits and leather-bound weekly calendars who, having driven themselves over on their lunch breaks, would take up position behind the big drooping coleus plants in the corner, talking soberly into their cell phones. Sisters, she'd think, observing them tenderly. Fellow passengers on the same vast, creaking ship, borne by the same inexorable tides toward the same unseen shores.

Today, however, she was in no mood for sisterhood. Today, with her swelling stomach, her threadbare jeans, her soiled socks—there had been no clean ones in her drawer either—she felt very much the solo tourist. Today, obeying some private, stubborn, unreconciled impulse, she passed right by the elevator and went into the gift shop instead.

To atone for this morning's bad scene, she picked out two expensive logs of Toblerone chocolate for the boys and, because she had a weakness for chocolate, one more for herself. She had a weakness for red licorice too, so she got some of that. Her weakness for fresh flowers, especially in midwinter, she had the force of will to resist for the moment; this freed her up to indulge yet another weakness, the art cards. There was a Tintoretto she did not recall from previous visits. She loved Tintoretto. Of course it was easy to love him: He was dead. He lived in Venice. His work was radiant and thrilling, he imbued everything he saw with a voluptuous glow, and those singular demands he made on the spirit—faith, abundance, the capacity for ecstasy and submission, sympathy and release—were the very terms of life's brief, all-too-binding contract she most craved to concede. For similar reasons it was easy to love his *paisanos* Titian, Veronese, Botticelli, and Raphael as well. And she did. She loved them all, the whole busy, prolific Renaissance crew, with terrific ardor and fidelity, slipping out to the Museum of Fine Arts in makeup, black leggings, and silk scarf to pass guilty but rapturous lunch hours whenever she could; that is, whenever the fickle gods that oversaw work, schools, parking, and the museum's ever-retracting hours of operation could be appeased; that is, about five times a year.

Well, she thought, handing half a dozen postcards, along with the chocolates and her Visa, to the woman who worked the register: Italy by proxy; it would have to do. She'd spent two weeks there once when she was twenty; the experience had nestled comfortably into a shadowed, fragrant grove in her brain. Her summer tour of the great cities, her breathless attempt to connect the dots, to sketch out, from the Old World's flaking chiaroscuro, a hint of a design. Having read Walter Pater at an impressionable age, Bonnie had come to think in such terms, to believe rather ravenously, along with the rest of her art history class, in the hard, gemlike flame. It remained the one immaculate ideal in her life. How she'd longed, in her slender youth, to immerse in that flame—peel off her too-white, too-tight, unmarked skin; burn up her mind's small dream of a world and enter the hot swarm of another, aglow . . . for we have only an interval, Pater had said (dutifully she signed her name to the receipt); one must wrest from life its very juice, seize every one of its latent pulsations.

Pulsations! Dear God, it made her shudder to think of all the pulsing she had done on that trip, all the pulsing and all the peeling and all the burning . . . and for what? She remembered a cool late morning in Florence, the sun wan and vague behind the mountains of Fiesole, towers rising over the cupolas, stone bins on the window ledges spilling yellow roses and oleander like ten thousand princesses letting down their hair. Back at the *pensione,* snoring dolefully, was a tall, uncircumcised French-Canadian she had met on the train. His name was lost to her now. But she remembered the curious and delicate sensation, as she closed the door behind her and tiptoed out into the hall, of his cold semen trickling inquisitively down her tanned, unshaved legs—how simple it was in those days, how mindless, being on the pill!—and then a moment later she was out, wandering off *isolata* into the cloven streets, in sundress and sandals, no map, no guide, only her slim, heavily annotated paperback Rilke to steer her across Ponte Vecchio in search of some crumbling out-of-the-way chapel the poet had cited for its gilded cherubim and frescoed ceiling, while around her the flies, the spotted pigeons, and the lean young men on scooters wove their noisy and somnolent arabesques. In truth, it had not been a particularly sublime experience, but it had remained with her over the years. She'd known it would, even at the time: a fossilized memory of traveling light, of the wide, ungainly wingspan that once propelled her. Something fluttery and ambitious and forever incomplete. Because she had never found that damned chapel.

At the elevator, she pushed the Up button and stepped back to wait. Her heart was pounding. Why? It was not as if she didn't know what lay before her.

Outside it had begun to snow. The flakes looked merry and fat, like some white, confectionary cereal. Restlessly she pulled her hair back into a bun and secured it with a scrunchie. She was no longer early for her appointment.

She glanced over the bulletin board, which was intricately tiered with announcements for workshops, classes, and support groups. Job Safety. Sexual Dysfunction. Stress Management. Adult Children of Alcoholics. Living with AIDS. Living with Schizophrenia. Living with Addiction. Living with Cancer. Living with Dying.

She thought of Larry Albeit and his wife, Kip. Noni Juice: What was that? So much to be learned in so short an interval. And then? The thing itself would not be mastered. There was always another class going on in the next room.

Living with Bonnie Saks. Now, there was a class, she thought. There was a fucking challenge.

A crew-cut, thin-lipped young man drew up beside her, carrying a yellow shopping bag. She thought she heard him sigh.

"I pressed the button," she muttered defensively, as if to herself. "It's very slow."

He gave a vague nod. "They all are."

There was something wise and smooth and overarching in his tone that both dismayed her and drew her attention from his face to what lay around his neck—a priest's ringed collar. Visible just above it were the dark pocks and crevices teenage acne had left like a glacial deposit on the pink slope of his jaw. Oh, she thought, the ravages of the flesh. Their eyes met. Behind the pale membrane that coated his pupils was a quizzical forbearance, like that of a dog responding to the call of an inattentive master. But perhaps he was only near-sighted, she thought.

"Visiting someone?" he asked.

"A doctor. And you?"

"A patient." He sighed. "I suppose that's easier. Though it's not my favorite part of the job, by any stretch."

"I know what you mean," she said. She meant it kindly; it was not until later that she realized how presumptuous she must have sounded.

Perhaps for this reason, or some other, the priest fell silent. She observed him carefully from the side, seeing in his profile, or imagining she saw, the boy he had once been—bright, gawky, ambitious, self-conscious, fenced off from girls by his skin's bloody wire, all those spiky hormones twisting and braiding like a cord. Curiously, the image did not evoke pity, but an odd kind of envy or covetousness. Could you be a normal person, she wondered, whatever that was, without a normal sex life, whatever *that* was? Could you stop wanting the usual things? Could you drive that desire away? Could you train yourself to want something else?

Nietzsche, she recalled, believed sexual abstinence did wonders for a man. Something about the reabsorbed spermatozoa heading up to the brain cells, steeping them in a rich, pungent mineral bath, a sort of high-protein diet. What hooey! No doubt Thoreau believed something equally stupid. These absolutists, she thought bitterly. These stupid, brilliant men with their stupid, brilliant theories. Transcendence was easy for such people. Of course when you were aloof and abstract of mind, it was easy to be pure. Of course when you stepped away, turned your back on the clotted domestications of the city, where things were not simple but relative, multiply determined; . . . of course when you denied yourself the common longings, bought a ticket for the high, unoxygenated spheres, took a cosmic shortcut right out of the gray zone . . .

She was beginning to feel a little gray and zoned out at this point herself. A sickly sweet odor of aftershave, deodorant, toothpaste, and Woolite—the many applied chemicals of the public self—came rising off the priest like a cloud. Woozy as a snowflake, she moved back a step, hoping he would not take offense. But he did, of course. He proceeded to glare at her as if *she* were the one who smelled, *she* were the one in the spooky, antiquated getup, *she* were the one who'd sworn off sex forever, *she* were the one who believed despite all earthly evidence in some ludicrous, medieval notion of a divine being.

Then abruptly, the young priest smiled, a brief but luminous flash, and a cold drizzle of doubt descended over Bonnie. Oh, maybe it was all true, she thought. Certainly she was guilty on the second and third counts, and, given the socks she was wearing, perhaps the first as well. As for the fourth, perhaps he saw something about her she could not see for herself. He cleared his throat and said, "It's on the way."

"What?"

"The elevator, see? It's heading down."

It was true; the numbers were running backward at last.

By the time it arrived—the whisk of the doors like the sigh of some weary, beneficent god—she had begun to tremble.

ANXIOUS? asked a notice taped unevenly to one wall.

ARE YOU SLEEPING TOO MUCH? TOO LITTLE? IS YOUR APPETITE UNEVEN? DO YOU FEEL LIKE THINGS ARE

OUT OF YOUR CONTROL? PERSISTENT ANXIETY AND INSOMNIA ARE MEDICALLY TREATABLE CONDITIONS. TEN MILLION AMERICANS SUFFER FROM THEM, AND YOU CAN HELP.

Right, Bonnie thought. I'm the one.

RESEARCHERS SEEK MALE AND FEMALE VOLUNTEERS FOR A THREE-MONTH SLEEP STUDY. COMPENSATION OF $250/WK TO BE PAID AFTER COMPLETION OF MEDICATION PROGRAM. CALL FOR DETAILS.

The priest got off on the third floor without saying good-bye. She rode up to the fifth, where she proceeded down the hallway to the east wing, holding her insurance card before her like a talisman. Above the gridded ceiling she heard the thudding booms and clangs of renovation, the high abrasive warble of metallic saws. A pale skin of dust lay over the drooping plant leaves. The heat was on full blast. Bonnie was glad for it, but the receptionist, a voluptuous, olive-complected woman named Christina, looked sweaty and laconic behind her desk. She sat slouched forward in her swivel chair, rouged cheeks plump as eggplants, her mouth forming a small languid pucker of unwelcome. Because Bonnie had some acquaintance with that mood herself, and because Christina appeared to be new to the rigors of the natalogy unit—or had not, at any rate, been working four years back, when she was pregnant with Petey—she tried not to get too pissed off at the rude, improvident way Christina went about her business, frowning ostentatiously and popping her chewing gum as she scanned the humming screen. "Twenty dollars," she announced like a verdict.

"What for?"

"Office visits are always twenty dollars."

"Since when? It used to be ten." For that matter, it used to be five. It used to be *free.*

"First of the year. Don't you read your policy updates?"

"Never."

"You should read your policy updates. It's important you be informed. That's how they announce these things."

"All that paper and postage," Bonnie said. "That's why costs are so high. If they'd just stop sending out so many updates, everything would be fine."

This improvisatory stab at microeconomic theory sounded somewhat lame and dubious even to her. In any case, it failed to elicit much of a reaction from Christina. "All the plans are charging this much for visits now," she said. "Not just yours. It's a way of containing costs."

"Well, they're not containing *my* costs."

"I'm sorry," Christina said, popping her gum, but in a muted, officious, barely audible way. Her eyes softened. It might have been all that incongruous heat, or perhaps she'd only just then noticed the black hole that had opened at the elbow of Bonnie's wool sweater; for a moment she really did look sorry. "You can use a credit card, if that helps."

And so Bonnie gave over her Visa again. Even before the morning's profligate spending she owed several thousand dollars on it, not to mention a considerable amount of interest; but she had already burned her American Express and had no choice. At least, after all the impulsive spending, the chocolates and art history and other wasteful froufrou, this was an investment in something serious and substantial, something *real.* Or so she told herself, looking over the baby-picture Christmas cards on the bulletin board, happy beneficiaries all, while she waited for her crinkly yellow receipt.

She followed the nurse—another new one—down the hallway, through the labyrinth of offices, and into an examination room in back. "He'll be with you shortly," the nurse said. A thin, long-faced woman with an irresolute perm, she paused at the door on her way out, examining Bonnie with something like interest. "There's a box of tissues over there," she said. "On the desk."

Bonnie nodded absently. Why on earth should she require tissues? They never used to offer her tissues in the old days, when she'd come here with Leon. Back then, the nurses would orbit like moths around the bright bulb of his head, laughing at his jokes, patiently answering his questions, nodding in bemusement and sympathy when his childish terror of needles sent him stumbling out of the room. How refreshing to see a man so sensitive, so in touch with his female side. Meanwhile she was the one splayed out on the table, giving blood. She was the one still here opening her veins, while Leon and his female side had run off together to South America.

When the nurse was gone, she tossed her coat and bag over a chair and examined her face vindictively in the mirror. Her eyes of course were sunken and red. Her nose was red too—a hot, neon, Times Square rendition of what increasingly seemed her own personal primary color—which, given the drawn, winter-pallid condition of her cheeks, nicely spotlighted her least attractive feature. As for her hair, it looked flighty and aspray, as if it had been shot out of a can. On the other hand she could console herself with the fact that all those free health club membership offers she'd tossed in the trash and all those restless nocturnal hours in the kitchen were really paying off: she now had not one chin, but two.

Then, wriggling out of her sweater, she felt something give along the seam, and found she had managed to drastically elongate the hole at the elbow, which now formed a garish scar halfway up her shoulder. A throb of panic announced itself in the veins of her wrists. The exam bed was cold. She could not get comfortable. Wrapping her arms around her own torso, she tried to rub herself warm, a gesture that was returned to her in the mirror as an odd hopeful parody of embrace. Whose hands were those caressing her shoulders, tugging at her blouse? Meekly she kicked off her shoes, undid the belt of her jeans, and was sitting there in a state of disheveled apprehension when Dr. Siraj rolled in with the blond nurse, who closed the door quietly behind them.

"My dear girl," Siraj trilled in his thin, mellifluent tenor, and she relaxed at once. She did love doctors so. "Where have you been, hmm? You must tell me everything."

"Well," she said. "I always do."

"Those darling boys. Have they grown very tall?"

"Oh yeah. Larger than life."

"Excellent," he said.

"How about you?" she asked. "How're things at home?"

"Only so-so." His smile turned momentarily inward at the corners. "I lost my father, you see. Last October. An attack of the heart."

"I'm so sorry. I had no idea."

"Rather a proud man, my father. I brought him over from Kanpur, you know. At the end. Every night he would sit there in front of the television set, complaining to my wife. The food, the cold, the pills, the pain, and so forth. My sister, the poor dear, has many problems of her own, but she left her three children in Houston and flew up to help. Right away my father began to complain to me about her. She in turn complained to me about my father. My wife complained to me about them both. There is no stoicism in my family, you see. This is why we're so close. We have no private pains. We share them freely among ourselves."

"You never told me you were Jewish," she said.

"Jewish? Ah." He narrowed his dark, moist eyes, not so much in mirth as recognition. "Marvelous. I shall remember that one."

He looked at his watch.

"So I gather you have something to share with me, hmm?"

"Oh, you know," she said. "The usual."

"How delightful. You've done a test, of course?"

She nodded. "I never did test well."

"Of course you do, darling. You always pass with flying colors; it is part of your charm. But shall we just take a look to confirm?"

"Might as well," she said. "I paid twenty bucks out there."

For a moment he looked blank.

"The plan," she reminded him.

"Ah, yes. The plan."

"Who *makes* these plans, anyway? I'd like to meet them. I don't think I understand the whole plan concept."

"No one does, my dear girl. That's why there are managers. One can't have managed care without the managers. Now," he said, "just relax, hmm?"

"I'm trying."

"Very good. Just lie back. We'll forget everything, all our worries and cares, our little burdens. We'll just see what there is to see."

Unlike most people, Bonnie actually liked going to doctors. She had a pretty fair tolerance for dentists, accountants, mechanics, hairdressers, and lawyers too. It was a professional age. She delivered herself with gratitude to their buzzing offices, sought out their informed opinions, their brisk and impersonal evaluations. They made her feel located; they made her feel *known.* She had been so long a student. People who not only talked about things but actually went around *doing* them seemed like evidence of some casual, secular miracle. In their presence she became calm and penitent, infinitely pliable, open to the ministrations of grace.

Siraj she liked especially. Tall and sharp-featured, he had long cunning hands and a yeasty, extravagant style. He wore a good deal more personal jewelry, for instance, than she did. Gold bracelets, fine rings. Italian shoes and suits of the latest fashion. A rich pomade clung to his hair, elevating the crown like a seawall. Below it his dark eyes glittered and schemed. For all his inner helium, his buoyant affability, there was something of the fox about him. In his garage out in Lincoln were two metallic-gray Jaguars, identical in every detail, which he alternated driving to work. It was, he'd once explained, his way of holding down the mileage. What with several teenage daughters, an agoraphobic wife, a Russian chess tutor in Needham, and a winterized cottage near Tanglewood, she imagined it made for a lot of driving.

"Oh yes," Siraj said, feeling around inside her. "Let me see . . . seven, eight weeks? Does that sound right?"

Bonnie closed her eyes a moment, tracing a backward path, through the clumpy terrain in her head, to Stanley's last visit. It had been, even by Gottfriedian standards, a rather perfunctory event. He'd arrived already exhausted, or so he announced, from his conference; then, paying zero attention to *her* exhaustion, which was both considerably more profound and historically determined than his, he'd kept on his down coat and wool scarf for the twenty or so minutes it took her to finish reading *Curious George* to Petey and getting both boys tucked in bed. The whole time she could hear Stanley pacing out in the hallway in his black snakeskin cowboy boots—to which were attached more layers of irony than she could keep track of—crunching his cherry cough drops and mumbling his way down a long, crabbed registry of vendettas and complaints. It was, she knew, only a rehearsal. The real performance would come later. First he'd deconstruct his three shallow and moronic copanelists. Then the insipid dullard of a moderator, who had failed to recognize him often enough. Then, as his internal generator gathered steam, he'd begin to improvise, expounding upon such worthy if familiar topics as his department chair in Toronto, his publisher in Princeton, his parents in Miami, his twin brother in Chicago, and finally, to complete the sullen geography of his worldview, the entire editorial board of the *New York Journal of Advanced Semiotics,* all of whom were guilty of holding him back in one or another petty, jealous, hermeneutically transparent way. At no point in the evening was Bonnie even tempted to raise, let alone wave, her own rumpled flags of grievance, like Alex getting a D on his math test, or Petey being on the verge of another in his continuing series of ear infections, or a certain steely irascibility she had detected that morning from her own department chair when the subject of her dissertation deadline came up. Why bother? She might as well have asked Stanley for the lowdown on his current live-in girlfriend, or for his intentions, such as they were, for the night ahead. Talk about hermeneutics! She might as well have insisted he take her out to dinner; he could have easily expensed it. But no. Tired, half numb, she had let the evening unfold in its usual unsatisfying and multiply determined way, falling into the sloppy casualness of old, semi-former lovers as they always had—even, it occurred to her, *before* they were old and semi-former—the radiator clanging its expensive tune, the domestic beer salvaged from the back of the fridge, the take-out ribs from Jake & Earl's with their gluey, bloody glaze, the take-home video that she was, as usual, too tired to follow, and then, somewhere in there between the somnolent scroll of the credits and morning's clamorous alarm, some rather sloppy and languorous sex.

Had she even come? There had been so little in the way of preparation that night—so little foreplay, so little forethought—it hardly seemed possible. But then that was how it worked sometimes. Release was granted when you weren't ready, when you'd done nothing to earn it, when you were operating under the messiest, most inadequate, least promising conditions imaginable. It was the body's own sick joke. Look, Ma, no hands . . .

"I knew it," she announced. "I fucking knew it."

"A woman always knows. Except, of course, when she doesn't." Siraj snapped off his gloves. "Well then."

"Well then what?"

"We must get you started, dear girl. Blood tests. Vitamins. Ultrasounds. We shall have a lovely spring, full of appointments. We must get to know each other all over again. Share our most intimate secrets."

"I'm not sure I can," Bonnie confessed.

"Then I will share *my* most intimate secrets."

The blond nurse, who had yet to say a word, cleared her throat expressively.

"That's not what I meant," Bonnie said.

Siraj smiled. "I know what you meant, dear girl."

"Oh."

Exactly what *had* she meant, though? Earlier that morning she'd thought she knew what she was doing; she had, she presumed, already plotted a course. But at the moment she found this course of hers difficult to retrace. What was happening to her? The touch of Siraj's fingers had undone all the pale ivory buttons of her resolve.

The doctor was regarding her steadily.

"It seems you have some thinking to do, hmmm?"

"I've already done that," she said. "It hasn't helped. It never does."

"You were not planning for such a development, I take it?"

She shook her head. "I'm lucky these days if I can plan a meal."

"Sometimes, of course, we plan without knowing."

"Thank you, Charlie Chan."

He smiled at her indulgently.

"Oh God." Her hands flew to her mouth. "What an awful, horrible, racist thing to say. I'm so sorry."

"Please, my dear girl, there's no offense. When one is under strain—"

"But it offends *me,* don't you see? And believe me, it's only the tip of the iceberg where bitchy remarks are concerned. What's the matter with me, Dr. Siraj? I can't sleep. When I do sleep I can't wake up. It's like a bad dream. I'm trying and trying to climb out of this hole, and every time I get near the top, which is where everyone else I know seems to have *started,* I fall right back in. Does any of this make sense?"

"Of course it does," Siraj agreed readily. "A great deal of sense."

"Please, talk to me straight, okay? Don't get all fatherly on me. I hate that."

"My dear girl, why so theatrical? A large undertaking lies before you. You are merely being sensible, asking yourself if it is something you are able, under present circumstances, to do."

"But why does it have to be *able* to do? Why can't it be something I *want* to do? Why can't the things I *want* to do and the things I'm *able* to do be the same for a change? Is that so unreasonable?"

"Perfectly reasonable."

"All right then."

"So," Siraj said, a bit coolly, she thought, "what do you want to do?"

"I want to have it."

The words had blown out of her like a jet of smoke. It was odd; she had been equally prepared to say the other.

"Forgive me, my dear. I seem to be a little confused."

"I want to have it, okay? But I don't think I'm able. In fact I *know* I'm not able. So, really, I don't. I mean, it isn't even a close call, in that sense. But the thing is . . . the thing is, Doctor . . ."

She looked at the nurse for help, but her expression was as dry and colorless, as impossible to authenticate, as her hair. As for Siraj, he continued to regard her thoughtfully, stroking his round chin with its tender, shadowed cleft. His solemnity at this moment perplexed her, if that were possible, even more. Meanwhile the second hand on his Rolex twitched and twitched.

"Oh, come on. Why don't you *say* something? You're supposed to be my OB, to say nothing of being my goddamn friend. Plus the twenty bucks to Christina out there. Can't you at least come across with a little advice? I promise not to sue you if it turns out disastrous."

"You want advice, my dear girl?"

She nodded gratefully. At last, someone to tell her what to do. Why hadn't she called Siraj a long time ago? He knew her better, from the inside out, than anyone else. Why did she always have to be so—

"Then I would recommend you visit our very excellent psychological clinic on the sixteenth floor."

Her heart flopped and sank.

"I will call up to them right now for an appointment. Perhaps they can get you in today. Of course they're terribly busy. But in cases such as this—"

"I'm *not* a case!" she all but shrieked. "I'm a thirty-nine-year-old woman, Dr. Siraj! I've got one kid on Prozac and another who wets the bed. I've got two jobs, no husband, and the one time I go ahead and have sex with something that isn't manufactured by GE, I get knocked up. You want to talk shrinks? I've had more shrinks in my life than I've had boyfriends. Don't you see? Isn't it obvious? What I need isn't a new shrink. What I need is a new *life*!"

"My dear girl," Siraj sighed, having reached at last the end of his patience. "You have one."

On the way out she was forced to go through her datebook and discuss her plans for the future with Christina. Finally, after several false starts, they settled on a time for the next appointment. "He gave you a prescription?" Christina asked.

"Yeah. Two, actually. For my advanced years." She tried on game, stoical smile with only limited success. There would be tim to perfect it. The prenatal vitamins, she knew from prior experienc would be both pricey and hard to swallow. Perhaps that account for her reluctance to push away from the reception desk just yet get back in the elevator and head home.

"What about you," she asked idly of Christina. "Any kids?"

"Me? Nah. Someday maybe, like with the right guy."

"You have a guy now?"

"Yeah. Hector. I don't think he's the one."

"What's he do?"

"He goes to school. Engineering. Three nights a week he drives his brother's cab. Airport runs."

"He sounds wonderful."

"Hector? He's still kinda young. But he treats me good."

"What's good?"

"Hah?"

"I'm just curious. Is it identifiable? Does it bear any resemblance to, say, a hard, gemlike flame?"

Christina scrutinized her carefully. "You look kinda down," she said. "Can you get home okay?"

"I've got my car," Bonnie said. Suddenly she had what seemed an inspiration; she dug in her bag for the postcards she had bought at the gift shop. "Here. I want you to have this."

Christina examined the card with some suspicion, front and back.

"It's a Tintoretto," Bonnie explained.

"Yeah?" Christina frowned. "It's pretty," she declared. Her voice, tinged vaguely with feeling, nonetheless lacked something in the way of conviction. "Thanks a lot."

"I like to put them on my refrigerator," Bonnie said hopelessly. "Or in the bathroom, beside the mirror. Sometimes right *on* the mirror. Oh hell, look, just throw it away when you get home, I don't care."

"I'll keep it right here," Christina announced. "Right here on the desk, next to my—"

But Bonnie, her lower lip quivering, had already turned to go.

Upon entering the elevator she pressed the *L* button and stepped back deferentially to allow other people in. As it happened, there were no other people. The doors shuddered closed and there she was again: herself. She read over the anxiety flyer again, or else a different copy of the same one, or else another flyer altogether.

When the elevator started to move, it did not escape her notice that despite her best efforts to go down she was in fact going up. She watched the light pulsing its way up the chart of numbers, one by one, making its maddening climb.

6

Quantifiably Fascinating Behaviors

THE WOMAN was already crying when she stepped into the elevator. He was reasonably certain of that. If his experience with Wendy Lesher, with Marisa Chu a few nights back, and with the female sex in general had taught Ian anything, it was that the origins of female grief were often private and obscure. Rarely had they much if anything to do with him. This was comforting in some ways, but in others disturbing. The fact was, Ian had reached the stage in his life where he would have liked to be responsible for causing more grief in other people. Particularly women. He'd have liked to shake things up a bit in that area, evoke some strong emotions, to seize the sky itself by its blue, billowy shoulders and make it rain. And then? Then he'd step forward with his promising future and his good intentions and his air of keen, can-do capability and, waving his white handkerchief like a magician, swipe the tears away.

Yes, one had to step forward, Ian thought. Because the behaviorists for all their dull schematicism had got it right: Existence precedes essence. One acts in order to become. Frantz's placebo studies appeared to confirm this. Chemically speaking, the body's metabolic changes were often determined by functions of the mind. Action first; *then* transformation. That was the whole nub of expectancy theory. Maybe even life itself.

All of which ran through his head as he eyed the woman two feet away, slumped against the back wall of the elevator.

He had a quick intuition, the kind one sometimes gets in elevators, that she'd entered on one of the lower floors and been drawn up to the high latitudes of the building against her will. Probably she hadn't bothered to look at the directional arrow. It was amazing how many people didn't. You could design a personality test around it, he thought. Determine what percentage of the population were willing to abandon themselves to processes beyond their control, when with the merest exercise of will, the smallest spike of attention, they could easily steer a more efficient course for themselves.

This woman here had obviously been far too busy crying to notice anything. She cried, he observed, in a perplexed and subtle way. It had a character of defiance. Her hands were balled into fists. The convulsions of her torso were muffled, repressed, the tremoring of her hair just perceptible. He could hear her breath leaking out in short, grudging, spasmodic creaks, like a balloon being tortured at the neck. Perhaps she was asthmatic. Or perhaps someone close to her had died. How was he to know? She was dressed like a graduate student, in faded jeans and shapeless black sweater, her earrings jaunty little toucans that swung loopily from their perches every time she moved her head. They looked to be the sort of earrings one bought on impulse for three dollars from a sidewalk vendor in Harvard Square, but maybe they were considered stylish. She had a wide, expressive, high-sloped face that in a different humor might have been attractive. On the other hand, the veins on her hands were prominent and stringy, the skin was beginning to line into folds at the nape of her throat, and, he observed, small colonies of gray had been established here and there amid the black tangled forest of her curls, from which evidence he concluded that despite her casual clothes she was considerably older than himself, a resident of that gated and architecturally uninspired development, middle age.

Maybe that was what was making her cry, he thought: not being young. Sometimes just the thought of not being young, just the prospect of having his life not ahead of him but all around and behind, made *him* want to cry. And he was still six months shy of thirty.

At last the crying appeared to have stopped. The woman wiped her nose along the torn sleeve of her sweater, then examined the results critically, as if even the trailing residue of mucus on her arm were in its transparency and formlessness a disappointment. It was not yet clear whether she knew he was there. So what? In a few moments they'd arrive down in the lobby, where the woman would step off the elevator and back into her unhappy, middle-aged life, and he'd proceed on alone down to the basement, where the Siamese fighting fish and their wondrous, quantifiable, fascinating new behaviors—*inspired sleep,* they had taken to calling it on the team—were awaiting his return.

The elevator halted at the seventh floor. The doors opened and closed but no one was there. They looked at each other inquisitively. The interlude of stillness gave their ride a context, a quiet moment of shared recognition. Two people plunging through space in a tight, shuddering vessel. And the ride was so short. One had to step forward. One had to grab hold. Otherwise all was chaos and dissipation.

He watched her rummage in her bag for a tissue. The elevator lurched, hesitated, then began to descend.

"Here," he croaked. He extended the handkerchief he had purchased the day before with his employees' discount from the hospital gift shop. "Take mine."

"Fuck off."

She had not so much as looked his way. Nor had her lips appeared to move. Obviously he had just imagined the words, the harshness of her response. A classic example of projection. Here he was feeling inadequate and defensive around women; of course his mind would write a script to confirm those same feelings. "I'm sorry," he said, clearing his throat, "all I meant was you should feel free—"

But now the doors were whooshing open, drawing back like curtains to reveal the bustling lobby, and the woman straightened her shoulders and fled into the crowd.

Watching her go, Ian closed his fist around the handkerchief. Something had fallen out of her bag as she'd stepped off the car. A postcard. The white diptych on the back was blank; no address, no message. "Hey," he called after her. But she was already pushing her way through the revolving doors, out onto the cluttered pavement.

Ian kneeled to pick up the card, which featured, on the front, some sort of painting, very busy and colorful, not his style at all. He preferred clean lines, good definition. Something modern, like photography. Nonetheless, as he rose from the floor, he wedged the card into his back pocket. The sudden flight of blood from his head disoriented him somewhat; perhaps this accounted for his impression, just before the doors closed again, of a world beyond the world, a world above and a world below, and himself a frail object suspended between. Then the computerized chime sounded, and the red arrow flared, and he was on the move again, headed down, with only his reflection in the chrome for company.

7

From the Files

USA Today, Dec. 19, page C3:
'ZO LONG, ZOLOFT
By Julie Kim

Move over Prozac, Xanax, Paxil, and all the other balms for the distressed in current vogue. As we near the end of the vaunted "Decade of the Brain," scientists are heralding a new generation of designer drugs, psychiatric medications more powerful, quicker acting, and with fewer unwanted effects.

A handful of the new medications are undergoing the first phase of tests in patients and should reach the market within the next three years; others are merely glimmers in the eyes of psychopharmacologists.

Neuroscience is poised to create "new medications both more effective and with fewer side effects than any before, by taking advantage of a wave of breakthroughs," said Dr. Howard K. Heflin, director of Experimental Psychology at Boston General.

Others are more cautious. "It's a big job," said Dr. Peter Sandusky, of the National Institute of Mental Health. "To fully understand the role of these receptors, we have to integrate everything from molecular biology and genetics to the study of behavior. You can't expect fast results."

Even so, the race to market is on. "We're betting on this strategy," said Dr. Richard Meier, senior vice president for clinical research at Sandar-Pyle Inc. in Atlanta. "We have medications in phase one trials in Europe, and will start testing them in the U.S. by the end of the year. And we're not alone. Look at Schering-Plough. Look at Merck and Lilly and Furst. They've all jumped in with both feet."

Dr. Sandusky, the mental health agency chief, cautions that more basic research is needed to discover precisely what

(continued on Page C9)

New York Times, Jan. 23, page A14:

Study Eases Concern on Pregnancy and Antidepressants

BOSTON, Jan. 22 (AP)—A new study has found no sign that taking the new class of antidepressants during pregnancy can harm a woman's unborn child.

The findings, based on data from nine medical centers in the United States and Canada, agree with research in animals and with previous studies of the use of Prozac-type antidepressants by pregnant women. Antidepressants are currently taken by more than 12 million people worldwide. While they were not thought to cause major birth defects, questions had been raised about whether they might cause subtle harm to babies' brains.

The new study turned up no evidence that any one of a dozen selective serotonin reuptake inhibitors, or SSRI's, taken by women during pregnancy affected their children's IQ's, language development, or behavior. A similar group of inhibitors has been developed for sleep disorders, and clinical trials are under way.

Dr. Howard K. Heflin of the Boston General Hospital Group, whose study is being published on Thursday in *The New England Journal of Medicine,* said, "I am very confident that if a woman needs one of these drugs, she should take them during pregnancy, because the risk of not being treated is much bigger than any risk of the drug."

The issue surfaced in October, when a team from the University of Pittsburgh published a study in the same medical journal raising the possibility that the new drugs increased the risk of premature delivery and some minor health problems in newborns. Because of shortcomings in the study, some experts discounted these results.

Dr. Arvin Peters of Johns Hopkins, acting medical consultant to the March of Dimes, called the latest study "great news," but added, "It doesn't wipe the slate clean of the concerns raised by the earlier study."

Boston Magazine, March issue, page 67:
"Prince of Darkness"
by Emily Rosner

"In dreams begin responsibilities," wrote the great Irish poet William Butler Yeats. And in the Hub, no man is more knowledgeable about the responsibilities of dreaming—or doing more to change them—than Boston General's Howard K. Heflin.

The acclaimed director of Experimental Psychology has hardly had time for his own dreams of late. Or for anything else. Fresh in from Washington, where he has been testifying before a congressional subcommittee on productivity in the workforce, he admits that in the past few months he's been no more than "an intermittent visitor" at the large, primitive art–strewn Victorian in Newton Highlands he shares with his wife, Gabriella, and two frisky Akitas.

"I have a very capable staff," he explains good-naturedly, rubbing his short, salt-and-pepper Van dyke, "but even they have their limits. When you're running three studies at once, someone has to be around to catch what falls between the cracks."

At 53, the Brookline native has the trim waist and ruddy glow of men half his age, a condition he attributes to a happy marriage, a good diet, and, he adds with a self-deprecating laugh, "far too much research." In a more serious vein, he adds, "I find research to be an impressive stimulant—it keeps you alert. You might say it prevents you from getting too dreamy yourself."

What's keeping Heflin alert these days—and nights—is a brand-new, two-million-dollar study known around the lab as "inspired sleep." The aim of the project, cosponsored by NASA and Furst Pharmaceuticals, is to find a way to simultaneously reduce motion sickness in traveling bodies and enhance REM—the scientific term for the state of rapid eye movements that signals a sleeper is dreaming—in arrested ones.

"We think REM sleep promotes changes in the brain that help astronauts adapt their motor system, particularly balance, to the near-absence of gravity," explains Heflin. "There is evidence of a feedback mechanism wherein adaptation to weightlessness increases REM sleep and dreaming, which in turn may enhance balance, orientation, and general mood. The overlap with antidepressants is clear. Obviously, if we can make some headway on this, it would be of immeasurable benefit here on the ground as well as out in space."

Too much of a chemical called acetylcholine in the nervous system is thought to promote motion sickness. Sleep scientists have discovered that the same chemical is responsible for bringing on dreams. Drugs given to astronauts to block motion sickness, therefore, could retard dreaming, which in turn might interfere with their adjustment to the confusing, sickening movements they feel in space. Hence the quest for a better, smarter drug.

To look into the possibilities for promoting more of "the right stuff"—in astronauts and earthlings alike—Heflin and his colleagues at Boston General have begun clinical trials with an as yet unnamed experimental compound, referred to by project staff by its code name, Dodabulax.

"It's a partial acronym," Heflin explains. "There's a line I'm fond of from Mark Twain's *Letters to the Earth*: 'Dream other dreams, and better.' It's become my inspiration, you might say." He gestures with familial affection toward the floor-to-ceiling shelves that line the walls of his study. "One finds oneself, as one gets older, more and more under the sway of the classics. Shakespeare, of course. Tolstoy, Chekhov. Keats. After all it's the poets, not the scientists, who are most adept when it comes to observing the human mind up close. They're the leaders. We physicians are just running along behind, taking notes."

So far the results of the Dodabulax trials have been, he admits with a worried frown, somewhat incon-(continued on p. 116)

Wall Street Journal, Feb. 11, page B3:

Newer Drugs Increase Sales of 2 Makers: Johnson & Johnson and Furst Benefit

by Sally Howe

Both Johnson & Johnson and Furst Pharmaceuticals reported fourth-quarter earnings gains of more than 15 percent yesterday, paced by strong sales of their newer medications.

Johnson & Johnson, which makes Band-Aids and the painkiller Tylenol, said earnings climbed 15.2 percent, led by sales of its schizophrenia drug Risperdal and its anti-anemia drug Procrit.

Furst's earnings rose 17.4 percent on sales of several newer drugs, including the antibiotic Zithromaz and the antidepressant Lycose.

Both companies are benefiting from expanding use of newer drugs by managed-care companies. "It's a bullish signal for the drug group as a whole," said Ian Perry, an analyst with Reston & Company.

Some analysts and investors had been concerned that unfavorable currency-exchange-rate movements, which lowered the dollar value of overseas sales, could hurt earnings growth. Furst said its revenue growth was reduced by 1.8 percentage points by such movements. Nonetheless, their shares rose 71 cents, to $85.375 on the Big Board.

Furst's portfolio of new drugs also includes the heart drugs Norvac and Caldula, and the antifungal medication Biflucar. The company began selling all five medications in early 1998. Phase two trials are currently being conducted on a new sleep medication, Dodabulax. Furst licensed the patents from Boston General Hospital, where the initial discovery was made.

Worldwide pharmaecutical sales rose 20 percent, to $2.88 billion from $2.40 billion, mostly as a result of sales of newer drugs.

"The new drugs show greater and greater promise," said Mr. Perry. "There's every reason to think the market will continue to expand."

Furst, which has gone several years without a significant new drug, has been under pressure from Wall Street to come up with a hit.

Subject: sleep medications
Library: Boston Public Library

The Lancet, Mar. 1, v. 372, p. 159:

Authors: P. Whyte, N. R. Lewellyn, and D. A. Cole
Greater Toxicity in Overdose of Xolar Than of Other SSRI Antidepressants

Abstract: Epidemiological studies have implicated Xolar, an ingredient in certain experimental compounds, in a greater number of self-poisoning episodes than would be expected from its use. We have prospectively assessed the clinical toxicity of Xolar in overdose. We followed up consecutively admitted patients with toxic poisoning managed by our department between January 1997 and August 1998. We used intermediate outcome measures: general seizures, tachyarrhythmias sedation, and QRS width on the electrocardiogram. 15 patients had seizures and 7 tachyarrhythmias. General seizures were more likely after Xolar than after other SSRI's (9/67 vs. 5/220), as were arrhythmias (4/67 vs. 3/220). Xolar in overdose seems to be proconvulsant. Consideration should be given to the use of other medications in patients at risk of seizures or suicide. Regulatory authorities should review the need for a 75 mg.–strength tablet.

Copyright Lancet Ltd. 1999, Australia
Subjects: antidepressants—toxicology
Poisoning—causes of

Transcript, Dec. 16,
NATIONAL PUBLIC RADIO *SCIENCE FRIDAY*
Interview with Dr. Elijah Frantz.

NPR: Doctor, you seem to be developing a large following in this country. Lately everyone I meet has your book under their arm or your website bookmarked on their computer. Are you at all worried by so much attention?

EF: Worried? I'm delighted.

NPR: Delighted even by the perception that you're some kind of New Age guru?

EF: All due respect, Ira, but that's just a silly label, the kind people use to dismiss things they don't like. There's a needless prejudice among Western scientists against anyone who can be understood by ordinary people. They think you must be driven by ego and greed. The need to be popular.

NPR: Like being featured on the cover of *Newsweek, Parade,* the *New York Times Magazine?*

EF: The media are the media. If they sense something interesting going on, they beam down their lights. Nine out of ten times the subject of their attention melts down quickly. So far that hasn't happened to me. But it could. To be honest, it would be a relief. I'd like to get back to what I really enjoy: time in the lab.

NPR: Our listeners will be calling in in a minute, but before they do, could you tell us a little about expectancy theory?

EF: Well, Ira, it's actually quite old and simple and commonsensical. We in neuropsychology have long been interested in the way the brain, the immune system, and the endocrine system are linked up at the molecular level. Expectancy is simply one way of exploring that linkage.

I'll give you an example. A few years ago in Japan they took 13 people who were extremely allergic to poison ivy. Each was rubbed on one arm with a harmless leaf, one they were told was poison ivy. On the other arm they were rubbed with a real poison ivy leaf, which they were told was harmless.

NPR: Wait: let me guess what happened . . .

EF: All 13 broke out in a rash where the harmless leaves contacted their skin. Only two reacted to the poison ones.

NPR: Fascinating.

EF: It's clear that what the brain expects about the future plays a key role in how the body will react. Not the only role, surely. But an essential one. And let me remind you, this isn't new. For centuries, Western medicine depended almost entirely on expectancy. Treatments like bleedings, emetics—they were only symbolic, not substantive at all. And yet it's remarkable how often they worked. Now, in the age of quote-unquote sophisticated medicine, we seem to have forgotten that.

NPR: So you're talking about some kind of placebo effect.

EF: The idea is to tap into internally generated brain states that are every bit as real as those from the outside world. For example, we train a lab monkey to expect a sip of apple juice every time he pulls a lever. By pinpointing the firing action of the monkey's brain, we're able to watch the cells fire 20 or 30 seconds *before* he pulls it. The expectancy, in other words, became conditioned and embedded in the brain chemistry. The question then becomes: What does the brain know and when does it know it?

NPR: So then, if this is all supported by research evidence, as you say, why are so many doctors out there enraged by you?

EF: Think about what happens, Ira, when you walk into a doctor's office. You smell the disinfectant. You see the white coats. The stethoscope. The prescription pads on the desk. You have expectations, based on your previous visits, that whatever the doctor writes on that pad will address your symptoms. What's actually written there, in other words, may not be as important as *the way* it's written. Or simply *that* it's written. Whether or not you get better is in part a function of the attitude of the physician. We want doctors to listen, to pay attention, to be allies, not antagonists. What's required is a whole new kind of training. A new medical vocabulary, if you will. So many doctors don't want to have to (cont.)

8

Getting Smart

AFTER CLASS—she'd let them go early again, even earlier than last time—Bonnie had a brief conference out in the hallway with Derek Toombs, one of her more desultory and recalcitrant freshmen. She'd have preferred to meet in her office, of course. But her office, which she once shared with Suzette and now with three other Expository Writing adjuncts she rarely saw, was located not in the stately five-story Tudor that housed the English and American Literature Department next door, but in a converted Quonset hut on the south end of campus, an area saturated with parking lots and Dumpsters and obscure materials of construction, known by its residents as the Valley of Ashes. Too far to go for a conference, she thought. *Way* too far to go for a conference with Derek Toombs.

Besides, she was used to conducting her professional affairs in this half-assed, improvisational manner. At her low rung of the academic ladder, every day was a kind of scavenger hunt for vocational dignity. One fed oneself on crumbs and dispensations that fell through the budget cracks. Between her two current contracts, she took home a little over nineteen thousand dollars. Her courses were remedial; she had no pension; she wandered from room to room toting heavy plastic bags like a homeless woman. In class she spoke in the same somber pedagogical tone of polite condescension she had learned from her own professors, but she could not quite bring it off; there was an absence of muscularity, of authority. It had something to do with being a woman, no doubt. Or with the fact that in the eyes of the administration, her future was more dependent upon her students' evaluations than theirs were on hers. The law of supply and demand was in effect. Fall out of favor, and there were hundreds of other impoverished humanities scholars to take your place, each nurturing the same rather winsome and fantastical notion that once their dissertation was finally over and done with, the *real* jobs would come. Bonnie had nurtured it too. Meanwhile she had been adjuncting for six years now.

Derek Toombs, of course, knew nothing of her history, but then history was not his subject. Alas, English composition was not his subject either. Lank-haired and diffident, with a small unhappy mouth and two stubborn, reddened, dogmatic-looking eyes, Derek appeared to be suffering a virulent allergy to his native tongue. His first, and still best, expository essay for her class—titled "Is Violins Ever Justified?"—had been a turgid Sargasso Sea of clichés, misspellings, malapropisms, faulty constructions, and glib generalizations, at the bottom of which, like a flat, discarded tire, lay the honest but impractical conclusion that the writer was in fact of two minds on this question: pro and con. After that, there had been a marked degeneration in Derek's style and output, along with a gradual but distinct escalation in his unexcused absences from class, to the point where now, a third of the way through the term, Bonnie had come to feel pretty single-minded about violence herself. She'd have liked to hit Derek Toombs, hit him square in the face with all her might. But one did not go around hitting students, of course. One went around failing them.

Which she had half resolved to do. Except he also fascinated her. Because when he did show up, Derek had a miraculous, almost mystical ability—it appeared to be his sole academic gift—to fall asleep at the twelve-minute mark of every class. Because he sat in the front row, and because he was so consistent when it came to manifesting this attention deficit disorder of his, she was able to observe the process closely. His lids would droop, his white jaw go slack. He'd prop his head up on his fists, where it would roll like a buoy on the soft tides of dreams. Should there be a loud noise or sudden movement, his lids would flutter open momentarily, but then they'd fall closed again, settling like olives at the bottom of a martini. This had been going on for weeks. They had discussed the problem once, midway through week two, though in retrospect Bonnie thought her comments had been too indirect. Still, students were students, she reminded herself: cocooned in their own lives, the snug synthetic of their youth. There was no reason other than sheer insecurity to take the kid's naps personally. Nonetheless it could not be denied that she was beginning to take them personally.

"Whassup?" Derek asked, striding toward her in his baggy, low-slung jeans.

"You tell me, Derek."

"Tell you what?"

"I want to know why you've been sleeping through class. It's insulting, it's distracting, and you're missing pretty much everything I say. It's what we in the teaching profession call bad form."

"Hey, man," he said. "I hear every word you say."

"Wise up, Derek. The truth will set you free."

"It's my contacts," he complained. "I got these soft lenses, they're burning my eyes, man. I got to rest them sometimes."

"You're asleep, Derek. You're unconscious. Catching *z*'s. How stupid do you think I am?"

He squirmed, thinking it over.

"Okay, yeah," he said. "Maybe once in a while I, like, nod off. It ain't nothing against you."

"I know that," she said, much too quickly. It was almost shameful, how eager she was to believe him. "You're probably falling asleep in all your classes, aren't you?"

A much more subtle and complicated look than she would have believed he was capable of flitted across Derek's face. "Not really," he said.

"Oh."

"I guess this is just like when it starts to hit me. Late morning. My blood sugar, maybe. I got soccer every afternoon, and my adviser's got me carrying sixteen units. And I've got this job at the Cantab, over in Central Square? They don't let me out till one."

"A lot of students work, Derek."

"Yeah, I know."

"We're all under pressure, right? We all have more responsibilities than we have hours in the day. It's part of that great glorious paradox, adulthood."

"Yeah, I know I got a problem," he said. "I gotta fix it."

"I hope you do. Because I don't want to sound unsympathetic, but if it keeps happening I'm going to have to resort to radical measures. I'll throw chalk at your head. I mean it. I'll stick your hand in a cup of warm water and make everyone watch."

"You wouldn't do that. You'd get in trouble."

"It'd be worth it, believe me."

"You're mean," he said abruptly. "Nobody likes your class, you know."

"I do."

"No, you don't."

"Okay, Derek," she said, raising her hands like a traffic cop. He was just like Alex, she thought, turning on her in an ugly way for no reason, missing the warmth in her tone altogether. Or had he? All of a sudden she was having to fight terribly hard just to catch her breath. "Have a nice day."

"Yeah," he said. "You too."

"I can't believe you're here," said Larry Albeit, dipping a crust of bread into the little plate of olive oil between them. "It's so unlikely."

Tell me about it, Bonnie thought. Or did she say it aloud? That after all appeared to be her big new talent: offending people, giving voice to her most disagreeable private thoughts. Letting the black birds fly.

In any event, Larry proceeded to tell her about it.

". . . I mean, we've been acquaintances for, what? Four or five years? And then one night we happen to walk out of a meeting at the preschool at the same time, and one thing leads to another, and now here we are having this intimate lunch at the Bacchae, sharing our deepest longings and fears. You have to admit that's relatively strange."

"Oh, I don't know. I'm pretty promiscuous, frankly, when it comes to longings and fears."

As if to attest to the veracity of this statement, she went on to recount her disastrous conference that morning with Derek Toombs. Across the table Larry nodded in that eager, placid way of his which appeared to be his substitute for actual listening.

"Maybe you should stop teaching for a while," he suggested. "Everyone needs a break from time to time."

"I need the money," she said.

"There are other ways to get money."

She shrugged. Though she believed this to be true, she'd had little experiential evidence of it. "Can we change the subject?" she asked. "Let's talk about something important."

Larry nodded, agreeable. He looked rather important himself today, in his cobalt-blue broad-shouldered suit. Were those pinstripes running down his sleeves? They were so thin and pale, so understated, it was difficult to tell. And yet Larry wore them lightly, as if he'd been pinstriped since birth. The man worked downtown, she reminded herself; he had lunches like this every day. Beneath the turbulent crest of his hair, his high forehead was shiny with solicitations. His eyes were bright, engaged. Tiny flecks of gray and brown were scattered like electrons around the hazel pupils, restlessly orbiting the dark stars at their centers. Larry folded one leg over the other, straightened his back, and cleared his throat significantly.

"Tell me," he said, "do you watch much television?"

Bonnie shook her head.

"That's good. That's very . . . admirable. Me, I watch a lot. It comes from being married, I suppose."

"Oh, single people watch TV too," she said, impatient. "They just work harder at lying about it." She had good evidence for both these claims, being single herself and having just lied to Larry about her own television watching, which like all her vices fell into the intermittent but prodigious range.

"Kippy says I should get rid of the thing. I have an addictive personality, she says."

"Aren't all personalities addictive?"

"Maybe so," Larry said vaguely. "Anyway, we don't let the girls watch. Kippy's really old-fashioned in that respect. No TV, no video games, no computer games. There are kids in Japan vomiting blood when they watch cartoons. All that computer-generated animation, the high-resolution screens. If you sit too close there's a risk of epileptic seizure."

"Really." She examined her busy salad. "I hadn't heard that."

"Of course it's safe for adults. We're immune."

"Why?"

"Who knows?" He finished his roll and reached for another. "Me, I like cruising the cable. It feels therapeutic. Sports, movies, doctor shows, cop shows, it doesn't matter. It's really just the movement I'm after. The shifting expressions, the flickers of action. The whole dark trance. Commercials are good too. Especially when you're high." He cracked open a pistachio shell and thoughtfully tapped out the nut. "When I'm straight, though, I like to watch something of quality. Preferably something British. I like to get really absorbed."

You're very deep, she almost said, aren't you, Larry? But she reined herself in. For all she knew he *was* deep. Anyway, she was tired of deep. She'd been down deep a long time. She was ready to come up for a little air.

"It's important to be selective," she murmured agreeably.

"Take last night. Cary Grant was on the cable, married to Deborah Kerr. They're very rich and happy, living in some English castle, when one day this tourist played by Robert Mitchum opens the wrong door by mistake, and *boom!* He and Deborah Kerr fall madly in love. It's very sophisticated and disturbing."

"What is?"

"The affair. The way so much comes from such a small accident. A door opens, a life is changed. *Three* lives. All because someone opened the wrong door. They joke about it, of course, but the film raises serious questions. What is fate? What is fidelity? Are these things relative or absolute? I mean, Cary Grant! It's the last thing you'd expect, isn't it?"

Bonnie shook her head; she was having some trouble keeping up. "What is?"

"Cary Grant losing his wife. And to Robert Mitchum! They're not even in the same class." He scratched at a water mark on his glass. "Of course he's got top billing, so he gets her back later, and things are all tidied up again by the closing credits. But I kept thinking, No way. The genie's out of the bottle now. It's all going to be different from here on in."

Larry, she saw, was staring at her in a new, needy, analytical way. As if she too were a movie of some kind. A raiser of serious questions.

"Would you look at this place," she said. "I mean, boy, is this something."

She was not, as these things go, much of a restaurant person. But she was capable of being one, she thought now, if she got more practice, if she found a way to dine at establishments like the Bacchae more often. Since, given her present lifestyle, this did not seem likely, she viewed the place through a wistful gauze of pre-nostalgia, the details already receding into memory's swarming and particulate haze even as she tried to fix them before her: the twinkling stemware, the rag-rolled ochre walls, the soft clatter of the enormous plates, the flawless rectangular mirror looming over the bar like a reflecting pool. Every surface seemed alive. Every object grabbed hold of the sunlight and did something vital and aesthetically interesting with it: broke it down, spun it in circles, doubled its speed. Even the gleaming black and white floor tiles were not content just to be stepped on; they reached out, enfolded you into their symmetries, put you through the paces of their elegant logic. The floor was like a chessboard where only the tall, swank, back-row pieces remained. The royalty.

Bonnie tried not to stare. She did. She dipped some bread in their little plate of olive oil and watched it gradually expand, a sight that filled her with longing and contempt. Because truly, when you thought about it, the Bacchae was so appalling, so shallow and decadent, such a sterling example of fin de siècle exhaustion, it was hard to take it seriously. When the revolution comes (the phrase rose fondly, reflexively to mind, a residue of her years with Leon) this will be, she reminded herself, only another smoldering ruin. But what if she was wrong? What if this *was* the revolution? This *was* history's dream? When Derek Toombs closed his eyes, was this what he saw: a bottle of Merlot, a basket of Tuscan bread, some wild-mushroom raviolis, an assortment of glazed pastries on a rolling cart? Two centuries of struggle had come and gone, and here they were again, she thought, eating cake, clinking glasses, the whole developed world chowing down around her, pausing between bites to bark out stock orders into their cell phones. Even the Russians. Even the Chinese! Meanwhile here she was, sulking like Fidel in her narrow island of a life, hungry and sleepless, holding her hard line. For what? History had passed her by. History was playing on another channel, another frequency. She had tried to catch the signal, she had tried and tried and tried, but it seemed she had been tuned to the wrong station all along.

In the end, of course, she wound up staring anyway. That was the cover charge, the toll one paid on these zooming roads. Just being there was like a contact high, a draft of secondhand smoke from the world's lusty, ongoing party. Watching the aerobic miracle women in their black skirts and spaghetti straps and improbable tans, flashing that single row of pearls they all seemed to have been born with, the men with their linen jackets and artfully stubbled chins, ponytails *tsk*ing over their necks like a groom's brush, talking markets, profiles, diversified options, she couldn't help but wonder, Where do they come from, these people? Where do they go? As both humanist and mother, she was inclined on principle to believe that human beings were fundamentally more alike than not. But later tonight she would be leaning over the sink, up to her elbows in hypoallergenic dish suds, trying to scrub the last traces of stew from her one good cast-iron pan while Alex did his homework and Petey banged his action figures together, and she would picture these people regathered here in this very room, enjoying their fizzy gins, their oaky single malts, their heady, unencumbered lives, and it would not be quite so easy to believe they were all members of the same, almost perfect union.

She felt a movement at the base of her throat. A throb, a second pulse. If only this were a real date, she thought. Then it occurred to her that in Larry's eyes, for all she knew, this might *be* a real date. If so, she should probably cut the hell out of there at the first available opportunity, unless of course she was willing to start thinking of it as a real date herself, in which case she should probably consider making at least a vague, token effort to act that way.

"I'm a little lost," she said. "I don't think I get the analogy."

"What do you mean?"

"Well, this film you're talking about. I don't have an English castle, I'm not married, happily or otherwise, and I don't like men with cleft chins. What's the connection?"

The thin brown jagged line that was Larry's left eyebrow shot up, like iron shavings under a magnet, at a seventy-five-degree tilt. The arc of confusion traveled across his face. "I never said it was an analogy," he said.

"Of course you didn't. Don't mind me: I'm a terrible bitch these days. Just go on with whatever it was you were saying."

"Bonnie."

"What?"

"Should you be drinking that, do you think?"

He was frowning at the glass of wine in her hand. She had ordered it without thinking when Larry ordered his.

"Oh God, I don't know." She shook her head, blinking back yet another tiresome and unsolicited visitation of tears. "No. No," she said, "of course I shouldn't be drinking it."

"I don't mean to sound moralistic," Larry said gently. "It's just all those articles, you know, in the science section of the paper, all those studies and statistics, they're really—"

"Terrifying?"

"I was going to say worrisome."

"Just one sip," she said, "that's all." Such was her mood and her general sense of weightlessness, however, that she proceeded to drain off a good quarter of a glass anyway, without so much as tasting it. "I must be getting old. Red wine gives me headaches these days."

"Me too."

"Then why did you order it?"

"God knows." He crinkled his eyes insouciantly. "I must've been feeling reckless."

Here we go, she thought. Larry the Reckless. Let the games begin.

"Mind if I smoke?" She reached into her bag. "I know I shouldn't do that either. And I won't. I've quit. But just one little puff."

"I don't think you're allowed to in here," Larry said. "But go ahead if you like. What the hell."

"Thanks. I seem to be a tiny bit desperate."

"I try to be tolerant," he said, watching her light up. "I'm not an either/or type."

"I appreciate that."

"My thinking is, we all need our vices. The world's full of risk. So be it. Let's get to know the enemy. Break a little bread with it. You can't insulate yourself, it doesn't work. Too many ways for the world to get at you. Like Kippy's tumor," he said.

Bonnie coughed. Unsurprisingly enough, the cigarette was turning out to be an even worse idea than the wine. And here came the maître d', shaking his handsome head.

"I can't even imagine," she said, stubbing it out.

Larry frowned. "You know what I thought when I found out? I thought: okay, fine. *Fine.* This is a terrible, completely inexplicable new reality in our lives, but there's a decent chance it won't kill her. And meanwhile, maybe *because* it's so terrible and inexplicable, it will sort of inoculate us against all the other terrible, inexplicable things that could. See what I mean? The homeopathic model. Like a flu shot. A little dose of the virus to keep away the big one."

"I don't think it works like that," Bonnie said. Though in truth she often caught herself thinking the same way, if not in ways even more transparently recondite and hopeless. "I think the big one comes anyway."

"Maybe so. Still, I make it a policy to practice moderation and harmony, even when it comes to the extreme. It's my own brand of chaos theory. *Partial chaos,* I call it. A small, measured dose of the immeasurable. Like an X ray, for instance. Or the Unitarian church."

"The Unitarian church?"

"Take the way you just smoked that cigarette," he went on. "Two puffs, then out. Very good. I used to smoke three a day, you know, before Kippy got sick."

"Three packs?"

"Three cigarettes. I didn't even *like* smoking. But it broke up the time."

"I was thinking of getting a patch," she said.

He nodded. "I admire that, the patch concept. The way it keeps coming all the time, flowing into your system, even when you sleep. But I don't care much for nicotine." He looked down at the broken cigarette spilling its contents onto a bread plate. "I used to have a weensy little methamphetamine habit, though."

"Oh?"

"This was a long time back. I was in law school, sort of stuck. I wasn't too happy with how the whole life-direction picture was coming out. I felt like I needed to speed things up. I'm in no way saying it was a good thing. But I got used to it. Now, though, I'm interested in going the other way. I want to slow down."

"I've slowed down," she said. "Believe me, it isn't so great."

"Depends on your attitude," he said. "Your cast of mind. I learned that back in rehab. Ordinary life didn't feel ordinary anymore. It felt painful, physically painful. I had to find new ways to deal with that."

"I hate pain," Bonnie said. "It's not that I'm a coward. I just don't have the patience for it."

"I know what you mean. I'm the same way. Kippy, though, she's tough. She gets very Catholic and severe about these things. Like when she came home from the hospital, she was really suffering. Take the Percocet, I kept saying. That's what it's for. She'd fix me with this look. *Stony* isn't the word. Like she was going to cut my throat."

"Percocet's great stuff," Bonnie reflected.

"Fabulous," Larry agreed. "But that's the thing. She *wanted* the pain.

Sixty thousand people in this country dropped dead from medications last year. *Legal* medications. That's more than died in Vietnam. She looked it up. So better a little pain, she says, than too much cure."

Right, Bonnie thought. Another guru heard from. She gazed out the window and down toward the street. Two joggers trudged past, headed for the river, wearing surgeons' masks against the cold.

"I hate pain," she repeated. Apparently the phrase was stuck in her head.

"More wine?"

"No, thank you." Through the phantom of her own reflection she contemplated the joggers, the river beyond them, and the northern sky with all its gray, linked-up freight balanced precariously overhead, a big jerry-built contraption waiting to fail. Maybe they really *were* surgeons, she thought. On the lam from some failed operation, playing hooky from the tedious indoor business of life and death. She remembered her visit to Siraj the other day. She remembered her first visits too, years ago—seeing Alex on the ultrasound, his tiny form upside down, as if an inversion of herself, his fists raised like a boxer's, floating heedlessly in his blissful amniotic sleep.

"Well," she sighed, "I admire her courage. Both of you. I really do."

He shrugged modestly. "We have a lot of support."

"Friends?"

"For her, yeah. Friends, her sisters, the girls, her mom."

"And for you?"

"For me," he said, with a shy, growing smile, "the support is more of a pharmaceutical nature."

"You know, for someone so into moderation," she observed, "you seem to do an awful lot of dope."

"No, no." He leaned forward conspiratorially. "This is different. I'm part of a study, you see. It's all very controlled. Scientific. Just the organizational brain power alone would take your breath away."

His tone all at once had become fervent, sheepish, wondrous, and solemn. The sound of a new way. Bonnie's women friends spoke like this too, after their first therapy sessions, their first shiatsu massages, their first poetry slams or extramarital affairs or shopping trips to

Costco. Conceivably she herself would use this tone someday, she thought, in recounting her lunch at Cafe Bacchae. "Alex," she said, "my eldest? He's on Prozac right now. Prozac and Dr Pepper."

"Interesting combination."

She shrugged. "He's got a lot of rage. It helps him deal."

"I've never tried Dr Pepper," Larry said. "Not that way."

"I have this friend, Suzette, I used to teach with. He picked it up from her. She came here to study nineteenth-century poetry, but her adviser said no, you don't study the poetry first, you study the period and then go *back* to the poetry. So she holes up in the library, finds out what they wore, what their furniture was like, what they took when they were under the weather, which for writers is pretty much every day. Turns out between all the cordials and syrups and patent medicines, they were even more self-medicating than you are. You know how people talk about Coca-Cola being full of cocaine? So was Dr Pepper. Also a little opium, to mellow you out."

"No wonder it was so popular."

"That's right. Especially with women. Aside from poets it was mostly women who bought the stuff. Suzette decided it was a big paternalistic government plot to keep the wives spaced out at home so they wouldn't demand the vote. She wrote three-quarters of a dissertation on it. Never mentioned poetry at all. Got a lot of interest from university presses too. Only then she met the man of her dreams and gave it up to raise sheep in Vermont." She frowned stoically. "Not that I resent her for it. Not that I want to tear her nipples off for deserting me like this."

"And you?" Larry asked mildly. "What are you on, Bonnie?"

She shook her head. "I'm not on anything. I don't even approve of that shit."

"You don't approve of biochemistry?"

"I don't approve of shortcuts. Not anymore. Every time I take one I wind up getting lost."

Coming from a woman who abhorred absolutists, who chafed at puritanical strictures of all kinds, and who, moreover, had wasted ten minutes over breakfast contemplating a cosmetic surgery ad in the newspaper, this was a curious declaration at best. Nonetheless it was true. She did not in fact approve of antidepressants, save for Alex and anyone else who required them, as he did, to function in the world. Perhaps she required them too; but, at thirty-nine, she had long ago worked out certain accommodations with her temperament. She had sued for peace, stumbling along with the usual crutches—coffee, cigarettes, licorice, books, and men. They had proved of only limited comfort, true. But she was used to them.

Besides, these smart drugs, these new, improved nerve tonics being hawked in the media's chautauqua tents, they frightened her. Their enhancements seemed unearned, overly direct. The whole millennial banquet of mood lighteners, breast swellers, hair growers, fat removers, dick hardeners—all the fast chemical solutions you could buy in a jar and swallow your way toward perfectibility—made her feel reticent and grudging, like a fat girl on a diet. Was there to be a remedy for everything, then? For life itself? Some pill or tablet to reconstitute the molecules of your fate?

Then too Suzette, when she'd first got into Xanax, had reported no small amount of weight gain. That wouldn't fly. Also she kept getting the names mixed up. Xoloc? Perzoft? Desperine? Somehow they all wound up morphing into alphabet soup.

"This one you're on now," she said. "What's it called?"

"Actually," said Larry, "I don't think it has a name yet. It's brand new. Experimental."

"Oh."

"I handled some insurance work for a guy over at Boston General; he's the one who got me into this study. It has to do with receptors in the brain. Some new activation agent they've worked up. Gives you fantastic dreams. Fantastic dreams that never end."

She remembered the flyer at the hospital. Could it have been the same sleep study? Probably there were studies going on all over the place.

"You wouldn't believe how great this stuff is, Bonnie. What the nights are like. Do you have any idea what it's like to have nothing but deep sleep and fantastic dreams?"

"Not a clue," Bonnie said.

"Well, you wake up feeling incredibly refreshed. Powerful. Sexy. Energetic. Capable of managing anything."

Larry cleared his throat and stared at her meaningfully from across the table.

"Which brings me back to our discussion the other night. That whole . . . situation."

Here we go, she thought. Absently she ran a moistened finger around the circumference of the fluted glass. It gave off a low, impersonal moan. The music of the spheres.

"Have you thought about it at all? What we talked about on the phone?"

"A little," she admitted, shifting in her chair.

"I'm glad. Because I was serious, you know. I really think, if you're willing, we could make this happen together."

"I realize that." Her finger skated another lap around the top of the glass, soundlessly this time, as she struggled to fight off a rare but virulent blush. "But honestly, Larry, I just don't think I could handle it right now. You wouldn't know it to look at me, but I'm actually trying to turn over a whole forestful of new leaves at the moment. Not just keep making the same old—"

"Listen, Bonnie, I completely understand."

"You do?"

"I know it's a long shot, no question. That's why you should take your time. Think it over. It's an enormous decision, with enormous consequences, and the last thing on earth any of us should rush into, especially you. But in this case, I mean if you really do think it over carefully and then decide what's best for, for everyone, and then all parties agree . . . it does seem like it might be uniquely, you know, *workable.* Especially given that we already know each other. . . ."

Workable? she was thinking. When had she ever had an affair—even with a man who wasn't married, who wasn't so hyper and earnest and substance-abusing—that was workable?

". . . one thing it would mean, of course, is there wouldn't be any of that awful, expensive research to do, all those preliminaries, building up trust—"

"Larry."

"What?"

"Can you pick up the pace a little? I've got thirty essays to grade and this more-or-less-permanent headache. How about you just go ahead and make your move already."

"My what?" She watched his left eyebrow shoot up again.

"You're trying to get into my pants, right? That's why you invited me here."

Now it was Larry who flushed. "Bonnie—"

"Look," she said, "it's okay. I'm not mad. As I said, I don't know what I want exactly, though when push comes to shove I do hate the idea of stealing someone's husband. Especially a husband I'm not even sure I like that much. No offense."

"None taken," Larry said, "but—"

"The truth is I probably *could* like you, if I tried. Because you do have a nice, open face, and compared to most of the adulterers I meet, you seem basically well meaning and sympathetic, which gives you a leg up on, oh, Christ, everyone else. . . ."

"I'm not trying to seduce you, Bonnie."

"You're not?" she asked. In the course of her long speech she had lost some breath; it came out as "*why* not."

"Don't get me wrong, you're a terrifically attractive woman. And I'd be misleading us both, I think, if I denied that underneath everything else there was some fundamental chemistry, some real pull of an erotic . . . an erotic . . ."

"So wait, then what *do* you . . ." She hesitated; one hand, on its own recognizance, sought out the trembling exposure of her mouth. "Oh."

"I'm sorry. I should have been more clear. I thought you understood."

"I don't know what to say."

"It's just that here you are with your condition, and your dilemma, and Kippy and I wanting another kid . . . I'm sorry, it just seemed like it might . . ."

"Don't apologize," she said. "It was my mistake."

There was a moment of silence. Her face felt crowded and hot. She placed both hands on her wineglass and stared into its depths. She did not feel humiliated, exactly, though she did feel the presence of something like it, some close cousin, some intimate relation or very dear friend. She was pretty certain, however, that when she got home and reviewed this conversation in the cold, unfriendly light of memory, she was going to feel *very* humiliated.

"On second thought," she said, "go ahead and apologize. You should be ashamed of yourself, you creep. You fucking ghoul. Be serious: You really think I'd give a kid of mine away? And to a *lawyer*?"

"Please," Larry said, reaching for her knotted hand. "Your voice, it's so l—"

"Loud? This isn't loud. This is *shrill.* Would you like to hear loud, Larry? Would you really like to hear *loud*?"

But now Larry was shaking his head unmistakably, no no no. So that was a factor. Also there was the question of the Bacchae's rather overeager acoustics, the effect of which was not so much to dampen the crowd noise as aggravate and atomize and intensify it to the point where everyone in the place was *already* screaming just to make themselves heard. She doubted her ability to make a scene here even if she wanted to. And finally there was the question of whether she wanted to. Whether she wanted to lose control or gain it. Lose this man's attention or gain it. Lose the baby or—

She remembered Siraj's advice, the flyer in the elevator, the young man flailing his handkerchief. She remembered what she'd said to him. She remembered Derek Toombs, and what he'd said to *her.*

"Would you excuse me for a moment, Larry? I'll be right back."

She went to the ladies' room, found an empty stall, and after a moment or two of reflection, discreetly threw up. It was Larry's partial-chaos theory in action: a minor explosion meant to forestall a larger, messier one. Surprisingly enough it seemed to work. Afterward, at the sink, patting cold water over her pale face, she did in fact feel moderately better. Also, paradoxically, a whole lot worse.

So much of both did she feel that on the way back to the table she paused at the pay phone and punched out the number Siraj had given her and which she had committed to memory on the way home. It was only a machine, of course, on the other end of the line, and leaving a message required the usual lengthy, complicated procedure of options, abbreviations, and codes, but finally it was done, and she could return to the table and the strange man who awaited her there in a slightly different frame of mind.

As if hoping to purify the relations between them, Larry had in her absence ordered a tall sloping bottle of Pellegrino. He cleared his throat as she settled back into her chair, and gazed at her apprehensively across the worried water. "Everything okay?"

She smiled. It wasn't easy, but neither was it altogether hard. She would stop fighting with everyone, she decided, tasting her hard, puckered lime. She would become philosophical, use her smarts. Even drugs were getting smart these days. So why not her?

"Yeah," she said, "I'm fine."

And she was. She was able to sit there for another several minutes, chatting about the preschool's new bylaws, and the current crop of seed catalogs, and the options for disposal of chemical weaponry, in all of which subject areas Larry seemed both passionately invested and extremely well versed, and the waitress came by with her short black skirt and impossible legs, flashing the bill in its black leather jacket, and with only a minor effort Bonnie managed to keep up her smile the entire time. It became easier and easier. And when Larry gathered up the folded slip, reached for his wallet, and casually, oh so casually extracted his platinum Visa, Bonnie made no move, not even in her head, to stop him.

That night at home she put on some headphones and a CD of "The Goldberg Variations," drank some warm milk, turned off the lights, unzipped her jeans, and retired to the sofa to masturbate. It was a new strategy. Suzette the Betrayer, who knew more about classical music than she did, claimed Bach had designed the entire intricate, cathedral-like structure of thirty variations and nine canons to relieve the insomnia of his patron, Count Keyserlingk, by roughly these means. The curative effect was a function of the timbre of the harpsichord, apparently, along with the tempo of the minor variations, particularly the twenty-fifth. Unfortunately the recording Suzette swore by featured Rosalyn Tureck, whereas Bonnie's version was by Glenn Gould, whom under normal conditions she adored. But now his feverish, irregular purring got in her way.

She went on to try Satie, Ravel, Ben Webster, and several moody and lugubrious tracks by Leonard Cohen, with no better results. She felt dry-grooved, static. The earphones clutched too tightly; her neck became entangled in the cord. Finally she turned off the machine and sat there on the sofa with her head in her hands. It felt a great weight. The day filtered back to her in whispers and suggestions, a murmur in the blood. Larry Albeit's big bright face adhered to her mind like a patch. *You don't approve of biochemistry?*

She would not fight it any longer. She let go her head with a groan.

At once, as if sensing a change in weather, her nipples rose and tightened. She gazed down at them inquisitively. They looked parched, unattended. She offered them the moisture of her palms.

After that the whole thing took only a moment. She came to the sound of her own shallow breaths in the dark.

9

The Hows and Whys

EVERY FRIDAY morning, someone on staff had to wake up early and drive down to Walpole State Prison to gather the week's data. The idea was to have a quick consult over breakfast with Big Don Erway, the resident chief psychiatrist, make whatever on-site adjustments were required, and get back in time to drop off the files on Howard Heflin's desk before he left for the Vineyard, where it was his habit to spend every weekend, weather permitting. That was the Friday routine. In execution, however, there would invariably be some crisis concerning the house or the dogs or the wife or the ferry or the traffic on Route 3—they would hear the whole lamentable story at Monday afternoon's staff meeting—which had prevented Heflin from getting to the files after all, so whoever's turn it had been to get up at five-thirty and drive an hour and a half to the penitentiary might just as profitably have slept in.

Today it was Ian Ogelvie's turn. Though the timing, all things considered, was in his opinion very poor. He had been hoping to devote the day to his grant proposal. With the deadline less than a week off, his proposal badly needed some polishing, to say the least, if not a rigorous revision, if not a drastic, substantive overhaul. If not—to say the dreaded most now—a fast trip down the incinerator chute. Something, at any rate, was missing; Ian was certain of that. Some flawed hinge at the center of the project, a connection not yet fully worked out between Point A (the Dodabulax effect) and Point C (expectancy theory). For weeks, up late at the computer, poring over his notes and files, he'd felt on the brink of B—its green breast lay just beyond the horizon of the monitor—but he wasn't there, not yet. The voyage was murky and strenuous; he was beginning to fear that no matter how much he labored toward it he'd never quite land. Or he would land but, like Columbus, choose for his discovery the wrong name. Not B but R, or F, or X . . .

What was missing, he thought, was the human touch. Ever since Marisa Chu had come strolling into his lab that night and bestowed upon him the surprise of her tears, something had changed. A cool shadow of irrelevance had fallen over his work. His animals did not, could not, say enough. And without expression, he thought, there was no true measure of expectancy, only a harsh, schematic outline, the simple product of biomechanics and chemical engineering.

He supposed this was what they meant by the sadness of science.

And then, as if his intellectual limitations weren't problem enough, he'd returned to Barbara's loft the night before, bone-tired and despairing, to find his sister in the grips of a formidable flu. She'd been up all night hacking, sneezing, and, when she wasn't vomiting clamorously in the echoing john, moaning like a wind tunnel; from his compromised position on her foldaway sofa Ian could not very well have interrupted all these urgent private noises to ask her to shut up. So he had to settle for lying there in the darkness, fully and resentfully awake, listening to the mail planes circling toward Logan, the delivery trucks downshifting onto the on-ramp of Route 93 like the cumbersome, slow-moving machines they were. At last, around two-thirty, the noise, or his attention to it, began to recede. The loft fell still. He was just moving into the vicinity of a light, indeterminate phase one sleep when Tuck, the household's mesomorphic calico, stirred, perhaps unconsciously, by the distress of his mistress, decided to chuck his usual nocturnal schedule and head off to the kitchen for breakfast three hours early. There, with great delicacy, patience, and industry, he proceeded to scratch out his own loud feline version of Morse code against the paper shopping bags wedged between the refrigerator and the oven.

"He thinks it's morning," Barbara had groaned from the other side of the makeshift wall. "You've got to . . ." she paused to honk mournfully into a tissue, ". . . feed him."

And so Ian had stumbled over to the kitchen to serve the needs of this stupid, selfish creature with his fickle circadian clock. Perhaps Tuck would enjoy a nice can of tuna, he thought, laced with a nice gram-and-a-half dose of Dodabulax. Perhaps Tuck lacked purpose in his life, and would enjoy the chance to devote himself to science. It was something to consider.

All the while he could hear Barbara whimpering across the partitions, "I won't, I won't, I won't . . ."

Poor Sis. Must have been some kind of weird fever dream, he decided now, driving south toward Walpole in the eroding dark. He made a mental note to bring her some soup from the deli near the hospital. It was the least he could do, given that it was Barbara's own rusty but reliable Jetta he was driving at the moment. But then she had always been free and easy with her possessions, even as a child. She'd never clutched on to things the way Ian had, hoarding his comic books (*Dr. Strange* was a favorite) in a locked trunk. Nor did she label every food purchase with her own initials, as he did even now, and confine it to a particular shelf of the fridge. She was looser than he was. It came from being an artist, he supposed. She was comfortable with mess. The fact that her career, compared with his, had for years lacked both shape and trajectory—though that could change, he supposed, with this upcoming show of hers at the Summer Street Gallery—or that her loft typically looked like a flea market after a rainstorm didn't seem to faze her. The warped, mismatched plates, the threadbare rugs and tottering end tables, the bright Milky Ways of paint and plaster whorling across the floor—Barbara, in spattered clogs, clomped her way right through it, preoccupied by things he did not understand. She did not appear to worry the same way Ian did, or about the same issues. The only major worry they seemed to have in common these days was Ian himself, his continuing occupation of the loft's sole piece of comfortable furniture.

The sky had begun to break into light.

Gradually his crankiness fell away under the drumming of the tires, the whoosh of wind against the windows. It was nice to be out in the liquid, massing sunrise. His protestations to Marisa Chu notwithstanding, Ian was, in truth, a morning person, a lark, and so tired and harried as he was, he was conscious too of not being altogether unhappy to be here, alert in the rising day, surrounded by brilliant transformations. The highway traffic was gentle, soundless. Beside him ran the river, the dun Neponset, its surface pocked by industrial foam and the rippled splash of breakfasting fish. Across the blue border of the windshield soared three large egrets, their wings falling as one. He pinched the last crusts of sleep from his eyes and tried to focus, but by then the egrets were gone.

At the penitentiary, he drove through the main gate and parked near the back of the lot, in one of the spaces reserved for medical staff. This early on a Friday morning, only a single car, a burgundy minivan, was in evidence. Big as it was, it looked like a toy beneath the enormous monolith of the outer wall.

Approaching the door, he heard not far away the dull, authoritative clang of steel on steel. The sound gave him pause. It had given him pause the last time, he remembered, too.

Inside, he showed the guard his pass and went through the first station. This led him down a green corridor to the second guard at the second station, then a blue corridor to the third at the third. Each time he flipped open the visitor ID they had given him, he tried to affect a look of knowing boredom; each time he faltered under the stare of the guards.

Jesus, he thought, they hate us here. Even the guards.

Perhaps because of the early hour, as he wandered the maze of corridors to the infirmary, Ian felt awash not in strangeness but recognition. The faded uniforms, the low hum of unseen generators, the smell of indifferent cooking on an industrial scale . . . it all seemed like some eerie, dreamlike extension of the hospital, of the life—the structured, institutional life—he himself lived. He had a sudden surge of empathy for the men behind the walls. And some guilt as well. For today it seemed only the thinnest, most papery of accidents that would allow him to be waved through the exit doors at the end of the morning and leave them behind.

Erway's office was deserted. Ian stood awkwardly in the clinic's open doorway, waiting for someone to appear. It was already eight-thirty. If he didn't get moving he'd fail to catch Howard Heflin before he left for the Vineyard.

The Vineyard. For all his collegial dealings with Howard Heflin, it had not escaped Ian's notice that in three years he had been invited to the Vineyard only once, and that time—there had been some deadline or other—he'd chosen to stay in the city and work instead. Since then no offers had come his way. Meanwhile Malcolm Perle had gone out several times. So had Marisa Chu. So for that matter had Roger Levis, Sukey Witherspoon, and David Brandt. All had on one summer Monday or another come strolling in late to the staff meeting, pink-cheeked, loose-limbed, and garrulous, exchanging the intimate looks and lazy, languid smiles born of private recreation, of shared and exclusive knowledge. The beach at the Vineyard was a two-minute walk. The tennis courts were clay. At sunset there were vodka tonics, goat cheese gougeres, strawberries dipped in white chocolate. A television actor had come to dinner—someone very famous whom Ian, naturally enough, had never heard of—and told a number of memorable jokes, none of which for some reason it was possible to repeat. That was how things went on the Vineyard.

But such thinking, Ian decided, was petty and unreasonable. He had, after all, chosen to work. That was the way you made progress, by working. Wasn't it?

Where was Erway, anyway? Why wasn't *he* working?

The trials this month were a new series with which Ian, preoccupied by his own affairs, was not entirely familiar. Fifteen subjects, double dosage, four weeks running. It sounded pretty grueling. Of course the men were all drug addicts to begin with, which was why they'd volunteered. Word had it that when supplies grew tight, there were junkies on the streets of Roxbury who intentionally got themselves caught committing small crimes, just to be incarcerated and then admitted to the experimental wing. The food was good in the experimental wing, the magazines current, the supply of drugs safer and better regulated and of much higher quality than it was on the street. The system worked like a bank: there was a small window by the stairs where the capsules were dispensed, and the prisoners had their accounts and made their withdrawals in a smooth, orderly fashion. Howard Heflin had designed it himself, then gone on to secure the funding from Furst Pharmaceuticals. Or had it been the other way around?

Outrageous, Ian thought, the way Erway left his door open like this. Why, anyone at all could just walk in, as Ian had, and plant himself behind the psychologist's desk, as Ian had, and go ahead and help themselves, as Ian now proceeded to do, to whatever files were on hand. Of course the desk, like the rest of the office, was so profoundly disorganized, what with all the folders, logbooks, old newspapers, half-completed requisition forms, antiquated memos, used coffee cups, and crumpled, sugar-crusted napkins from Dunkin' Donuts, one was hard-pressed to *find* any data. The man needed an assistant badly. His working conditions were substandard. The carpet smelled of mold. A pile of CD's—Sarah Vaughan, Chet Baker—lay facedown on the file cabinet, naked of their cases, their silver shine clouded by dust. According to Marisa Chu, who made it her business to know these things, Big Don Erway had been a hot young comer himself back in the sixties. Second in his class. Taught at Penn, thesis accepted for publication, limitless future. And now here he was. Explain that.

To pass the time, Ian began flipping through the files and charts he unearthed from the desk. Blood pressure readings, rectal temperatures, eye-pupil diameters. Nothing particularly interesting. A bottle of prescription pills fell out from between two files and into his lap. Verloxx. The instructions on the label were in German, not one of his languages; moreover, they were obscured by a rust-colored smudge, dried ink, perhaps, or blood. He capped the bottle and set it back on the desk. He would look up the name later back at the lab.

There was an old television set in the back of Erway's office, propped on a metal stand. Very well; he would settle in to wait. He picked up the remote and leaned back, crossing his legs at the ankle and setting them gingerly on a corner of the desk. *Nova* would be good, some science or nature program, not too trivial or time-wasting. But the screen was a blizzard of static.

He noticed a videotape poking out from the black mouth of the VCR. *Eddie,* the label read, *2/27.*

Ian punched Play.

At once a man's face filled the screen in close-up. It was a handsome but numb-looking face, round, very dark, with a scar on one cheek shaped like a blotchy nebula and an adornment of droopy, convoluted dreadlocks. The eyes were puffy and vacant. They held the last traces of what appeared to be a rather played-out suggestion of amusement.

". . . right, well, that was pretty good, man. That was all right. But then it got kinda wild. Like my head, it started to get all big and all. Blew up like a balloon. You know those blood pressure cuffs they got in the army? Like that. It got bigger and bigger, and then it just kind of like, you know, *detached* itself, man. Went AWOL. Just sailed off by its ownself, levitating up there, and I didn't get too bothered about it or anything 'cause I figured it's just the shit you gave me that's doing this, right? Just the shit. So I didn't mind. It was kind of cool watching my head float away like that. 'Cause I knew that room wasn't going to be able to hold me no more. I knew that for a fact."

There was a pause. An off-camera voice, one that Ian recognized as Don Erway's, could be heard asking a question.

"That's right. Then, whoosh, it just, you know, kept on going. Through the window, out past the roof, wound up way up in the clouds, man. It was heaven. I mean the church kind of heaven, that's what it was. And it was great up there, all blue and peaceful, just like they say. And I looked down on y'all, my people, my flock like, and I took pity, man, I took pity. I was Jesus Christ, see. I knew that now. I been Jesus Christ all along. I had this huge head, and this long beard and everything, and nothing bothered me, and I just hung out up there in the clouds looking down and forgiving you motherfuckers. 'Cause y'all were stuck on your bodies, and I was free of that. But then, I don't know, I guess I kinda got tired of being Jesus after a while. I started missing the rest of me, my dick and all. So I figured I'd just come back down, be like everybody else again, see what that's like. Maybe I'd appreciate it more, once I got back. I was thinking maybe I would.

"When I started to freak? That's when, man. 'Cause I got *stuck* up there. I couldn't *get* back down. I could see my neck and arms wriggling around down there like a bug, and I couldn't hardly breathe on account of the air, the atmosphere being so thin and all. So that's when I started screaming. Man, I was terrified. But none of you croakers'd help me out. You just sat there staring, like you didn't care if I got down or not. Just left me *hanging* up there . . ."

There followed a brief interlude that consisted of Eddie burying his face in his hands and mumbling inaudibly.

"So you felt fear, is that right, Eddie?" It was Erway's voice again, off-camera, nasal and thin. "A significant degree of fear?"

"Oh man. What the fuck do you think?"

"You say you knew it was the effect of the drug. And yet it frightened you anyway."

"Man, I knew it was *some*thin' got me way up there. That ain't the same as knowin' how to get down."

"I see."

"Man, you don't see shit. You want to see, why don't *you* try shootin' up some of that shit next time. *You* be Jesus for a while. Then maybe I'll listen to *you*."

"That's all for today, Eddie."

"Look, man, I got news for—"

"I said that's all for today, Eddie."

Eddie leveled a cold glare in the direction of the camera, perhaps contemplating some wayward act of vandalism. But then his eyes turned soft, as if made sullen by the sight of his reflection in the lens. "Okay with me," he said.

Ian hit Stop. He sat staring thoughtfully at the static on the screen. In the frenzied collisions it was possible to detect patterns and shapes, intimations of meaning. He continued to see Eddie's ghostlike face, his flat nose and blobby scars, his sagging halo of braids. His voice too continued to stumble around in Ian's head, knocking things over, banging on doors. . . .

Then Donald Erway walked in.

"You're in my chair," he said.

Ian sprang to his feet. Thirty years back, Big Don Erway had played offensive tackle at Colgate. Since then his waistline had softened considerably, and the wire bifocals he'd taken to wearing gave his huge moon face an expression of dainty, owlish humor. Nonetheless he retained the talent of very large people to physically intimidate others, especially in a room as small as the office. *His* office, Ian reminded himself. "Sorry," he said, "I was just—"

"Ogelvie, isn't it?"

"That's right."

"I'm good with names. It's true. That'll be my epitaph one day: the big fat fuck was good with names." He settled heavily into the chair behind the desk and, frowning, propped one creaky knee over the other. When he took off his glasses to rub at his eyes, his features slackened; suddenly the big fat fuck looked worn and ironical as a teddy bear. "You've brought the Danish?"

"Sorry?"

"They usually bring Danish on Fridays. It's kind of a tradition."

"I'm sorry, I didn't know."

"You guys should communicate better. No team can function without good communication skills. Take that Korean gal," he said. "I told your boss, keep your eye on that one. Her almonds and apricots are excellent. The raspberries speak for themselves. But her poppyseeds, whew. Inspirational."

Ian resigned himself at that moment to being late getting back. Interestingly, he found he didn't much care. "She's actually Chinese-American," he said. "If we're talking about the same person. She's from Baltimore originally, I think."

"You don't say." Erway blinked sleepily behind his slitted glasses. "And how is our man Howard? What's he got to say for himself?"

Ian considered his position before speaking.

"Dr. Heflin is working hard on the new trials," he said. "He's eager to publish."

"Eager to pub-lish," Erway sang in a light, tuneful falsetto, *"eager to know-w-w . . ."*

Politely, Ian tried to force a laugh. It came out yippy and lame, like the bark of a small dog. Here we go again, he thought: whatever gene or helix in the human organism was responsible for ironic capacity seemed to be missing or fractured in him. He lacked the talent for banter, for malicious gossip, for whatever it was that Donald Erway and the rest of the world appeared to hope for or expect from him. But he was still thinking of that man on the tape. "That one of ours?" he asked, indicating the dead television.

"Who, Eddie? Yeah."

"I didn't see his name on the roster."

"You wouldn't," Erway said. "Not Eddie. He's part of what we call a special subset."

"How special is special?"

"Triple dosage. Ninety days. It's called accelerated commercialization," Erway said. "Roughly translated, it means throw the whole pot of spaghetti at the wall and see what sticks."

"I didn't realize things had come this far."

Erway's eyes narrowed. "Things?"

"Are there others?" Ian asked. "Other subset people in this kind of shape?"

"What kind of shape do you mean?"

"Jesus, do you have to ask? Paranoid delusions, profound disorientation, delirium tremors, nightmares of panic and powerlessness—"

"They weren't nightmares," Erway said.

"Excuse me?"

"The word *nightmares* implies sleep. Eddie wasn't asleep."

"You're joking."

"We have it on tape, amigo. Wide awake. No PGO surge. Eyes

open. *Wide* open. A fair bit of crouching under the bed. Otherwise no different from you and me sitting here."

"I'd like to see his acetylcholine level. Was it very low?"

"Yeah. Got it here somewhere." Erway frowned, leafing fruitlessly through a file. "But there are other factors. We found traces of pyridostigmine in his blood. And Eddie's a vet."

"I don't follow."

"Pyridostigmine was a nasty little number they dug out for the Gulf War. The thinking was it'd negate Saddam's nerve gas. Turns out it negates acetylcholine too."

"You think that accounts for his response to the drug?"

Erway shrugged.

"What about REM behavior disorder?" This was a syndrome Ian had read about, where patients got up and performed the content of their dreams. A man in Chicago, thinking he played fullback for the Bears, had run through a bedroom window and killed himself. "He might fit the profile."

Erway smiled. "With these quickie studies, you're always guessing. Half the time the condition turns out to be iatrogenic anyway."

He cocked an eyebrow, waiting for Ian to ask him what iatrogenic meant. But he knew what it meant.

"Here," Erway said, "take the charts. Read up. Normally as site manager I'd hang on to them, but you look like a young man on a mission. What the hell, we're all on the same team, right? Doing R-and-D for the big pharma?"

"That's kind of a cynical way to put it, don't you think?"

"I beg your pardon, Dr. Schweitzer. I've offended you." Erway examined his cuticles, frowning. "Heavens."

Ian remained silent. He was trying to lay out a path in his head, one that led away from here and back to his lab, where the light was good and the offices clean, where spiders toiled benignly on their webs and cats licked sleepily at their paws and fish went round and round in their gurgling tanks, performing silent, elliptical ballets. But something kept getting in the way. "This special subset. Are you saying Dr. Heflin approved it?"

Erway's eyes flitted about the desk, looking for something. "You know, for a minute back there I almost thought I was talking to an intelligent person."

"But if the human trials are in any way hazardous, surely—"

"What? We'll give those nice people from Furst their money back? Three thousand plus per patient? Ah, there you are, you rascal." Erway picked up the bottle of Verloxx and began to roll it back and forth between his meaty palms. "A friend over in Munich sends me these little beauties. Anti-inflammatory, for my knees. A bona fide miracle drug. But you can't get it here. They've held it up in clinical trials—too many ibuprofen products on the market would go belly up."

"They?" Ian asked.

"Sure. There are vested interests, you know, who'd prefer us to be in a little pain. Not too much, but some. It could happen to this new compound of yours too. What's he calling it now anyway?"

"Dodabulax."

"Dumb name."

"It stands for something," Ian said. "I forget what."

"Look," Erway said, "my advice, for what it's worth, is forget about Eddie here. Believe me, if this drug does get approved, and my guess is it will, no one's going to thank you for being cautious. No one'll say, Sorry, we're tinkering with nature's most delicate and inscrutable mechanisms here, let's come back in twenty years when we've got the kinks worked out."

"I don't know," Ian said. "Maybe we *should* wait."

"It's too late." Erway rattled the pills in his hand; they made a sound like gunfire. "Hear that? This is war, my friend. Now, the war on drugs, that was a nice phrase, but come on: it's been a war *for* drugs all along. Those guys at Squibb and Merck, you think they don't know about war? They're pros. They've got it all rigged. First you score the treatment, then you find the illness to match it. Sign up some white coats, create a little psychological dependence in the user, and bingo. You're in business. Just say yes."

"Let me ask you a question—"

"You're not listening, are you?"

"How did you wind up working in the state prison system? I looked up those articles you published when you first started out. You were part of that whole Penn project; people still talk abou—"

Erway waved a hand to cut him off. "Look, my young friend. I hardly know you. I've had no Danish this morning and no Verloxx and I was in only a marginal mood to begin with. I'd prefer not to start trading life stories at this point." He leaned forward moodily and began a slow, cetaceous rise from his chair. "Let's just call it a case of Rush's dream and leave it at that."

"Rush's what?"

"You're a research guy. Look it up. Now, if you'll excuse me, I have a lot of unbelievably tedious busywork I need to start pretending to do."

"What happened to Heflin, anyway? You knew him before. How did he get so much influence?"

"He was lucky," Erway said. "It happens all the time. You're probably too young to understand the hows and whys."

For years people had been telling Ian Ogelvie he was probably too young to understand the hows and whys. In a sense it was almost liberating to have so little expected of him. But in another sense, a newer and deeper one, it had really begun to get on his nerves.

"Here," Erway urged, "take the charts and go. You'll find ten or twenty shocking violations of professional ethics, mostly by me. I'm tempted to use the familiar excuse that we're understaffed, which happens to be true. But I refuse to be defensive. So let's just say that if you were to express to your colleagues up there some concerns they might want to address in the area of methodology, it would not, in this old man's opinion, be unwarranted."

Ian looked around the meager office with its surfeit of trash, its peeling walls and threadbare carpet. He felt an odd, satisfied detachment, glad for a change to be himself and not Donald Erway, nothing like Donald Erway. Given a choice, he'd have even preferred to work for Howard Heflin than this fat, passive, embittered old cynic who could hardly work his way out of his chair. "They're perfect, you know."

"Who?"

"My spiders. The webs they're spinning. They're perfect."

"What's the matter with you? Are you stupid? I've been as rude as humanly possible and you're still here."

"I just wanted to tell you that there's another side to this thing. The drug is exceptionally interesting. I've got Siamese fighting fish who've completely stopped fighting. I've got mice swimming around all day in plastic buckets. Swimming *cheerfully.*"

"This you call interesting?"

"Mice *hate* water. Just the stress of being near it should throw off their entire choline production. But there's no sign of a degrading enzyme. We're beating it off. Come up to the lab and see," Ian urged. "There's a lot of excitement."

"I don't trust excitable people," Erway said. "I see too many of them here." Smiling wearily, he patted Ian on his shoulder, simultaneously steering him through the doorway.

"Hey, do me a favor."

"What?"

"Tell that Korean gal hello."

When the tiresome young idiot had finally gone, Donald Erway settled back behind his desk with a grunt. Fishing a small key from his pocket, he opened the lock on the top drawer and drew out his works. The flesh-colored tubing was like an enormous comma, the dangling midpoint between two difficult clauses. He wrapped it around his arm, pulled it tight. The last thing he noticed, before he took a break from noticing things for a while, was the television glowing in the corner, soundless, receiving no channel like a window onto a furious void.

10

Group Think

SHE HAD expected it to feel stranger than it did, entering a world this way, as a faceless visitor, a virtual being. But in fact it was all too easy. The smoothness of access was mildly disturbing. Was the self just some bulky, insulated coat one could leave out in night's anteroom, folded over a chair? And would it still be there when she got back?

She turned on the computer, adjusted the lamp to reduce the glare, and settled in behind her desk. Slowly the monitor filled with light. There were a series of benign clicks, and then after a brief hesitation the modem, engaged, spewed out its hawking, guttural noise, as if something were being mangled beyond recognition in the workings of the machine. And then she was in. It was like falling asleep. Slipping past the interference, shrugging off the ropes of physical law, getting free.

She typed out the code she'd been given and hit Enter.

At once the screen turned busy and significant with light. Who were they all, she wondered, these coded names, blinking messages back and forth like so many stars in search of constellation? She imagined people vaguely like herself, only worse, of course, more pent-up and isolated and damaged, hunched at their desks, sleepless, heads bowed under penitential cones of light, tapping away soundlessly at the keyboard, composing discordant little melodies of rage, loneliness, and fermented desire; trying to conjure, from the tower of stacked components and the grid of inlaid circuits, some sort of fledgling, improvisatory community.

Oh, she had entered, all right. But entered what? A neighborhood of solitaries. Some fun.

Or else, she thinks experimentally, it's all a hoax. The machine's a hollow box, the plug is dead, the wires do not connect, and this is only a sweet, tender fantasy we've all agreed to share, a reverie of linkage. No Web, but only spinners . . .

Well, she tells herself, everyone needs a place to go. Even an imaginary place.

She browses the sites in a restless, greedy trance, looking for shelter, consolation, advice—she has no idea what to call it. Perhaps there's no name. She suspects this may make it harder to find.

Subject: LONG STORY
From: cherylk@aol.com

Hi Guys,

Finally I've gotten up the courage to tell you why I've joined this anxiety group. It's kind of a long story so I'll shorten it. I was abused as a kid by my stepfather. He wasn't even my stepfather, just some asshole from the power station where my mom worked who she used to sleep with when she was lonely, which was pretty much all the time I guess 'cause he sort of moved in with us for about five years until he finally split.

So I told my mom about the abuse but she said it was just a phase and I'd outgrow it. I think about that a lot now. I can't figure out if she meant what he was doing to me was just a phase or me telling her about it was just a phase or what. Anyway, I got my ass out of there the second I turned 18. Joined the military, which is not such a great place to avoid men, by the way. The good thing was I met my husband. Except now it's the bad thing too. We've been together 7 years, three kids, but he never touches me in bed and says he thinks he wants to maybe take a vacation sometime to go down and see his ex-wife in Tampa. She's getting divorced, going through a bad time, etc., etc. Hey, you know what? I'm going through a bad time too. How about taking a vacation to see *me?*

Anyway I've decided to stop being such a victim all the time. I quit my job and went to a therapist and got some really helpful drugs into my system.

At least the kids are doing well at school, and I've found you guys, and that's been really supportive for me, and I got turned on to this great new psychopharmacologist downtown who wants to put me on Effexor. Which is supposed to be great stuff. Though I hear it causes lower bowel problems.

I just need to talk, I guess. Just throw the words out and not care where they're going. Is this what they call a talking cure?

Thanks for being so patient—

cheryl

Subject: SEXZONE
From: donrz@aol.com

I have a history of depression and had tremendous results from Nortriptyline and Prozac for 4 yrs. I felt so good I didn't mind giving up my sex drive. The way I felt was better than sex. It was calm and peaceful and there wasn't any wet spot to deal with. But then I started to get kind of bored not having a girlfriend. So I asked my psychiatrist to cut back the dosage.

Guess what? My sexual appetite came back but so did my symptoms.

Yesterday I went to a new psychiatrist and we agreed to try Serzone. I turned down Paxil because it's in the SSRI family, and from what I've read about it I thought I wanted to try a different class. I'm hoping I can get some relief from the insomnia and obsessive ruminations. I'm also hoping I can have a normal libido one of these days. It's always either way too much or nowhere near enough. Anyone out there have any experience with this? I'd appreciate feedback, especially from males.

don

Subject: ATYPICAL DEPRESSIONS
From: valerie@aol.com

I wonder if anyone else out there feels like I do.

I've been diagnosed with both social phobia and atypical depression. The *DSM-IV* says you're supposed to differentially diagnose between the two because the extreme rejection sensitivity of atypical depression can look like social phobia. But I wonder if for some people, like myself, social phobia might be a *form* of atypical depression. MAOI's are effective for both, right? So couldn't social phobia come from an exaggerated rejection sensitivity?

This is me: When I'm depressed (i.e., not on Nardil), I:

sleep 12–15 hours/day;
eat ten times what I should;
have miserable self-esteem;

am constantly obsessed with mistakes I've made and ways I've embarrassed myself in the past;
am crushed when criticized or ignored or put down and then obsess on how terrible I am;
have to push myself incredibly hard to do anything productive, and then torture myself about what a lazy slob I am;
am flooded with suicidal or self-destructive thoughts;
everything seems incredibly difficult, especially the rain (I live in Portland);
I think everyone is disgusted with me;
I'm irritable and impatient and anxious;
although I do find things funny, enjoy a good movie or book or CD, etc . . .

Which fits incredibly perfectly with atypical depression. Which supposedly includes hypersomnia, rejection sensitivity, leaden paralysis, all with mood reactivity. Makes you wonder, doesn't it?

I've been enjoying being part of this group. For a while I was part of a panic group but the people in it made me really, really nervous. This one seems a lot more mellow.

Valerie

Subject: SOCIAL PHOBIAS REVISITED
From: merle.t@aol.com

I don't take drugs, which I realize makes me sort of an odd bird in this chat group. But hey, I'm a weight lifter. I bench-press 340. I've got shoulders like the young Brando. I don't even do steroids. I figure my body is a sanctuary and I should treat it right. Though if anyone out there has something really *good* to recommend, I may be interested. Because I've been having a real rough time lately.

Just to let Valerie know she's not the only one, here's my personal hit parade of social phobia symptoms:

I'm incredibly nervous in groups of people or in public;
I think people are judging me and/or will dislike me and/or reject me and/or take no interest in me whatsoever;
I never go to parties, or other optional social events;
If I have to go I dread it weeks in advance;
I always sit in the back or corner of a theater or bus so people won't see me;
I avoid eye contact;
I avoid gossip or talk about politics;
I avoid bright colored clothes;
I avoid mirrors;
I avoid restaurants;
I avoid aquariums and zoos and sporting events of all kinds;
I avoid bookstores that sell coffee;
I avoid discussions that take place in the men's room;
I avoid telephone solicitors;
I avoid letter carriers, UPS trucks, FedEx packages, and pizza delivery;
I don't go out on a whole lot of dates.

Which is pretty much *total* social phobia, right? Which I've got. But I think Valerie's theory is right—it all comes out of that whole negative-thinking system you get from depression. Self-disgust, inability to deal with rejection, and so on.

Also I've been kind of addicted to cyberporn lately. I'm up all night with that shit. And I don't even *like* it. But all you have to do is hit that button and there it is, the promised land, all these nasty beautiful girls with their mouths hanging open and their legs parting like whatever you call it, the Dead Sea, and they're right there in your room and it's dark and nobody even knows about it, and they'll do practically anything you want.

I know, I know: obsessive behavior, super unhealthy any way you look at it. I feel a shitload of guilt and shame about it. I do. But how do I stop? How do I *want* to stop?

Merle

P.S. Hey Valerie, want to have dinner sometime? I live in San Jose but I'd be happy to drive up on a day that's not too rainy. Let me know . . .

Subject: GETTING RESTLESS!!
From: deejay@aol.com

Hi! I've been on Wellbutrin and Cytomel for about 2 months! How long does it take before it really starts to work??? I don't feel so good sometimes but other times I really am starting to think it's working! I'm sleeping better but I'm still sooo tired sometimes though not right now actually! I was on Desipramine for about 6 months but couldn't get up to a good dose, the side effects were so harsh! Then my shrink tried Paxil, which seems to lessen my anxiety some, but not enough! Now I'm on these new meds, and I haven't had a panic attack in a while, and it definitely helps put a curb on all that obsessive thinking I was doing, that little voice inside your head that constantly worries and thinks and goes around and around in circles and drives you nuts half the time—

But I still feel like my attention is kind of bad! Like a lot of the time I'm not aware of things around me like I know I'm here but it doesn't feel like i'm here! Sometimes I can't really connect with my environment! The shrink says exercise, so I'm riding the stationary bike at least ten miles a day, but I'm not sure it's doing me any good! I hate the way things don't gel in my head! Like i look at stuff but it takes a few seconds before i realize what the hell i'm looking at, or i get so tired i have to remind myself what i'm doing and where i'm at!

I don't know, maybe i should go back to Desipramine? It's supposed to have more attention-boosting properties, but i also have this problem that i think too much, and i don't really like that! But maybe there's nothing to do about it, I don't know. Anyways, someone e-mail me some good news!

Anybody have any luck with Norpramin or Mapelor? I hear good things about Medafoxamine, but is it true you can only get it in France?? How long is this stuff supposed to take anyway????

That panic group Valerie mentioned is starting to sound pretty good to me! Maybe I should hook up with them????

dj

Subject: DIPPING A TOE
From: bsaks@aol.com

I've never done this before . . .

A friend of mine suggested I look in on this information group you people have going. My best friend, before she moved away to Vermont with the man of her dreams, used to suffer from anxiety and depression a lot. She said you guys were very helpful to her in ways she couldn't quite explain. So anyway, here I am.

I don't quite know what I'm looking for, frankly. I've never been on the Internet before—wait, I think I already said that. It's just that I'm not all that computer oriented in general. I generally prefer to write longhand, even though it's slower—it's just that feeling of primary contact, holding a fountain pen, I don't know, it just seems more grounded and trustworthy to me somehow. Plus I'll admit to some ecological misgivings about the fact that you can't even sit down and write a letter these days without all this hardware set up, burning some precious, nonrenewable fossil fuel. I'm kind of an old-fashioned liberal, I guess, in that respect.

But my friend said this news group can be a valuable resource for people trying to cope with anxiety and insomnia and what-have-you, compare notes and treatments, etc. Not that I'm actually getting much treatment right now, other than checking out a sleep clinic at the hospital—a man I know is recommending me for some new study—to see if there's something wrong with the way I go about it, and if they can give me something to help. But from what I've read here it looks like a lot of people are struggling with problems a lot worse than mine. Still, I thought maybe I'd just try and dip a toe in here and see what happens.

What I'm looking for, I suppose, is something to help me sleep, and maybe lift my mood a little. Maybe more than a little. At the same time I don't want any side effects. I don't want to get nervous or manic or any more put off from sex than I already am. Any suggestions? I'm not really up on the literature pharmacology-wise and I've developed this aversion to shrinks so I'm kind of stuck at the moment. But it seems like you guys out there are as good a place as any to start.

And oh, I'm pregnant too. Which is probably a deal-breaker all by itself. But if anyone has any advice, I'd be more than grateful.

hopefully,
bonnie saks

P.S. Am I supposed to use my real name, or some kind of nickname or handle? Not sure what to do . . .

P.S. Forgive me if this sounds presumptuous—I'm not really up on the protocol—but if I were you, Valerie, I think I'd consider keeping at least a state or two of distance between you and this guy Merle.

P.S. No offense, Merle. I'm sure you're a perfectly nice person. It's just that I think she'd be better off with someone less troubled.

Subject: SHUTTING THE FUCK UP
From: merle.t@aol.com

Hey, Bonnie, welcome to the group. I'm sure you'll find it a valuable and supportive and all-around empowering experience, like the rest of us, for coping with what are obviously in your case an impressive set of debilitating social problems—like not being able to distinguish between helpful advice, say, and freelance meddling into other people's business.

You don't need a pill, lady: you need a muzzle.

merle

Subject: LIGHTEN UP
From: ccarnegie@aol.com

Hey, Merle, down boy. Chill. Stop taking out your infantile macho passive-aggressions on the rest of us. Besides, I pretty much agree with B. (Weird coincidence . . . one of the ladies I baby-sit for is named—oh never mind) about you and Val. She's got enough problems. And you're like the worst possible thing for her, dude. You've got this whole muscles-and-shyness thing going on, and that's a pretty creepy combination if you think about it.

Sorry to be coming down so negative tonight. I'm kind of freaking. I've got all this English homework but I pretty much totally can't concentrate. Macbeth. I'm so sick of that guy. And his wife: what's *her* problem? Does she have to be such a serious bitch all the time? She's so much like my mother it isn't funny.

See here's my problem: I was on these really cool meds for a while, but I ran out. It's a downer, you get all stoked on some great new pill and then one day, zip, it's gone. Problem is I don't have a clue what they even were. I sort of stole them from my brother's girlfriend Emily, who I pray to God never finds out, but she probably will, cause I'll probably tell her, with the way things are going. Emily's in this really fancy graduate school learning to be a shrink, they do all these research projects so she's always getting to try out the newest stuff, but she's also totally messy and absentminded so when she loses a sample or two she never figures out where it went. But I can't just go up to her and be like, hey, Emily, can you get some more samples of those blue meds so I can steal them from your purse? Or can I?

Anyway what happened was, I was crashing at their apartment last week cause things were getting so evil here with that great heaving bitch who calls herself my mom. I was trying to do my homework, too, which was definitely getting me stressed, and Mark and Emily were having this major argument in the kitchen about some weird work thing she's involved in. It has to do with sleep, sleep and motion sickness. Like I guess barfing in the car and all that. I don't know what the big conflict was but it pretty much completely drowned out the TV. Mark was trying to push one of his stocks on her—he's into money, he's kind of a capitalist scumbag in general, though he has his good points I guess—and Emily was like no way, it's totally inappropriate and besides she could get in a lot of trouble. I think the reason they're not getting along is because Mark works so much at night, they never see each other, he's always down in the financial district at three in the morning talking on the phone. He hardly sleeps, in fact. He has to stay on top of the Nikkei, or the Hang Seng, I forget which. If you fall behind you're out of the game, he says. That's what he calls it: a freaking *game.*

Whatever. Anyway, I started thinking about how lousy and ragged I feel sometimes when I'm riding in the backseat of the car. I think I actually *have* motion sickness. A bad case. And I have a lot of trouble sleeping too. So in a way that kind of made it legitimate for me to boost her purse when she went to bed, right?

So anyway. I don't know what these things had in them but they were totally potent. Even better than that great tranq Special K they used to have at all the raves till the asshole governor decided to make it illegal. You can still get it but it's a lot harder now. It's not the same. Brendan, this guy I'm seeing, he says that's their MO, those government types. They let you try some cool new med and get way into it, then they take it away. Just to show who's boss. He has an uncle who works for the tax service so he knows a lot about the whole fascist government vibe.

Anyway, these pills are totally *sweet.* About twenty minutes after you take them everything gets all melty and there's this great positive energy that just rolls right through your head and out, sort of like music does sometimes when the band is really mellow. I gave a couple to Brendan, and he agreed with me. He said it was like having this really cool party with all his best friends every night, all night long. He said he got so stoked on his own dreams he didn't want to get up again, ever. For me it was pretty much the same way. Your basic party concept, only better. And then when I woke up, they didn't fade out like they usually do, they sort of slopped over into the day, like the party was just going on and on, and I was the center of the whole thing, and everyone was gathered around me in a really cool and beautiful way, and I was like the queen of the world. It made me get all meditative. I kept thinking, does Emily take these every day? No wonder she's so hip and confident all the time. No wonder she's got so much energy. Me, I got a whole lot done, and did real well with people for a change. Even my mom didn't seem so completely Caligula-ish as usual.

Only problem is now I've run out.

I can't sleep at *all* now. I just lie there. I mean the party is way over. And Brendan, he's not doing so great either. Like he keeps flunking his math quizzes, and he's really good at math.

Anyone have a suggestion? Seconal doesn't do it for me anymore: I've got some weird resistance. This health food freak at school said he chews valerian root three times a day, but I don't like the sound of *that.* Someone else said melatonin but I hear that's just some completely bogus airport rip-off. Then Lucinda Markowitz told me about her dad. He's got something called apne that keeps him up at night and according to her is actually kind of dangerous. I don't know, maybe she said *acne.* Which I do have plenty of, unfortunately. So does Brendan, it's like all over his shoulders and down his back. It's kind of disgusting if you look too close. But the rest of him is really cool.

Anyway thanks for listening. I feel a lot better now, even though I still don't know what to do. If things don't improve pretty soon I'm going to have to go to Emily and beg for more. And then it'll all come out, which'll be really bad.

cress

Subject: OH NO
From: bsaks@aol.com

Cress? *My* Cress? My *kids'* Cress?

Subject: WHOOPS
From: ccarnegie@aol.com

Um . . . hi. I didn't know you stayed up this late.

For someone who doesn't even have a boyfriend, you sure get pregnant a lot. What's up with that? Can't you get on the pill or something?

Maybe *you* should get in touch with my brother's girlfriend. Call if you want her number. We can go 50-50 on anything you get.

cress.

p.s. are you going to be like all pissed at me now? Cause you still owe me $6.50 for that cab last week.

II

Minor Infatuations

THEY WERE talking about mentors. That is, Marisa Chu was talking about mentors. Ian Ogelvie had little to contribute to the discussion. The grim fact was that for all his internships, residencies, and collaborations, Ian had never actually *had* a mentor. Not a proper one, the kind who watched over and advised you, who made important calls on your behalf, who invited you to dinner and looked on affectionately as you played with his children and/or dogs. No, everything he'd accomplished he'd accomplished on his own. This was something to be proud of. And yet he did not feel proud of it, exactly, but resigned. It seemed one more thing that set him apart.

Marisa Chu, on the other hand, had both found and remained in touch with an impressive number of mentors along the way, and in an impressive number of subject areas: artistic (dance teacher, ceramics teacher, cello teacher, assorted others), spiritual (Sufi RA in college; old friends Lev, an orthodox Jew, and Murad, an orthodox Muslim; assorted others), sexual (best teenage friend, best teenage friend's big brother, dance teacher, ceramics teacher, cello teacher, Sufi RA, Lev, Murad, assorted others), and professional (college adviser, grad school adviser, dissertation committee, several distinguished researchers she'd met at conferences and now communicated with by e-mail, Howard Heflin, assorted others). It made a difference, it seemed, being a woman. Women understood the need for guidance, for role models. Women, like all outer-directed personality types, required timely boosts up the ladder of ego-identity formation. Eventually of course the mentors must be shed, a painful but necessary business if one was to grow. Here, in Marisa's opinion, was where men went wrong. Men, deficient in sensitivity and self-awareness, would invariably blunder through a series of tiresome patricides that left them hobbled by guilt and doubting their own instincts. Meanwhile women would do the smart thing: go into therapy. "I know it's ridiculously slow," she conceded, "but it's still the best way to deal with separation issues. A safe, supportive space. Only let's face it, traditional practice at this point is a joke."

"I agree," Ian said.

"And analysis! Forget that. For women the results've been scandalous. But you'd be amazed how many in my cohort are still playing around with those Stone Age tools. Mom and Dad, countertransference, interpreted dreams."

"You can't blame them," Ian said judiciously. "It's how they've been trained."

"That's right. They've been trained that way by the old guard, and the old guard *wants* it slow. They want women whining on the couch about their fathers, not up and functioning well. It pays the bills. Plus they get to feel all big and potent at the same time."

Ian, straight-backed in the red vinyl booth, nodded forcefully, doing his best to appear a vigorous exception to this trend, someone who understood about outer-directed women and their countless ongoing struggles for identity. He was struggling a bit at the moment himself. His eyes were burning. Apparently some selfish, inner-directed person nearby had lit up a cigarette, the toxic smoke of which was now being directed outward, toward their table. Ever since the fire in his apartment building he'd been acutely sensitive to smoke; now, with its dark weight filtering into his lungs and his eyes tearing up involuntarily, it made the process of engaging Marisa Chu in meaningful dialogue even more taxing than usual. In her presence he felt thick-tongued and clumsy, impatient to go ahead and start saying the wrong thing already.

It would not take much effort either. All he had to do was point out that many of the iconic models of womanhood Marisa Chu was now citing as ego-identity influences were not so much individually as culturally determined, like the postcards tacked to the wall above Barbara's worktable. Frida Kahlo, Simone Weil, Amelia Earhart, Margaret Mead. Fly-girls, he thought. Solo acts. Martyrs in long scarves. Was that the freedom they craved? Freedom from male gravity? Or from quotidian life itself, the dull smog of cause and effect, the humdrum logic of *and then, and then*?

"Ever hear of a man named Rush?" he asked abruptly.

"Who?"

Across the table, Marisa had dipped her head to inhale the fragrant steam rising off her black tea. Behind the rippling vapor her dark eyes shone. They were tiny, intricately veined, inexpressive as marbles. The skin on her cheeks, he could not help but observe, was flawless. Even up close her nose was all but theoretical, the subtlest of speed bumps on the smooth paved road of her face. With each inhalation, the ruby in her nostril flared like a stoplight. He tried to see past it, to her urban heart, the swerves and loops, the flickering directional signals of her inner traffic. "Rush," he said.

"First name or last?"

"Last, I think. He had some sort of famous dream."

"What kind of dream?"

"I'm not sure."

Who *were* they, other people? What *did* they dream about? Why was their behavior so maddeningly veiled? At times such as these, quiet times, it seemed possible to Ian that for all his labor and investment in the field he might know nothing, have learned nothing that truly mattered. But such doubts were natural, he thought. Necessary. Doubt was one of the fossil fuels that drove you.

Though Marisa Chu appeared to have very little of it in her tank. Nor was she much given to quiet times in general. She seemed to lack Ian's gift—or curse, he often thought—of sitting still. Even now, stuck within the sloping contours of the booth, she continued to vibrate in place, throwing off her erratic, subliminal buzz, like a radio set, either by accident or design, between stations, picking up the washy, wave-tossed rhythms of a distant frequency. Occasionally she'd seem to forget where she was altogether. Her face would harden like a mask, and then she would fall into brief, alternating interludes of humming and silence, the existence of which Marisa herself did not seem quite aware.

"I've heard the name Rush," Marisa said. "I know I have. Did you look him up on the database?"

"I haven't been able to carve out the time. This grant application's due in four days."

"Mmm." She swished over to the end of the seat. "I know."

"You're applying too?"

But she had already squeezed out into the aisle and was on her way to the bathroom, her purse banging against her slender hip. He watched her go. Even poised atop her thick black platform shoes, she had a low center of gravity, one that made her adept at negotiating sharp turns.

When she returned, she took one look at the table and asked, "Where's our soup? They didn't bring it?"

"I think the waiter's having a cigarette back in the kitchen."

"Too bad," she said. "I'm starving."

There was a short silence as they contemplated the absence of food before them, one that gave Ian time to wonder both what in the world he was doing here and whether Marisa was wondering the same thing. Was this a date? They had already talked lengthily about movies, so perhaps it was. Marisa, he'd learned, preferred independent films with challenging structures and smart, vulnerable heroines. She'd listed a number of these films, most of which Ian had for one reason or another not yet seen. No, she'd never seen *Redbeard,* she told him, or anything else by Kurosawa either. Was he good? The foreign films she liked were from underrepresented countries like Iran or Chile or Bosnia, cultures that lacked a voice. There was an urgency of expression that moved her. Though occasionally she enjoyed French comedies too, the ones where the women left their fussy bourgeois husbands for Gérard Depardieu. She had a crush on Gérard Depardieu, she said. He reminded her of her father.

Ian, listening to this, had fallen almost against his will into the neutral, nodding affect of the clinician. Stripped of her studded motorcycle jacket, Marisa, with her slim hips and clipped hair and shapely biceps, her baggy button-fly jeans and faded black T-shirt and round chalky heat-rippled face, looked, he decided, more like a boy than a girl. A longing to assimilate the male, possibly a function of unresolved issues with the father. And here was the result, he thought: This naked urgency. This gallery of rogue heroines. This longing to merge and burn and implode like a bomb.

Across the table, Marisa, running her tongue along the ends of her small even teeth, had gone on to acknowledge a minor infatuation with Václav Havel as well.

He watched her playing with her Visa card, tapping it up and down on the gold-veined Formica like a chef mincing garlic. The black stripe on the back of the card was streaky with use. His suite-mates back in New Haven, he remembered, used to chop their cocaine the same way, with their parents' Visa cards, then pass it around on a vanity mirror in bleached meticulous lines. He would have tried some, he thought. But he was always coming back to the suite late from the lab, exhausted, and he supposed he had not looked receptive. Or possibly he'd looked *too* receptive. Uncool. Whatever cool was, that dark, winning formula, it had eluded him. Something to do with wearing black, the negation of nature's rainbow. Something to do with hardening yourself to certain things, not wanting, not needing them. Apparently that was how you advanced in the world, how you got things you needed and wanted—by not needing, not wanting them. Nonetheless he did not see how it was possible, given all the things he still needed and wanted, to stop needing and wanting long enough to get them.

Meanwhile Marisa Chu was relating her adventures in Prague, which along with tens of thousands of other young people she had visited the previous summer. The houses were painted a thousand colors. There was music in the churches, jugglers on the street. "It's wide-open territory," she said. "The opportunities are fabulous."

"For what?"

"Research," she said. "I saw some brilliant presentations over there. Groundbreaking stuff."

"Wait," Ian said, "there was a conference?"

She gave the tiniest nod of acknowledgment. "Howard thought it'd be good experience for me. He gave me a paper to read."

"Funny," he said, "usually I know about the big conferences. Usually I know all about them."

"This was very small. Low-key. You didn't miss any—ah," she said, "here's our soup."

They were served one bowl of hot-and-sour soup and a double order of scallion pancakes. It was Marisa Chu's favorite snack. The restaurant, it transpired, was her favorite restaurant. In her car, heading over, they had driven in her favorite gear, fourth, past her favorite area of the Common, the swan boat lagoon, at her favorite hour, just post-sunset, coming up on her favorite part of the city, Chinatown, from her favorite direction, the west, all the while listening to her favorite tape, Bach's cello suites numbers 1, 2, 4, and 6, played by her favorite cellist, Mischa Maisky, at her favorite volume, unbelievably loud. To spend time with Marisa Chu was to be drawn into an enormous, mystifying web of judgments and distinctions. Her preference for this dingy little rathole on lower Beach Street, for instance, as opposed to any of the two dozen other Chinese establishments nearby, struck Ian as at bottom a rather whimsical and arbitrary affectation, a mere preference for its own sake. Still, he had seen enough willful, obsessive people over the years to know that this was how they went about the world, dividing it into binary oppositions—the real and the fake, the square and the cool, the sublime and the pedestrian—drawing lines in the sand between one thing and another, trying to impose the design of their will upon the shifting, shapeless dunes.

On which side of the line, he wondered, would she place him?

"Here," Marisa said. She dipped her imitation-china spoon with its adorning dragon into the bowl, lifted it to her lips, and blew. He remembered the way she had blown dry the Polaroids at the lab, when was it, just a couple of weeks before. So tenderly, so lovingly: as if all it took was her breath's cool, temperate moisture to flesh out the images and summon them to life. "Taste this. It's extraordinary."

Actually the soup was very good, if one liked hot-and-sour, which Ian didn't particularly. He supposed that if one liked hot-and-sour one might even say the soup was extraordinary.

"Fabulous, right?"

"Uh-huh." He tried to recall how many sexual encounters he had had in the past two years, since Wendy Lesher. Was it one, or zero, or was there some kind of ambiguous fraction involved? Then too a part of him was furiously registering Marisa's tactile proximity as she leaned in close, black eyes shining, and slowly withdrew her inlaid spoon.

"It does something to you, this soup," she murmured in an awed, theatrical tone. "It expands your perceptions."

"Oh, that's just the MSG," he heard himself say, unable as usual to stop the noisy pedagogue in his head from elbowing the rest of him, the silent majority, aside. "Glutamate has an excitotoxic effect on the hypothalamus. I've read the literature. In some cases, on the neuroendocrine level, it can get pretty dangerous. You wind up with something that looks like Alzheimer's or Parkinson's."

"I've read the literature too. And you're right. Except for one thing."

"What's that?"

"There is no MSG. They don't use it."

"Oh."

Marisa took a bite of scallion pancake, closing her eyes the way people do to savor things better, to receive them in full. It was beginning to wear him out a little, keeping track of all her preferences and appetites. The pancake itself looked unpromising. A film of grease shone dully on its pocked surface. Fried foods, he thought.

"What about you?" she asked when the first pancake was gone. "You didn't tell me yours."

"My what?"

"Your role models. Wait," she said, "let me guess. Freud, naturally. Not Jung. Too fuzzy and mystical. Adler? Horney?"

"Actually," he admitted, "the only role model I can think of off the top of my head is John Cade."

"Who?"

Just having to explain who John Cade was, and to a colleague, no less, felt like an indictment of his whole life path. It made his head heavy; it was all he could do to support it with both hands. "He discovered lithium."

"Oh, right," she said. "I knew that. South African, right?"

"Australian."

"Want the rest of this?"

"No, thanks. You can have it."

"Sure?" Without waiting for an answer, she set to work polishing off the rest of his pancake, her pale lips taking on an orange gloss from the chili oil, which was also, he couldn't help but notice, about to drip down her chin. He had an impulse to reach across the table with his napkin and wipe her face. It took all his strength not to. What was wrong with him? He recalled that woman crying in the elevator the week before, his offer of aid, her rebuke, the handkerchief dangling limply between them like a flag. His own motives seemed to him strange and open to question, his inner life a double-jointed, ambiguous affair.

Primum non nocere, he thought. First do no harm.

It was important to distinguish between helpfulness and intrusiveness. Perhaps Marisa could help him there. She was an acute, worldly creature. There were a number of things he could learn from her. Perhaps it followed then, if one did not examine the provisional, semicircular logic of this too closely, that there were a number of things she might learn from him as well.

"The impressive thing about Cade," he said, "was he wasn't even *interested* in research. He was just a simple practitioner, out in the sticks. A guy with no budget, no funding, no sophisticated training or equipment. All he had were a few bipolar patients stuck in a manic cycle whom he wanted to help and had no idea how."

"I love this sauce," Marisa said dreamily. "They use fresh ginger."

He was boring her. What else was new? And yet one had to be true to one's nature. Even if one's nature was dogged and thorough and earnest and responsible—all the wrong things, in short, in life if not in research—one had to be true to it. He was certain of that, even though he could not quite remember at the moment why this should be so.

"Basically," he went on, "Cade followed the Hippocrates paradigm. Mental illness as a symptom of toxic imbalance. He figured he'd test for toxicity in the urine, only uric acid is insoluble in water. So he looked for the most soluble urate he had lying around. Which happened to be lithium salt."

"Lucky," she said.

"How could he know it would erase the toxicity altogether? The whole thing was counterintuitive; it should have increased, if anything. But it didn't. Then, on a hunch, he switches from lithium urate to lithium carbonate, and *bang!* He's got hypermanic guinea pigs laid out on their backs like sunbathers."

"Lucky again."

"Maybe. But there was a structure. An elegance. Cade was just following the Greeks. Health as equilibrium. The four humors. Blood, phlegm, yellow bile, black bile. All he did was go after the yellow. Everything else followed."

"He did human trials, I trust?"

"Ten patients, chronic mania cases. It took less than a week. The only hard part was getting them off the ward fast enough. Some had been inside for twenty years; they didn't want to go, even though for all intents and purposes they were fully functional. And the rest is medical history."

"I'm not wild about the methodology," Marisa said. "He could have used a larger test group."

"He only *had* ten patients. What was he supposed to do? Import them from somewhere else?"

"Sure. Or export himself. Why not?"

"He had no money. This was just some horrible backwater in 1948. Nobody was funding this. Nobody cared. He did it all on his own."

"How about the sea cucumber?"

"What?"

"They do a sea cucumber here that will change your life."

"Fine." He had no idea what sea cucumber was.

"So," she said, after she had ordered for them, "let me get this straight. You're saying this guy's your all-time hero and role model because of one serendipitous finding?"

"But this one serendipitous finding," Ian said, with mounting irritation, "has helped millions of people live normal lives! It's relieved them of immeasurable pain! This one dumb ion of salt has changed their whole lives!"

"You're shouting," Marisa observed coolly.

"Am I?" He looked down at his hands; they were bunched into fists. "That's really unusual for me."

"Well, stop, okay? I'm tired of being shouted at. I was shouted at all afternoon."

"I'm sorry. I'm kind of wrought up, I guess. That damned deadline."

This seemed, between two researchers, a frank enough request for sympathy, but none was forthcoming. The sea cucumber had arrived and she dug into it hungrily.

"Who shouted at you?"

"Just a lady at the clinic. Nobody important. But it came at the end of a real gonzo day." Marisa sighed and set down her chopsticks. "I had Shirley Foy *and* Ray Steinmetz back to back. After lunch was Little Elvis, in full regalia. Then Mrs. Resnikoff."

"Mrs. Resnikoff? I thought we sent her to McLean."

"The HMO sent her home."

"But the woman's crazy as a bedbug."

"That doesn't cut it anymore. You have to carry an Uzi. And it has to be loaded." She frowned. "It got worse too. Remember Mickey Turko? Fat guy, apnea, night sweats, worked for a cable company?"

"Was he the one with the recurring nightmare about losing his genitals?"

"Yes. And guess what? His dreams have come true."

"Meaning?"

"He's got testicular cancer," she said. "Metastasized. A matter of months."

"Good God."

"Oh, you should have seen me with poor Mickey. I was really great." She stared mechanically at the whorl of green tentacles on her plate. "I listened. I empathized. I clarified. I helped him identify and explore his feelings. Of course his feelings weren't too positive, needless to say. But we explored the hell out of them. Yes, sir, we gave those feelings of his a real fifty-minute workout."

"There's no treatment for that kind of misery," Ian said. "There will never be a treatment for that kind of misery."

"Well," she snapped, "there should be."

The waiter came and took away the plates.

"Anyway," Marisa waved her wrist vaguely, "finally I gave up. I wrote old Mickey a scrip for some industrial-strength Xanax, and sent him on his way. The second he's out the door this new patient walks in—a referral from Siraj, up in OB. What a bitch. Hated me right off too. Wanted someone older. Or a man. You know," she said accusingly, "I tried to call you, but you were away from your desk."

Ian attempted to conceal his pleasure at this information behind his napkin. "I had to drop off my sister at her gallery. She has this big show coming up."

"No big deal," Marisa said. She began tapping her foot absently. "It's just I hadn't had a break all day, and I was hoping to put in a call to Stanford, and she comes in and starts whining about her insomnia and her kids and her career issues. And, oh yeah, she's pregnant too. Siraj thinks she might fit our profile. Anything for a finder's fee, right?"

"Other symptoms?"

"Headaches, early morning awakening, anxiety, impulsivity, mood swings, anhedonia. Classic borderline. They're usually women."

Ian nodded. It occurred to him that he was suffering at the moment from several of these symptoms himself, as was Barbara, as was most everyone he knew. Either they were all afflicted with borderline personality disorder, or else nobody was, or else, he thought, the diagnosis had grown so broad as to be of no practical use.

"I'm thinking Zoloft," Marisa was saying, "unless it's contraindicated for pregnancy, which I'm pretty sure it isn't. Plus five or six weeks of therapy if her insurance signs off, which they probably won't. She's basically a normal." She frowned. "Half the scrips I write these days go to normals."

"Pain is pain," Ian said philosophically. "Does she know?"

"About the study? She's seen a flyer. And she's got a friend in one of the test groups. So she's interested. Of course I told her no way."

"I could run a lit search for you. I haven't seen anything to contraindicate pregnancy."

"Why bother? She's not even sure she's going through with the pregnancy. And I don't think she'll come back anyway."

"How do you know?"

"Because I gave her an appointment slip for next week and a stress reduction sheet, and watched her toss them both in the garbage on the way out." Marisa blew out, as if it were contaminated by this image, a short, bitter breath."You're lucky." She nodded toward the fish tank in the window of the restaurant. "Most of your work is with animals. They're a lot easier."

He nodded. It was true. Especially now, with the Siamese fighting fish having put down their dukes, or so it seemed, for good. Even after being taken off the drug for two days, they continued to exhibit their heightened affect of sanguinity. The mice and spiders too. It was as if their receptors were still receiving their inspirations, still hearing the music well after the band had put away their instruments and climbed in the van. Mistaking echoes and longings for the real thing. Emily Firestone, his brilliant, noisily combative new intern, was back at the lab right now logging the results, a task she performed very competently when she wasn't too busy complaining, as she often did, about being underutilized. Even so, it was nice to work with someone, Ian thought. To have another voice in your head beside your own.

Maybe there *was* something in the soup after all, or in Marisa's proud, pallid face looming across the table—was she transferring to Stanford? was she still involved, in some cross-continental way or other, with Malcolm Perle?—but Ian was beginning to experience a little heightened affect himself at this point. He felt what he only rarely felt outside the lab: zero inclination to be anywhere else. "Have you considered subaffective dysthymia?" he asked her. "It's a simpler diagnosis. Of course you'd want to check her REM latency to confirm."

Marisa regarded him evenly. "Why don't you treat her? If she comes back. Then you can check out all her latencies personally."

"I've offended you."

"Not at all. It's in the best interests of the patient. She seems to have a problem dealing with women."

Who doesn't, he was tempted to say.

"Or maybe it's me," Marisa said. "Lately, I don't know, I just seem to be in this phase where I find men more interesting. Men like to talk about work. And work's what I really care about right now. With my women friends it's all relationships this, relationships that. It gets stifling. I mean, look at us."

"Us?"

"This conversation. Notice the word *relationship* hasn't come up once?"

"I'm never exactly sure," Ian admitted, "what people mean by it."

"Generally they mean death."

"Ah."

"In the small sense, I mean. Clarity, comfort. Settling down. When we talk about emotional maturity, isn't that what we're saying? Settle down. No more struggle. No more tension."

"Is that so bad?"

"It's not a question of good or bad, I don't think. It's a question of genuineness."

It occurred to Ian, listening to her, that all the richest and most fantastical human constructs—marriage, science, religion—rested upon the same wobbly, two-legged sawhorse: that something is wrong with us as we are, and that we can be saved from that wrongness. The unease and the solution.

"And love?" he blurted, heat rising to his cheeks. "Is that death too?"

"Just the opposite. Love is highly volatile. Highly dangerous and impersonal. It's like the ocean—you can't tame it, you can't cork it up, you can't build your house on it. You have to make yourself a vessel; let it pass right through you. But no," she said, "people are greedy, they want to own love like a piece of furniture, and they can't, and it makes them unhappy. Which is why if you ask me there are so many wonderful opportunities in the mental health area these days."

"But if you don't try and contain it," Ian said, "how do you make it last?"

"You don't. It doesn't."

"Then how do you *live?*" he demanded. "Alone?"

"Not necessarily. For people like me, who can't handle multiple partners, serial monogamy is as good a solution as any. Most people end up that way anyway, more or less. How about you?"

"How about me what?"

"What's your methodology? Do you do multiple partners, or are you more the serial monogamy type? Or do you just rent porn videos a few times a week? Not that these are necessarily exclusive of each other."

"I don't—"

"Then there's the kids issue. Kids are a complication. They mess up the paradigm. Still, I'm only twenty-seven. I figure I've got ten or so years to figure it out. And by then the factors'll probably be different. I might be gay by then too. Or famous. Or dead of some incurable disease. I might even be married to a stockbroker and living in West Newton. Throwing dinner parties with matching plates. It sounds horrible, but it could happen. Can't worry about it now, right?"

Ian was silent for a moment.

"What do you mean," he said finally, " 'gay by then *too*'?"

She shrugged.

"You think I'm gay? Is that what people say about me? That I'm a gay person?"

"This may come as a blow to you, Ian, but I don't think people spend a lot of time speculating about your sexual orientation. They're busy with their own problems. And when they do gossip, they're probably way too busy talking about *me.* They do," she said, "don't they? Especially now that Malcolm's gone off to India."

"He has?"

"Him and that spunky Quaker of a wife. Miss Can-Do. Miss Let's Help the Poor Downtrodden Third Worlders. She's filled his head with that Friends Academy shit for years."

"No one's said a word to me."

"Oh well. They probably assume you're occupied with other things."

"Like what?"

"Like your work. And being gay."

"But I'm not gay."

"It doesn't matter," she said. "Gay, straight, bi, it's all one continuum. There's no need for the whole denial-and-repression syndrome, where you avoid sexuality in general so as not to be confronted by your true makeup."

"But I don't *have* a true makeup," he said. "Or wait, I do. It just happens to be the true makeup of someone who's not gay."

"So what are you then?"

"Pardon?"

"What attracts you? *Who* attracts you?"

The truth was scrawled on Ian's face, he felt sure, in great messy gobs of red ink. But he did not say a word. Marisa's expression as she studied him was jointed but opaque, like a folding screen. He found it painful, almost literally painful to look at.

"Scratch that," she said. "Bad question. Completely unprofessional. Also none of my business."

"It's okay."

"No, no. I hate it when people I work with do that to me, get personal about my life like that. It's obnoxious."

Ian nodded and frowned, though in his view it was not all that obnoxious. He had been about to do it to her himself. But he changed his mind. "If your patient does come back," he said finally, "I'll be happy to treat her."

"Great," she said at once, amiability now restored. "That's really nice of you."

"No big deal."

She shrugged. "It makes me feel better, though. About the whole thing." Regathering herself in an athletic, not entirely unselfconscious way, she stretched, arching her back, uncoiling, inch by inch, her creamy shoulders and her low, barely perceptible hips, a languid flower straightening in the light. *Which whole thing?* he was tempted to ask. All at once, with practically zero effort, he felt he knew her very well, knew just who she was, could practically sketch out the floor plan of her entire funky one-bedroom apartment back in Jamaica Plain—the old, comfortable furniture, the obscure black-and-white photographs on the walls, the futon humped away stoically in the corner, the little tchotchkes from Peru and New Guinea on the coffee table, the dozen or so magnets of a kitschy, ironical nature that were spread across the refrigerator. On the counter would be bottles of wine, candles burned to erratic heights, wicker baskets full of lemons, kiwi, pomegranates, pears, all the lumpiest, most colorful fruits.

Mentally he paced down the hallway and into her tiny but light-soaked and serenely cluttered bathroom, where he began to nose through the contents of her medicine cabinet, ticking off the little bottles, each one an answer, or was it a question, in the tough pop quiz of her identity. . . .

"So," she said. "Shall we?"

His heart raced. "Shall we what?"

"Head back to the lab."

"Sure," he said. "Why not?"

"We'll go along the river," she said, pulling a crumpled bill from the front pocket of her jeans. "It's incredible at night. And I know a great new place we can stop for coffee."

"Here." He reached for his wallet. "Let me get this."

"What for? You didn't eat anything."

It should cost me something, he wanted to say. It was bound to, he thought, sooner or later.

But Marisa was already marching off toward the register, arms half drowned in the black sleeves of her jacket. Ian followed along behind. At the cash register he waited for her to receive her change and finish trading pleasantries with the owner—a dialogue, he couldn't fail to notice, in which she seemed no more nor less invested than she had been with him. Still, he was with her, he had come with her; they were leaving together; that was something new. In her car earlier, as they'd whizzed past the Common, he'd looked out at the well-dressed people strolling home from work in the failing light, dusk dropping over them its rapturous net, and a sharp, fleeting pain went through him that, walled up in his glass tower, he had missed so much unclassifiable behavior. He felt right then that he understood the city on a more intimate basis than he had previously—what drove it, what sustained it, what wove together its constituent parts. He did not feel quite the same proximity to knowledge when he was alone.

It had left a trace on the tongue, that moment in the car, a savory tang that had not gone away. He was grateful for it. He would offer to buy Marisa Chu coffee, of course, once they arrived at this new great place she spoke of. And a pastry to go with it, some sugary stimulant to speed up the brain. A croissant, a muffin, a chocolate biscotti. Whatever her favorite was. He did not doubt that she would have one.

12

Questions and Answers

1. Please state the principal reason, in your opinion, that you would make a good candidate for the Sleep Study: *Persistent insomnia.*
2. How did you hear of us? *A flyer. Also a friend.*
3. What time do you usually try to fall asleep? *11–12 p.m.*
4. How long does it usually take you to fall asleep? *Two or three hours. Sometimes more.*
5. How late do you normally sleep? *3:29.*
6. When falling asleep or trying to fall asleep, do you (never/sometimes/often):
   a. have thoughts racing through your mind? . . . *often.*
   b. feel sad or depressed? . . . *often.*
   c. have anxiety (worry about things)? . . . *often.*
   d. feel muscular tension? . . . *often.*
   e. feel unable to move? . . . *often.*
   f. feel afraid of not being able to sleep? . . . *often.*
   g. have crawling, aching, or twitching feelings in your legs or feel like you must move them? . . . *often.*
   h. feel afraid of the dark or anything else? . . . *often.*
   i. suddenly become awake or alert? . . . *often.*
   j. sleep with someone else in your bed? . . .
   k. get up at night to attend to your children or something else? . . . *often.*

l. sweat a great deal? . . . *often.*
m. feel your heart pounding? . . . *often.*
n. wake up screaming, violent, or confused? . . . *often.*
o. grind your teeth at night? . . . *often.*
p. have a hard time getting out of bed? . . . *often.*
q. have dreamlike images when waking up even though you know you are not asleep? . . . *often.*
r. wake up with a headache? . . . *often.*
s. wake up nauseated? . . . *often.*
t. wake up over two hours before you have to get up? . . . *often.*
u. feel sleepy during the day? . . . *often.*
v. have anxiety (worry about things)? . . . *often.*
w. wish you could take a nap, but can't? . . . *often.*
x. feel weakness in your muscles when laughing, surprised, angry, excited, etc.? . . . *often.*
y. lose control of your emotions for no apparent reason? . . . *often.*

7. How much coffee do you drink? . . . *a lot.*
8. How much chocolate do you eat? . . . *a lot.*
9. How much tobacco do you smoke? . . . *a lot.*
10. How often have you used:
    a. marijuana? . . . *often.*
    b. cocaine? . . . *often.*
    c. hallucinogens? . . . *often.*
    d. stimulants? . . . *often.*
    e. depressants? . . . *often.*
    f. narcotics? . . . *never.*
    g. list others . . .
11. Note what strategies you have employed in the past to remedy the problem, and what the result was:

EFFORT	WHOSE SUGGESTION	RESULT
ignore it	ex-husband	none
hot milk	ex-husband	none
chamomile tea	ex-husband	none

EFFORT	WHOSE SUGGESTION	RESULT
relaxation tape	ex-husband	none
L-Triptophane	ex-husband	none
melatonin	ex-husband	none
slept alone	ex-husband	made more anxious
meditation	friend	made more anxious
over-the-counter drugs	friend	headaches
single-malt scotch	friend	headaches
psychotherapy	everyone	none, headaches, made more anxious

12. When would you PREFER to be sleeping? (circle one) Day. Night.
13. Please check the appropriate box for each statement about yourself:

	NEVER	SOMETIMES	OFTEN
a. I feel downhearted, sad, and blue:			x
b. I have crying spells:			x
c. I enjoy looking at, talking to, and being with attractive people:		x	
d. I notice I am losing weight:	x		
e. I find it easy to do things:	x		
f. I am irritable:			x
g. I find it easy to make decisions:	x		
h. I am hopeful about the future:		x	
i. I have unusual fears:			

14. Are there any advantages to your problem? Any ways in which you think you may actually benefit from it?
15. Please describe, as fully as possible, the principal STRESSORS in your life:

Pausing, she reached for another twirled, waxy stick of licorice. She would have to come back to these last questions. The space she'd been given for her answer to number 15 was, she thought, insufficient; to do it justice would require turning over the sheet and writing on the back in a very small hand. She would have to go back to 6j, 10g, and 13i too.

Unusual fears, she thought. How was one to distinguish between those and the other kind?

"Mommy?"

"Just a second."

The questionnaire was extremely thorough. It ran eleven pages, single spaced, in the tiniest, most clinically precise of fonts. She gave it her full attention. She was hoping to prove herself worthy of study. Dr. Gogolvie—or whatever his name was, the guy whom Larry's psychopharmacologist, that snippy little bitch at the clinic, had referred her to—had advised her to be candid and forthcoming. In addition to the sleep drugs, they were also paying $250 a week, he'd said, tax-free. So she sat there filling in every blank space with her good blue fountain pen, neatly and crisply, trying to be as candid and forthcoming as possible.

It was like building a pyramid, stone by stone, a chiseled monument to her own sleepless, demanding god. Her *disorder,* they called it. One used to be afflicted with an illness, something overarching and mysterious upon which war must be waged; but now one merely had to cope with a *disorder.* It seemed to her a falling off. Nonetheless she tried to do it, this disorder of hers, justice. She was as complete in her answers as space would allow. She described it as she would an objective, independent being to which, like some boorish cousin at a family reunion, she was related only accidentally. She cut no corners, shirked from no embarrassing revelations. They would take her as a subject, or they wouldn't; whichever way it fell, she was determined that the person who read this document—her Dr. Gogol—would come to know her. Or if not her then her disorder. He would at least come to know her disorder.

"Mommy?"

"Get your clothes off, Petey," she called over her shoulder. "I'll be right there."

The clock read eight-fifteen. She had been at it for over an hour. And she was not yet halfway through.

"Mommy!"

Capping her pen, she laid it down with reluctance. Between the questionnaire, the dishes from dinner, and the student essays she had long since promised to return, it was shaping up to be a long evening. But then insomnia was good for that, she thought. Insomnia had a talent for stretching out the workday, pulling the hours from its dark mouth in a long, skinny string, like so much tasteless taffy.

"Mommy! Come turn on the bathroom light."

He was afraid of the dark. Who wasn't? Fear was their thing, all right—their night flower, their black rose. Time to raze the garden, she thought. Time to turn over the soil and plant afresh.

She could hear the boy calling for her again, for Mommy. He kept intoning those same two syllables over and over, until they began to sound, to her at least, like only another phrase of fraudulent magic, another arbitrary and nonsensical appeal to an absent being.

"Hold your horses," she said. "I'm on my way."

Though the water in the bathtub was a Miami-like ninety degrees, and infused with three expensive pearls of bayberry-scented oil from the Body Shop that made it feel even warmer, it did not prevent Petey from whining, as he always did, that he was cold. To prove his point he sat there shivering theatrically and turning as blue-lipped as possible while Bonnie washed him. This involved the usual slow, grave process of erasure. First she rubbed out the clouds of dirt storming across his forehead; then the crescents of shadow that had accumulated, puffy and unseen as mushrooms, behind his ears; and finally, the elliptical purple discoloration from the evening's grape juice, which had dried into a mournful clown mask around the corners of his mouth. The boy was a walking tabula rasa, his skin a soft plaster on which all the world's vagrant impressions left their mark. Carefully, so as not to erase too much, she moved the cloth down his long neck and bony, concave torso, over his slender hips, and, with great solemnity and deliberation, between his legs, where the pale equipment of his future lay intricately coiled.

"Are you *done?*" he asked.

"Almost."

"That's what you always say."

"Well, it's true," she said. She was determined not to be rushed. She'd heard a scientist on the radio claim that young rats licked by their mothers were better at handling stress than those who weren't. Apparently the licking caused their brains to manufacture a calming chemical, some sort of homemade Valium, that eased their way through life. She tried to keep this in mind whenever she gave Petey a bath.

Her own mother had been doting and affectionate; she wondered what this said about the general applicability of the study.

Beneath the wet cloth Petey shivered and moaned. Despite if not because of her attentions, he would be, she thought, a delicate man. Perhaps one day he'd find himself writing bad plays in a foreign country, like his father. But no, chances were he'd be out in the audience instead, stranded in the dark, enthralled, feeling implicated against his will in the plight of every character, no matter how thinly drawn or sparsely costumed, sharing their luckless fates. His emotions were like water: they assumed the shape of whatever surrounded them. Unlike his father, unlike his brother, unlike Bonnie herself at this point, the boy was not by disposition steeled for adversity, and so every experience of it would continue to come as an unhappy surprise—the way it did, for instance, right now, when she pulled down the drain lever and ordered him to step out of the bath just as he'd finally begun to acclimate to it.

Despite her command Petey hesitated, one foot in and one foot out, and with the same concentrated, pursed-lip, vaguely disappointed expression he brought to bear on all things elemental, watched the water whirl magnetically above the tiny grate, hover for a moment, then disappear with a gasp. Some transparent flakes of himself, he seemed to realize, were going with it. Where to? At his age the workings of the bathtub must be, Bonnie thought, as large, as stubbornly senseless as the ocean.

"Let's read a book," he announced breathily through his nose when the last of the water was gone. He was getting another cold.

"Yes," she said. "But which one?"

"I choose."

The book he chose was not a surprise; he'd chosen the same one for several nights running. Still, he delivered it unto her with joyous apprehension, a treasure unearthed, as if accidentally, from the bright disorder of his shelves. "Read," he instructed, and snuggled up beside her.

At once a wet spot, like an anemone of shadow, bloomed on her blouse from the pressure of his head. But then the blouse was already stained to begin with, from vinegar and mustard and olive oil and tomato sauce and Christ knew how many other constituents of the day's hastily assembled meals. The cost of living, she thought.

She began to read.

The book, *The Gravity Company,* was the tale of a prosperous hamlet named Cayuga Ridge. Among other local industries, Cayuga Ridge had been blessed with the utility of the title, a big, well-toned establishment devoted to the manufacture, maintenance, and distribution of gravity. One fine day, after Mortimer, the manager of the company, goes off to lunch, the cleaning woman ("a Gravity Company runs well when it is clean") inadvertently trips the automatic switch on the Gravity Machine with her broom ("a Gravity Company does not run very well when the gravity has been turned off"), at which point all hell breaks loose. Actually, it *floats* loose, in a form so riotous and amusing, to Petey anyway, it's indistinguishable from heaven. Baseballs fly into space. Roller-coasters sail off their tracks. Zookeepers play yo-yo with the elephants. The Cayuga River departs its banks and flows into the sky. Gravity has fled, and yet no one in Cayuga Ridge seems to miss it. It's as if by invisible coup a tyrant has been dethroned; the people begin quite literally to walk on air, to test out new laws, new powers of worship, assembly, and self-determination they did not know were theirs. For a while, life is a party, their lives as sportive and unbound as gods'. If not for Mortimer, that killjoy bureaucrat—who, seeing the pizza that was to be his lunch float like a Frisbee out the window, raced back to the office to reset the lever—they might have gone on enjoying their hallucinatory weightlessness forever.

But Mortimer was a professional; he had a duty to perform, whether civic or personal, or some hybrid of the two, it was impossible to say. Ruefully Bonnie read the last page, wherein the town reverts to the quiet, humming efficiency that characterized it previously, and closed the book. Odd, but she did not recall from her previous readings feeling quite so downcast at the way it turned out.

"Well," she said, "that's that."

"Good book, huh?" said Petey. It was what he said every night, about every book. He appeared to be, in this respect, even less discriminating than she was.

"Yep. It's a good one, all right."

He yawned. As she straightened the quilt to better contain him, she saw his eyes cast uneasily about the room, settling, at last, on the silent upper bunk. "Where's Alex?"

"I told you. He's on a sleepover at Jamey's house."

"Why?"

"Just for fun." Because this last word seemed just then, in the shadowed gloom, oddly inadequate and abstract, she added, "It's fun, sometimes, to sleep over with your friends."

"You don't," the boy observed.

"True."

"Do you want to?"

"Not so much. Not lately."

"Why?"

She shrugged. It appeared this was to be her night for questions and answers. But one can only answer so many. It was important, or at any rate necessary, to leave some blank.

"Why can't *I* have a sleepover?"

"You will, honey, I told you. When you're older."

"I'm older now."

"I mean years older," she said. "Remember? We talked about this at dinner. How sometimes little boys can't do all the things their big brothers do. They have to wait. Remember talking about this?"

"Uh-huh."

She could see that he remembered nothing of the sort. Unlike his older brother, however, this one, by virtue of both temperament and birth order, was able to concede right away that there might in fact be provinces of truth that lay beyond the range of his perceptions. So he did not put up a fight. He continued to observe her carefully as she hovered over the bed, arranging his inseparable trio of stuffed bears—A, B, and C—so they formed a line of lexical defense around his pillow. Against what she didn't know.

When she was finished, she reached behind her and flicked off the overhead light. At once, dozens of plastic stars they had affixed to the ceiling the previous summer in whimsical constellations began to shed their cool, artificial glow. "Night-night, lovebug. Sleep well."

He nodded amiably, and lay back to receive her kiss. All of a sudden, now that he was letting her go, she couldn't bear to leave him. She did not need another child, she thought. All she needed was for this one and his brother, the ones she already had, to stay close, to not leave, to sleep well. Perhaps she should have the abortion after all. There was so little time left to decide.

Tomorrow, she thought.

She rose from the bed. The room was swimming in stars. The walls were scalloped from the diffused sepia blush of the night-light. An artifact from their last trip to the Science Museum, the night-light was shaped like a starfish, and so perhaps that helped account for the slow, tidal feeling of reluctance that afflicted her on her way out the door. She had found it difficult to leave the questionnaire too, she remembered, an hour before. She supposed that, no less than her children, she simply did not do well with transitions. Did anyone?

"Wait," Petey whispered, "where will you be?"

"Right down the hall. Like always."

"Not always," he reminded her. "You went to that meeting last week."

"True. But I came back."

"Why?" he asked.

"Why did I leave, you mean, or why did I come back?"

He shrugged. The question had become rather too complicated for both of them.

"I knew you'd come back," he said after a moment. "Know how?"

"How?"

"Daddy told me."

"Oh honey, I don't think so. It was probably just a nightmare."

"Uh-uh. He called on the phone. He's coming to visit. He told me. He even told Cress."

"He did, huh? When was this?"

"Last week."

Which given his present stage of mental development might have meant anything: last night, last month, last year. Conceivably it might even have meant last week. "That's strange. Cress didn't tell me."

He tugged at her arm. "Are you mad?"

"Of course not. It's just funny, that's all."

"You sound mad."

"Well, I'm not. I'll talk to Cress. I'm sure there's a good explanation. Why would Daddy call and nobody tell me? It's downright peculiar, don't you think?"

The boy appeared to weigh this question for a while, staring up at his eight-dollar galaxy as if the answer might be inscribed somewhere in its dim, particulate sprawl. Eventually, however, his thoughts moved from cosmology to commerce, alighting upon what was, for him, the heart of the matter. "Think he'll bring toys?"

"I don't know, honey."

"But what do you *think*?"

"I think let's talk about it tomorrow," she said. "Okay?"

"Okay."

No sooner had she arrived in the doorway, however, than she heard a tiny sucking sound. "What is it?" she asked.

"You forgot the magic," he wheezed.

"Oh honey. You don't need the magic every night. The magic's just a sometimes thing."

"I need it," he said, sniffling.

"Things don't work as well if you use them too often. Even magic loses some of its magic, you know, if you take it for granted. Then it's not quite so special anymore."

"I need it," he maintained.

Though she did not often wish to have Leon back, there were times when the rusty, rattling Rube Goldberg contraption that was her own gravity machine kicked on, and such dubious and regressive longings became unavoidable. Once in a while it would be nice to glance across the bed into that drawn, distracted face, as she used to when Alex was this age, and exchange one of those subtle messages parents evolve by way of Darwinian adaptation to get through their nights. What would Leon say if he were here? Go ahead, add to the light, spin a shaman's cloak of protection for the child, what harm will it do? Or conversely, No, don't indulge his fears, let him fall asleep under his own power, learn to pass through the border between fantasy and reality himself? Either course of action would be better than this paralyzing doubt of hers.

But there was no one to consult. Only the plastic stars, and the blank wall behind the bed, with its trembling skin of shadow and light, for company. Here was where his movie played. Here was the screening room where writhing snakes and long-nosed dragons, all the phantom legions of the Underworld, were cast out by his mind's hot, twittering bulb. No wonder he needs magic, she thought. Who doesn't?

She should fill out a questionnaire for Petey too. A mother-son act. That would surely be a first.

A branch tittered at the windows.

Do it, she thought she heard him say. But it might have been the wind.

"*Lumma-yumma-rumma-zah,*" she intoned quickly. "You are hereby protected from evil dreams."

Then she kissed him three or four more times, and a couple more after that, and though she was if anything keeping the poor kid up now, several additional times as well, as if by so doing she might exhaust their need for each other, the weight of her lips sufficing to iron down once and for all the lumps and furrows on his brow. And her own. Then, abruptly, she let him go, and hurried down to the kitchen, where her paperwork still lay in its messy piles, nowhere near complete.

13

A Science Lesson

THE TECHNICIAN was named Boris. This struck Bonnie, clutching her overnight bag in the empty office, as a rather freaky and inauspicious portent. She scanned the calligraphy on the framed certificate from the Association of Polysomnographic Technologists, hoping she'd merely heard wrong when Doctor Gogolvie had referred to the technician who would be assigned to her case. But no, there it was on the wall above the desk, in baroque black letters: *Boris Zenko.* The name of a madman, she thought. A demented troll. A leering hunchback. Nocturnal, hollow-eyed, wild-haired, late-late-show Boris Zenko. A man who skittered across dark rooftops, who killed neighborhood dogs and roasted them over crackling fires in the backyard.

Oh, what the hell, she thought: bring him on. After Leon, after Stanley, after Larry Albeit, after that snippy Chinese girl with the pierced nose at the clinic, after the nervous, intense (and at the same time oddly and inexplicably familiar) voice of Dr. Gogolvie himself, she almost preferred at this point to deal with an outright lunatic as opposed to a covert or provisional one. She was tired of hermeneutics; tired of gray areas; tired of guessing, indecision. She was tired, period. Oh boy, was she tired. Which was why she was here: to find a way to stop being so tired. And this Boris creature, if he ever deigned to show up, was going to help her.

The office itself, though small, did inspire a certain incremental confidence, crammed as it was with sleek and expensive-looking computer equipment. That the brand names were uniformly foreign encouraged her further. Running her eyes over the gleaming hardware, she found it easy to believe that once all those fine state-of-the-art beams of sound and light were pointed in her direction, her problems, those large and formless ephemera, would dissolve at once.

At least the research study was picking up the tab. The money for the baby-sitter, on the other hand, would come out of her own tattered pocket. Twelve hours, at seven-fifty a pop, for the services of a drug-crazed kleptomaniac who spent half her life swapping prescription advice with psychopathic strangers on the Internet. And the other half? She'd never get to sleep thinking about it. Still, this was midwinter vacation; none of the other sitters was available, and besides, the boys adored her. Why shouldn't they? She was blissed out on chemicals. Except, of course, when she wasn't.

"You're straight tonight?" Standing under the kitchen light earlier that evening, Bonnie had glared deep into Cress's eyes, seeking out rogue substances. The pupils, though granite-hued and stubbornly unfocused, looked normal enough to her, but then she no longer trusted her ability to tell what was normal from what was not.

"Actually, no," Cress had said. "I'm strung out on horse. I'm gonna burn the place down."

"Ha ha," Bonnie said. "And lower your voice. The boys'll hear." She noticed a paperback, shorn of its cover, lying facedown on the couch. "Homework?"

"Macbeth. I've got this big paper to do," Cress said.

"What on?"

"Whatever," Cress said with a sneer. "Whatever I want." Her tone was at once vengeful and indifferent, in the contemporary student mode, as if their intellectual freedom was a burden. Better to sleepwalk from assignment to assignment than to wrestle with the white, tangled sheets of their own minds. "I'm thinking maybe the weird sisters. They're like the only ones I can relate to in the whole stupid play."

"Why am I not surprised?"

"I've been getting this cool stuff about witches," Cress went on, "off the Net? Those hexing herbs they used, hemlock and mandrake and whatever? They were full of these chemicals. Alkaloids, I think they're called. That's what gave them all those weird, you know, visions."

"No kidding," Bonnie said, pulling on her coat. Where were her keys?

"And like when they'd go flying around on broomsticks? That's because what they'd do was, they'd make this sticky paste out of that stuff, and then they'd slab it on a stick and rub it up and down against their cunts. Drove them out of their minds. I mean, completely batshit."

"Your English teacher's going to love this," Bonnie said.

"They thought they were, like, flying. But it was just the sex and drugs."

"Far out."

"Shakespeare was no dummy," Cress sniffed. "He wants people to think he's making it up, but he's not. He did research, you know. Like those possets Macbeth's wife puts in everyone's drinks to knock them out? Those're real too. I bet you didn't know that."

"Never thought about it, truth be told."

"Well, you should. You're the one who can't go to sleep." Her face took on the light of an idea. "Maybe you could ask at the college. They must have some possets lying around somewhere."

"Give it up, Cress."

"I'm just saying it might be worth trying, that's all."

"Listen," Bonnie said, fastening the Velcro cuffs of her jacket, "just don't get any ideas about sharing this research of yours with the boys. They're batshit enough as it is."

"Yeah, well, whose fault is that?" Cress frowned indelicately at Bonnie's stomach. "Do they know about you, by the way?"

"No. And don't you dare tell them."

"Jesus, what do you take me for?"

"Look, just keep it together, okay? If you fuck up on me, I'm going to have to call your mother. And I hate talking to your mother almost as much as you do."

"You're so hostile," Cress hissed. "I thought we were *friends.*"

"We are friends. Which means we have to be able to depend on each other, stick together through thick and thin. And boy," Bonnie said, "this had better be as thin as it gets."

She hunted frantically around the kitchen until she found her keys. *"Guys?"* she called down the hallway. "Come kiss me, all right? I'm going."

Silence.

"I think they're watching a movie," Cress said. "I heard them yelling at the TV when I came in."

"They're mad," Bonnie said. "They heard the word *hospital,* and now they think I'm sick."

"Are you?"

"No, I don't think so. Are you?"

"Probably," Cress snorted. "I wouldn't be surprised."

"Neither would I." Bonnie struggled with the zipper of her down coat and shook out her hair; you'd have thought she was readying herself for a night out with a man instead of a labful of recording instruments. "All right. I'm ten minutes late. You sure you can handle this?"

"Chill," Cress had offered by way of a final, all-purpose word on the subject, and then Bonnie had opened the door and scooted through.

On the front step she paused to confirm that the lock had clicked shut behind her. It had. Then she heard a brief, inquisitive cry of betrayal that, though muffled, was strong enough to travel through the door's two and a half inches of unstained pine and penetrate her chest. Petey. Apparently the boy had looked up from *Fantasia* to find her, the Master Wizard, gone. And now he was getting yet another tedious science lesson, the kind no child ever takes voluntarily, learning how time, that nervous fugitive, having neglected to wait for him as usual, has slipped out through its hidden aperture just beyond the screen.

*   *   *

"Sorry I'm late. We can. Get started. Now."

Bonnie turned. "Dr. Gogolvie?"

"It's Ogelvie. Actually. But feel free to call me. Ian. If you want."

The sight of him puffing and wheezing in the doorway was more than a little alarming. She had waited all this time for someone to undertake to help her, and now here he was: this skinny, long-faced young man in his oversized lab coat, his pale head reckless with hair. He fought for breath, his cheeks red from the effort. Possibly he'd just come in from outside, where freezing winds tore up and down the Fens. Or else, she thought, he'd been down in the cafeteria or somewhere and forgotten their appointment, and had to run down the hall to make it, the way she herself did so often, both in reality and in dreams.

Pretending to be insulted, she folded her arms. "I was supposed to see this Boris guy. That's what you said."

"Apparently Boris had to. Go down to New York. Today. For some reason. Short notice."

"I'll say."

"It won't affect your workup. I'm familiar with your. History. I have the chart." Now that his breathing had begun to regulate, he sighed, swiped the hair off one cheek, smiled with brief, unconvincing jauntiness in her direction, and turned to scan the contents of the file in his hand—which from the rueful solemnity that now inscribed itself on his face must indeed have been hers. His eyes, she noticed, managed the difficult feat of being both sunken and bulging at the same time. How old was he? His neck was slender, the apple high-riding and taut, unripe. When was the last time an iron had been passed in the vicinity of his shirt? No need to bother checking for a wedding ring with this one, she thought. Nonetheless she felt obliged for reasons of thoroughness to go ahead and check.

"Are you sure we shouldn't wait for this Boris guy to get back?"

"Oh no." He scribbled something on her chart in the minute, rapid-velocity style of a professional. She tried to peek over his shoulder to see what he might be writing. But between the doctor's surprisingly broad torso and the black toppling waves of his hair, she was held off, denied access. "It's not that complicated actually, once you've got everything set up. It's all pretty routine."

"Oh. Okay."

"Why don't you sit down?" he suggested. "It might help you relax."

"I am relaxed. It's just my face that's nervous. It sort of goes its own way sometimes."

He nodded soberly, as if she had said something very interesting. Was he deaf, or was he utterly humorless? What difference did it make? She was determined to be a good sport about this thing. Restless, she looked around the room for something to start being a good sport about.

"Who *is* that?" She pointed to a busy, colorful piece of abstract art on the wall behind his head. "I know I've seen it before. Kandinsky?"

"Who?" Vaguely he inclined his big distracted head to regard whatever she was looking at.

"The artist who did this. Paul Klee?"

"No one did it," he said. "Well, maybe God."

"Who?"

"It's a brain cell," he said.

"No kidding." She looked it over wonderingly. It appeared she had stumbled at last into the presence of something real. Perhaps this was her usher, she thought. This unlikely young man. He had the solitary stillness, the air of indrawn patience, one finds among the docents of a museum. Standing beside him, she felt a tiny, precise movement inside her belly, a little winglike fleck of recognition. "But it's *beautiful,*" she complained.

He nodded. "We like to think so."

"I suppose it came from someone famous? Like Einstein, or Freud, or, I don't know, Enrico Fermi?"

He paused, frowning. "I think," he said, "it came from a pig."

"Oh." She looked it over again. "Well, pigs're supposed to be very intelligent, right? Orwell and all that."

Dr. Ogelvie merely gazed at her, his face blank and shiny as a CD. Orwell and all what? Increasingly Bonnie experienced just this sort of embarrassment in making reference to a novel. And that was outside the university. It was even worse, of course, inside, especially in the English Department, where her fellow graduate students appeared to suffer pangs of sorrow and discomfort whenever she had the bad taste to cite an actual work of fiction in an otherwise abstract and highly profitable discussion of literary theory. Movies, of course, were fair game; comic books, sitcoms, and music videos even better. But somewhere along the line the novel had lost its grip, come to seem tediously rear guard, arcane, burdensome and top heavy, like the dinosaurs. How had she missed it? What had she been doing? Probably reading, she thought. It was the source of many of her problems.

She examined the photograph of the brain cell again. "You actually know your way around one of these?"

"Not completely." He waved her chart before him casually; it was, after all, for him only so much paper. "But we're starting to get a handle on it."

"And once you've gotten it? Then what?"

He stared at her.

"I mean, you know, where do you go from there? How about the heart?" she asked, hopeful. "There's a lot more to be done with that one, right?"

"With the brain," he said, making an effort at patience, "there isn't a then-what. There's never a then-what."

"Oh."

"The brain's like the universe. It's inexhaustible. Your curiosity can't ever possibly be satisfied."

"In other words," she did not bother to conceal her disappointment, "you never get it."

He stared at her blankly again, his hand dreaming in his white pocket. It was her own fault. She had wanted to provoke him and now here he was, provoked. Meanwhile here *she* was, trying to be playful but managing in the process only to sound petulant and dense. Why? Because she was nervous about spending the night under his supervision? Because his black curls and pallor, his long, hairless hands, his passionate insularity, reminded her of Leon as a young man?

But then he had always been young, Leon had. No doubt he still was.

"We don't really think in those terms," the doctor said curtly.

"Of course you don't. It was a naive, stupid thing to say."

"You don't do research for the results." He seemed intent on explaining himself regardless; it was, she thought, one of his gender's duller and more prevalent traits. "It's a process. You invest yourself in that process. You pose fundamental questions. Not to answer them necessarily, though of course you hope for that. But to find connections. Something to help explain them to yourself. Naturally you hope some greater good will come out of that process along the way. Even if it's only accidental."

"Speaking of accidental," she said, desperate now to change the subject, "have we by any chance met before?"

His eyes went slitty and gray. As if she had insulted him. "Why do you ask?"

"I don't know. I keep thinking I've seen you. Maybe across the river?"

"Well," he said abruptly, returning his attention to the file in his hand, "it's possible." The pen he stuck behind one ear for the moment, smoothing the hair back, rather delicately, she thought, to accommodate it.

On the top sheet of her file she could make out the words "PRESENTING COMPLAINTS." She was a novice in these matters, but they seemed to her needlessly pejorative.

"I left a few blank," she offered. "On that questionnaire. I ran out of time."

"Don't worry about it," he said.

"It's just I wanted to do things right this time. I want to be, you know, a good subject."

He examined her sternly, his head tilted at an inquisitive angle. He might have been a policeman with a flashlight, peeking in through the window of a deserted house, trying to track down the source of a mysterious noise. "Why don't you go ahead and change into your night things," he suggested.

My night things, she thought. The words, against all logic and context, brought forth a little chittery rain shower of erotic sensation. "Where?"

"In there." He indicated with a nod the room next door.

It was, she saw at once, the sleeping room, where she would pass the night. There was a twin bed, neatly made; atop the floral-patterned quilt someone, Boris maybe, or Ogelvie himself, had placed a small teddy bear—more or less wittily, she thought. The pillows were flat and medium soft, comprised of synthetic down. Above the headboard sprang a template of outlets, presumably for the electrodes, or whatever neo-Frankensteinian apparatus they intended to attach to her while she slept. The carpet was light blue. So were the walls. There was no television. In lieu of a closet, there was a tiny armoire—it might have been purloined from a doll's house—for her clothes. The narrow window along the west-facing wall afforded a narrow, west-facing view: a sickly sliver of moon, a dull swath of cloudless sky, and a dark, singularly uninteresting quadrant of the parking lot. Still, all things considered, if you were able to ignore, as Bonnie was not, the video camera on the ceiling and the infrared lamp by the bed and the tall, silently suggestive presence of the oxygen tank in the corner, the room was certainly pleasant enough, and in its bland and tidy way refreshing.

She sat on the edge of the bed, kicked off her shoes and unsnapped her jeans. They fell off her legs easily. Padding around in her socks, she might have been preparing to enter a cathedral, a gleaming mosque, someplace grand and coherent where people fell on their knees and spoke in whispers. A constructed world. A second sphere. . . .

"Let me know when you're ready," Ogelvie called from the other room.

"Just a sec."

Dutifully she slipped into her new pajamas, purchased the day before with this excursion in mind. Her socks she left on not so much for comfort—the room was if anything too warm, what with the carpet and the low-blown heat humming efficiently through the rippled ducts—but out of self-consciousness for the odd, involuted contours her toes had assumed over the years. She was a visitor, not a patient. She would only expose herself so far.

"Ready," she announced.

No answer. What had become of him? When did everyone decide to stop responding to her call?

Finally she poked her head into the observation room, to find Ogelvie pitched forward in the swivel chair with the phone pressed to his ear, staring morosely into the hypnotic comings and goings of the computer's screen-saver program as he listened to what Bonnie concluded, via his glum, guttural body language, to be either no answer or the wrong answer on the other end of the line. A plug-in coffeepot trickled on the counter behind him. She could tell from its color that the coffee would be weak. But perhaps he preferred it that way.

Poised in the doorway, she watched the coffee rise to fill its receptacle, slowly but inexorably, and then stop. Someone had measured it out. This was a lab, she reminded herself, a place of routine procedures, of applied scientific knowledge. The coffeepot had been programmed to do what it did.

It was then she noticed the rectangular window on the wall above his head. He would be observing her through it, she realized, all night. Perhaps he'd been watching her change into her pajamas just now. If so, the sight had failed to inspire him. His shoulders were hunched, his eyes twin scoops of shadow above the bony, aspiring flare of his cheekbones. When he put down the phone he looked spongy, depleted. His mouth was tight, his gaze wan and moist. He tried, not altogether successfully, to clear his throat.

"Hey, Doc," she said, "are you okay?"

"Oh sure." He waved his wrist in the air uncertainly. Was it trembling?

"I don't mean to pry. But you look a little distraught all of a sudden."

"Oh no. Just minor fatigue. I've been trying to get a proposal in shape. It's made for some long nights."

"Well, I know what that's like." His eyelashes were beautiful and extravagant in their length, their delicate delineations. What a waste, she thought.

"Also," he allowed, "there's sort of this other, interpersonal thing going on at the moment."

"Oh." She willed her face not to fall. Very well, she would be granted no usher. She would proceed alone.

"Or maybe not going on is more like it," he said.

"I know what that's like too, sorry to say." She felt obscurely moved by his distress. At the same time, it did not relieve her of a certain measure of apprehension when it came to turning herself over to his care.

"Amazing, isn't it, how draining these things are. How destabilizing. Just in a physical sense, I mean. The way when you like someone, one word from them can make you feel powerful, and another takes all your strength away. Like you've been drugged."

"Yeah," she said. "Life's a hoot."

"It's a chicken-egg question, isn't it? Goes way back to the Greeks. Does the mind drive the body, or is it the other way around? Does consciousness only record physical reality, or does it actually *create* it? There's so much contradictory evidence."

"I heard this story on the radio," she began, "about baby rats—"

"Take sleep," he went on vehemently. "It may be we sleep badly because we're depressed. Or it may be we get depressed because we're sleeping badly. They might be parallel phenomena, or they might causally intersect, or there might be some third explanation we can't account for. It's hard to say." He reached into his pocket and shook out a pack of sugarless gum. "Want some?"

"No, thanks."

"There was a man down in San Diego. Randy Gardner. He went without sleep for two hundred and sixty hours. That's eleven days. It's in the *Guinness Book.* World record."

"He must have gotten a lot of stuff done."

"He was a volunteer in an experiment."

"Oh."

"The last night of the study, he played a game of basketball against one of the researchers. It was three in the morning, and their skills were roughly equal. But he won. A remarkable thing. No weakness, no hallucinations, no mood shifts, no anomalous phenomena. Can this be explained? No. Some people need more sleep, some less. Why? We don't know. Is REM just some fossil of early evolution, a mistake that got locked in by accident maybe, somewhere between the reptiles and the birds? We don't know. Do we actually *need* it? Hard to say. It depends how you define need. . . ."

"You better work on your rap," she said. "You're not exactly inspiring confidence here."

She locked her jaw, fighting back a yawn. He noticed it anyway.

"Sorry," she said. "Long day."

She watched a shadow deflate across his face, a sight that both bored and depressed her. Here she was again, insulting people. It would be a great thing, the best thing possible for the collective good, when she was finally put to sleep.

"You're right," he said coldly. "We should get started."

Five minutes later, she was sitting, uneasy, on a hard metal stool, trying to enjoy or at least tolerate the sensation of having her forehead dabbed with a foul-smelling cotton ball. "Ugh. What's that?"

"Industrial alcohol. I know it's unpleasant, but it's an important lubricant. Facilitates contact with the electrodes."

"Okay," she said. "Lay on, then."

Laboriously he began to attach the electrodes, holding them in place with strips of gauzy tape. Two under the chin. Two near the eyes, two behind the ears. One at the front and center of the forehead. The young psychologist, she observed, worked methodically, with an air of gathering concentration that resembled anger. He kept wincing and frowning as if dissatisfied with someone—perhaps her, perhaps himself. "It's been a while," he admitted, pausing to wipe his brow. "Tell me if I make the tape too tight."

"It's fine."

"I always did like working down here," he murmured, peeling off more tape. "Sitting in the dark, watching people sleep."

"I can't imagine anything more boring."

"You'd be surprised. The brain's extremely active all the time. Even when you're asleep. It's something you learn down here—the night brain isn't so different from the day brain. The energy still gets put out. It's just a question of who's paying attention. Who's listening in on the big secret."

"Mmm. Sounds like a power trip to me."

His eyes turned thoughtful. "There *is* a feeling you get when the sun's coming up and everyone's just dragging themselves out of bed and here you've put in all this work already. There's nothing like going out for breakfast after you've been up all night accomplishing things. The food tastes better. Enhanced. Or biking along the river at sunrise. The air, the light, the dew on the grass. Incredible. Nothing like it."

"Yes," Bonnie said. "I remember."

She was aware of a growing desire to touch this man, to partake of his earnestness, his hunger for enhancement. *Libido sciendi*: the lust to know. Was that Milton or Descartes? Stanley would remember; he'd been a Miltonist when they'd met, had been only too happy to show her paradise in his room at the Hyatt—her moans rising like birds over the artificial waterfall in the lobby—and prepare her for its loss. But that was how it was with her: knowledge and sex intertwined. Like Eve she could not have one without the other.

And maybe that was the problem, she thought. After twenty years in the academy, learning had lost its heat for her, its erotic drive. Knowledge too was a chemical reaction: if the elements weren't balanced, it went toxic. She had studied too many of the same things. At some point she had stopped learning altogether. Perhaps it followed then that she had pretty much stopped having sex altogether too.

"I used to do a lot of all-nighters," she admitted, wistful. "Back in college. I'd take a couple hits of speed, and that would be that."

He began to prepare a syringe. "Was this the sixties?"

"How old do you think I am?" She feigned, or half feigned anyway, an expression of dour petulance. "It was a few years later. Which was not exactly dull times either, believe me."

He shrugged. "I missed all that, I guess."

"Well, it wasn't so great. Though sometimes it seems great to me now. Comparatively, I mean. A lot seemed possible."

"Judging from your preliminary exam, it must have been. That's quite a drug history you have."

"Is it?"

"I don't think I've seen anyone break it down alphabetically before."

"Well," she said, flustered, "I was just trying to be thorough."

He tapped the syringe with his finger. It leaked a little clear fluid at the tip. Like love. She closed her eyes to receive it.

When the needle went in she clamped her jaw shut. A wave of heat passed through her veins. She refused to think of it as a puncture, a loss. Something, she told herself, was being added to the mix.

"I should explain what I'm doing," he said. "You probably want to know."

"That's okay," she said brightly. "I'm not really much of a materialist. I'm just as happy being ignorant of the details."

"I think it's better if I tell you. That's the normal procedure, I think."

"Fine." She waved her hand. "Go ahead."

"There's a brain hormone we've identified called CRF. It's related to anxiety. It increases when a person is under stress. Now, the shot I just gave you is a synthetic compound we've devised called Dodabulax. What we've found is, in the overwhelming majority of cases, the drug blocks the action of the CRF. It's what we call a perfect specific."

"A what?"

"Something that does just what we ask it to do and nothing else. Now, once the CRF is blocked," he said, "there's nothing to damp down the endocrine receptors in the hypothalamus that connect to the REM mechanism. So we see a lengthening and deepening effect on the patient's sleep."

"But I thought it was going to be a pill. That's what my friend takes. A blue tablet."

"We prefer to administer it by syringe the first night. It's cleaner. More immediately effective. But we'll give you some pills to take home with you."

"Great."

"One every night," he instructed, "just before bed. Take it with water. It's crucial you be consistent. Think of it as a contract you're signing. You hold up your end, and the drug will too."

"What happens if I take more than one?" she asked impulsively.

He stopped for a moment; he appeared to be assessing her. "For the purposes of the study," he said, "we'd like you to take one."

She nodded, abashed.

"The side effects should be negligible. Dry mouth, maybe a little numbness in the extremities. You may feel some mood lift as well. Probably it's no more complicated than the benefits of a decent night's rest."

"You checked about the pregnancy, like you said? You're sure it's safe?"

"I've done a thorough search of the literature. I assure you, there's no danger, either to the fetus or to you. Of course," he added, pausing, "if you want to be absolutely certain, the best advice is always to take nothing at all. But even then there are environmental factors. One can be only so pure. And if it's urgent for you to find relief—"

"And where will you be all this time?" she asked quickly, lest she change her mind.

"Right here."

Gently, he pinned up her hair in the back, which, because of its unruly weight and mass, kept spilling over as he attached an electrode to the base of her head.

"I'll be watching the polysomnograph. The computer will register the data, analyze it, and, after I've done some annotating, print out a finding. We'll have a colored graph of your sleep. We'll see how much time you spend in each of the stages, REM included. We'll also see your periods of wakefulness. This may give us some diagnostic clues as to why they're occurring. If they are."

"*If*? You think I'm making it up?"

"Of course not. But people often misread their own patterns. I've had apnea cases who swore they slept soundly when they've actually woken hundreds of times during the night. And vice versa. Insomniacs as a rule tend to exaggerate how little sleep they get. We think we know our deepest mechanisms of self, but we're often wrong. Our subjective experience is very different from the facts."

"Great," she said. "So not only am I lying awake at three-thirty in the morning listening to animals eat my trash in the backyard, you're saying it may not even be objectively *happening*?"

"Probably," he said, choosing his words with care, "it is."

"Now you're patronizing me."

"It's perfectly normal to be anxious," he said. "Sleep is an intimate experience. It can feel awkward and strange to share it with someone else. You may find yourself fighting it some."

"I usually do."

"Meanwhile I'll be watching it on the screen. Looking for unusual activity."

"You'll be there all night?"

He nodded.

"What if something unusual happens when you're on a break? I can be sneaky that way," she added, trying one last time to charm him. He had yet to address her by name. It was beginning to really bug her.

"I told you, the computer will record everything that happens. I'll review the whole thing later and score it."

"You mean I'm going to be graded?" Why bother finishing her dissertation, she thought. You never graduate. The tests go on and on.

"Scoring," he explained, "is our term for marking what we call sleep events. Leg kicks, incidents of arousal, changes in position, that kind of thing."

"Oh."

"There. How does it feel?"

"Not bad." The electrodes, to her surprise, were cool and light as dimes. She closed her eyes and imagined herself covered with coins, her entire body having facilitated contact with legal tender, while across the river in Cambridge her tiny, underfinanced house with all its creaks and cries, its laborious relations, floated off into the ether. Dimly she recalled her dinner, a pot of condensed clam chowder, wrinkled and congealing on the stove. Could Cress be trusted to put it away? She had to remember to call Leon too. Find out when he was coming. *If* he was coming.

"Let's get you into bed then," Ogelvie said.

He led her through the doorway, plumping the pillows for her, adjusting the sheets. Critically he examined the video camera, blowing away some dust he saw, or imagined he saw, on the lens. Then he went over to the heating unit and placed his hands palms down on the grille. "Does it feel cold in here?" he asked. "To me, I don't know, it feels chilly."

He bent over to adjust the dial at the base of the unit, brushing the hair back out of his eyes with a certain irritation. It began to seem possible to Bonnie that he was as nervous as she was.

Yawning, she glanced at her watch. Eleven-thirty.

"Never mind," she said. "I sleep better in a cold room anyway."

"How's that tape? Too tight?"

"Fine," she said. "Look, can I get into bed now?"

"Sure, go ahead." He straightened, looked around the room one last time. It appeared to pass inspection. He began to plug the ends of the dangling electrodes into the panel behind the bed, one by one. "All set. Unless you want a glass of water?"

"No, thanks."

"I'll put one out on the table in case you change your mind. That's the procedure down here."

"It's entirely up to you. I won't drink it."

"You may find it easier to sleep than you think. Sometimes just being away from your normal conditioning pattern can have great effects."

"I better," she said. "I have to get out of here early. The kids have school at eight-fifteen." And their sitter might be in a coma by then.

"Or you may want to read for a while," he suggested. "Get really tired. Facilitate the transition."

She shook her head. "I'm really tired right now."

"Okay then. I'll shut off the light. If you need me, there's a buzzer near your head."

"Fine." She nodded sleepily. "Night-night."

"Night-night," he murmured stiffly, lingering at the door. His sudden reluctance to leave her, along with the phrase they had used, gave her a quick jab of melancholy, of tenderness. She missed the children. "Pleasant dreams."

She closed her eyes. She could feel her tension rising up, as it did every night, to do battle with her exhaustion. Vague sounds of traffic swished by in the distance. Night people, headed home. She thought of the young man next door, somber and alert, bathed in light, monitoring every flicker of response on the scrolling screen. Up and down: it seemed all her nocturnal complexities could be reduced to that. Patiently he had explained the many exquisite functions of the recording equipment—how they tracked the alpha and delta waves, the eye movements, the muscle convulsions, K-complexes, oxygen saturation, and sleep spindles. What had he called them? *The deepest mechanisms of the self.* It was a comfort to know they were at work, minding the store in her absence. It gave her a pleasant feeling of security. She began to feel very far from things, and at the same time oddly immanent, on the verge of a salient truth.

She'd been wrong—it was not sleep but the waking life that was the interlude between the acts, the bright but meandering intermission. Because now, with the lights off, that whole state of being simply collapsed, as crumpled and disposable as a coffee cup. She had been lingering out in the lobby much too long. Now the intermission was over. Now she was back, facing the stage where all her heart's noisy operettas were playing and playing, forever trying to complete themselves. And now the house lights were going down, and the curtains drawing open, and she was being ushered in, and all the separate players in night's contentious orchestra were rising up in concert with their finely tuned instruments, getting ready to welcome her, the errant maestro, back to the podium at last.

14

Better Living

A MAN in a lab coat stood over her, jiggling her shoulder in a muscular, insistent way. She had no idea why. She was aware of a cool trickling in her head for which there was no language or logic. Her ears gurgled like a fountain. She lay there blinking back the daylight as if from the wrong end of a kaleidoscope, her eyes flooded with fanciful colors and random, twisting geometries.

She felt like Alcestis. A foot in each world.

The man in the lab coat was not the one she'd been expecting. He looked like a dark Santa. He was fleshy and round-faced, his jawline lost in the tangled black insurgency of his beard. Two bushy eyebrows threatened to meet and fornicate in the center of his forehead. Below, behind frameless glasses, his eyes were milky gray. They examined her with the peremptory, otherworldly gaze of a clerk in a used bookstore.

"You must be Boris," she said. She found the name right there on her tongue, already formed. "Boris Zenko."

"And you must be trespasser."

"I had an appointment," she said. "Bonnie Saks?"

"Saks?" Boris frowned. Or rather, since he was already frowning, he allowed his frown to darken and grow. "This draws for me a blank."

"I had an exam scheduled. Last night." She scratched an itchy place on her leg, an area where the skin had stretched oddly in sleep.

The itch, and her capacity to relieve it, began to suggest to her the possibility that she was in fact awake. "Didn't Dr. Ogelvie talk to you? He made all the arrangements."

"Here we have another blank."

"Actually," she said, "the exam was supposed to be with you. But you had to leave for New York, so Dr. Ogelvie covered for you. Not that he was mad about it or anything. He said he had to stay late anyway."

"Nobody covers for Boris," Boris informed her. "Boris is the technician here. And I don't go to New York, never. Once in the Dinkins administration I am visiting a girl at Columbia University, I am beat up and left for dead in Morningside Park. I can show you scars."

She shook her head to discourage him. "So wait, you mean he isn't here?"

"Ogelvie? How should Boris know?"

"He said he was going to stay. A break or two, maybe, he said. But he said he'd stay."

"Shrinks," Boris said meaningfully.

"Yeah, I guess so."

"Anyway, you will be taken care of. There is a record of the polysomnogram in the computer. Unless he was so stupid to erase it."

"Why would he do that?"

Boris shrugged. This was not his province, other people's motives. He was the one who connected the wires, monitored the machines. Never mind that he had been superseded in this capacity for some unknown reason the night before. Never mind that Ogelvie had for some unknown reason broken his promise to remain by her side. Lately, everyone she dealt with appeared to have some obscure, unacknowledged plan that guided their actions and inactions, all of which seemed to implicate, or at the very least indirectly affect in an alarming way, Bonnie herself. Was this paranoia, she wondered, or was it simply and objectively the case? She no longer knew what to hope for.

"You know what?" she said. "You better check."

* * *

She was late getting back, and so a small miracle of administrative competence was required for her to get the lunches packed, the breakfast dispensed, and the boys swathed in their scarves and coats and offloaded onto their respective school buses before she ground to a halt amid the bright wreckage of the kitchen, her mind as blank and cool, as perfectly weatherless, as the morning sky.

The house was still. Sunlight poured through the windows, falling onto the table in garish streaks. She patted her pants pocket absently. The bottle of pills was there. Fingering the plastic cylinder, she regarded everything—the cereal bowls, the juice cartons, the rings of puddled milk on the table before her—as artifacts of another, hopelessly primitive culture. Before her life she now stood watchful and deferent as a tourist. So this was the kitchen, she thought. Where the meals were cooked. And this was the table where the children of the household would gather to pick noisily at their food and then quarrel over who should clear. What quaint customs. What odd rituals of behavior. She did not see how they would ever catch on.

An odor of nicotine was in the air, acrid and colorless. Under normal circumstances, Bonnie had no aversion to secondhand smoke—if anything she welcomed it—but today the smell oppressed her. The night in the lab had done something to her, she thought. Softened her up. Made her more permeable. Besides, a baby was present; one had to take care.

She patted her pocket again. At least Ogelvie had left her the pills, as promised, before he ran off. Already she was eager for the night ahead, when she could start taking them. But there was the day to be got through first.

She heated some water in a pot and took the carton of eggs from the refrigerator. She kept meaning to buy the brown ones, but the white were cheaper; and besides, she told herself, whatever bleaching agents were responsible for their color, or their absence of color, surely after four decades her body had learned to assimilate. Still, she would switch to the brown kind after these. It was the day's first decision.

Humming, she extracted an egg from its cardboard niche and cradled it in her palm. It felt sticky. Pale yellow juice had leaked through the shell from some hidden hairline fracture, oozing out nutrients and minerals and, for all she knew, salmonella as well. But she could not bring herself to throw it away. So she left the bad egg on the counter, took out another, and proceeded to stand there watchfully over the stove, in yesterday's blouse, barefoot and pregnant in morning's bright quilted light, listening to the water rumble and turn over in the Calphalon pot.

She could hear Cress sleeping in the other room, giving off a low, spasmodic snore. Among other deviations, the girl appeared to have a fissured septum. The world was full of cracks.

It occurred to her that the boys, as they'd wolfed down their breakfast, had not once paused in their labors to inquire about her night at the hospital. Why should they? Here after all was their mother, fully dressed save for shoes, occupying her usual domain, engaged in her customary mode of A.M. service. Nothing visible had changed. One could read their total absence of curiosity about her as a good sign, she thought, as evidence of the steady, unblinking flame of emotional security she had kindled in the boys against long odds. That was one way of reading it. There was another way of reading it too, of course.

A moan rose in the living room. Calmly Bonnie collected her eggs and toast and sat down in front of the newspaper. The headlines were meaningless. How long had she been away? It felt like years.

Awhile later Cress emerged. "You're back," she yawned.

"Mmm. Better get going, you'll be late for school."

"Big whoop."

"It's up to you. If you want to hang out, you can shower here. I'll even make you breakfast."

Cress appeared to consider the offer. "Nah. I'll just get my stuff together and boogie."

"Suit yourself."

But the girl remained right where she was, face puffy-lidded and vacant, her lank, hennaed hair tumbling sleep-mussed over her oversized T-shirt. Squinting, she lifted one hand to block the sun from her eyes as it streamed through the paneled window. Two bars of light played across her knuckles, her silver rings. "I dreamed I was scrubbing the counter," she said. "Like, all night. I could not get that thing clean."

"Maybe you need more practice," Bonnie said. "Try doing it once in a while when you're awake."

"It's got something to do with my mother, right?"

"Work dreams are always masturbatory," Bonnie observed, heaping some egg onto her toast. "It's something you learn in college."

"No way." Cress giggled.

"Believe me. I'm an expert on the subject."

Cress peered at her.

"You look funny," she declared. "What'd they do to you down there, anyway?"

"Watched me sleep." She wiped her mouth, put the silverware on the plate, and pushed back her chair. Her eyes took in the bright, disposable detritus around the sink. The unscrubbed counter. "I slept all night."

"Is that all?"

"For me that's a lot."

"Don't you want to know what happened around here?" Cress offered.

"Was anyone hurt?"

"Uh-uh. Not really. A little rowdiness is all."

"In that case, no. Don't ask, don't tell is my policy. Just like you with my phone messages."

"Look, I told you I was sorry about that."

"Forget it. I'm not mad anymore."

"I mean, so the guy calls. Big deal. Who cares about that creep anyway?"

"His kids care. Sad but true."

Cress grew almost pensive for a moment, as if glimpsing, somewhere in her cramped, swaddled closet of a mind, the sheer fabric of a selfless thought. But then she shook her head and padded into the living room to don the clothes she'd worn the night before.

When she returned, Bonnie was scribbling out a check, to which she added, at the last minute, five extra dollars. "I'm going to shower," she said. "Thanks for helping out."

"Yeah."

"Really, Cress, you saved my life. I don't know what I'd have done otherwise."

"Sure. No problem." The girl seemed a bit put out by this show of employer gratitude, no doubt assuming it would translate into additional work for her down the road. Sullenly she hoisted her bag over her shoulder. "By the way," she announced, "you're out of toothpaste."

"No, we're not. I had it with me."

"I meant the kids."

"Well," Bonnie said, "their teeth won't fall out from one night."

"You sound like my mom," Cress said crankily. "Kids are resilient, that's her favorite expression."

"A wise saying. Let's give the woman credit."

"Want to know her second favorite?" Cress asked, already trudging toward the front door.

"Not really, no."

"Her second favorite is, Get the fuck out of my face."

The night, she decided in the shower, had been an event. Some hard line, some calcified bone of her being had been fractured and reset in the lab. Now the cast was coming off, the pink, unblemished surface being exposed to the light. She was no longer quite the same. She did not know how to interpret this information, whether it constituted a hard scientific fact or was just another vague, private myth she had conceived for herself. She did not know if it was even necessary to interpret. Despite what they told you in grad school, things did not always signify. Sometimes they just happened. Though rarely enough, it had to be conceded, did they happen this way to her.

Eyes closed, the hot pulse of the shower massaging her face, she floated like a cherub on a cloud of steam. When she emerged, her skin looked like a sunrise. Condensation had pooled over the windows, running in pale, erratic streaks down the mirror and walls. She could not see her own face in the mirror to put on foundation.

She decided to go without. She would go without earrings too. Without bracelets and barrettes, without even her watch. She would just exist for a while unadorned. She had no plans to go anywhere anyway.

In the bedroom she put on jeans and a workshirt and brushed back her hair. Her hands felt tingly and numb. Ogelvie had mentioned something about numbness, she recalled. A side effect of the drug. She could not recall what the others were. She decided to call him and find out.

The card he'd given her was executed in the contemporary style of numerical Esperanto, with a forbidding series of ten-digit numbers listed at the bottom—for his lab, his beeper, and his fax—above the busy, convoluted cryptogram that was his e-mail address. She left messages at every one. Her voice was patient and controlled. No matter how many times she was cut off or put on hold, her mood, no less becalmed than the phone Muzak itself, remained cool, evanescent. Not once did she slam down the receiver, or yank open the fridge and stand there nervously wolfing a pint of hummus or half a pound of prosciutto while the icemaker whirred and the generator hummed its maddening, judgmental song. She simply waited, and then when the line engaged she explained to whoever it was, person or machine, that she had found the pills he had left for her, along with the directions, but as she had a couple of questions remaining about what to expect and would still like to debrief at least a little about the whole sleep-lab experience, given that it was her first time and everything, she would appreciate him calling her back at his earliest convenience, thank you very much. And here is the number. As it happened, there was only one number where she could be reached, a sad, parsimonious reality that often made her feel, in her relations with professional people, rather outgunned and defensive. But that was how things were.

The phone book listed only four Ogelvies in the metropolitan area, two out in Medford, one in Brookline, and one in Somerville. Choosing quickly and at random—the same strategy she employed for lottery tickets, restaurants, movies, and, it often seemed in retrospect, lovers—she tried the Brookline number first. It was disconnected. There was no way to be sure, but from the grainy and querulous quality of the NYNEX tape admonishing her to check the number and try again, it had been disconnected for some time. The voice on the machine in Somerville was neither grainy nor querulous, though it too was female, a husky-sounding woman named Barbara, who offered to take messages for Ian too. So the handsome young doctor was married after all. It was a familiar disappointment. The age of divorce, for all the noisy hyperbole, just wasn't panning out. No one had the stamina for it any longer, not even her.

Nonetheless she went ahead and left a message on the machine. She was beginning to enjoy leaving messages. Her own voice in her ears sounded tuneful and pleasant, infinitely likable. A much nicer voice than the one she remembered having yesterday.

Because she was on a roll of sorts she made several additional calls to various friends, even to Suzette up in the snowy, remote Northeast Kingdom of Vermont, if only for the pleasure of leaving messages on their respective voice mail systems. She'd have been almost disappointed if they'd answered; it would have thrown off the clean, linear mechanism of the morning. Still, she could not help wondering, as the hours passed in their frictionless fashion, where in the world everyone had gone.

The sky, she observed through the window, was an amazing, arterial blue. It was as though she'd never seen it before. But of course it had been there all winter, biding its time. So had the bluejays, the cardinals, the chickadees and finches and buntings, the upside-down, hibernating bats. None had gone away. They were only lying low for a while. Soon they would start making their reappearances. Already out in the yard, in the barely delineated garden, the first tips of the crocus leaves, sharp and meticulous, were preparing to break through. Just because you couldn't see them didn't mean they weren't there.

What was required was patience, a measure of faith. Or were these in fact the same thing?

What was the loss of her polysomnogram to her anyway? Especially given that she retained only the vaguest of ideas at this point what a polysomnogram *was*? Then too it bore remarking, if only to herself, that she had just experienced the most glorious sleep of her entire adult life.

She could not have said if it had been dreamless or dream-drenched. She recalled a slow passage as through deep woods: her progress uncertain, her limbs rubbery and strange, the very air a kind of pale, trembling jelly that offered resistance and envelopment both. And then after an interval of wandering she'd arrived at last in a clear space, where nothing could touch her, and the colored lights came washing down in a flood, and all that had been shadowed and recessive during the day—the dense, interwoven profusion of things—was transformed into iridescent brightness and definition. Good Lord! It was like entering a Rothko, she thought. Borne up by an ineffable heat mist, immersed in sunbursts of yellow and red, the primary colors of being. All her life she had been looking for light, but in seeking it straight on had only managed to blind herself. Now, under the influence of the drug, she began to look not at the light but at the things around it, the things lit by light, and what they revealed, in their clustered, temporary arrangements, of the darkness between. And then a silent trumpet blew, and the mortar of opposition in her head began to crumble, and what had been her consciousness—that walled, overrun, siege-ridden city—came tumbling down, and suddenly they were no longer separate things, herself and the world, but were shown to be comprised of the same stuff, one slow, spiraling emanation, like God's own peculiar pipe smoke. . . .

Then she'd awoken to find Boris Zenko hovering over her like a storm cloud, and there were no words in her head—no syntax, no grammar, no residual memories—to help identify either him or herself. A weird sensation. Not unpleasant, just weird. The only ugly part was the man's insistence that she did not belong there when she knew for a fact that she did.

Now, standing at the sink, preparing to swallow her daily dose of prenatal vitamins, she felt the need to talk about all this with someone who might just conceivably understand. Her mother. But her mother was gone. Neither Leon nor Stanley was appropriate for this sort of consultation. As Ogelvie wasn't available, as Suzette wasn't available, as, this being a Friday morning, no one she knew seemed to be available, she went ahead and called Larry Albeit.

Who was in a meeting, but came to the phone anyway. "So," he said wearily, "how'd it go?"

She told him more or less how it went. Out of respect for whatever clients might be lined up behind him on the other end of the phone, watching time tick away like a taxi meter, she tried to be concise.

"Maybe he had another patient," Larry suggested. "An emergency that came up. This is a hospital situation, after all."

"You'd think he'd leave a note."

"These medical types, who knows. They're even worse than us on the niceties."

"Actually he was *very* nice. One of the nicest guys I've met in a long time," she said. "At least that's how he came across."

"Did he have you sign anything? A release form?"

"I think so," she said. "Why?"

He sighed. Clearly it was fatiguing for lawyers, the relative ignorance of everyone else. "What about right now?" he asked. "How do you feel right now?"

"That's the funny part. I've got all this energy."

"That's great."

"It's like I'm a baby. Like I just had my bath, and now I could go do something or just hang out in my crib. Either way's fine with me."

"Great. That's really wonderful, Bonnie."

Odd, how this simple deployment of her name, and the reservoir of feeling she sensed fenced off behind it, brought tears to her eyes. The world seemed determined to penetrate her. Somehow when she wasn't looking this man had insinuated himself like a weed into her life. Moreover, and here was the really shocking part, he seemed at the moment to be her best friend.

"Look, I'm going to have to get back to this meeting in a minute."

"Sorry." She remembered his case, those stalled trains with their chemical freight, waiting for a signal. "We can talk some other time."

"If you like," he added in a low voice, "I could stop by later on my way home."

"Oh no. That's not necessary."

"What is it, Friday? I think Kippy's taking the girls to the ballet tonight. I could come by around nine."

"Listen, I'm fine, really. I was going to spend some time with the kids tonight anyway. Tomorrow's my birthday," she added. "Or wait, no, Sunday's my birthday. Anyway, it's coming up soon."

"Which one?"

"Forty." It was only after she said it that she realized she hadn't, as was her custom, lied. "Four-oh."

He whistled through his teeth.

"I guess it's kind of a big one, huh?"

"Congratulations," he said. "Or what have you."

"It's sort of snuck up on me," she allowed. "Normally I try to work up a major depression for these things."

"You don't sound depressed."

"I'm not. I mean, it doesn't *have* to be this big, traumatic event, right? I can just go ahead and celebrate for a change, and refuse to get all gloomy and preoccupied, can't I?"

"Hey, you're a grown-up, Bonnie." He sounded weary again, preoccupied. "It can work any way you want."

"Well, I'm going to make a huge dinner," she declared. "I'm going to cook up a goddamn storm." No sooner had she made this strange, seemingly arbitrary declaration than she discovered it was true. "Thai, or Vietnamese, or Malaysian maybe. Somewhere out on the Pacific Rim, where it's really steamy."

"I do wish I could come." He paused. Perhaps he was thinking, as Bonnie was, that only a week ago she might have replied with an acerbic *what for?* But she did not do so now. In fact she was a little perplexed that he had given up so easily on her and her high spirits, that he had missed her dinner invitation, however covert or half-conscious; that her virtue, and his, were to remain unchallenged. "The truth is I feel responsible. I'm the one who turned you on to this stuff in the first place."

"Hey, Larry, I'm grateful. No kidding. Better living through chemistry and all that."

"It's just I want to make good and sure you're in capable hands. I'd hate to see anything go wrong."

His concern was beginning to feel a little burdensome and irrelevant to her, a bit of freelance lugubriousness he was manufacturing on his own.

"I've got hands too," she said. "Don't worry. I'm on top of it now."

Typically on Fridays she worked on her dissertation, trying to squeeze in a good day at her desk before the weight of a long, unproductive weekend was upon her. But lately, between her writing block, her sleeping block, and her pregnancy, good Fridays at her desk had become something of an endangered species. Lately most of her Fridays were bad Fridays. On bad Fridays she tried to convince herself that, all appearances to the contrary, her time was not going to waste, that she was simply conserving her energies for essential things. But she could not be fooled so easily. Not when these essential things turned out to be leafing through catalogs, doodling at the piano, and listening to the BBC.

But today as she settled in behind the desk she felt purposeful and sure. Some of the night's lucidity still clung to her, illuminating runways in her thesis that had previously been fogged in by jargon or vagueness. In the space of a few hours she cut four pages, rewrote two others, added two more. In the process it became possible to forget how little she currently believed in or for that matter even understood her dissertation. A flicker of hot, concentrated light at the back of her brain was impelling her forward, burning through the foliage, the overlapping fronds of muddled meaning, and reflecting off the hard object that lay shrouded at its heart—*the mirror in the hut.* It was still there, after all this time, gleaming like a key. Nothing had been lost. Here he still was, her Thoreau: "I should not talk so much about myself if there were anyone else whom I knew as well." Oh, that phony, she thought, that dreamy, romantic, shamelessly self-indulgent hypocrite, holed up out there in his fool's paradox, his tidy, bean-counting life of the mind. . . . She supposed she was still a little in love with the guy even now.

Yes, love. Why kid herself? It had been that all along. The whole interminable, misbegotten project had been conceived in love, no less than Alex had, than Petey had. There had been so much love to go around then. Even now, through time's dulling haze, she could feel the experimental thrill, the heady engagement of playing house with Leon and Henry David, arguing heatedly over suppers of lentils and rice, trying to work out a triangular system all their own, something large and coherent and true. There had been an offer, vague but tantalizing, of connection. As a result of their efforts, something would be delivered unto the world. Something new. But then Alex was born, and her career had stalled, both her marriage and her thesis unraveling like a slipknot, and then awhile later, like some attenuated reprise of the chorus, Petey had poked out his wet, slippery head and begun to cry. And now she was alone. What was one to make of that?

She looked around the cool, sunlit bedroom, attempting to read an answer in the jumble of forms. A queen-sized bed, only half employed. An oak dresser of obscure, possibly antique vintage. Five pairs of serviceable shoes. Three belts. Nine and a half pairs of earrings. Books, magazines, monographs, and catalogs piled on the floor. A pair of Rollerblades, as yet untested, the kids had given her for her *last* birthday. On the bedstand, a fountain pen, a teacup, a ripe pear. Was this not an abundant life? Was her allotment of adversity any higher than most? Why then had she allowed it such a privileged place, a front seat at the banquet of her expectations?

Lilies that fester smell far worse than weeds.

Shakespeare, she thought, one of the sonnets. But which one? She would have looked it up, but her *Complete Works* had mysteriously gone AWOL from the bookshelf. Anyway, what did it matter? She had read and read and read. Time was scudding past like a cloud. Her friends, her mentors, her cohorts from school—all had long since moved on. Even Leon; even Stanley, in his way, had sailed off to other harbors. Meanwhile her boat remained in dry dock. Self-pity had built its nest in her bow; anger's forced, inefficient steam heat had warped the planks of her stern. Before very long the boys too would be shipping out, steaming around the world—Petey, who couldn't steam his way around a bathtub!—under their own, testosterone-fueled engines. And then what?

The phone was ringing. One of her calls being returned at last.

Had she waited too long? She had always been too expectant of life. Or perhaps not expectant enough. Either way it came to the same thing.

Now she could hear the phones in the kitchen and living room ringing too, in their loud, not-quite-harmonious tonalities, the echoes traveling conscientiously back and forth along the walls like messengers on some mad, impossible chase. She fished the bottle of blue tablets from her purse, tapped one out into her palm. She remembered seeing them for the first time in Cress's shoulder bag that day: small, round, and clefted in the center, as if touched by a benevolent finger. Baby blue. She was only supposed to take one at a time, she recalled, and only at night, half an hour before bed. But what would the harm be if she took it now?

Swallowing it down, she remembered that other baby-blue capsule inside her, shrouded in hazy, amniotic sleep. She was not alone. A new promise was inside her, a new chance. As Siraj had said, *a new life.*

She pulled her chair up to the desk. There, on the blue screen, she found her own words waiting for her, twitching and restless, like the children of a haughty, self-absorbed mother who was forever running late.

She looked at the tiny Band-Aid on her biceps. Somewhere beneath it lay the little hole where the dreams had gone in.

The boys will be home soon, she thought.

Carefully she adjusted the light.

15

The Thing Itself

IAN OGELVIE was home that day too. That is, his sister Barbara's home. Which was not quite a home in the conventional sense, but rather a narrow, high-ceilinged industrial space in lower Somerville, with a thin drywall partition separating the cluttered work area from the equally cluttered living area, and a gray, geometrical view out the soot-streaked windows of the FedEx building's loading dock; and was not in *any* sense his at all, as Barbara herself had taken to reminding him every so often, with progressively eroding good humor. Indeed, had he been paying a little more attention, it might have occurred to Ian that between her recent flu and her impending solo show at the Summer Street Gallery, his sister was operating under considerable pressures of her own. But somehow the idea had failed to penetrate his inner fog. He was not a particularly egotistical person, but he was a very tired, overworked, and undersexed one, and in his current state it *did* seem almost counterintuitive to Ian, the notion that other people might have problems too. Other people's problems were boring anyway. Like—though the Freudians hated to admit it—other people's dreams.

For that matter other people's successes were boring too, the most boring thing of all. Take Barbara, for example. One of the many dubious features of the artistic vocation was, in Ian's opinion, the abysmal lack of quantitative standards. There was no objective methodology, no fact-based system for judging achievement. An artist like Barbara worked alone, in the dark as it were, rarely knowing, let alone actualizing, her own intentions, and even when she did profess to know what she was doing and did in fact succeed in doing it, this miraculous breakthrough was only rarely perceived by her peers, who could be relied upon to be even more grudging and amorphous on the subject of other people's achievements than they were on their own. So then what to make of the fact that after eleven years of near-perfect obscurity, sculpting what looked like oversized birds' nests out of iron and driftwood, Barbara had acquired a prestigious new dealer, been taken up by a prestigious new gallery, and had won three enormous and prestigious grants in the past six months to design what she now called, without any apparent irony, "invisible environments"?

Suddenly her work had gone entirely "conceptual"—piled stones, transparent walls, found objects deployed in random clusters. To accompany her installations she wrote a few lines of nearly impenetrable catalog copy, citing the influence of Joseph Beuys, claiming that given the world's descent into a condition of "pure simulacra," she was attempting to provide in her work "a clean new lens."

"They're not meant to be *looked* at" was her quote in the *Globe*. "Looking's overrated anyway. Everybody looks and nobody sees. My ideal audience would sit around on benches with their eyes closed, nodding off."

Which was pretty much what Ian had done when she'd unveiled her latest installation. The project, and Barbara herself, had been featured in a special year-end edition of the Sunday Arts section called "The Next Wave: Twenty Mavericks for the New Millennium," a photocopy of which, he knew for a fact, had been taped to his parents' condo refrigerator down in Florida for the past eleven weeks. Was it just him, Ian wondered, or were there getting to be an awful lot of mavericks out there these days? Mavericks and waves. Whenever you turned your back, another ten or twenty of them came crashing over your head, sweeping away your grant money, rushing past you with a long, lazy hiss to mingle with their friends on the sand.

"Twenty Psychopharmacologists for the New Millennium"—now *that* was an important list. But who would ever bother to read it?

Still, he would suggest the title to Charlie Blaha the next time they spoke.

Sleepily he opened his eyes and looked around the loft. The video jackets piled on the television, the Gauloises butts broken in the ashtrays, the empty pie tin on the coffee table with its lurid cherry glaze, the dull, metallic scent of warm Chablis lingering over the jelly jars . . . the next wave, he thought, had obviously enjoyed having the beach to herself last night. No doubt she'd have enjoyed having it to herself this morning too, were it not for the inconvenient fact that her normally punctilious kid brother was still sprawled crossways on her foldaway sofa at 11:43, half conscious, his breath a forlorn whistle through his dry, parted lips.

At some point he must have dozed off again, because when the phone rang he stirred momentarily, and the frayed thread of a dream fell loose. His mouth was parched. This was, he discovered, but one small piece in a larger puzzle of loss and abandonment. A massive headache was another. So too an aching, cumbersome erection. Some vast project had been undertaken in sleep and left physiologically messy, unresolved. Perhaps there was still time to finish. He burrowed deeper into the cushions, trying to reenter the labyrinth, retrace his steps, down, down, down, into the darkness, following the echoes of the creature who hid there, the half-man, the—

The phone rang again. Where was Barbara? The woman's voice that filtered through the message machine, though familiar in some sense, sounded nothing like his sister. He concluded he must be wrong. Perhaps, even if he didn't know it, still asleep.

Or maybe what he was, was still drunk from the night before. Presuming that he had even *been* drunk, which, given his limited experience in the alcohol-intake field, remained open to debate. Did his little hit-and-run experiment with Boris's vodka constitute drunkenness? He didn't think so. There'd been none of the traditional (and perhaps, he thought now, apocryphal) symptomologies: no lurching-through-a-spinning-room, sex-with-a-licentious-stranger, passing-out-in-a-puddle-of-one's-stinking-vomit to reassure him that he had gone about this drinking business in the correct way. No, he'd done very little lurching to speak of. He could recall no puddles of any kind. And as for sex . . . as for sex . . .

He wished he *were* gay. He did. Because if their somewhat stylized testimonies could be believed, all the gay people he knew—there were at least four of them—led sex lives of singular appetite and abundance. They had other enviable attributes too. They tended to be in excellent shape. They had good taste in clothes, a wide circle of friends. They had their own congresspersons, their own advocacy and support groups, their own churches and synagogues and fitness centers, their own history and literature full of their own heroes, villains, and martyrs, even their own shelves at the video store—all the threads of social fabric that bound a community together, that wove a net around the self and held it in place. His one lesbian acquaintance, Jutta Banks, even had a child now, a chubby, sloe-eyed baby she and her lover, Margaret, had manufactured in some industrial park out on Route 2 using God knew what kitchen utensils. Occasionally in good weather he'd pass them on his mountain bike as they strolled along the Charles, proudly fondling their denim Snugli and smiling at him, at everyone, in that dreamy, knowing way, as if they were all in on the same joke, all Equity actors in the same noisy and significant production. Only where were his cues, his directions? What had become of his script?

Yes, he thought, gay people were altogether admirable, and he'd have liked nothing more than to enlist in their ranks and thereby be delivered at last from the misery of chaste confusion that was his life. After all, it wouldn't take much. A certain flexibility, a willingness to submit, to cross over borders, enter unknown provinces, conduct the private, intricate transactions of the species in other currencies. The mysteries of *down there* . . .

He had felt closer to them, those subterranean riddles, those *triste tropiques,* the night before, in the quiet aquatic stillness of the sleep lab. Marooned at Boris's desk, watching the patient's biorhythms scroll monotonously across the black screen, he'd had plenty of time to ponder these issues, what with all the final polishing up of his grant application he wasn't doing. There simply wasn't time. He was much too busy staring into space. He was much too busy doodling tiny interlocking trapezoids down the margins of the logbook, and consuming the weak, tepid coffee that trickled down with such miserly slowness from the machine, and punching out Marisa Chu's home phone number with a trembling index finger as he rehearsed all the witty and spontaneous things he'd say should she ever break precedent and actually pick up the phone.

She had to be home: it was one in the morning. Having studiously researched her clotted, frenetic schedule, Ian knew for a fact that in six and a half hours she had her supervision session at the clinic. Did she never sleep? Perhaps she was screening her calls, as Barbara and for all he knew every woman did, trying to filter out the undesired noise of what did not immediately concern her from the select and useful information of what, or who, did. As for Ian, he was determined to cross over tonight from the former category into the latter. He would declare himself. He felt the impulse rising in him, formless and irresistible as the ocean, as the black, turbulent night itself. Tomorrow would be different from today. That was tomorrow's golden whisper, its promise. For too long he had taken what had come his way. Tomorrow that would change. He would do what he should have done with Wendy Lesher, what he should have done with Howard Heflin, what he should have done with the insurance company after the fire in his apartment. He would force the issue.

But apparently some issues cannot be forced. Apparently some issues force *you*—force you to restrain yourself, humble yourself, negate yourself. *Make yourself a vessel,* Marisa had said. And he had. He'd made himself a plane, a small, buoyant, hollow-winged glider, sailing along blithely on the breathy singsong currents of her message—*Hey, it's Marisa, I'm not home but you know what to do*—and then, after the beep sounded, enjoying a moment of perfect vacancy and silence, of poised, airborne attentiveness, before losing his nerve and spinning tremulously out of control and finally crashing the receiver down into the sheer rock face of his embarrassment.

And so the night limped forward on its bloody useless feet. *You know what to do,* he thought. Right.

His loneliness was a sea that refused to part; he would never make it across to another shore.

He thought about writing a letter. It was a quixotic and old-fashioned idea, ludicrous on the face of it, but in addition to being at least marginally better than nothing it would give him the opportunity to compose his thoughts in peace, without the interference of Marisa's actual breathing, inscrutable self. He could be artful, subtle; could fine-tune his self-presentation, stylize it somewhat. Clearly in its natural form his self-presentation wasn't working. It was time to lend nature a hand.

He picked up his notebook.

Dear Marisa, he began: *I hope this doesn't make me seem too weird or forward, but I just wanted to say*

He paused, frowning. Like many shy people Ian was appalled by his own penmanship, the cramped hesitations of the vowels, the ungainly consonants and their improvident assertions. Then too, this opening disclaimer *did* sound pretty weird and forward, thus managing to call attention right away to the essential weirdness and forwardness of the entire project. It wouldn't do. He tore the page from his book, crumpled it into a ball, and threw it at the trash basket. Missed.

To fetch the errant wad of paper he had to get down on his hands and knees and feel around behind the desk, down at the bottom. Which was how he'd discovered the Stolichnaya.

The sight of that round-shouldered quart bottle, with its cheery red-and-white label and its fancifully exotic Cyrillic lettering, kicked off an elaborate sequence of Kübler-Ross-type stages in Ian's head. First denial, then anger, then negotiation. Then a cautious, incremental acceptance. This led in turn to one last, as it were, final phase, wherein it became irresistibly clear to him that the vodka and he had been placed in the same room as part of an enormous controlled experiment in human behavior. But whose?

He spilled his coffee in the sink and washed out the mug. As with all the mugs down here, it was embossed with the snazzy blue-and-black Furst logo. Wiping it dry, he noticed, stenciled on the porcelain underside, three initials. CHP. Consolidated Heart Pumps? They were a company out of Dallas, revered for the elaborate barbecues they threw four times a year in the cardiology ward, to which the entire staff was invited. Maybe Furst owned them too. They were into all kinds of areas these days. Diversifying. Nothing was just one thing anymore.

He drew the vodka forward. The snap of the gold seal was a confirmation. This too, this primitive bit of plastic hardware, had been designed for a double purpose: to contain and to release. He was simply making good on its potential.

He took a long drink. The injection he'd administered, he noted with satisfaction, was making good on *its* potential as well. From the wild zigzag of her brain waves on the monitor, the patient was reacting precisely as one would expect to a fifty-milligram dose of Dodabulax. Blood oxygen levels were high. EEG racing. EMG perfectly flat. The first REM episode had lasted twelve minutes; this, the third, had already gone on for twenty-five, with no sign of termination. The forebrain areas of her limbic system, the ventral tegmentum, the nucleus accumbens, all the quadrants associated with pleasure and emotion were lit up like a city. A Paris of the mind.

Homo Faber, Ian thought proudly, draining his drink. He would call Charlie Blaha down in New York tomorrow, tell him the article was a go. His ticket would be punched.

One of the more provocative and intriguing characteristics of imported vodka, Ian decided, was how fast it went down, how it managed to feel, passing through the throat, almost as weightless and transparent as it looked. No doubt this accounted for its popularity over in Russia. Of course it was popular here too, he knew that. *Very* popular. Which was why he chose to go ahead and have another drink. Because he wished to associate himself with popular things. It was high time. He too was a maverick, a new wave. A top-twenty man. The rush of blood in his head as he snapped the drink back was rowdy and swelling, altogether indistinguishable from applause.

Emboldened, he punched out Marisa Chu's number again. No luck. So he poured another finger or two of vodka into his mug.

Did Boris drink on the job every night, he wondered, or only on special occasions? He must remember to ask him. He didn't know Boris very well, only the surface facts, that the man was smart and brusque and about twenty pounds overweight, and that the sight of Boris's stained, disorderly teeth—had there been no fluoridation where he'd grown up?—jutting out of his jaw reminded Ian of gravestones in an overgrown cemetery. To conceal them, Boris was in the habit of keeping his lips pursed when he spoke, which made his low, mumbly voice even lower and mumblier, and lent the lower half of his face a fixed, ventriloquial expression of withheld amusement, as if life were an old joke he'd heard a much better version of the day before. Once, Ian recalled, a few years back, the two of them had chatted for a few minutes at the engagement party for Kim Wachtel, a surgical resident, at a club on Lansdowne Street, after which Boris had distinguished himself by his prodigious energies and uninhibited choreography on the dance floor, and Ian had distinguished himself by leaving before half the guests so much as arrived. He and Boris had exchanged a few forced pleasantries in the bathroom that night, about what he couldn't recall. It was sad when you thought about it, how many people he saw all the time whom he hardly knew, who hardly knew him. Everyone was so alone. Or was it just him?

What about the heart, she had asked him.

Well, he thought, it's a big house, with a lot of windows. One has to choose a place to stand.

Sipping from his mug, he watched the woman on the monitor for a while, noting the rise and fall of her brain waves. The sight awoke in him a great, murmuring tenderness.

He shouldn't have lied to her, he thought. He should have told her what he was up to. Already he had implicated himself in something questionable. And yet, these double-blind experiments were so restrictive. Wouldn't it have been equally questionable to turn her down? *Primum non nocere . . .*

He remembered the postcard that had fallen from her bag. He still had it somewhere in his desk, upstairs. He should have told her that too, how he remembered her from the elevator. How her misery that day had infected him. Stayed with him, moved into his cells. He longed to banish it, to dissolve it in a solution. But the vodka would have to do.

By now it had become undeniable that the level of liquid in the bottle had dropped precipitously, to the point where even an insensitive fellow like Boris might notice. He thought of Boris's dark, shrewd face, his thick wrists, of the crucial formative years of early development he had passed in an altogether rougher, more vodka-savvy environment. No telling what Boris might do if he found out. So Ian resolved to go down to the liquor store and procure another quart.

His ascent from the swivel chair, however, did not go quite as smoothly as he would have hoped. No sooner had he gained his feet than he began to teeter like a seesaw, his legs buckling at the ankles, his knees gone watery and vague, and his head—that large, mysterious, stupendously heavy object—spinning lazily on his neck like a globe. The lab was spinning too. Its furniture and hardware, its windowed surfaces . . . he watched them all fly by, waving his arm in a stoic gesture of farewell.

As for what happened next, that was not entirely clear. A heroic expenditure of effort seemed to be required just to keep him erect all of a sudden, to prevent his body from doing what it wanted to do: lie down on the floor. To minimize the dizziness he closed his eyes. Time passed; or rather time politely stood still and allowed Ian to pass through it, like a man crawling through a tunnel on his hands and knees, chasing some distant, refracted memory of light. When the tunnel ended and he finally emerged, he discovered that he had not in fact made it all the way down to the liquor store just yet. For that matter, he had not made it all the way out of his chair.

Maybe, he thought, he would not go down to the liquor store quite yet. Maybe he would just stay where he was a while longer, in the cozy darkness of the sleep lab, doing what he said he would do, watching over the woman next door. Guarding her sleep. Hadn't he promised her he would stay? Hadn't she surrendered herself to his care? He pressed his nose against the one-way window, and cast his moist gaze over the room. Her face was blank. Her lids shuttered tight. The merest tremor moved down her limbs, like the ripple of a water spider. What music was playing in her head? He tried to hear it, the buzz of the receptors, the frenzied hum of the ions, the basso trembling of the membranes, the sounds of the great organ performing its swinging, tireless jazz, full of improvised rhythms and harmonic convergences. . . . He tried to listen, but he was on the wrong side of the glass. He could only imagine.

He looked down at his open notebook, the white page laid out like an unmade bed.

Let's suppose, Marisa, he wrote, *that our operating principles are right. Suppose the hormonal paradigm holds, and the brain really* is *a gland. This means brain energy must be fluid. It must travel through the body, can't be fixed or corked up. Sound familiar? Isn't this what you were saying about love? What some people say about God? That business about God being everywhere, present in all things . . . could they be right? Because we know, down at the molecular level, there's no such thing as aloneness. Down there it's all patterned recognition, multiple interdependencies; no one thing separate from everything else. And it follows then, doesn't it*—he could feel the vodka oiling the gears in his head—*that the stuff of consciousness isn't set inside the brain but scattered in pools throughout the organism, all organisms, flowing around, always on the move, impossible to quantify. . . . I mean, what do you call* that*?*

Was this the point that Malcolm came to? Why he left? Oh, he was going to need, Ian thought, a *lot* more vodka than this.

You were right by the way about Rush. I looked him up. He was one of the founding fathers, the first great American shrink, an altogether admirable guy. Anyone who changes their whole life plan on account of one dream: that's admirable. And that's what Rush did. He dreamed one night about a man who climbed up the steeple of Christ Church and started waving around the weathervane. He'd point it at the sky and tell it to rain. It wouldn't. He'd call for the wind to blow. It wouldn't. He'd yell for thunder. Wouldn't. Then he started to sweat and curse, until the weathervane broke off in his hands, and that's when Rush must have woken up I guess because the dream ends there.

Or does it? Because that dream stayed with Rush the rest of his life. He quit politics and devoted himself to his practice. And now, I don't know, it's weird, but I think maybe I'm starting to dream about him too. Except in my *dream the lunatic on the weathervane is* me. I'm *the guy on the roof.* I'm *the bug in the software.* I'm *what's flailing around and out of control at the center of*

"So how's she doing?"

Ian's throat closed like a fist around his Adam's apple. Some drunken hallucination, he thought. Another lunatic, wayward, uncontrollable dream. For here, standing only a few feet away in her long black coat and white scarf, was Marisa Chu—peering in at him from the doorway of the technical office with her pale, calculating gaze and her creamy little melancholic half-smile.

"Hey," he called a good deal more loudly than he'd intended. "You're home!"

"Just stopping by on my way out." She nodded toward the monitor. "That's my referral in there, right? That Saks person?"

"Yes. Yes indeed."

"How's she doing? Calmed down any yet?"

Quickly he closed his notebook, bound it with a rubber band, and stuck it in the top drawer of the desk. "Not a peep," he said. "REM three. Forty-one minutes and counting."

"You're a magician."

"Nah," he said, flushing. Oddly, he had been a good deal happier a moment ago, addressing the Marisa Chu in his notebook, than he was now, with this other, more corporeal Marisa Chu standing over him, squinting to read the printouts over his shoulder. Her lips, he noticed, were thin as creases. Her cheeks lacked color. The Marisa Chu in his notebook was better-looking than this one too.

"She thought she was alone," he explained. "That was her problem. But it's perfectly obvious she's not."

"Really." A thin, translucent membrane of worry fell over her eyes. "Where's Boris?" she asked.

"Boris?"

"Boris isn't here?"

"Boris's strictly diagnostic. Wouldn't approve. Would feel compromised maybe."

"Compromised by what?" She peered over his shoulder into the next room. "You *are* doing a diagnostic."

She must have seen it then. The empty vial on the counter, and the spent syringe beside it, dewy and glistening at the tip.

"Jesus, Ian. Have you lost your mind?"

"It was supposed to be a surprise," he said.

"You know the protocol. She has to be selected by the Human Subjects Review Committee. Nobody discussed this. Nobody even prepped her."

"I did. We talked the whole thing over. She was very eager to proceed."

"She's also pregnant."

"I know. I did a lit search. No increased risk, just like we thought. I've got the file right here somewhere. . . ."

"A lit search? A bloody lit search?"

"I know what I'm doing," he maintained, not altogether forcefully. This conclusion seemed just a wee bit less supportable all of a sudden than its opposite. "I've got it covered, believe me. She's in absolutely no danger from the drug."

"I don't see how you can be so sure."

"Trust me."

"Do you know what'll happen if Howard finds out about this? Do you have any idea?"

"Howard's in Japan," Ian announced.

"He is? He didn't tell—"

"Howard's in L.A. Howard's in Montreal. Howard's in Basel, Switzerland."

"What's the matter with you? And why are you talking so loud?"

"Loud?" Leaning backward in his swivel chair, Ian attempted to put his feet up on the desk, hoping to convey some of the manly insouciance he felt under some pressure at the moment to embody. But he miscalculated either the height of the desk or the weight of his legs, and his feet swung down again, sending the bottle of Boris's vodka to the floor with a clunk. There was almost nothing left inside it. Sorrowfully, he watched it roll around on the beige carpet.

"Tell me you drank that whole thing," Marisa said. She too was gazing at the bottle, which had come to rest like a supplicant at her feet.

"No way. Uh-uh. Nosirree."

"You've got some kind of death wish, Ian? You want to screw up your career?"

"Just taking a break," he explained. "It's been sort of an all-work-no-play situation around here, if you know what I mean."

"I better get you home."

"Just do it. That's what Howard would say. Join the team."

"Where's your coat? It's freezing outside."

"I've been thinking about that guy who lost his balls, you know? Terrible thing. Zip and they're gone."

"All right, look, hang on. I want you to drink this coffee first, okay?"

"Uh-uh," he said, shaking his head. "Coffee's a stimulant. Highly addictive."

"Just a couple of sips."

"Lemme ask you something," he said. "Why'd you put that thing in your nose? What for?"

Marisa shook her head in disgust. It was the only evidence she gave of having heard the question.

"Isn't there enough pain already? Or wait, do you *want* the pain? All that feeling—what, some kind of flooding of the nerve receptors, is that it? Please, I've got to know."

She continued to shake her head in an unpromising way.

"Here's my theory," he said. "My theory is it's all that keeps us going. Pain, I mean. Keeps us awake. My theory is, if not for pain we'd just, you know, float around like jellyfish. Nothing on our minds."

"Look," she said, "help me out here. Try to stand up. You're heavy."

"Let me feel what you feel, Marisa. We're all one thing. No good pretending we're not."

"Shhh. Stop bellowing. I'm taking you home now."

"Home? I'm not home. . . ."

"Where are you staying? Somerville, right? Come on, don't make me do this all by myself."

"I'm not home," he said, "but you know what to do."

* * *

As they cross the bridge it trembles and groans, registering the weight of their passage. The river is still. The moon dangles overhead like a stopwatch. Around it the sky shows a nasty bruise—purple and black, a smear of orange in the middle—as if from some violent altercation with a sunrise. It is unbelievably late. He is unbelievably tired. But unless he is dreaming, and he half suspects he is, he is also doing approximately what he has been fantasizing about doing for several weeks now—racing through night's dark tunnel with Marisa Chu.

He has not as yet declared himself, he realizes. So he takes care of that right away.

"I love you," he says.

"You what?"

"I realize you're still hung up on Malcolm and all that but I don't care. I have strong feelings for you. It's all I think about anymore."

"I have to be honest with you, Ian. There are a lot of men in the picture these days. And even if you aren't gay, you're definitely on the nice-but-boring end of the spectrum."

"A man can change."

"Well," she says, "don't change for me."

"What better reason?"

She is silent. The ruby in her nose flares into visibility every so often under the transient impressions of the streetlights, like some fickle but luminous firefly. He leans his head back against the seat. They are listening to the tape of Bach's cello suites again, which might account for the déjà vu he's experiencing at the moment, the sense of having been whirring through the city enclosed in this small vehicle for a long, long time. Beside them the Charles unfurls like a cape, adorned by bright reflected stars. Smart new Lego-like biotech plants line one side of the river; along the other spread the white neoclassical porticoes of MIT.

Every window looks dark. No one home in the house of knowledge. All the busy students are asleep.

The scent of refined sugar fills the air. It billows out in clouds from the Necco factory, where, Ian recalls, they make those tiny candy hearts that melt on your tongue. His heart too is tiny and thin. He can feel it trying to dissolve.

The cello bow is sawing him open, prying him apart. A gull swoops past the car.

Pull over, he says.

Without a word Marisa Chu turns onto a side street, parks. She switches off the ignition. It is very quiet. He can hear her breathing in the dark, see the pale mingling clouds of vapor. The smells of the river—its dank compound of growth and decay—come washing in through the vents. He would swear they are still moving.

Look at me, he says.

She inclines her head to see him. Her face is round and immaculate, with a thin fissure of shadow in the center, like an enormous aspirin.

He presses against her, kissing her with a raw, shameless hunger he only distantly recognizes as his own. He kisses her neck, he kisses her hair, he kisses her mouth and jeweled nose and the clefted area of softness that lies between. From somewhere close by, one of the dark houses that line the street, he hears the ringing of a phone, insistent, intrusive. He tries to shake it off. A woman is waiting, Marisa, or wait, no, Wendy Lesher, or wait, no, the woman from the elevator, with her tangled-up black hair, her dark, sunken, unsatisfiable gaze. *What about the heart.* He will lead her through the chambers and hidden valves, he will show how it liquefies on the tongue. Pushing the restraining belts aside, he moves forward, burrows into her like a dumb, sightless animal, crosses her hills and plains, dips into her valleys, builds a nest for himself at the warm, plush center of her being. . . .

Ohh, she says, crumpling under his weight. Ohh, man.

Through the walls of his chest he can feel a mad pounding, like an inspiration. Each beat is a two-step, a coupled, incantatory thud. No *dream.* No *dream.* No *dream.*

16

The Sandman

English 11B
Mr. Oxenhorn
Rough Draft

The Weird Sisters
an analysis of *Macbeth*
by Cress Carnegie

In William Shakespeare's long, five-act play *Macbeth* (1605?), he uses the witches in a number of ways and for a number of reasons. Some people find the way he uses them completely unbelievable, and say because of this the whole play is sort of bogus, like a fairy tale. I, however, find the witches to be very convincing, though, and also very meaningful.

Witchcraft was a real important issue in England back when Shakespeare was alive. There was a lot of witchcraft going on then. For example, King James, who was the ruler of the country at the time and was married to Queen Elizabeth, published a whole book about it. It was called *Daemonologie* (chk spelling?) and was about all these weird and sometimes highly gross ceremonies that witches liked to try when they hung out together. If you practiced witchcraft back then and you got caught by somebody then you could get killed or thrown in jail, for example the way they did in that really intense play by Arthur Miller we read, *The Crucifix.* There were laws about this.

So to not believe in witches back then would also have been against the law, because it would have put you against the king, who did believe in them, and the king was considered the law back then and was also incredibly stubborn and opinionated. So you see, Shakespeare didn't really have any choice. He *had* to include all that witch-and-enchantment stuff, and he *had* to make it realistic, just to be able to keep having his plays put on.

In addition, some of the most important scenes in the play have to do with the witches. For example, in Act IV. "The midnight hags" is how Macbeth, who's extremely negative and insulting most of the time and not only toward women, calls them. They are preparing one of their "potions," which has in it things like "fillet of a fenny snake" and "eye of newt and toe of frog" (p94).

This sounds very disgusting and unbelievable, I admit. But it turns out that there is nothing unbelievable about it. For example, a man named Alberto Magnus wrote an extremely ancient book called *Mirabilibus Monday* (chk. spelling, date?), where he lists all these ingredients and a lot that sound even worse, and talks about how the witches used them to make their "potions." (add more here next draft?)

When you think about it, what Shakespeare does in this play is just like what people like J. D. Salinger and F. Scott Fitzgereld and Lorraine Hansbery do all the time: exaggerate all the bad things in life to make their work more exciting. This is what is known as "tragic literature." That's what Banquo means when he talks about "the cursed thoughts that nature gives way to in repose." Cursed is another word for negative. What he's saying is, the more you lie around thinking about things, the more negative and weird and "tragic" you get. Another example is when Macbeth says (p97), "if I had *three* ears I could still hear thee," when in fact he only has two, obviously. It's bogus statements like this that make the witches tell him, "Seek to know no more." Because they know he'll keep getting in more and more trouble if he learns anything else through their powers, instead of finding things out on his own the way he should. They're actually trying to *help* the guy. But he won't listen, so unfortunately he ends up dead.

In conclusion, I would like to say that though the witches are used for a number of good reasons in the play, they are also the most trustworthy and believable characters in my opinion. I don't think it's a coincidence either that they happen to be women. Women know things. It's not their fault the way Macbeth and all those other men put their advice to use. I also believe if there was more about the witches, the play could have a more realistic ending. For example, Macbeth's wife is very depressed and mean, maybe because she's all alone in the castle and nobody even knows her first name. If *she* met the witches, they might all become friends, and they could hang together sometimes and the witches might be able to give her a potion to help her stop sleep-walking so much. If she got more rest, then maybe she'd have a better attitude, and she wouldn't be tempted so much by all those "black agents" (page?) that Shakespeare talks about coming in the night, and then maybe she'd be able to concentrate more on the really important stuff like her kids and her career, so she wouldn't get on her husband's case all the time to go around killing people like Duncan for example. Even people in castles need to get out sometimes, and talk to someone who understands the way they think and

There was a light, irresolute rapping at the front door. Bonnie hesitated. She had only a paragraph to go in Cress's paper and was reluctant to set it down.

"Hold on," she called.

She'd been lying on the sofa, listening to some Chopin while she waited for the angel food cake she had just baked from scratch for her own impending birthday to cool. Shifting her weight, she'd felt something tear; and, reaching down, had discovered Cress's paper, folded vertically down the center and tucked into the wedge between the sofa cushions. Below it lay her errant copy of *Complete Works of Shakespeare*—a book she (Bonnie) recalled plunking down three-fifty for, oh, about a century and a half ago, at Paul's Used Books in Madison, Wisconsin—both the text and annotative marginalia of which she had herself liberally appropriated on more than one stressful academic occasion. A fat number 2 pencil lay embedded roughly midway through *Macbeth,* breaking what was left of the spine.

Cress's paper, and the rare show of resourcefulness that had yielded it, impressed her. As a practicing thief, a reflexive gender warrior, and a borderline moron, the girl was well-equipped for literary criticism, Bonnie thought, already. Moreover the draft, though rough, had its merits. It had passion. It had focus. It had its own weird brand of New Historicist fluency. It was also, if you factored out the spelling and the grammar and the baroque teenage calligraphy with its odd, ornamental loops and curlicues, semireadable, which was more than she could say for her own students' efforts. Yes, you had to give Cress credit: the paper was an enviably substantial product for one night's work—particularly a night spent in the company of Petey and Alex—and Bonnie was sufficiently taken with it that she resolved to write its author a glowing recommendation for college next fall, presuming she in fact applied to college, and did not wind up in jail or drug rehab instead.

What time was it? Nearly eleven. She took off her reading glasses, turned down the stereo, and went to the door, squinting through the peephole to see who it was. Cress, she thought, back to reclaim her lost words. But no: encased like a specimen in the bulb of the lens was a handsome man with a yellow tie and a high, rising forehead.

"I know, I know," said Larry Albeit. "I said I wouldn't come and here I am. How to explain?"

"Don't bother," she said. "Just come in."

Though she hadn't been expecting him, his presence before her now seemed an inevitable development, the logical but unforeseen consequence of a dream the night before. There had been a rigorous ascent up an icy slope, one that left her dizzy, gulping for oxygen. At the summit were a ring of eucalyptus trees with fine, needlelike leaves. Within that ring was a white dome. She'd approached it barefoot and trembling. Inside, sitting cross-legged in a cone of light, she found Larry Albeit. He'd been waiting for her, he said. And then he rose, and took her hand, and ushered her inside, and when they arrived at the inner chamber he laid her gently backward over the silk embroidered cushions, and then he . . . he . . .

"Here," she said. "Let me take that coat."

"Thank you." He shrugged off his long coat, which fell easily into her arms, and ran a hand through his spiky graying hair. Perhaps as a result of her dream—the causality of the matter hardly concerned her—there clung to him now a shadow of subtle enhancement, an inflection of something timeless, enduring. A second life. "Are the boys in bed? I hear rumbling."

"It's just Alex. He's famously noisy at night. God knows what he's doing back there."

"Well, I hope I'm not interrupting," Larry said. She followed his gaze around the living room she had—such was her energy that day—dusted, straightened, and vacuumed just before dinner. She had missed a few spots, she saw now. "There's nothing worse than having someone come to the door when you're snuggled up in bed with your child, reading a story or talking about what happened to the dinosaurs or where you go when you die. All those big abstract questions that haunt them so. Intimate moments. Precious."

"You seem a little tense, Larry."

"Do I? How strange."

"Are you hungry? There's about three pounds of chicken curry left in the fridge. You're welcome to it. Or maybe a glass of wine?"

"These are good questions. I'll have to get back to you. Mind if I just sit down a sec?"

"Suit yourself."

He fell, making a somewhat noisy and self-conscious production of it, into the white depths of sofa, still creased with the outline of her own occupation. "Kippy and the girls," he announced, "are at the ballet."

She nodded; she had not as yet sat down herself. "I thought that was yesterday."

"I had it wrong. It was tonight."

"Oh."

"You should see how they look, all dressed up in their best black clothes. Stockings, painted fingernails, the whole works. I mean the word *cute* doesn't even come close."

She looked at him assessingly. "Something troubling you, Larry?"

"Nothing major. A rough patch at work, that's all. Lost a case or two."

"Not your fault, I hope."

"Hard to say. In the big scheme of things, who knows. Anyway," he said, "with corporate stuff I can't really justify getting all worked up. Twenty years ago I was boycotting half these companies for their shoddy labor practices anyway."

She nodded absently. His boredom with such matters was refreshing; nonetheless it had a long way to go before it approached her own.

"Of course, some of the other partners don't see it that way. They tend toward more of an uptight, little-scheme orientation."

"Little scheme?"

"They're very caught up in the whole win-lose aspect, for one thing. It's very tiresome."

"They're mad at you, I take it."

"Not in the technical sense, no. But questions have been raised about my focus. My level of commitment and so forth."

"And at home?" she asked mildly. "Have questions been raised there too?"

He shrugged. She noticed an extra line under his eyes, a horizontal crease as from a pillow. "I think maybe I will have some of that wine," he said. "That is, if you can spare it."

"Oh, I can spare it all right. I'm off the stuff."

He looked at her closely. "The baby? So you've decided, then?"

She nodded, almost demure. The baby. For the first time the words, and the reality they embodied, gave her a small, delicate thrill. She was having a baby. She had never quite consciously decided to do so, but then for some decisions, consciousness wasn't the point. Some decisions just went along without you, bypassed the consciousness station entirely. Wasn't that a miraculous thing?

"I see," Larry said, rubbing his smooth chin.

But how, she thought as she went off dutifully to the kitchen, could he possibly see? What did he have to see with? Only the usual male mechanisms, that paltry jumble of twitching nerves and blobby floating organs that passed for sentience. She had twice as much of everything. There was no comparison, really. At times she found it almost pitiable, the male nation—its geographical remoteness, its barren constitution, its top-heavy militias and underfunded arts, its flat, one-way roads. No wonder Larry needed a glass of wine. As for her, not having a glass of wine was the easiest thing in the world. It felt so heady and elating and at the same time so natural, not having a glass of wine, that she wondered why she had waited so long. Why hadn't she thought to start not having glasses of wine years and years ago?

The buzzer over the stove went off. The cake was ready.

She took the Bundt pan from the oven and laid it out on the counter to cool. The warmth of the kitchen, the smell of vanilla and eggs and risen dough, the low rumble of the dryer in the basement, the photos on the refrigerator, the scarves and coats and baseball hats laid out along the back wall, dangling like flags on their pointed hooks—for a moment she forgot how cluttered and oppressive her life was, and took heart from it instead. Because braiding these things together, assembling them into a whole, this too was a kind of vocation. You had to pour into it everything, hold nothing in reserve. If you held back, the thing withered in your hand, became useless and faded as old currency. You had to keep investing yourself, again and again. Spending it all.

"Bonnie?"

"Coming."

When she returned, wine in hand, Larry, as if completing a thought, said, "I'm really happy to hear it."

"Hear what?" she asked. She could not for the life of her remember what they had been talking about.

"You know, the baby. I wasn't sure you were going through with it."

"I wasn't either," she said.

"Can I ask what happened?"

"Nothing," she said. "Nothing happened."

Larry nodded helpfully. He appeared to be waiting for her to continue.

"Really," she said. "Nothing happened. It's just, I guess you can only take so much of that. Nothing, I mean. Then something takes over. And so," she announced, "there you are."

She was aware that her behavior in this moment was, no less than Larry's, increasingly cryptic and paradoxical. She did not fully understand why she had allowed him into her house just now, to take just one small example, instead of sending him back out to his heat-efficient Saab and on his way. Because of one brief, rapturous dream? But then life was full of riddles that could not be resolved. You could only hope to be delivered from them by the operations of nature.

Behind her came a thud in the kitchen. She could feel the refrigerator trembling and shuddering like a thing abused.

"Baby?" Alex asked, wandering in lazily in the tearaway sweat clothes he liked to sleep in. "What baby?"

"Hi, honey," she said, with pointed brightness. "What're you doing up?"

"Couldn't fall asleep." He scratched himself thoughtfully with his left hand. From his right dangled one of his lurid, tangerine-colored sports drinks: Gatorade, or Powerall, or Electroflex. Empty bottles of the stuff were piled high in the recycling bin. Discarded weapons in the athlete's ongoing arms race, the replenishment of every wayward sugar and salt, every missing acid and electrolyte. "What baby're you talking about?"

"Honey, you remember Larry Albeit? From the preschool?"

"What preschool?"

"Petey's. The one you used to go to, remember?"

"I went to preschool? When?"

"When you were the right age. Anyway, as I was saying, Larry is Caitlin's dad."

"Who?"

"One of Petey's classmates. You met them at the picnic last fall, remember?"

Before the words "What picnic?" had time to form on the boy's lips, Larry jumped to his feet.

"Forget it," he said, extending his big hand toward her son. "It was months ago. I've pretty much forgotten it myself."

From behind the dark, drooping curtains of his hair, Alex pursed his lips, staring at the proffered hand with a near seamless lack of comprehension. He was not yet in on it, Bonnie thought, the handshake conspiracy, the reflex to lock palms with another Y chromosome. Sullen, evasive, fearful of exposure, Alex had developed no dance moves, no political instincts. Among his peers he remained a loner, too shy for the clamoring extroverts, too forceful a presence to abide the introverts. A nation of one. No doubt it was Bonnie's fault somehow, his aloofness, his intractable betweenness—the absence of a live-in father and all that—but the truth was she took some stubborn pride in it too, saw a tiny pearl of integrity gleaming through the crusted, carbuncular shell of his manners, and so she could not help but detest herself a little for wanting, as she did right now, to yank his big graceless hand right off his goddamn wrist and turn it over to Larry Albeit—who was still standing there in the same awkward, touchingly hesitant posture, waiting to receive it.

"I'm not stupid," Alex maintained. "I'd know it if I went to some stupid picnic or not."

"Fine, dear," Bonnie sighed. "You never went."

"Wait, when was it again?"

"It doesn't matter," she said. "Now do me a favor, shake Larry's hand and say a nice good night, so when he goes home later and his wife asks what the older brother is like, he won't tell her you're surly and rude beyond all belief."

"I really hate it," Alex said, "when you make fun of me."

"I'm sorry, honey. You know I love you like crazy. Now go to bed."

"I was just getting a drink," he said defensively, putting down his sports drink to allow Larry to shake his hand. "But I heard you out here talking."

"Larry and I have business to discuss. It concerns the preschool. He's on the board, you know."

"Huh. Cool." Alex gave Larry and his wineglass a measuring look. "So, what? You just had some kind of a baby or something?"

He pronounced the word *baby,* Bonnie observed, with the aggressive propriety of a firstborn, as if he would forever hold the patent on any further use of this concept. All he wanted, it seemed, was one small thing that remained his own.

"Baby?" Larry's face, which had been almost cravenly congenial a moment before, folded up like an umbrella. "Oh no, not at all. We were just talking about . . ."

"Someone else," Bonnie said.

"Yes. A mutual friend."

"What does that mean, mutual?" Alex asked.

"It means someone we both know."

Alex thought this over, frowning in his usual ostentatious, heavy-browed way. "The only person I know that you know is my mom."

"I mean someone your mother and I both know."

Larry's tone at that moment was patient, deftly pedagogic. Fatherly. So this is how they talk, she thought. Without too great an effort she could imagine such conversations going on night after night in this very room, with this very man. . . .

"Who?"

"You don't know her," Bonnie snapped. He was beginning to mess up her tranquillity. "Now would you please go to bed?"

"It's not fair. It's Saturday night. Why can't I stay up?"

"Tomorrow's a big day, lovey. You've got basketball at eleven-thirty. Then we're going out to do something outrageously fun to celebrate my birthday."

"Again?" he lamented. "I thought we celebrated that *tonight.*"

"Tonight was just a warm-up," she said. "Tomorrow's the big one. And after that, watch out. It's going on for weeks, months. Ever hear of Leon Trotsky? This'll be our own little permanent revolution."

"Yeah, right."

"Now go to bed. I mean it."

"This sucks," Alex said. "This is so totally unfair."

Watching him stomp off down the hallway on his unwieldy, thick-thighed legs—already as long and heavy as her own—Bonnie felt a familiar inner tearing. She had created this being in all good faith; he was her pride, her adventure, her own hut in the woods. And yet it was harder than she wanted it to be not to turn her back on him. The problem ran very deep, she thought, past the standard Oedipal issues, down to some dark fetid species pool below the psyche. Way down there, in the primordial chemical soup, a twist had occurred, a tiny, cancerous quirk of the cells, a jagged fork in the genetic road that led to proper individuation. And now here they were.

She was reminded of an article she had read in *National Geographic* about a desert tribe, the Pitjentaras. With their second children, the mothers of the tribe were extraordinarily affectionate and easygoing. They'd croon to, dance with, stroke and caress the child, sleeping in the same bed, breastfeeding for up to five years. The first child, on the other hand, they would eat. It was a way, she supposed, of accelerating the natural progression of things.

Larry cleared his throat.

"A nice boy," he said after a moment. For which effort, were she in an altogether different mood, it would have been necessary to hate him.

"Fairness is a big issue around here," she explained. "The general consensus is there isn't quite enough to go around."

"Well," Larry said, "I suppose you can't blame him."

"Oh, I don't. It's completely age appropriate. There's a whole chapter on the subject in *Children and Divorce.* Our standard reference."

"Well, I'm sure we'll be getting there soon enough," he said.

"Divorced, you mean?"

"No, no. God, no." Larry blushed; the effects of which were concentrated on his big forehead, in the area between his eyes, which was usually so white. "I mean that angry age. You know, with the little ones."

"Mmm."

They sat in awkward silence for a moment. Larry began to pick at the sleeve of his shirt; an errant thread, whether real or imagined she couldn't tell. But she admired his industry in tracking it down. From her perch on the arm of the sofa, she had the advantage of six or so inches of height over him, and so was able to see running like a vein of soap through the piled steel wool of his hair a stripe of scalp. The pale, the unholy whiteness of it was a shock. She had to restrain herself from leaning over him like a shade tree to cover it. But why? Her own hair was graying too, her once-proud breasts softening at the folds, losing mass, succumbing to gravity's slow, inertial pull.

"I should tell them, shouldn't I? I'll be showing pretty soon. It's time."

He looked up at her, eyes sunken and distressed. "It's not for me to say, Bonnie."

She nodded. He was absolutely right, of course, but that did not prevent her from being disappointed in him, in everyone, for not even trying to tell her what to do.

"I almost said something at dinner tonight," she admitted. "I've been working up to it. Probably I'll say something tomorrow."

"You should do what you think best."

"They'll have to be nice about it, won't they? It's my birthday. Isn't there some rule about being nice to someone on their birthday?"

Larry looked stoic and thoughtful in his wrinkled shirt, his erratically knotted tie. "If only people could be depended on to follow the rules," he said wistfully.

"Probably the incentives aren't good enough. It's like communism," she said. "There's always a brain drain. A black market."

She heard a toilet flush down the hall. Alex. Could he possibly be jerking off already? She thought she had at least another year.

"Not that I'm anyone to talk," she admitted. "I was in the Socialist Workers Party for about three months once. We had some fantastic strikes. And great songs too. Really kept us going."

"It's tragic, isn't it," Larry said, "how our political energies fade with age."

"I don't know. It was kind of an artificial situation back then, with the war and all. I guess our heads were full of smoke."

"And what're they full of now?" he asked. "Movies? Catalog copy? There's still smoke, Bonnie. It's just another kind."

"Now you sound like Leon," she said, neither embracing nor resisting this turn in the conversation. At least it was a conversation. "He's still down there fighting the good fight. Bringing Brecht to the masses."

"Good for him," Larry said. "I respect people who work for a cause. Something bigger than themselves."

"Leon? Are you kidding? There's nothing bigger than himself. That's his gift," she said. "He's the most selfish selfless person in the world. He's got to roll his own cigarettes, never mind it's cheaper to buy them. He's got to buy the cheapest wine, the drabbest, ugliest clothes on the planet. God forbid his plays should have an intelligible plot, or be less than three hours long. That's the thing: he can't just be a loser, it has to be a huge, world-historic statement. Meanwhile whenever he needs his teeth cleaned he flies up to Miami courtesy of Mom. How's that for the city on a hill?"

"You sound a little angry," Larry observed, with his typical sparkling acuity.

"Bingo."

"But, and excuse me for playing devil's advocate here, I hardly know the guy—but couldn't you argue it's better to act inconsistently than not at all? To believe in a system of *some* kind—even an imperfect one? Be willing to sacrifice a little?"

"You want sacrifice? Let's talk about two kids sacrificing their father, who's too fucking high-minded to stick around and play house. You see, kids actually *like* having two parents, Larry. It's boring, it's completely reactionary, I know. But they can't help it. All those dumb, conventional, petit bourgeois things like dads and movies and baseball games: they really *like* that stuff."

"People use kids as an excuse," Larry said. "A reason not to do more. I never believe them."

"That's because you're a man." She was tempted to point out, by way of illustration, that his presence in her house at this very moment had only been made possible by a generous grant from the

Kippy Albeit Trust. But she feared he would be shamed into leaving. And she was not quite ready for that.

"Sometimes I think that's why we have kids in the first place," he mused. "To prevent us from doing things. It's a lot of work, doing things. This way we can tell ourselves our lives would have been really extraordinary if not for these kids of ours, when the truth is they probably would only have been ordinary in a different way."

"Gee, Larry, I'm confused. I thought you were so *into* kids."

"I'm just trying to think clearly, that's all. Challenge my own assumptions a little. That's the first step on the road to change."

"The what?"

"We say we want freedom," he went on, "but do we? Freedom is so problematic, so confusing. We're no good at it. Maybe we'd rather have this sleepy little half-life than the real thing."

"Speak for yourself," she said. "Who are you to talk, anyway? You're Mr. Snooze. You're the Sandman himself. Look at you: you're half asleep right now, aren't you?"

"You know, Bonnie," he said carefully, "I didn't get into this sleep thing as an escape. Just the opposite. I'm trying to go *inside,* not out. Toward, not away."

"How can you tell the difference?"

"Forget it," he said. "Let's not spoil things by arguing."

"Things? What things?" She was willing to forget, she thought, just about every word they had exchanged. She was even willing to forget her dream, the aura of change that had hung around her visitor when he entered; it no longer seemed present, let alone urgent. "Why are you even here, Larry? Would you remind me?"

"I wanted to give you something."

With some ceremony, he set down his wineglass on the coffee table and leaned down toward his briefcase.

"No way," she said. "No more hash named Bonnie. I'm off that too."

"Relax." He snapped it open. "This is a real present. For your birthday."

"That's even worse."

"Why?"

She looked at him sternly, more sternly, in truth, than she felt. "You know why," she said.

"Don't be silly. It's just a little token between friends. I've got it right here."

Watching him hunt through the crisp accordion folds of his inner briefcase—nothing, from his expression, seemed to be quite in the order he'd left it—Bonnie brought two fingers to her lips involuntarily, holding her breath, as if approaching a roadside accident. In a sense that's what it was. Her driving hunger for erotic attention was plowing right through the guardrail of her disinclination to accept compromising favors from married men. The collision, though soundless, made her feel woozy, morally unsure. Her limbs went numb, the skin on her face heavy and slack. As if from behind shattered glass, she watched Larry extract a square white box from his case and put it in her hand. "Open it," he urged.

Just the tiny weight of it in her palm caused her will to crumple like a fender. She lifted the lid. "Oh my."

Inside, resting on a cloud of fine spun cotton, was a tiny antique bottle of perfume. The glass was pale blue, intricately faceted with colored gems and buttressed with running bands of silver, like a tiny cathedral window. That the liquid was obviously tinted water, and the baubles, and perhaps the silver as well, were obviously fakes did not dampen Bonnie's joy in the gift but nourish it. Tenderly she cradled the bottle in her hands. Her love of found objects, her taste for cheap, useless luxuries, for elegant, otherworldly compositions—she thought of Cornell's shadow boxes, those cutout paper birds in their gilded cages—how could Larry have known? Perhaps he really was the man in the white dome. The gift's gratuitous beauty was somehow enhanced by the knowledge that it could not possibly have set him back more than ten or fifteen dollars.

She put her reading glasses back on to decipher the label. *Wan Frauen Traumen.*

"I know," Larry said quickly. "You don't know what to say."

"Something like that."

"Don't say anything. Just try it on."

She unscrewed the metal cap and laid it on the oversized glass coffee table she had inherited from her parents. "You don't mean to tell me there's real perfume in here?"

"Of course it's real."

She sniffed at it warily.

"Now, now," he said with mock severity, "careful not to spill. Every drop is precious.

"You dear man," she said.

He looked up at her shyly. There had been a reedy, indeterminate quaver in her voice, a runaway note of vibrato feeling that had caught both of them by surprise. From the open bottle rose a cool cloud of scent, like a concentration of some natural substance, rainwater dripping off a eucalyptus tree. . . .

"I got it at Filene's," Larry said, picking at his thread again. "The saleswoman spoke very highly of it. It's from the Czech Republic."

"I've never smelled it before." She dabbed out a drop and began applying it to her pulse points.

"They mix in some sort of chemical. A pheromone, she called it. It's very subtle, the way it works, but apparently it sends out a message that gets received through an organ in your nose and transmitted to the brain. She said that's how animals communicate. Japanese beetles and so forth. They have this whole pheromone system."

"And the message?"

Bonnie felt a bit aswoon, her head losing altitude in the cloud of scent, coming in low like a jet toward the big flickering runway of his face.

"The message?" Larry asked.

"Yes, the message. Did she happen to mention what it was?"

He tried to look away, but she was right there in front of him. She seemed in that moment, even to herself, a great deal to contend with—her searching eyes, her tumbling, two-tone hair, her cool glaze of scent with its hidden animal messages.

"Something to do with, um, sexual attraction, I think she said."

"So?" She could feel herself drifting free of words, slipping the tethers of their implications. "What do you think? Is it working?"

"Bonnie," he said, "listen, I want you to know I've got very strong—"

"I know."

". . . wouldn't want to abuse your trust . . . but do you think—"

"Don't," she said, putting a finger to his lips. "Don't think at all."

For a moment their bodies appeared to hesitate in space, two planetary bodies orbiting—and resisting—the attractions of a black hole. She was unable to catch her own breath. Despite her resolve not to think, she could not help thinking that here was another answer for that questionnaire, another hidden luxury of depression: this zero gravity, this free fall through the vacuum of consequence. All she had to do was let go, she thought, and she'd fall and fall and fall. If you never hit anything, if you never touched down, was it really falling? Or was it rising?

Of course under normal circumstances, she would never let herself think this way. Under normal circumstances, she'd spend another hour or two making small talk, conducting all the while a harsh, tediously thorough examination of her conscience; after which, if the past was any indication, she'd ignore the results and do whatever she felt like and then get on with the business of regretting it all later. But tonight was her birthday, practically, and what with the cool purr of the Dodabulax in her veins, and these big sweeping currents of lust and idealism and perfume, her usual tight neurotic circuitry had shorted out. So she proceeded to skip right over the conscience exam, which she was bound to fail anyway, and into the lavish embrace of doing whatever she felt like.

She felt like fucking. The impulse, strictly speaking, transcended the personal, in the sense that it was not focused upon Larry Albeit exclusively, though as it happened it was more than large enough to encompass him too. Thus while the person she fucked did not *have* to be Larry Albeit, it *could,* she thought, be Larry Albeit, which was a timely and fortunate development indeed. Because from the look of things, Larry Albeit wanted to fuck her.

Their mouths came together, and locked. Thankfully, this time her head did not bob right back up like a cork, but stayed down instead, like a sponge, soaking in the warm sanguinity of Larry's breath, growing heavier with it, fuller, larger. Larry too seemed to be benefiting from the transaction, accruing both body weight and psychic mass, as evidenced by the growing confidence of his movements, and the impressive width and definition of his torso under his shirt and, even more impressive, the elongating ridge of pressure she could feel—*ah, she remembered this now*—straining dependably against the fabric of his trousers, like a high wind into a sail. Yes, something was being launched at last. She began to float out a ways, clear of ambivalence's cramped harbor, through the crosswinds, past the bobbing buoys, and into the high, salty seas. . . .

Boldly she drew her turtleneck over her head and tossed it onto the floor. Larry, issuing a gasp so audible and spontaneous she nearly came from that alone, buried his nose in her cleavage and began to root around hungrily, like a bear in a tree stump. His lips found her breasts and fastened on. She groaned. At once a kind of humidity engulfed her. She felt deep and fecund as a rainforest. Her back arched, her arms twined sinuously around Larry's broad shoulders, and her nipples, those pallid wallflowers, began to ripen and stir. It had been a while since she had slept with anyone save Stanley Gottfried, the deconstructionist, and so in addition to all the other benefits, there was the relief of finding herself flung clear of theory's gaunt, lawless orbit and deposited back on solid earth—where, she was gratified to discover, such late-Romantic conventions as foreplay still enjoyed a hegemonic run. For a while she was almost unconscious with pleasure. True, as Larry drove her back into the cushions, she was aware of a certain wavering hesitancy in his movements, as if he were anticipating patterns of gesture and response that only his wife *(his wife,* she thought, *his wife)* could know. But these oscillations did not last long. Soon the questions, answered or forgotten, went away, and Larry was moving down her body again, and the ease with which she escaped her jeans and her panties, and the pillows assembled themselves into a low wall of protection around them, seemed only to confirm to her that this was not a selfish or heinous or desperate act *(his wife . . .)* but in some way just the opposite: a highly moral journey of imaginative discovery. Another found precious object, like a rosebud, or the bottle of perfume, that glowed unexpectedly with inner light.

First you found it; then you had to do something with it. Like love. The finding wasn't enough; you had to polish it, maintain it. That was the test she'd always failed in the past. But this was not the past. The past was asleep in the back bedroom, musty and still. She closed her eyes and it was gone. In its place was only the slow, unhurried motion of Larry's tongue between her legs, her rising and subsiding hips, the mellow, milky sway of her swollen breasts in perfect synchrony with the ballad dreaming through the stereo speakers, and then she pressed her face against the pillow and something whooshed out of her like a sob, a groan. The roof of the white dome shuddered open; the light came pouring down; and there was the world, laid out like a buffet. And then something tore beneath her—*(his wife)*—and she lost her rhythm, and was thrown halfway off the sofa as well.

"Whoa." Larry, red-faced, laughed uncertainly. "What happened? I thought we—"

"Mother of God."

It was Cress's paper again. Having now been sat on twice in one evening, the essay was getting pretty ragged around the edges; it was torn conspicuously in at least three places. "Would you look at this thing?" she said.

"What in the world is that?"

"Just give me a minute, okay? I need to fix this."

She leaned over the coffee table, trying to smooth out the paper with the flat of her hand. She could not have said why it was so important to her, why she was prepared to leave Larry hanging fire that way, with his hair disheveled, his lips glistening and plump, while she ran off to fetch the Scotch tape. But it was. And then, on her way back from the kitchen, she caught a glimpse of herself in the coffee table (how stupid, she thought, to have held on to it for so long, a glass table in a house full of boys), saw a face which, for all its flushing heat, seemed oddly innocent of darkness, and she paused, in a sort of trance, to contemplate it, wave a last farewell to that skinny, knob-kneed creature who had been hiding there, she realized, all this time: bonnie old Bonnie Saks, of Scotch Plains, New Jersey, her earnestness and industry, like her hymen, still intact; as yet untouched by literature, adultery, and the history of communism; just a clean-living and responsible girl who has been dutifully self-sufficient all year—earning A's in school, coming home from Girl Scouts at five o'clock to cut the honeydew into wedges for dinner while her parents quarreled upstairs—who has waited patiently month after month, hoarding the brilliant coins of her yearning like a miser, for just this moment, when nothing is expected of her but pleasure, when being good and dutiful is no longer necessary, when it is enough, more than enough, merely to be herself. And now the lights go out, the cake is set in front of her with its garland of cream roses and its bright flickering crown of candles, and the girl closes her eyes and draws in her breath and makes a simple, ardent wish. . . .

Something rushed away. When she opened her eyes the girl, the cake, and the candles were gone. She saw a grown woman with droopy tits shivering in the pane of glass.

". . . so sorry," Larry was mumbling from across the room, tucking in his shirt. "I shouldn't have lunged at you like that. I don't know what's the matter with me lately."

"Forget it," she heard herself say. "It's my bad."

It was a sports expression she'd learned from Alex. My bad. Like most of his colloquialisms it was bracingly direct, suitable to an almost infinite range of experience.

"No, no, it's me," Larry said. "I'm out of control. I'm disappointing everyone these days."

"Okay, fine. It's you." She struggled back into her blouse. "You're a terrible person."

"Don't be angry, Bonnie."

"I'm not. Basically, I'm just going with the flow here."

"I appreciate that," he said.

"Well, maybe you shouldn't. I'm not sure I do."

She thought of Leon, of Stanley, of all the weak, feckless men she had invited into her life, who assumed they were good because they lacked power, force of will. If that was goodness, she thought, let me be bad. Their kind of goodness did damage to everyone.

"You're an amazing woman," Larry said, as if that explained everything. "You have this wonderful, ultimate clarity about you. I mean it. Tonight, when you opened the door, it was like going into the Supreme Court."

She frowned. "That's your conscience talking. You brought the court with you. Everyone does. Don't try to lay it on me."

"You're right," he said. "Forgive me." He sighed. "I don't know why I'm being like this. I seem to be kind of spaced out these days. Sleeping a lot. I haven't gone near the gym in two weeks. I just don't have it in me right now."

"I hate gyms. I never have that in me."

"It does get crowded in there, all those machines. People puffing away, listening to their music, their books on tape. Everyone in their own separate world. What's the point? I used to like it but lately all I want to do is sit in the park with the au pair girls and watch the little kids play on the swings. It's incredibly interesting."

"Come here, Larry."

He sat down beside her. She stroked his long face.

"Stop feeling sorry for yourself. It's a drag."

He nodded, somber. "That's what Kippy says."

"Oh? What else does Kippy say?"

"She says I should drop out of the sleep study. She thinks it's screwing me up big-time."

"She has a point."

"She says I go to bed at nine o'clock and then can't wake up the next morning. She says she wonders if it's the sleep that's so good or the life that's so bad. The thing is," he continued, "she's right. I do get impatient during the day, waiting for it to end. All I want is to climb back into bed as early as possible. It's a nice bed. A king-size. There's a lot of space to maneuver. Lately the law feels so confining."

"Maybe the dosage is too high."

"Maybe," he said. "It's just that I've always had such good tolerance."

"Don't be vain. As you said, age wears you down. Talk to your doctor, the one who got you in there."

"I will. You're absolutely right."

"I keep trying to talk to mine, but he never returns my calls."

"It's a pretty intense workplace," Larry allowed with a frown. "Seems to me, though, the dosage must be the same for everyone. It's not too high for you, is it?"

"Uh-uh. For me," she admitted, "it's just about perfect."

He stared down at his hands.

"I'm afraid," he said. "It's been so good for months. It's gotten me through some very tough times."

"There are other drugs."

"I've tried them. This has been the best by far. *You* know how good it can be."

"Yes."

"So you see. It's worth a little sacrifice."

"Losing your job, your family? Watching everything you've built go down the tubes?"

"I've been a good builder," he said. "I've done it for a long time. But people are complicated, is my feeling. There's this tendency after a while to go the other way. To just sit back and watch the wrecking ball swing."

"Well, don't go swinging near me, okay? I've got my own midlife crisis to deal with at the moment."

He cocked his head to look at her.

"Maybe this *is* dealing with it," he said.

"Let's face it, Larry. I'm not good mistress material. I have very little potential in that area."

"You didn't seem to feel that way a couple of minutes ago."

"I was carried away. It happens when I'm feeling tender. Let's not make more of it than it is."

There was a pause. She looked at the clock. Five to twelve. The arrangement of the hands seemed vaguely significant to her for some reason.

"Are you feeling tender right now?" he asked, circling her labia gently with the back of his finger.

"Um, not very."

He stared at her as if taking a sounding.

"What?" she said.

"Your pheromones," he ventured shyly, "say something else."

"They're not mine. They're not even real, they came out of a bottle. You told me so yourself."

But there they were again, her breasts, defying the long odds of gravity and experience and, as if obeying some inlaid code of instruction, aspiring upward one more time toward his open, knowing mouth. She felt no inclination to stop herself any longer. There seemed so little point. She knew about the wrecking ball. The destruction was only a prelude, like night itself, to the hammering industries of daylight. Or perhaps it was the other way around, she thought (Larry's mouth having fastened over her left nipple), perhaps it was the building that was only a transient phase, and the darkness and undoing what endured. The art and the science. But all this was for Larry to puzzle out, not her. He had lost his way in the dark wood; as for her, she had just begun to find it.

She was not to be penetrated tonight. So be it: she would be welcomed and received. This mouth, for the present, would be her point of entry. This mouth that opened to her, that lifted her up on invisible wires; this mouth that babbled the soft timeless nonsense of the body; this mouth that traveled over her tender, swelling belly and zeroed in to locate her at last.

17

The Minutes

ADVISORY COMMITTEE ON FUNDING, NEUROSCIENCE DIVISION.
DATE: March 15.
LOCATION: Conference Room, National Institute of Mental Health, Bethesda, Md.
TIME: 10:30 A.M.–1:30 P.M.
ATTENDING MEMBERS: Dr. Arthur Kaplow (NYU); Dr. Lionel Macy (Harvard University); Dr. Howard Heflin (Boston General), Chair; Dr. Barbara Hiddlestein (Stanford University). ABSENT: Dr. Arvin Peters (Johns Hopkins).
RESULTS:

Out of a total of 49 proposals, 11 were granted, 38 rejected. Seven applicants were encouraged to revise and resubmit for the June 30 deadline. This shows a moderately lower rate of acceptance than we have seen over the past four years. However, as the agency has fallen victim to no less than three severe budget adjustments in that time, the chair felt, and the committee as a body, after some discussion, concurred, that there was a pressing responsibility to reduce the overall number of grants awarded for the foreseeable future, pending the time funding is brought back to its previous levels.

PROCEDURE:

Dr. Macy opened the meeting by proposing a two-week adjournment to accommodate Dr. Peters, who was scheduled for eye corrective laser surgery that afternoon. However, Dr. Heflin, chairing the meeting, proposed that the meeting go on as planned, citing his own scheduling conflicts later in the month. In the interest of expediency, the other members of the committee voted to support Dr. Heflin's proposal, and the meeting was held.

The committee achieved unanimous agreement on all 11 of the final grantees, and on 35 of the 38 rejections. In view of time constraints, discussion on each proposal was limited to five minutes. This period had to be extended in several instances to accommodate more spirited exchanges of opinions. In two of these cases, issues were raised in regard to applicants whose proposed projects, however valuable and interesting in conception, were judged to follow too closely along the lines of the one of the committee's own members—or, as was demonstrated in one case, at once too closely and not closely enough. It was decided by a majority vote that while the potential for conflict of interest did not necessarily require the member to recuse himself from the discussion, Drs. Hiddlestein and Macy wanted to note for the record that future committees be advised to set up guidelines on this matter before their meetings to avoid any undue and time-consumptive conflict. In the end, though each of the three proposals was judged to have obvious merits, none was deemed suitable for funding by a majority of the members present at this time.

CONCLUSION:

Ultimately it was the committee's feeling that, despite the unusually high incidence of contentious debate among the participants, this was an extremely productive session, and should yield some valuable and provocative results.

Letters will be sent out to applicants within the week, notifying them of the fate of their proposals.

* * *

Ian Ogelvie was at his desk on the sixteenth floor, leafing through the various mail and phone messages that had piled up over the previous few days, when he came upon the envelope from the NIMH. Immediately he put it aside, unopened. There was no need to look at it. One does not spend half one's lifetime applying for things—schools, fellowships, grants, post-docs—without learning to decipher the signs and symbols, the whole ruthless runic code of binary separation that distinguishes desiring subject from desired object. Ian knew at a glance into which camp he'd fallen, and with what sickening and decisive force. While it was true, he supposed, that the inversion of the postal stamp in the upper right corner of the envelope could be interpreted in any number of ways, the bulimic slenderness of the contents was itself a loud and damning clue, as was the odd, free-form improvisation on the spelling of his last name (Ovalgie). Most fateful of all was the letter's arrival date, a good (that is, bad) two weeks after the fifteenth, when, according to his one source privy to such good (that is, bad) information—Marisa Chu, whose talent for information gathering, like her talent for all other forms of acquisition, was both virtuosic and borderline maddening—the committee had definitely met.

The acceptance letters, Ian thought, must have gone out first. This was how it worked. Good news traveled quickly. Good news flew express. Bad news, on the other hand, always came late, chugging along second-class or parcel post, laden with its clumsy freight of misspelled names, obscure forwardings, and topsy-turvy postage. It all made a mean, desultory sort of sense.

Though he had not, relatively speaking, encountered such a great deal of rejection in his life, Ian had been slapped by that cold black hand just often enough—Wendy Lesher a still-stinging example—to develop his own unique strategy for coping with it, and he wasted no time employing that strategy now. He put his head down on the desk, and fell abruptly, ponderously asleep. In the end it was not so much a matter of conscious choice as it was a physiological necessity, resulting from the convergence of three chronic conditions: his low blood pressure; his mild case of hypoglycemia, exacerbated recently by all the late hours, bad meals, and work-related stress in his life; and his keen if not neurotic sensitivity to rejection. Two, maybe three times a year, these precipitating factors combined like a Mickey Finn to lay Ian out cold. He would have been helpless to resist them even if he wanted to. And why should he want to? From the perspective of, say, an evolutionary biologist, his response to the envelope's stimulus was perfectly rational and justified. Animals think with their bodies. Should an animal's attempt to reach its goal be met with utter failure, that animal will either change its pattern of approach or else return to its lair to lick its wounds. This was one of nature's most primal dynamics, fight-or-flight. Ian of course had *tried* to fight. But now, as the stolid pugilists at the NIMH had seen fit to block his jab, and sent him reeling back to his corner with a bloody towel, he decided to try some flight instead.

And so he flew: right into the soft, pliant arms of sleep. Pitched forward in his squeaky, WD-40-resistant swivel chair, his head folded into the bony oblong cradle of his own arms, he slept for half an hour or so, oblivious to a sky gone asphalt and dull as a parking lot, and the slow misting drizzle that seemed to emanate as much as fall from it, swallowing the lights of the surrounding towers in a puddled blur. There is nature, and there is nurture; occasionally they drop their tiresome antagonisms and work side by side in collaboration, like the fraternal twins they are. And that was how it went for a while. Ian did his thing, and the minutes did their thing, and then came the peremptory staccato knock of a hand against the cheap brass of his nameplate, and the door, suddenly and annoyingly enough, was doing *its* thing—lurching backward on its recalcitrant hinges and banging hard against the six-drawer file cabinet behind it—and he was thrust awake again. "Dr. Ogelvie?"

"Mpph."

"We had an appointment for today. Remember? You asked me to come in." She waved her appointment slip. Exhibit A.

"Of course." Ian rubbed his big sore extruded eyes. "Ms. Saks. How are you?"

"Fine. Excellent, in fact. But would you mind calling me Bonnie? It's not important or anything, but I'd prefer it."

"Why don't you call me Ian, then. It's only fair."

"Whatever you say. Mind if I sit down?"

As she was already insinuating herself into the chair beside him, which had not been sat in for God alone knew how long, and casually flinging her shoulder bag onto his desk, managing in the process to displace by a few centimeters both his In/Out box and the small pile of paperbacks (Bataille, Foucault, and two or three other French writers with musical, challenging names whom Marisa Chu had lent him the week before, "in case you want some help," she'd said, "with the whole sexual identity thing") that had been leaning, rather precariously, it turned out, against its black frame—none of which he'd yet had the time or inclination to read, and all of which now tumbled onto the floor—Bonnie Saks managed to miss or ignore the fact that the entire time he'd been involuntarily shaking his head no.

"Sorry," she said, managing somehow to not sound particularly sorry.

"Never mind," Ian said. "I wasn't reading them anyway."

She was examining one of the book covers.

"Oh, Bataille," she murmured, in the tone of someone encountering their own parents at a party. "How do you find it?"

"Mmm," he said. "Interesting."

On the other hand maybe he would read the books after all. Who could tell? In the face of his failure with the NIMH, this odd ongoing infatuation with Marisa Chu, the mixed-results experiment he'd conducted with Boris's vodka, and this new, uncharacteristically brazen, perhaps even foolishly compromised way he'd begun to go about his research, the lines between predictable behaviors and the other kind had begun to fade, to the point where Ian was no longer able to theorize with any certainty what he might do and what he might not. This was especially true right now, given the proximity of his star patient, the volatile and demanding Ms. Saks, and the direct visual contact he was enjoying, despite his best efforts not to, with the ruddy dimpled twins that were her knees. He watched her cross one leg over the other carelessly, her skirt riding up her thighs with a soft, fabricy sigh. Was it possible she had worn that skirt for him? And what if she had? She was both a good deal older and a good deal taller than Marisa Chu, and her legs were commensurately a good deal heavier and longer, and yet the stimulus-response patterns set off by the presence of both women in his office were remarkably alike. How odd. And yet Ian knew that a certain amount of countertransference was to be expected in cases like these; the locus of desire being less the desired object than it was the mind of the desiring subject: i.e., himself. Thus he reasoned that his licentious and wholly unprofessional feelings toward his patient at the moment were not in any way specific to her, but rather a generalized state of being in himself. This was good. This was swell. It made him feel, among other things, a lot less out of control. At the same time, something about the process of watching her yank an elastic band from behind her head and shake out her hair, the black waves tumbling over the white, sloping shoreline of her neck, made him feel a lot *more* out of control.

The rubber band she slung carelessly around her wrist, like the annoying constraint it was. It dangled in the air, frayed and loose, like the pink rubbery strings of his wretched heart.

Oh, he really *was* an animal, Ian thought. He was a small, lustful, vulnerable creature who thought with his body, should be off hibernating in a log somewhere, not messing around with people's lives. This must be what failure does to you, he thought. It turns you into an animal. Then it catches you by the neck, and pummels you like a butcher's mallet, until you're boneless and tenderized and squashed almost flat, and then it rips the heart from your chest and sends it splashing and fluttering onto the floor.

"Nice office," his patient said. "There's something really comfortable about it."

"Thanks."

He commenced a quick internal review of the voluminous, intricately detailed guidelines about sexual harassment in the workplace that had filtered down from the administration in recent months. Should he open his office door a bit wider, or would that be too obvious? Or should he close it all the way, and would *that* be too obvious? He was not cut out for these transference issues. At least with the animals they never got in the way.

Her face, he observed, was dimpled too, though only on one cheek. This lent her features a poignant and appealing lopsidedness.

"What's that?" she asked, pointing to the specimen cage on the window ledge behind him. "Some sort of spider?"

"Yes."

"It's so still."

"He's asleep," he said, without even bothering to look. Molloy had been off the drug for over two weeks now, but it made no difference. He dozed all day anyway, in a shaded corner of the cage, while his webs grew crumbly and tattered from neglect. "He sleeps quite a bit these days."

"Is he on what I'm on?"

"More or less."

"How strange. It's like looking in the mirror."

"How are you feeling, then?" He remembered watching over her in the lab that night, the rise and fall of her brain currents, the steep, private oscillations. "As well as you'd hoped?"

"Better," she said.

His mouth felt rank. The nap's dull backwash coated his tongue. He should keep a bottle in his desk, like Boris. Vodka, or mouthwash—something tangy and chemical to burn through the gauze.

"The best thing, really, is how it's affected my work. I have this dissertation I've been tinkering with for years. But these last few weeks, wow. You wouldn't believe the progress I've made. Thanks to you."

"It's not my doing," he said. "You've done it yourself."

"You want to hear something funny?" she asked, suddenly growing expansive. "I was never even *interested* in literary criticism. I only got into this racket because I like books. But given how competitive the market is these days . . ."

"Market?"

"The job market."

"Ah."

Earlier that afternoon, Emily Firestone, the outspoken young intern who'd been assigned to him by Howard Heflin, had come by to drop off her CV, still warm from its trip through Kinko's light machines. It was six pages long, which in addition to the enhanced paper quality and the sharper font made it half a page longer than his. He'd pushed it away. It had not been necessary to read that document either, to know what it contained. He'd already heard in the willful jangle of her bracelets and the smooth, musky blend of casualness and presumption in her voice that Emily Firestone had either gone to an Ivy League school or should have, and would in any case wind up going to one, if not teaching at one, if not *running* one, in the not-so-distant future. Emily too had talked a great deal about the market. Though in her case she meant the *stock* market. Apparently Mark, her fiancé, was busy brokering some speculative stock transaction concerning pharmaceuticals, and though it all sounded very complicated and boring to Ian, he'd nodded along anyway in his best autopilot listening mode. The same way he was nodding along with Bonnie Saks now.

"It was my ex-husband's idea, actually. He kept saying the academic job market's going to get worse before it gets better. As long as I stayed in school I wouldn't have to start paying back my loans. That's how his mind works. He likes to think he's beating the system. I guess he figured I should just stay in school until retirement age, and then start collecting Social Security."

She looked to Ian expectantly, as if waiting for him to summon John Kenneth Galbraith himself to refute this strategy. But he didn't. Her ex-husband, he thought, was probably right, and this cost him a moment or two of gloomy contemplation regarding his own prospects for the future. Then too he could not help musing, on a lower though parallel track, what it would be like to be an ex-husband; to know that somewhere out there another woman with another man might lay such a claim to *him.* He would have liked to have been an ex- by now. A big, mysterious variable in someone else's life equation. But of course you had to be a husband first. You had to go out and make some mistakes before you could set about accumulating distance from them.

Bonnie Saks, perhaps misreading the inner-directed darkness of his expression as an outer-directed indictment of herself, said quickly, "Oh, I know it sounds cynical, talking this way. But I can't help it. I've got kids, and all these loans out, and I can't afford to do anything that's not going to pay off later. You understand, don't you?"

"Sure."

"I feel like I'm babbling here."

"Oh no. Not at all."

"I can't help it. It's been so long since I felt this good. Is babbling one of the side effects?"

He smiled. "You may be the first."

"Well then. I'm earning my pay already. Making a contribution to science." She laughed. "So what now? Want me to roll up my sleeve so you can draw some blood?"

"That won't be necessary."

"I thought you'd want blood," she said. She sounded more than a little disappointed.

"Next time," he said. "Next time we'll do a complete workup. Okay?"

"Okay, fine. Whatever you say."

"What I had in mind today was a little talk. That's all. Make sure you were doing okay. No ill effects. Maybe answer any questions you might have."

She thought for a moment, swinging her legs. Some coins had spilled out of her bag and onto the desk. He must remember to tell her.

"Will it wear off?" she asked finally. "That's the big one. Will it just stop working one of these days?"

Ian glanced involuntarily toward the spider.

"There's no reason it should," he said. "As long as you keep taking it."

"Oh, I'm taking it, all right."

"Then you should be fine," Ian said.

"And when the study is over? What then?"

He paused. This was turning out to be more difficult than he'd expected. He thought of Charlie Blaha, tapping his desk impatiently down in the Manhattan offices of *Neuropsychopharmacology Now.* He looked at the unopened envelope on his desk, with its alarming guarantee of no future grant support, and at the woman before him, the dark bags of fatigue gone from her eyes, simply wiped clean, as if by erasable fluid. She was his responsibility now, in a way that almost no one else was. He must tread that thin line between doing good and doing harm.

"Hopefully," he said, "you won't need it by then. That's our goal: for your circadian rhythms to regulate themselves."

"And if they don't? I'm fucked, right?"

"Not necessarily." He paused. "I could try to get you into the next study."

"You mean there'll be more of these?"

"Oh, undoubtedly."

"So I could just keep *do*ing this? Going from drug study to drug study? People do that?"

He nodded. "For some, it's the only kind of treatment they can afford."

"Mother of God," she exclaimed with a laugh. "What a country."

Ian was irritated by her tone. He did not see anything humorous about all the desperate ways people sought treatment for themselves. Pain was pain. If necessity was the mother of invention, surely pain was its abusive father. What was funny about that?

"By the way," she said, "shouldn't I have gotten a check by now? I thought I was being paid by the week."

"Yes," he said. "I'm glad you brought that up."

"You don't sound glad."

"You've been put into a special subset. A special category. Just for bookkeeping purposes. That's why you haven't gotten your first check yet."

"Or my second."

"If you'd like, I'll see what I can do to speed up the paperwork." He glanced wearily at the papers that lay over his desk like so much flaking skin. "Now, if you have no other questions, maybe we should—"

"What about sex?" she asked.

He looked up.

"Suddenly, I don't know, I just *want* it. Desperately. All the time. It's kind of a new feeling for me. I'm not sure what to make of it."

"I see," he said.

"I thought these drugs were supposed to turn you *off* sex. That's what I heard. Or am I into something new and different here too?"

"You've begun to relax," he said, in his most soothing and officious voice. "For a long time, probably longer than you even realize, your body's been full of tension and discomfort. Once that dissolves, you begin to come in closer contact with what's been waiting beneath it.

"Which is what?"

"Energy. Sex. Hunger. All those primary drives you've been repressing. It can make for a pretty profound change."

She nodded vaguely. "It's very confusing."

"I imagine it must be."

"I don't know how I feel about this. I guess I'm still trying to process it. I mean, it's great and everything, sleeping this way, don't get me wrong. But . . ." She ran her eyes over the books on his desk. "When I couldn't reach you after that night at the lab, I got nervous. So I went on the Internet and looked up some of your articles."

"You did?" The light of this revelation blinded him for a moment; he did not know whether to feel flattered or exposed.

"I wanted to see how your mind works. It's a trust thing. I like to know who I'm dealing with."

"And? What did you conclude from your investigation?"

"Well, I don't know," she said. "I guess I've got some questions."

He nodded for her to go ahead, though in truth he would have liked her to stop. He was already tired of her questions. They kept spilling out, knocking things around on his desk. She was having sex with someone, but not with him. So what? He was the one improving the quality of her life, and she did not even know how. She understood so little.

"Well, take this guy Heflin you publish with. He's sort of mechanistic, don't you think? I mean, according to him, dreams don't have any meaning or content at all. He makes it sound like they're just this random, silly activity that goes on at night."

"Oh no, not silly. And not random either. They're very specific, very purposeful. Like the mess a cleaning lady makes when she's—"

"Cleaning up the room. I know, I read it. And then afterward the brain organizes the information into a story that may or may not have some bullshit arbitrary meaning imposed on it from the outside."

"The brain," Ian explained, "tries to make a narrative from the facts at hand. That's its job, which it performs very admirably. Even when the facts don't cohere as well as they should, even when there are gaps and incongruities, the brain copes. It provides a story. Of course it's *only* a story. Not, objectively, the truth."

"So wait, you're saying we have to toss out the unconscious completely? The whole thing's just a pile of memory trash we take out at night to keep the mind humming along efficiently, and the rest is commentary?"

"In a sense."

"But look," she cried, suddenly exasperated, "where's the *room* in your system?"

"Room?"

"I had a therapist once, this was a long time ago, who was into Harry Stack Sullivan. There was this phrase he used, *The Uncanny*—"

"I'm afraid, Ms. Saks, that whatever Harry Sullivan might have had to say on this or any other subject lies outside the range of relevance."

"Oh, I know. He's out of fashion. Freud's not scientific enough, Jung never worked with rats. It's all biology now, right?"

"Please, these are complex issues. There's no way to do justice to them in a brief d—"

"Because reading those pieces of yours, I kept wondering, Gee, why'd he even bother becoming a shrink in the first place? Why doesn't he just put on a blue smock and stand behind the counter at CVS? That's the state of the art, isn't it?"

Ian's back drew straight. "It seems to be an art that's helped you, Ms. Saks, enormously."

"True." He watched her blink back what must have been a wandering contact lens. "I'm sorry, I don't mean to be argumentative. The truth is I *am* grateful. It's just—" She looked at him imploringly. "Don't you ever go to museums, Ian? Don't you ever see something that looks completely real and completely dreamlike at the same time? Something by de Chirico, or Magritte, or anyone, really, that's both meaningful *and* crazy?"

He sighed. "The benefits of the manic-depressive tendency among our creative artists, Ms. Saks, have been well documented. As has the pain and misery they've suffered and caused. Let's not romanticize psychosis and addiction into things to be treasured."

"But who draws the line? Who says what's okay and what's pathology? Because there are an awful lot of us in the middle, you know, who don't know *what* to call what we've got. What're you going to do, go around treating *everybody* for *everything*?"

"Of course not. It's an issue of being able to function in the wor—"

"I hear they've got a pill for shyness now. What next? One for obnoxiousness? For boredom? For . . ." yanking on a strand of her own hair, she cast around for the word, "*love*?"

For a moment he imagined he saw tears in her eyes. But perhaps that was merely their own insulating fluids, their own protective membranes. He was tired of trying to figure out women. He rubbed a northwestern quadrant of his forehead, where a migraine, like a submerged continent, was drifting toward the surface. He looked again at the too-thin white envelope from the National Institute of Mental Health. There it was: his future. It was almost a relief. As with all operations of gravity, there was an inevitability to failure, a grateful acceptance of natural law. It was like slipping into a cold pool an inch at a time; suddenly you're in, and it's absolutely fine, really, just trolling along, half floating, half sinking—the way, you realize, most people do for most of their lives—and there's no pressing reason you can think of to get out of the pool ever again.

Yes, it was a relief, all right, a real step forward, fucking up.

"I have this student, Guiliana"—here she went again! For all their talk about love, it wasn't love, but talk, he thought, that they really cared about—"she grew up on Cyprus. Her cousin died when she was twelve. She wrote a paper about it for my class. Her aunt was in mourning for five years. Hardly slept, hardly ate. Never went out."

"That's a long time," Ian said obligingly, "to lose to grief."

"I never said it was a loss."

"What is it, then?"

"That's what I want to know. Tell me, Ian, what would *you* do if she walked into this place? What's the procedure? Run a CT scan? A little Paxil, maybe? Some Zoloft?"

He was aware of being tested, if not insulted again; his tone grew flinty and cold.

"Frankly, we haven't had the luxury to indulge this sort of reflection. Our focus to this point has been on basic feasibility. The length and quality of the REM sleep itself. The hard science, as we call it."

She smiled sadly.

"Personally I'm happy to debate these issues with you anytime. Though I'd like to remind you that it's not uncommon to have doubts and second thoughts about taking medication. Still, if you're beginning to feel it's too much of a compromise with your humanistic principles . . ."

"Okay, okay. Don't get so defensive. I'm just playing devil's advocate." She looked out the window. The rain was now falling in hard, discrete lines, like pinstripes on the gray suit of Boston. A muscle pulsed silkily in her throat. "I like to look at both sides of the issue. It's an irritating tendency, I admit."

"Not at all," he said. "It's very valuable and endearing."

He watched her turn over this odd phrase like the ungainly, pear-shaped thing it was.

"Lately I've had this fantasy," she mused, "of ditching it all and moving out to Santa Fe. I could throw pots. I think I'd be good at that. Or make jewelry."

"And your children?" Ian asked. She was not so much looking out the window, he realized, as studying herself in its reflecting surface, trying on an attitude to see how it fit. "What would they say?"

"They'd say stay here and take an extension class."

"I see."

"They'd say finish the damn degree. They'd say follow through on something for once in your life. They'd say I'm at that stage where it's easy to lose sight of why you went into your field in the first place, but that doesn't mean there wasn't a good reason. Everyone in grad school goes through something like that, right?" She looked at him hopefully.

"I'm sure they do," Ian said, though in fact he had never gone through something like that, in graduate or any other school. He wondered, however, if in some sense he wasn't beginning to go through it right now.

"Kids are more conservative than you think. They don't like to gamble."

"I wouldn't know," he said.

"Of course not. Why should you?"

"Though I do think about it sometimes," he said. "Other ways, I mean. To live a life." She was staring at him as if he'd begun to speak in tongues. "I imagine we all want—"

"What?"

He flushed, unable to complete the thought.

"Tell me, are you a gambler, Ian?"

He lowered his eyes. For one furtive moment, such was the promiscuity of his inner life—which seemed forever inversely proportional to his outer one—he imagined the two of them stepping through the small rain-darkened window of his office as through the aperture of a plane, descending a bank of shining stairs, and emerging, blinking like newborns, into the warm, lucid sunlight of New Mexico.

"What do *you* think?" he asked.

"Hard to tell." She shrugged. "You never know."

The phrase fell lightly, easily from her mouth. It had the sound of a philosophy, he thought. A mode of perception as passive and enduring, as seemingly benign, as the jellyfish that drifted in the ocean.

Bonnie Saks gathered up her pigskin bag and slung it across her shoulder. "Well, I better go."

He nodded.

"Same time next week, right?"

"Right."

"I may need more pills by then. I'm running low."

"Whatever you need," he said. "Just let me know."

Because he had her file spread open beside him he did not, after she was gone, experience the usual descent into aloneness. The chair across from him did not seem too empty, the office did not seem suddenly too large. It was as if she were still here. Between the manila covers he had possession of her pulse rates, her blood pressure readings, her polysomnograms, the whole hidden record of her nights. He knew her critical numbers, the vaults and dips of her expectations. In a sense they had a relationship after all. A singularity, a closeness. They had researched each other, explored their fundamental premises, the materials of their minds. They had chosen each other, in sickness and in health.

He noted the time of her visit in the logbook. Under her name he wrote: *Enhanced REM. Heightened sense of well-being. Marked increase in written productivity, verbal responsiveness, sexual energy—*

Yes, he had chosen well. She would make a fine article, perhaps even a series. He picked up the phone and dialed New York. Charlie Blaha wasn't in. He had not been in all week. But Ian left another message.

Just then he spotted, out of the corner of his eye, the sealed envelope from the NIMH. Immediately the blood drained from his head. What if the experiment took a wrong turn? What if Blaha wasn't interested after all?

Are you a gambler, Ian?

Just for a minute, he laid his head down in the space that had opened between those documents it was no longer necessary for him to attend to and those, like his mail and phone messages, it was. He closed his eyes. There on the back of his lids, waiting for him, was an unbound, shimmering horizon. The sun a bright eye of morning, the moon lingering, stubbly and unwashed, above the reddened bowl of the mountains, with their sugar dustings of snow . . . just the clarity and expansiveness of the sky, its abiding emptiness, would lift the fog right out of your head. Nature unmediated. No clouds, no mist, no shadow between you and what's there.

The ultimate reality. Or the ultimate illusion?

There are an awful lot of us in the middle. . . .

We forget our dreams, he should have told her, for a very good reason: because forgetting spares us pain. The mind likes to minimize pain if it can. The mind prefers a clean house, one that's tidied up at night. The last thing the mind will stand for is a crowd of idle useless memories loitering around its offices in the middle of the workday, sprawling over the furniture, scribbling on the stationery, making long-distance calls on the phones.

18

Time Passes On

SHE SLEPT. It was easy now. The blue pills she carried with her everywhere, not to take them necessarily—she tried to restrict herself to one a day—but to have them close by. They were something to hang on to. An organizing principle. A paradigm.

As if the nights were not enough, she'd begun to take naps after lunch too. Her bed she laid out like an altar, with fragrant candles, sepulchral music. The white sheets ironed smooth, quilts tucked in tenderly at the corners. The drug had been her sacrament, her ticket of admission; now that her foot was in sleep's door, and the noise of the streets had clicked off behind her like a banal and raucous movie; now that, hearing the first sonorous blasts of that stately organ, she'd looked up to see the hanging tapestries and vaulted arches, the colored light streaming like holy breath through the stained-glass windows, she had taken to it, the well-slept life, with all the zealotry and fervor of the twice-born. It made her feel humble, susceptible to awe, part of some ancient ceremonious practice of worship. She wanted to be worthy. The more she slept, the worthier she felt. The more stillness she practiced, the faster the pace of her change. It all seemed very complicated—was this courage, she wondered, or its opposite?—and at the same time as simple as erasing a blackboard. This was her time. She had earned it. She had given and given and given. From now on she would be a taker, a recipient. A *bride.* The night her dark groom.

She'd climb under the quilt and close her eyes, offering herself like a sacrifice. When she opened them again the world seemed new.

She had found a higher calling. She bore the knowledge in her like a seed, a spore. Her long depression had fossilized; she was able to look down on it from afar, trace its dried, concave imprint on her skin. For a couple of weeks she floated through time like a posthumous being, like someone who has emerged, shaken but intact, from a wrecked car. Her former life was revealed to be a poor, sleepwalking thing, a festered wound crusted over with scabs. The flesh below was pink and smooth as a baby's bottom.

Around her the city itself seemed oddly submissive. Winter had abused it. The streets buckled and heaved, the sidewalks were ravaged by huge, forking cracks. Pale clouds of salt lay like a judgment over the parked cars. Even the shops held no attraction. Her itch to purchase was gone. The arrow of her attention to the material world—that flickering bulb with its wan corona—tilted toward zero. At home, dishes dirtied themselves and collected quietly in the sink. Laundry piled up at the foot of the silent washer. One day she opened a volume of poetry and found fuzz spots of mildew, dormant but visible, feasting on the starch in the binding. She threw it in the trash. After all, she reasoned, the book was only paper, chemically treated wood pulp; it belonged to the earth, not her. Once this had been determined, she walked around the apartment in her bare feet, surveying the rooms with a fresh eye. Yellowed catalogs and magazines, outdated calendars, expired coupons, these countless scraps of paper she'd been holding on to without being conscious of—that had been holding on to *her*—all went tumbling into the recycling bin. She emptied her closets, swept off her desk, put her thesis in a binder and the binder in a drawer. All the progress she had made amounted to so little. To Thoreau too she'd become indifferent. If not to him, then to her antipathy for him. Give the man some space, she thought. Let him tend his sparse little crop of beans. She had her own life to inhabit.

Only where was it?

She kept catching glimpses of it, impressions of some vast, radiant design that shadowed the hours like the gilt underlay of a mirror, just out of reach. A membrane had risen between her and the world, or else the membrane that normally separated them had slipped away. In any case their relations were different now. Idly she wafted along the humming avenues, vagrant as a mote in the sunlight. Around her the city clicked and gleamed like spokes on a wheel. Sometimes every face she passed seemed that of a distant stranger; at others they all seemed terribly close and connected, a family of sorts, trembling to the convulsions of her own heart.

One bright afternoon she drove out to Concord and, for old times' sake, went tromping in her boots around the muddy, half-thawed pond. She had not been to Walden in years. The woods, perhaps because they were seasonally bare, looked smaller to her now, more domesticated, exposed. There had been talk of development across the road. People were suing and petitioning each other, fighting over claims. Everyone wanted a piece of it. A *great good place of the mind.* Was it here? She looked up at the pines and bristled spruces, the willows hanging their leafless heads, the squirrels tumbling like circus clowns, and the swallows wheeling in a delirium. Had it ever been here? Or had it only been an idea the man had brought with him like a picnic lunch, and tossed out when he was through?

And yet this had been their place too. She recalled languid summer evenings and sunset swims, parking for free (Leon's favorite if not only mode of parking) in the lot across the road, coffee cans for berries slung on strings round their necks; the sand working its way into the curried chicken salad sandwiches she'd prepared, with a loving sprinkle of almonds and raisins, earlier that afternoon; Leon wheezing along behind her, oblivious, whistling one of his tuneless Chinese marching songs in a manner that still somehow made her believe, stupidly but insistently, he was lost in thoughts of her; and Bonnie in front, meticulously picking her way down the path, waving off gnats and mosquitoes with the back of her hand, giving names to all the foliage. She liked to label the wildflowers, decode the inscripted ferns, find metaphors in the trees, read commentaries on their progress in the songs of birds, the wispy arabesques and daisy chains the clouds formed in reflection over the pond. Had she read them wrong? At some point along the path of years the signs, or her manner of perceiving them, had blurred. Leon had wandered, first in theory and then in fact; Bonnie, losing confidence, had turned outward to Stanley Gottfried, then inward to no one at all; and after that the drug of disappointment had kicked in for good, smoking up her head, numbing out her extremities. And the berries, the ones they'd harvested so carelessly in their coffee cans, had aged, of course, as berries do: some turning withered and stringy, others mushy, overripe; a few at the bottom, like Bonnie herself, going both ways at once. What a waste, she thought. In her disdain for the commonplace, her greedy pursuit of an extraordinary life, she had slipped through the crack between and been buried there. It was a failure of vision, or imagination. Somehow she had failed to perceive, woven inextricably into the Nothing, that other experimental half-truth: the Everything.

She began to cry a little, right there and then, kneeling in her stretched-out jeans before the cold uneven stones of Thoreau's fireplace, the only trace of the original structure that still remained. It was almost three. The sun was winking through the trees. Traffic swooshed by, fluent and insensate as wind. Far off in the budding entanglements she could hear the hollow *pong* of a woodpecker knocking itself senseless. Though for the bird, she knew, it wasn't senseless in the least: only the sound the bark made when it yielded what was hidden.

Then all at once, as if a spell had lifted, she was ready to go back.

Because it wasn't enough, she thought. The woods, the glittering pond, the jeweled facets of the afternoon light . . . even Thoreau had grown bored with it finally. *It seemed to me I had several more lives to live and could not spare any more time for that one.* One could only transcend for so long. Eventually there came the itch to transcend that too.

And so she returned to the clamor and congestions of the city. She fetched Petey home from preschool—where he'd had, his teacher reported, a super day—and read him several absorbing picture books. Then Alex came in, having aced a math quiz he'd expected to fail, and climbed into her lap to give her a warm, completely gratuitous hug, and suddenly they were all having a super day. To celebrate, she made popcorn and hot chocolate, and allowed Alex to put on one of his awful, honking, cacophonous CD's, and as the last daylight washed off the window in runny streaks, like soap off a washed car, the three of them got down on the carpet on their hands and knees to play Chutes and Ladders. The game, with its arduous mazes, its fickle swoops and concavities of chance, proved not just suspenseful and interesting but also fun. Even Petey, who could be relied upon to shed tears whenever he lost ground, was easily persuaded to pick up the dice and try again.

Watching him regather himself, lean frowning over the busy game board with his drippy, delicate nose, his avid long-lashed eyes, Bonnie knew all at once that this must be what happiness was. This moment. No sooner had she identified the feeling, however, than she felt it rush past, a winged creature evading the light.

"Great," Alex said to Petey. "Now she's crying again."

"She's not crying," Petey said. "Are you, Mom?"

"I'm fine," she said. "Really."

"See? Told you."

"Told *you,*" Alex said. Nonetheless he got up and fetched her a tissue from the bathroom, like the mature, helpful young man he sometimes was. Then, when she didn't take it right away, he waved it frenetically in front of her face, like the angry, impatient brat he also sometimes was. "Here. Don't you want it?"

"Thanks, love."

"You're welcome," he said. Sullen now, and confused, he sat down to finish the game, which was almost over. But then what did he expect? Family happiness was fleeting. A temporary form of pain relief; an interval, not a cure. Maybe that was all you could hope for.

Anyway, they were together. And growing. And the baby too was growing, like a fever, an insurrection of the blood. And she was able to sleep now, to negotiate the world calmly. It was possible, distinctly possible, that everything she'd been waiting for, in the way of transformation, had already occurred.

* * *

At school too there were signs of a renaissance. Derek Toombs, though he still contrived to lose consciousness in every class, no longer lost it quite so early in the period, nor for quite so long, and occasionally during his brief interludes of alertness his huge, brow-heavy, Piltdown Man–ish face actually began to show signs of human comprehension. Changes were under way around him. Bonnie watched, with fascination and pity, as Derek struggled to comprehend them. The way his instructor (Ms. Sucks, he'd taken to calling her privately) had come out from behind her blockish lectern and begun to spin like a dervish around the room. What was *that* about? Also she'd begun to wear, over her usual low-budget uniform of khaki and denim, a lot of bright, Day-Glo-colored scarves that fluttered around behind her when she moved like tropical birds. And, what was really troublesome, she actually seemed to be taking this expository writing crap *personally* all of a sudden. Like it *mattered.* But hey, even crappy state colleges like this one were full of talkers and pencil-necks, maniacs of abstraction—people who stayed up late reading late-German philosophy, or putting on experimental plays where nothing ever happened, or handing out leaflets in the student union protesting things going on in countries they'd never been to. True, Ms. Sucks had not been that sort of teacher in the first part of the term; if anything, she seemed even more cynical than they were. But strange things happen over the course of a semester. You start out all bundled up in sweaters, coats, gloves, and hats, and by the time you're through, the girls are wearing halters and short skirts and the guys're walking around in flip-flops.

Was she getting laid, finally? Was that it? Because from the way she went on about word choice and sentence structure and clarity of expression, she must have been fucking Strunk and White. *Make every sentence a window,* she told them, *and see the world true.* Whatever. This Windex obsession of hers was only the beginning; there was also her annoying new habit of reading passages from Chekhov and Flaubert and about twenty or thirty other eggheads out loud in every class. Sometimes these readings—sometimes one *sentence*—took up half the period, until the eyes of even the really good students glazed over like winter ponds. Not that she cared. For too long she'd watered down the whiskey with these kids, seemed to be her attitude; time to give them the good stuff, or else close down the bar altogether.

Bonnie, from her own point of view, did not fail to notice how tight and wary her students looked as they fell into their seats, their heads tilted at grudging, suspicious angles. Here they had come back from a relaxed midterm break to find that someone had replaced the cast, put up new sets, and rewritten the play. What for? They were state-college students; their time was not to be trifled with. She watched the calculators whirring in their heads, the private balance sheets, the cost-benefit analyses. The numbers were against her, she knew that, but she was too far in to stop. One day, arriving late, she caught Lisa Vujanovic, one of her few really good students, performing for the class a cruel though rather accomplished parody of her elaborate new teaching style—her windmilling, Evita-on-the-balcony arms, her abrupt, aphoristic declarations—and she laughed. A month before she would have been devastated. But now she received it like a compliment.

Even when it became apparent that for all her inspirational efforts, her students' compositions were still as plagued as ever by lazy mistakes, near-total self-absorption, and the absence of any identifiable subject matter beyond the erotic hothouse of the dorm, she refused to despair. No, if anything it was the assignments themselves, the weekly tasks she had inflicted on them, that appalled her now, that struck her as arbitrary and graceless, ill-conceived. Describe a lake from the point of view of an old man? Good Lord, why? They'd be old soon enough themselves and would lose all sureness. Whatever bodies of land or water stretched before them then would be capturable by no known language.

Still, they were beginning to awaken to her. She could feel it. Outside the mercury was rising, the planet turning its big fat face to the sun. She was gorging on existence, basking in its warmth like a housecat. After school, walking to her car in the flickering dusk, she was like someone with a secret, a password. *Dodabulax.* She did not know what it meant, but every time she took one, the doors of possibility swung wide open, and she awoke the next morning as someone alive in a dream.

Where if anywhere Lawrence Albeit, Esquire, fit into this picture, she didn't know. Nor it seemed did he. The man had developed in recent weeks a magnificently grave, haggard, watery stare. His hair was wild. His clothes were shapeless and creased. His Saab, untuned, made loud faltering noises. It was as if the chains of his ecstasies had slipped their gears. She watched him tumble downward in a spiral like a lethargic, displaced angel. Though in his own eyes the direction remained upward, and rising.

In the three weeks since their first sexual encounter—she tried not to probe too deeply into the causes and effects—a number of alarming trends had gained momentum in Larry's life. He had, if his own reports could be believed, pretty much given up conjugal relations with his wife. He had pretty much given up professional relations with his clients and colleagues at the firm as well. Other things he had pretty much given up included, though were not limited to, home maintenance, car maintenance, weight maintenance, shaving, dental hygiene, deodorizing, racquetball, weight training, *The New York Times, The Nation, Consumer Reports,* and perhaps his most reliable and enduring passion: coaching noncompetitive girls' volleyball, ages five to seven, at the West Cambridge Y. On the other hand, he spent a lot of time in bed these days. That was what he was into—sleeping, listening to talk shows, and watching the occasional violence-free cartoon with the girls.

Still, it was important not to dwell on these developments, Bonnie thought. Larry was working out his own paradigm, just as she was working out hers. Besides, he could afford some time off. He was a full partner at the firm. Kippy, like most Connecticut girls, had some obscure private family income. Also there was money socked away in T-bills, annuities, the Asian market. No, if the structures that held the man's life together were giving way, she figured it was up to him to make the adjustments.

Nonetheless when he showed up at her door one night, in woolly pants and a wrinkled shirt bereft of collar stays—the black of his loafers an indictment of the puffy white sock-bare ankles above—she found it hard not to wonder if their friendship, or relationship, or whatever one was tempted to call it at this point (she herself felt beyond such categories), was really as healthy as he claimed.

"Honey," he crooned, spreading his arms in a gesture of welcome, or despair, "I'm home."

"You're late, dear. You had me worried."

It was a little game of greeting they had been working up, a sort of postmodern exercise designed to reassure them that they were in control, riding herd over their intentions. Neither of them was very accomplished at it yet. The game's ironic artifice seemed to intensify with every repetition, gaining new wrinkles of stridency and brittleness that were like stretch marks from the effort of willing itself toward being. Despite if not because of this, neither of them had yet been able, or inclined, to quit.

"Couldn't be helped." Larry flopped down noisily onto the sofa. Whether his exhaustion in that moment was genuine or feigned for the sake of their little playlet wasn't immediately clear. "So how're the kids? Did they make the team? Are they in the play? Did they get the girl?"

"Of course," she said.

"That's swell."

"By the way, did I mention I'm having an affair with Caitlin's father?"

"Good. Best thing for you. How's the sex?"

"Depraved." She noticed that he was kneading through his shirt the soft dough around his navel. His belly had lost its tone. "There's only one thing."

He looked at her calmly.

"He won't fuck me. He's got the tongue of a maestro, but when push comes to shove he won't come across. Why do you think that is?"

His gaze slid past her.

"There must be an explanation," he said. "I'm sure he wants to. Who wouldn't?"

"I'm thinking maybe it's his weird way of staying faithful to his wife."

"Interesting theory."

"Don't get me wrong, I love cunnilingus. It's one of life's greatest pleasures. And he does it very well."

"Does he?" There was a slight tremble of concentric lines—a grimace, perhaps a smile—at the corners of Larry's mouth.

"*Very* well. In fact the first few times I kept thinking, Boy, is this ever nice. But the fact is there are other times, and I'm afraid this may be one of them, where going down just doesn't cut it."

"Sure." He clucked his tongue. "I know just what you mean."

By now their penumbra of irony was a torment for her. It was beginning to feel terminal.

"Are you holding back for Kippy?" she asked suddenly. "Is that the idea? Do you think it somehow makes it less adulterous if you don't actually go ahead and stick it in? Because I have to tell you, that's one very slippery slope."

"It's not for Kippy," he said.

"For who then?"

He bent at the waist to examine his ankles. The process was not uncomplicated.

"It's difficult," he mumbled toward his shoes. "I don't know if I have the words."

The words, she thought. It always comes down to the words with these guys. And they're never there.

Stanley had told her once, in the course of a hot, indolent summer matinee, about a Pacific island named Lifu. In Lifu, the male sex organ was called his *word.* "Sort of like Christianity," he'd murmured, casually slipping her flowered panties down her thighs. "In the beginning, the Word. Only in the Lifu creation myth it's the word that creates the Father, not the other way around. Then the Father heads off into the Great Emptiness, touches it with a dream-thread, and *Shazam!* The world."

"What about the mother?" Bonnie had demanded. "Where does she fit in?"

"Who knows? Probably she's the Great Emptiness."

"Typical."

"Now, now. Don't be cranky." He'd teased her nipple in slow, maddening circles with the palm of his hand. It was one of his more effective debating strategies. If Harvard were a single woman, Stanley Gotffried would have been hired with full tenure already. "Obviously the whole myth is just a substitute for the repressed concept of parental coitus. The penis, the seminal fluid, and so forth. Your Big Bang."

"All right," she'd groaned, "go ahead."

"What?"

"Give it to me," she'd said. "Give me your word."

The problem, looking back, was that she had more faith in language than Stanley did. Words would issue from his mouth like soapsud bubbles, swimmy and rainbowed, free-floating. It was only later, after he'd ducked into a cab and was halfway to Logan, that they popped, leaving you out on the sidewalk, sticky and wet and choking on exhaust, to sort out what he meant. But then what could you expect, she thought, from a man whose idea of intimacy—like the rest of his ideas, it bore remarking—had been liberally appropriated from Lacan. Love was giving something you didn't have to someone you didn't know. Words too. Words to guys like Stanley were just spatial clusters of noise. Sound bytes. He flung them around like poker chips wherever he went.

Meanwhile here was Larry Albeit, a more literal person altogether, sitting before her with his lips pursed, shaking his high-domed head. "I'm sure it's just a question of the dosage," he said mildly. "It's never been an issue for me before."

"Yeah, yeah. That's what they all say."

"Anyway, they've got pills for this sort of thing now."

"I've heard that."

"They're supposed to be very effective," he said. "I'll check with my insurance about coverage."

"It's not fair," Bonnie complained. "For me it's just the opposite.

I'm horny as hell. Off the charts. Ogelvie says the drug got rid of all my tension, and now my primary drives are coming out."

Larry smiled wistfully. "I felt that way at first too," he said. "At least I think I did."

"Good Lord, Larry. Give it up. Isn't there anything worth keeping from your old life?"

"It's not like that, Bonnie."

"What *is* it like?"

"Don't you know?" Beseechingly, he lifted his eyes to hers. "It's like travel," he said.

"Right," she said, manifesting through the exhalation of her breath a bit more skepticism than she felt. To be fair, the concept of it being like travel seemed remote but not entirely unfamiliar. She too had traveled once.

"Every night I'm out there exploring, like Jacques Cousteau. Worlds within worlds. Uncharted territory. Way down deep."

"Uh-huh."

"But I'm not there yet. I'm hoping to go deeper. Stay down longer. I want that power you get when you control the dream. Prolong it at will. Because going in and out every day, it's problematic. You lose a lot of the good stuff."

"A little in and out," she muttered, "is all I'm basically asking for here."

"My goal," he declared, "is total immersion. That's the ideal. In a perfect world I'd sleep twenty-four hours a day. Nothing else. Just that."

"And then?"

"Then I'd come back."

"To what?"

He smiled. "Whatever's around."

"Brrronkk," she said. "Wrong answer."

"There," he said eagerly. "That's it in a nutshell. I *know* the right answer; I've *done* the right answer. I've had it up to here with right answers. What I want is to *not* know for a change. Just jump in headfirst and flounder around. It's the uncertainty, the risk, that wakes you up to things."

"Things? What about people?"

"People." He blinked serenely. "Sure. But people, how do I put this? It's something you learn from talk radio. People are things too."

"Gee, thanks a lot."

"I don't mean that in a pejorative sense," he said. "Things are just things; it's the connections between them that're important. That's where the energy is, the secret life. Take plants," he said. There was something cool and creamy in his tone that was beginning to alarm her. "Plants sleep all the time. It's how they experience the world. They have this deep sonar that records what's going on around them. That's what I want. My big goal. To be like a plant."

"I've got news for you, Larry. You're closer than you think."

Larry Albeit watched this remark wing right by, his face unstirred by the breeze.

"Look," she said, "isn't there any easier way? Can't you just drop acid once in a while like most people?"

Now Larry gazed at her tolerantly from the heights, or depths, of his sonar consciousness. "Acid's just a light show," he said. "Something for kids to do at rock concerts. It isn't the real thing."

"And this is?"

"I'm not sure. Maybe. I admit it's slower. More demanding. You've got to shed some baggage to make it work. That's the key. Let go. Find the zero. Travel light."

"But what if you get lost? How do you get back?"

"There *is* no lost," Larry opined smoothly. "Don't you see? There's only our small, localized anxieties, all the bullshit surface tension we rely on to hold us together. What to make for the dinner party, what to do about the car, what the weather's going to be tomorrow. We've got to break through that stuff. Find the water in the rock. Break down the ego. Become not one, but thousands. Not one. No one. None one. None."

"Jesus Christ." She stared at him in horror. "You're beginning to sound like *Finnegans Wake.*"

"Is that good?"

"You're losing it, Larry. Jacques Cousteau! You're having a fucking breakdown."

"On the contrary," he said, "a break*through.* The fact is I'm seeing things a lot more clearly now. They're all in pieces but there's a unity too. Like the law. Now, the law's a very good system, I agree. But it's awfully fragmented, and that's where the problems come in. What I'm looking to find is the law *below* the law. What they call in physics a unified field. 'Cause it's down there somewhere. I've read about it. On the subatomic level it's all particles and waves. A great, timeless ocean. One big flux."

Suddenly she had a craving for a drink. A drink and a cigarette.

"You should go back to work," she said. "You need structure, Larry. We all do. Too much freedom wears you out."

"But I am working, Bonnie. It's just my office has changed. My hours." He yawned. "Though when I do go back," he added, "I'm thinking I may teach."

"What, become a law professor? That's a great idea. You'd be good at that."

"No, no. I mean *real* teaching," he said. "Kids. Pledging the flag. Assemblies. Field trips on the bus. Answering simple, straightforward questions about forests and pond life. I had a dream about it the other night. It was terrifically pleasant."

A thought occurred to her.

"This thing with me," she said. "Is that work too?"

"Absolutely," he said, beaming. "The very best kind."

"Well, I'd like to see you work a little harder at it then. How about taking off your pants."

"Fine." Obligingly he undid his belt and began to work his trousers down his hips. "But can I just ask you something?"

"Sure."

"You know those big droopy stalks with scarlet blossoms, the ones you see in the park in the summer? You know what they're called?"

She nodded. "Love-lies-bleeding."

"Amazing," he said. "Me, I had to look it up, but you already know."

"Mmm." Unbuttoning her shirt, she frowned down at her dimpled belly. Was she beginning to show?

"It's only now that I've stopped going to the office that I'm starting to learn about all this stuff I never paid attention to. Isn't that strange? You, Kippy and the girls, all those young mothers and au pairs who hang out in the park—you're my teachers now."

"What makes you think we want to be?" she snapped. "Do you have any idea how tiring it is, having to instruct you guys all the time?"

"I see your point," he said. "But what's the alternative? Business as usual? Because believe me, when it comes to middle-aged men, you've got your work cut out for you. Not much room left on the hard drives, I'm afraid. They're all cluttered up with sports, mutual funds, mortgage rates, cholesterol counts. Basically we're talking numbers."

It appeared sex was on hold for the moment. His pants had snagged around his knees. And she was beginning to get chilly without her shirt. "It's because they're afraid," she said.

"Afraid of what? Tumors?"

"Women."

"Well, can you blame them? You're so demanding, you women. So exhausting. I'm not saying it's your fault. Probably it's hormonal, all those monthly surges, the ebbing and flowing . . . the way you're always trying to *do* things, *improve* things . . . it's very admirable in some ways. I mean, you never see a bunch of women sitting around on a nice day watching golf on TV." He ran a hand through his hair and sighed. "The fact is, nowadays when I go to a dinner party, I don't even bother with the husbands anymore. I go straight for the kitchen. That's where you find out the good stuff. Whose mother is dying, whose kid has a learning disability, who's getting divorced because her aunt left her a thousand shares of Pfizer and a big apartment on Waverly Place. It's a whole different language in the kitchen. Books, food, parents, children. Relations between one thing and another. Sexual secrets. There's nothing quite so compelling as the sight of a mature, intelligent woman in a sleeveless dress arranging flowers in a vase." He paused. "Why so sad?"

"Because," she said, "that used to be me."

"It will be again. I promise."

"No, it won't. Someone has to be watching. To notice."

"*I'll* notice." He reached for her hand, stroking it tenderly, absently.

No, sex was not in the cards, she thought. Not tonight. Perhaps, from the way things were going, not ever. "That's going to be my mission in life," he said. "To live among women and notice the way you do things. Salad dressings. Halloween costumes. So much ingenuity, such technical know-how. Just sitting down when you pee—I mean, what a nice, efficient way to go about it. So meditative."

"I've never thought about it that way."

"Of course not. It comes naturally for you, so you take it for granted." He scratched his stomach thoughtfully. "I like the female approach. I'm thinking of joining Kippy's book group, on the condition they don't let in any other men but me. They seem willing to consider this. There's just one drawback."

"What's that?"

"I can't seem to read anymore. I'm too high up. The words are like ants marching across the page."

"Maybe they'll let you audit. Sit in the back and listen."

"Really? Can you do that?"

"Half my students don't read the books we discuss in class. It has no effect on the absorption rate, from what I can see."

Larry nodded thoughtfully. She noticed he was holding his stomach again.

"What's up with you, anyway?" she asked. "You look awful."

"Stomach problems. I was on the potty all day. Dribble dribble. Can't keep things solid down there."

"And Kippy? Where's she tonight?"

"Home," he said. "Kippy's home with Caitlin and Rebecca. I, on the other hand, am not."

"May I ask what you told her that allowed this to come to pass?"

He shrugged. "I said I was coming to see you."

"How candid of you."

"Oh, she wasn't surprised. She knows I like you. She's heard your name a lot these past few months."

"She has?" A small flame leapt in her chest. "Why?"

"Can't be helped. Apparently I talk in my sleep. Apparently I talk *a lot* in my sleep." He yawned then, as if the very mention of sleep was enough at this point to summon it forward. His breath smelled stale. "And I've been sleeping quite a bit lately, as you know."

"Goddamn it, Larry. You have no right."

"Right?"

"This involves me too. Can't you be a little fucking discreet?"

"Don't worry." Larry waved his wrist. "It's all part of the plan. I give Kippy a little truth, and that distracts her from the larger one. Partial-chaos theory in action."

All of a sudden she was reminded of the parent meeting. Nothing had changed. He was still using her to certify his courage, to license his escape, and she was still allowing it. "You've lost your sense of proportion," she said. "You're confusing partial chaos for the real thing."

"Could be," he said absently. "Mind if I sit down for a minute? My eyes are burning."

"I think you better go."

"Just for a minute," he said, leaning back. "You have no idea how good it feels."

"You know what'll feel good? When you and your limp dick dribble right out of here."

Larry nodded serenely. "I understand, of course. It's still early for you. One foot in, one foot out. You haven't committed yourself. But if you trust me I can help."

"Look at you, Larry: you can't even hold up your end of a conversation without falling over. Would *you* trust you?"

The man on the sofa, his eyes closing now, appeared to give this question some careful thought before he spoke. Or perhaps he was asleep. Before he could arrive at a response, in any case, the phone began to ring. The answering machine was on, but Bonnie sprang out of her chair instinctively to get it. She did not reach the kitchen until the fourth ring, so she and the machine picked up simultaneously, which ensured that the short, none-too-friendly conversation that followed was not just recorded for posterity but also heightened by a quantum factor in volume and pathos and reverberatory strangeness.

"It was for you," she said when she was done.

"What'd she want?" he murmured groggily.

"To remind you about the Outliving Cancer meeting tomorrow night."

"I'd have seen it on the kitchen calendar anyway."

"Not unless you can see through walls."

He opened his eyes. "She's kicking me out?"

"Not in so many words."

"How many does it take?" A dull light burned in Larry's cheeks; for a moment he almost looked angry.

"What's the matter?" she asked brightly. "Wasn't this part of the plan?"

Larry didn't answer. He had the look of a man considering some new and provocative idea.

"Uh-uh," she said. "Don't even think about it."

"Not even one night?"

"No way. What's that saying? You slept in that bed, now make it?"

He looked puzzled. "I think you've got it backward."

That flower was in her head again, the one whose name she already knew but Larry, she thought, had only just begun to learn. "No," she said. "You're the one who has it backward."

19

Salts and Sugars

THIS TIME Ian did not forget the Danish. This time he was waiting in front of the bakery when it opened in the dismal, agate dawn, his nose pressed to the steamed-up window, trying to rub the glass clear with the palm of his hand. It was half past six. Inside he could hear a phone ringing, doors slamming open and shut, metal trays rattling into slots. A radio was playing, not music but talk—a couple of A.M. personalities swapping loud, jocular banter. For those who woke up early, the world was full of amusing jokes. Woke up early or stayed up late.

Ian meanwhile had just done both: worked until two on the project, then rose again at six for the drive down to Walpole. Had things been going even a little less badly with the shamrock spiders, he'd have felt entitled to knock off at a reasonable hour the night before. But the spiders had stopped responding to the drug. To *every*thing. Their metabolisms were way off, their energies depleted. Ian had taken to elevating the dosages on an almost daily basis, but it was no use; the most rudimentary functions—eating, drinking, sleeping—seemed beyond their powers. And the webs, they were a joke, not even remotely serviceable at this point. It would be a very feeble and disoriented fly indeed that allowed itself to be ensnared in such pitiable, tattered ruins. The spiders themselves seemed embarrassed by their efforts. They had taken to cowering lethargically in the back corners of their cages while Ian, pen in hand, stared at them dolefully, his logbook full of cross-outs and erasures, trying to find a language that would convey what had happened, a strategy that might somehow convince Howard Heflin or anyone else on the planet that this was, or could be made to seem, a favorable result.

Luckily he was far too stressed out at the moment to worry about Howard Heflin. He had Big Don Erway and his rapacious appetite for sweets to worry about first.

A red-haired woman in an apron came and unlocked the bakery door. Ian stepped inside. At once he was enveloped by a moist, yeasty cloud that might have been the earth's own breath if the earth, he thought, were a much nicer place. He breathed it in gratefully. Though as a rule he did not care for high concentrations of sugary carbohydrates, in his haste to depart the loft without waking Barbara (she'd been up most of the night too, clomping around in her paint-spattered clogs, getting ready for her show) he'd skipped breakfast, and now he was starving. And besides, the Danish looked so merry in their festive displays, so puffy and light and full of color, with their ridged sockets of shell and their wide glazed pupils of congealed fruit—like eyes in search of a face, he thought—he found it almost hard to believe they were real, and not some fantastic, impossible confection born of whimsy and desire.

"Can I help you?" The woman in the apron reached for a piece of wax paper. Helpfulness appeared to be her specialty. Behind her bright offerings she hovered, almost shy, a fine smoke of commerce in her gaze. The first sale of a new day. It seemed a responsibility of sorts. Because Ian was enjoying her attention, and because he was famished, and because this would be, he hoped, his last visit down to the penitentiary for quite some time, he lingered at the counter somewhat longer than he intended, running his hands over the sloping glass—which soaked up the overhead light and dispensed it in graceful benediction over the goods below—before at last giving voice to all the many things it occurred to him to want at the moment: specifically, a brioche, two almond croissants, a pain au chocolat, a cinnamon roll, a maple bar, a bear claw, a lemon scone, and, strictly as an afterthought, two onion bagels topped with a pale, stubbly, fake-but-appealing-looking substance called Asiago cheese.

Who said he wasn't a spontaneous person? Here he was, Ian thought, spending all this money he couldn't afford to part with on all these pastries he didn't care for, and thoroughly enjoying every moment of it. He watched the woman fit them into bags with her long, knowing hands. The bagels she put in last, which meant they were on top, which worked out exceedingly well an hour later; bagels with Asiago cheese being, it so happened, a particular favorite of Big Don Erway's, especially washed down with the double cappuccino Ian had also been thoughtful enough to bring, though in a separate bag, of course, so as to avoid any spillage or soaking action in the car that would ruin both his $18.65 investment in pastries and the good impression he hoped to make this time, as opposed to the bad impression he was fully aware he had made last time, for reasons too numerous and depressing to recall.

"Has it already been a month," Erway asked when he walked in, "or are you just anxious to see me?"

The chief psychiatrist was tilted backward in his swivel chair, feet crossed on the corner of his desk and fingers tented over his belt, like a man awaiting a shave. He needed one too, Ian thought. The stubble on his neck, brown and profuse, might have been scrawled there haphazardly by a child's crayon. His cheeks looked stoved-in, volcanic. Absently he held up his arm and scratched a spot just below the fatty biceps, where it tapered down to his elbow. He gazed over toward the door. His eyes held a glimmer of distant sadness. He might have been observing Ian through the wrong end of a telescope. It seemed equally plausible that he was not observing Ian at all.

"It's been a month," Ian said.

He set his two shopping bags full of pastry upon the desk, the surface of which was, he noticed, somewhat less disheveled than last time. Islands of gray blotter could now be seen amid the white sea of paper. Someone had either been working harder than usual, or else throwing more things out.

"Oh boy." Erway unlaced his fingers, leaned forward, and peeked into one shopping bag with satisfaction. "Treats."

"I kind of went overboard, I guess."

"No need to apologize. The point is, you cared. Message: you care."

Was the man drunk? Ian watched him pick out the coffee, peel off the lid, and breathe the steam in deeply, with a connoisseur's expression of withheld judgment.

"I take it you've heard," Ian said.

"Heard what?"

"The FDA. They're set to approve."

"Oh," Erway said. "That."

"They're saying it's for motion sickness. That's how the drug is being licensed. They don't even mention the other applicabilities."

"Multiple uses," Erway said. "Well, you can't blame them, amigo. Not with all that money at stake. It's human nature to hedge the bet."

"Human nature?" Ian asked bitterly.

"Motion sickness is your Trojan horse. It gets you in the gate. In a few years, no one'll remember what the original license was for. The facts'll be on the ground." Erway took a noisy, not altogether efficient slurp of his coffee. A residue of milk foam attached itself to his mustache and clung on; it gave him an air of Falstaffian jollity. When he set down the cup he began extracting the various baked goods one by one, inspecting them with the quick, inquisitive eye of a customs official. "You've bought in yourself, I hope."

"Bought in what?"

"Jesus, man. Don't you read the paper? Furst went up eighteen points, thanks to that little blue night-light of yours. And it hasn't even been officially announced yet."

"I'm afraid I don't really follow the market, Dr. Erway."

"Of course not. Forget it." Erway waved his hand. "I'm feeling cranky today. Pay no attention to that man behind the curtain."

Ian found himself entertaining the very appealing prospect of never having to see Don Erway again. On the other hand, there was always another study. "I thought you'd be relieved," he said, "to have the trials over."

"My wife says I'm a repressed person. In her opinion I'm not as in touch with my emotions as I should be."

"Maybe you still have reservations? What we talked about last time, that Gulf War vet? You were concerned about him, you said."

"Was I?" Erway hesitated; he fixed his gaze on the black stapler at the corner of his desk. "Was I really?"

"Eddie, his name was. You gave me the file. You seemed to think he may have suffered some kind of irreparable damage as a result of the trial methodologies."

"Yeah, Eddie," Erway said gloomily. "Eddie the Great. Well, what did you find out?"

"Actually, I've been incredibly busy these last few weeks. It's been a crazy time. I haven't even got—"

"Forget it," Erway said, waving his hand. "I'll save you the trouble. A modest increase in the catecholamines. Vasopressin, endorphin, prolactin. Some gastric and intestinal motility. You'll see it in the reports."

"But those symptoms all indicate acute fear response."

"Is that so." Erway took a bite of his bagel and chewed it with laconic thoroughness before swallowing it down. "Well, maybe he was a little spooked, at that."

"I'd like to see him, please," Ian said. "Today. Right now. I have some questions, maybe some tests I could ru—"

"Sorry, amigo. He's been released."

"From the program, you mean? Or the whole prison?"

Erway wiped his wide mouth daintily and then crumpled his napkin into a ball. "From everything." Taking aim with one eye, he fired the paper at the trash can in the corner. It bounced noiselessly off the rim and onto the carpet. There was something about the way it bounced, the height and the angle of it, the accidental distance, that made Ian suddenly afraid.

"You don't mean he's dead, do you? Because there's something about the way you just said 'from everything' that sounds a lot like the way you might talk about someone being dead."

"Eddie's up in East Lowell. That's where he's from."

"Thank God."

"You wouldn't say that, I don't think, if you'd ever been to East Lowell."

"It makes no sense," Ian blurted. "How did they get it approved this fast? There are supposed to be several reviews."

Erway gave him a cool glance of assessment.

"All right," he said, "I'll give you a hint. Check out who's on the review board. I know, it's supposed to be a big secret. But with a little ingenuity and about ten minutes of computer time you can crack it."

"So?"

"So memorize the names. In six months, look again. You'll notice a number of intriguing changes."

"People move on. Is that unusual?"

"Not at all," Erway said. "Neither is it unusual if, say, a little ways down the road, one or two of those same names happen to turn up on the executive council of Merck, or Sandoz, or SmithKline-Beecham. Or even, lo and behold, our very own Furst Pharmaceuticals. International consultants or some such. Highly remunerative work. The junkets alone would blow your mind."

"But that can't be legal."

Erway made a desultory *comme ci, comme ça* gesture with the flat of his hand. "Borderline," he said.

"So," Ian said, "there's pressure from Furst."

"Not from. On."

"I don't understand. I thought Furst was this huge multinational corporation."

"You should read the business pages once in a while," Erway said. "Furst got bought five months ago by Trianon. Now they're the pharmaceutical division of a much huger multinational corporation. But that won't last either, because Trianon's about to be merged into Central Home Products."

Ian shook his head.

"There's no reason you'd have heard of them," Erway said. "A no-name coffee packager out in Ohio or someplace. Cups, filters, second-rate beans, institutional supplies. Middleman stuff."

"Coffee?" Ian remembered the three initials on the bottom of his mug back at the lab. *CHP.*

"That's how they started. Only one day the founder of the company gets a brain embolism, and his son comes into the picture. The son went to Oberlin, fancies himself enlightened. Everyone tells him to sell out to his competitors and retire. But no, he's got big ideas. He *buys.* Corporate progressivism, he calls it. Capitalism with a human face. Industrial self-reliance. Pretty soon he's gone and scooped up a coffee farm, a fleet of trucks, a Styrofoam factory. To deal with lighteners and sweeteners he brings in a couple of chemists from Parke-Davis. What does he care if he exhausts his capital? It's his dad's money anyway. But he gets lucky. The chemists come up with something they can sort of get away with calling organic. The food co-ops and nonprofits go wild for it. Then after a year or two the economy takes off, the company goes public, and *Boom!* Suddenly the kid's richer than Croesus and he's got this fancy new board of directors, the very best names. So what do they do? They kick Mr. Young Visionary out on his ass and bring in a new guy, very tough, very practical, to negotiate with Trianon."

"I thought Trianon was an agricultural concern," Ian said.

"It's nutraceuticals now. Chemically enhanced foods. The idea is you shouldn't have to make separate trips to the drugstore and supermarket. Two for the price of one." Having finished off all the pastry, Erway began to nibble at the brioche. Savory to sweet, and then back again. Beneath their heavy lids his eyes were lit up like lanterns, fueled by salts and sugars seeking harmony, alignment. "So now they'll have the whole thing covered, won't they? They'll wake you up, they'll feed you, they'll put you to sleep. Money round the clock. A perfect cycle."

"You make it sound like some kind of conspiracy," Ian said.

"Not at all," Erway said. "It's the free market."

"Is that all anyone talks about anymore? The market?"

"The market is a wondrous thing," Erway said. "It's worthy of respect. You should see my last quarterly report. Hell, I may be able to retire next year."

"So why dig up all this dirt on Trianon then? What do you care?"

"I don't. It's just that I've got this fancy Pentium computer the governor bought me, and sometimes in my lunch hour I like to hunt and peck and see what turns up. That's all. Information's a spectator sport, amigo. Nowadays, you can do it from your chair."

"I better head back," Ian said. He was beginning to feel the early hour of his waking; it made him spacey and light-headed just when he was in need of the opposite, of extra gravity and sureness. But so be it. He picked up the files, the final reports on phase two trials of substance D. They were lighter than he expected. But then why shouldn't they be? The whole thing was riddled with holes.

"Rush's dream," he said.

"What about it?"

"I looked it up in the library," Ian said. "I just wanted you to know that. I understand what it means."

"I doubt that." Erway's mouth made a small pucker. "Yessir, I doubt that very much."

"Look, whatever you may think, I'm not the bad guy here, Dr. Erway. I'm working really hard to do the right thing."

"You're a young man with potential, we all agree."

It was useless. Ian opened his briefcase and stuck in the files.

Erway smiled sadly. "Back to the spiders, eh? And the mice. How are the little cuties? Still doing the backstroke?"

"As a matter of fact they are."

"Had to double the dosage, though, right? Or was it triple?"

Ian stared at the calendar, avoiding the man's eyes. March was a gray landscape, the white squares below clotted busily with pencil marks. Soon it would be April, bright and blue. Soon they could all turn the page.

"Ah well," Erway said, magnanimous. *"C'est la vie."*

Ian cleared his throat. "I can get Eddie's address from the warden's office, I assume."

"Sure. Ask for Natalie. She's my favorite down there."

"I will." Ian paused. "There's just one last thing."

"Jesus Christ."

"A patient I've been treating the past two months. She's about forty. Single mother. Pregnant. Her presenting complaints were early morning awakening and prolonged depression."

"Who wouldn't be depressed? The poor woman's exhausted."

"Exactly. That's why I accepted her into the study. I've got a copy of her polysomnogram right here. There's just this one irregular component that I wanted to discuss with you. Something I did on my own."

"Uh-oh."

"No, no," Ian said. "Everything's under control. It's just, this thing I did, I can't talk about it with anyone up there. Dr. Heflin, he . . . The study's supposed to be strictly double-blind. But I wanted, I had this feeling, you see, that she was the perfect—" He looked up to see Erway shaking his head. "What?"

"How much?"

"How much what?"

"How much do you intend to pay me for this consult?"

"Why should I pay you anything?"

"Isn't it obvious? I'm a licensed professional with two advanced degrees."

"All right," Ian said, "here. I spent eighteen dollars and sixty-five cents on this food you're eating. The coffee was another two and a quarter. That's over twenty."

"With tax," Erway pointed out generously, "it would be more."

"Call it twenty-two then. What'll it buy me, you son of a bitch? Five minutes of your valuable time? Ten?"

Erway was silent for a moment.

"Fuck it," he announced, as if concluding an argument with himself. "Don't you know when you're being kidded? C'mere, c'mere. I'll do it for free."

20

Couriers

"YOUR APPOINTMENT," Christina informed her at the reception desk, "was for nine-fifteen."

"Sorry. I overslept."

"By three hours?"

"I've got a lot of sleep loss stored up," Bonnie explained, fidgeting with a recalcitrant pen at the sign-in clipboard. She let out, as both symptom and illustration, a huge, not quite voluntary yawn. "That must be what it is."

"I heard of eating for two," Christina said. "I never heard of sleeping for two."

"Well, I'm doing both."

"So I see," Christina said archly.

Bonnie flushed. Because she had been so brazen as to mess with the fine print of the schedule, she would now be forced to endure insults from this petulant young woman and her twenty-eight-inch waist. "Maybe it's the vitamins," she said. "Or those amniotic hormones they talk about."

"You look okay," Christina said, by way of apology perhaps, or accusation. "You're not showing too much."

"It's on the inside," Bonnie said.

She noted the continuing presence of the Tintoretto postcard on the corkboard above the desk. A good sign, she thought. Christina's sunken and judgmental expression, however, was a bad one. Were her scheduling duties really that important to her, or had she fought with her boyfriend again? Hector. She wondered if the girl knew how heroic and doomed-inflected that name was. Would it be too presumptuous—too teacherly—to ask? For they were all on epic journeys, she felt certain of that now, all the women in the waiting room, on all sides of the desk. Sailing off from burning, plundered cities, winding their way toward some elusive distant promise of home.

"I'll try to work you in," Christina said reluctantly. "But it's not up to me."

"I understand."

"Friday afternoons are the worst. People are in a hurry."

"That reminds me, I need to be back by three," Bonnie said. "My kids."

"I'll do the best I can," Christina said evenly. Was she getting pissed off all over again? "Why don't you have a seat?"

But instead Bonnie went down to the coffee shop in the lobby, where, making an immediate enemy of the waitress by plunking herself down at a table for four, she occupied herself with her second tuna sandwich in as many hours. With it she ate a small bowl of salad, crunchy but tasteless, despite its decorative sprinkling of Bac*Os; followed by a wedge of glutinous pie topped with Reddi-Wip, the fruit of which appeared to bear some kind of vestigial and attenuated relation to the apple. And a glass of milk, laden no doubt with BHT. Somehow all these additives combined to leave her hollow and unsatiated.

Restless, she wandered back through the lobby, pausing to conduct a slow, comprehensive survey of the hospital directory. Siraj was listed under Building A, Ogelvie under Building B. The sleep lab was on the eleventh floor of Building B, but the anxiety clinic, to which it was connected by referrals, was on the nineteenth floor of Building A. It all seemed needlessly stupid and confusing, like her setup at the college. Perhaps this was the guiding principle of institutional life, she thought: to keep you perpetually on the move, nosing your way like a lab mouse through the maze of corridors, chasing some moldering promise of reward. Often, as she made the rounds of her vocational appointments, Bonnie felt like little more than a glorified courier. A busy but passive conveyor of specialized instructions, written by others, directed toward others. Running here and there with her bag of hastily written, hastily evaluated papers, tossing greetings over her shoulder, forever on the verge of arrival.

She was down to her last three pills.

Since their last appointment, she'd left half a dozen messages on his machine, but Ogelvie had not called her back. Nor had he put in an appearance at any of her subsequent follow-ups, leaving her instead to the ministrations of his young, gum-chewing, bottle-blond intern, Emily Firestone. Fortunately, considering her youth and inexperience, Emily was a terrifically soothing, competent presence—much more so in some ways than Ogelvie himself—once you got past the fact that she did nothing but complain about the projects she was assigned and the careless way she was being supervised by the senior staff, Ogelvie foremost among them. "They're smart people around here," Emily had said last time, "but they're really inflexible. They think they know everything."

"Well, you can't leave," Bonnie replied. "This is practically my second home these days. I couldn't bear to be orphaned."

"Oh, Dr. Ogelvie hasn't forgotten you. He's monitoring your case very closely."

"He is?"

"Uh-huh. Sometimes he's here all night at the computer. He's incredibly focused."

"Think he's cute?" Bonnie had asked.

Emily shrugged. Three bangled bracelets slid down each arm. Her coloring, whether a product of makeup, blood pressure, or some recent out-of-state solar exposure, was approximately that of a cantaloupe. "He's okay, I guess."

"There's just this way he has of looking at you," Bonnie said. "Like he's reading your brain waves. What's his wife like?"

"He's not married."

"Are you sure?"

"Uh-huh. He lives with his sister. Someone told me he was gay."

"I don't think so."

"Me neither. Know what he said last week? He was talking about you. He said: 'She's the key. I'm sure of it.' "

"The key to what?" Bonnie asked. The idea was both attractive and unsettling.

"Who knows? Probably this big paper he's been working on. He's got all these notes he lugs around in his briefcase. But you should ask him yourself."

Bonnie intended to do just that right now, today, while she waited for her appointment with Siraj. All the way over to Building B she counseled herself to remain civil and accepting. Three pills left: it would not do to antagonize him.

She recalled Ogelvie's face as he labored over her that night. He had not seemed very adept, very together. At the time, of course, she had been focused on all the ways in which she herself was not together. But looking back on it, she began to wonder if she hadn't somehow managed to infect him with her own anxieties; if, as in the second reel of some old black-and-white horror movie, she and Ogelvie had during the course of that night accidentally switched brains. Perhaps that was why he had been so difficult to reach these past weeks. She pictured him skulking around Boston, hollow-eyed and stooped, laden with the baggage of sleeplessness and despair that had formerly been hers.

To whom did the sleep doctors turn when *they* couldn't sleep? Who oversaw the overseers?

Naturally when she got to his office Ogelvie wasn't in. From the multiple layers of pink Post-it sheets over his office door, he had either not been in for a couple of days or was paying no heed to his messages. She found one with her own name on it, tore it into pieces, and left them scattered on the floor, so he would have to walk over them to get inside. For all the good he had done her he had proved feckless, irresponsible; she wanted her name to stick to his shoes.

Downstairs, the sleep lab too was quiet and dark, save for the kaleidoscopic screen-saver program unfurling languidly on the monitor. Boris Zenko wasn't in either. Night workers: she supposed they answered to a different authority. She remembered the smell of booze in the technician's office. Probably they were all on something. Uppers, downers. Whatever helped them listen in on what Ogelvie called *the big secret.* But no doubt they could get away with things, under cover of darkness, that other people couldn't.

Feeling aimless, dispossessed, she roamed the corridors. Pediatrics. Orthopedics. Radiology. She did not know what she was looking for, or if she was looking at all. She merely walked the floors, trudging dutifully up and down the stairs, viewing each ward—Cardiology, Internal Medicine, Neurology—as though it were a station on some obscure private pilgrimage. All the beds were full. People lay with their eyes closed in the unwavering light, dreaming of health. IV's trickled silently in their slings. Televisions hung from the ceilings, murmuring dolefully, the anchormen dangling like genies in the air. She tried not to listen. No news, she thought. No news, and no weather. To everything there was a season and goddamn it this was hers. She was swelling with life; she wanted no close encounters just now with the other side.

Geriatrics. Oncology.

She stopped to drink from a fountain; the water, shockingly cold, tasted of chemicals.

Only in the obstetrics ward did she allow herself to pause, to linger, curious, before the wide windows. But no, it was here too, everything she'd been trying to avoid—the bald heads, the writhing, undersized bodies, the gummy, voiceless mouths—the whole furious flailing project of the species. Once you entered the hospital, there was no getting free. The hospital was a closed system. The end present in the beginning, the beginning present in the end. All one thing.

Her head was swimming. Her belly, that swelling globe, felt abnormally tight at the equator. A name echoed through the corridor. Someone was being paged. Though she knew it could not be her, she hurried back to Siraj's waiting room anyway.

And a good thing she did. Because Christina had squeezed her in after all.

* * *

"You are one of the lucky ones," Siraj told her, fitting on the gloves. "Some women look worse as the weeks go by. The impression, if I may say, is of a war being lost. But you, my dear, look better and better."

"Liar," she said. Nonetheless her mood began to lighten at once.

"Not at all. There is a radiance. It's a matter, dear girl, of simple physiology. A second heart now beats inside you. Because of this your circulatory capacities are enhanced. Hence more blood is sent up to your face. And so we have the proverbial glow."

How thrilling, she thought, to be given such a clear, rational origin for such a vague and intangible effect. It reminded her of how she used to feel browsing through the OED, finding the root of some obscure, heavily corrupted word.

"I've always wanted one," she confessed. "A radiance, I mean."

"Everyone does, my dear. That's why there are so many babies. Babies and obstetricians."

"I suppose you're right." She tried to fight back a yawn.

"Tired, hmm?"

"Actually I've been sleeping a lot better lately. A lot better and a lot longer."

"Excellent." Siraj unhooked the fetal monitor from its speaker and breathed on the end to warm it. "And your appetite? It is satisfactory, you would say?"

"Voracious. Almost scary."

"Heartburn? Flatulence? Swollen veins? Nasal congestion? Vaginal discharge?"

"Hardly any at all."

"Marvelous."

"It's so strange. It's completely the opposite of last time. I feel like I'm getting younger, not older. Have you ever heard of such a thing?"

"One hears," Siraj allowed generously, "a little bit of everything."

"I suppose you would."

"The body is like weather. It defies our best efforts at prediction. Doctors know this, but to admit it would effectively weaken our authority. So instead we have this fantastic conspiracy of bullshit. Isn't that so, Cynthia?"

Cynthia, the blond, voiceless nurse who was always around and yet whose sole apparent function appeared to be to provide Siraj with a foil, gave one of her impassive and recessive nods.

"Can I quote you on that?" Bonnie asked.

"Ho ho. You certainly may not. But you may go over to the table and lie down."

She followed his instructions. Loosening the buckle of her pants, she squirmed them down past her hips. With every movement the slick white sanitary paper beneath her crinkled and snapped, registering the imprint of her body like a text.

"Sixteen weeks," she declared, shaking her head. Beneath her tone of weary incredulity, she felt a secret, inexpressible pleasure in saying it aloud. "Hard to believe."

He glanced over his shoulder. "You have already given Cynthia your urine?"

"Got it," Cynthia said.

"Marvelous."

"I've always liked peeing into a cup," Bonnie admitted. "There's this nice feeling of usefulness."

"Do you hear, Cynthia?" Siraj beamed. "I tell my nurses: handle every urine sample with care. They are nature's haiku. The compression of data, the little dance of sugars and proteins. Quite miraculous. One knows when one looks at a urine sample that nothing in life is ever wasted."

"I'll try to remember that," Bonnie said, "if I ever finish my dissertation."

"Ho ho!" Siraj chanted. His eyes narrowed appreciatively, not so much from mirth as recognition. They had been having these exchanges for some years now.

"So then," he said, checking his watch, "shall we move on to business?"

Smiling expectantly, he placed the monitor on her belly and moved it around in a slow, expert circle, as if polishing the skin, buffing it to a translucent shine. She closed her eyes. There was nothing to do but lie here. She was a courier, truly; she had only to carry this weight for a while, clear it through customs, and then she would be free to go.

Through the ultrasound speakers she heard nothing at first, or rather, the sound of nothing—an empty roar, loud and formless though not, she thought, uncontained, as if when you got right down to it the self was just a cave after all, a hollow space given over to primordial darkness, random gusts of wind. Was it possible to climb out, she wondered, or did one have to be lifted? There was no way to know. And then, her limbs became very light, very fluttery and useless, and her mass began to dissolve, her skin peeling like a fruit's—with every wave of Siraj's wand, another layer seemed to disappear—until she began to feel as if she were slowly being emptied into the machine. Whether this was something to be sought or feared she didn't know. But she had stopped fighting. She would welcome whatever came.

As if in reward for this placidity, a sound began to rise out of the emptiness and labor toward her, solemn and steady as a drumbeat. When Siraj moved the wand up her torso, the drumming rose with it. When he pulled back, it subsided. The rhythm was deliberate, full of purpose, like a busy and well-managed construction site. She listened to it approach with a kind of impersonal awe.

At last her eyes went moist with recognition.

"Oh," she said, "she's a good one, isn't she?"

"A darling," Siraj murmured above her.

"I could tell. I mean, once we started to get used to each other, I just knew. She's going to be the kind you can really talk with. The kind you can take to art museums and flea markets and the ballet, who won't pitch a fit at the Stop & Shop when you pass the Cap'n Crunch—"

"Try not to move, please."

"With boys," she burbled on mindlessly, "with boys you never rest. Not for a second. They're so skittish and fragile, there's always this danger you'll either wound them or smother them and then the rest of their lives they're in therapy. But with a girl, I can tell, it's going to be completely—"

She stopped. "What?"

"Mmm?"

"You're still fooling around with the monitor. Usually you've finished by now."

"One moment." He was palpating an area on her belly and cocking his head to listen. His almond eyes, under the fine black arches of his brows, were still. And yet the expression on his face remained scrupulous and pleasant, as if poised to receive a funny if rather obvious joke.

"Just breathe," he instructed her, "in the regular way."

"What's the regular way? I don't think anyone ever taught me."

"Less talking, my dear, would be a start."

"See," she said uneasily, "this is what I mean. Usually I'm done breathing by now."

"Sometimes there is this little game they play. Hiding and seeking. We must catch the slippery rascals just so as they swim around."

"Why are you all of a sudden talking to me like I'm the child?"

"Please, you must be quiet. I am trying to hear."

It was then she almost broke down and told him about the pills. Really, she would have said anything at all to erase the twin deltas of concern that were beginning to inscribe themselves at the corners of Siraj's mouth. "I don't understand. Didn't we just *hear* her? Wasn't that her being so assertive a second ago?"

Siraj smiled wanly. A quizzical disturbance had stolen into his eyes.

"Well?" she demanded.

"That was yours, my dear."

"Exactly what I said. That—"

"I mean your heart. Not the baby's."

"Oh," she said. "I see."

But in fact she saw nothing. How could she, when her eyes were closed? Obviously they had been closed the whole time. Obviously she was not in Siraj's tidy, sterile office at all, but still in her own bed at home, cocooned in her down comforter, still drifting through the warm, weightless universe of oversleep, only vaguely aware that in some other, parallel galaxy she was running late for her appointment at the hospital. She wasn't there, obviously. Obviously she was still at home, still sleeping, still drifting through the warm, weightless, et cetera, still operating under, still being operated upon, by the low, ruthless compulsions of a dream. Which was good. Which was fine. Because it meant that the sound she heard, or rather did not hear, or rather imagined she heard or did not hear washing through the tinny speakers of the monitor—that too was nothing. Just a random magnetic signal from inner space, cast off by some old, guttering star. A bit of cosmic flotsam, signifying nada.

Poor Siraj, of course, had no way of knowing it was only a dream. Siraj was only a translator of knowledge, a courier like herself; he had no power to generate its shape. He could only do what doctors always do to fill up empty space: he could only talk. So that's what he did. Apparently he had a great deal of additional information to convey on the subject of heartbeats and who they did or did not belong to and what this might or might not mean, and he went ahead and conveyed it, speaking with such an air of calm, reasonable assurance, of implicit coherence, that it began to occur to Bonnie after a while that the man was insane. Or if he wasn't, then her dream Siraj, her inner Siraj, was. The only other possibility, which had now begun to push its way into the crowded elevator of her mind, was that perhaps this wasn't in fact a dream after all. But then why could she not persuade her eyes to open? And why did the sound of nothing come flooding back now, that huge, impersonal roar with all its anger and indifference, and carry off his words?

"Cynthia? Do you have a minute, darling?"

And now, look, here came Cynthia again, plodding through the door in her white flat shoes. Cynthia, with her drably vacant eyes and her lank, uncongenial hair and her neat stack of manila charts cradled to the very latitudes of her torso where her breasts would be if she only had them . . . and then she could not hold it back any longer, the panic came whirling through her in a maddening, hypnotic spiral—had she swallowed that screen-saver back in the sleep lab?—lighting up her face in a series of bright, undulant flashes over which she was able to exercise, it seemed, zero control. And now Siraj was speaking to Cynthia in his lowest, quietest voice, asking her, no, telling her to make some calls, and Cynthia was nodding, yes yes yes. What choice did she have? Cynthia had no power to make or decide things. She too was only a courier. Everyone was. Cynthia dutifully took her message and went away, and now Bonnie was alone again, and Siraj was stroking her face with his long, clever hands, saying something wonderfully sensible about there being no reason to worry, none at all. Much of what he said after that was swallowed up by the noise of the machine. Something about the vagaries and vicissitudes of the equipment. Something about the ultrasound clinic on the third floor. Something about scheduling issues that applied to that hour of the afternoon, that day of the week, that month of the year. Something about there being no reason to worry. Something about tomorrow. Something about there being no reason to worry at all. Something about tomorrow and tomorrow and tomorrow. Something about there being no reason, no reason whatsoever, none, none at all—

21

Caped Crusader

As the clock on the VCR read 4:02, and there was no one around to instruct him otherwise, Petey went ahead and turned on *Batman.*

It wasn't, unfortunately, the *real Batman*—that is, the movie *Batman*. He had only seen the movie *Batman* once, the time Alex brought it home from the video store when he wasn't supposed to. Though Alex had also seen it a number of other times too, as he'd informed Petey in his usual mean, superior way—at the movie theater, and at his friend Jamey's house, Jamey being, it went without saying (though Alex said it anyway), a lot more fun to watch it and all other movies with too. Anyway, this wasn't that *Batman*. This was the cartoon *Batman,* the one on TV every day when he got home from preschool. Petey liked the cartoon *Batman* a lot, and tried to watch it as often as he could, though, because his mother didn't approve of watching TV, that turned out to be not very often at all.

But now his mother wasn't home, so he could do what he wanted. And he wanted to watch *Batman.*

He reached for the remote. Just pushing the red Power button with his own thumb gave him a cool, weightless feeling in his bones. He burrowed down into the cushions. The thing was, though he did not like to admit it even to himself, the cartoon *Batman* sort of frightened Petey a little, too. Oh sure, Batman was a good guy, trying to save the city and all that. But he could also look pretty mean when he wanted to, swooping around in that black mask and cape, with his square jaw and thin, colorless lips. Sometimes Petey wondered if Batman was really such a good guy after all. Could you be a good guy and a bad guy at the same time? He considered the question for a moment. Superman, of course, was good all the time. So were the X-Men, the Power Rangers, Scooby-Doo, and the Ninja Turtles. All good, all the time. Spiderman, on the other hand, had kind of a scary mask, and crawled up and down buildings a lot, and had a secret identity, just like Batman, where he was really two people at once. Yes, Spiderman was the same way: another good/bad guy who did a lot of weird stuff on rooftops at night.

That was another thing that sort of bothered Petey, now that he thought about it: the darkness. In the show it always seemed to be nighttime, and meanwhile outside it would be getting dark too, right at the same time, so what was happening on the screen seemed like part of this larger, darker thing that didn't end when the show did but settled over the whole house, like the night itself, and then later—much later, when he was alone in bed—soaked into his sleep. Maybe that was why his mother didn't like him to watch. She knew it scared him.

But it wasn't always easy these days to sort out what his mother approved of and what she didn't. Like most grown-ups, she *said* she didn't approve of watching TV—especially the kind of show he and Alex liked the most, which she called dark and violent and disgusting—but sometimes when she was reading papers for school it turned out to be all right, and sometimes when she needed to lie down for a little nap in the afternoon (they kept getting longer and longer, her little naps) it was all right, and whenever Cress came over to baby-sit it turned out to be all right, and if there happened to be some boring old kissing movie on that his mother liked, it was all right too. So it was hard to know when it really was all right to watch TV and when it wasn't.

Though it was probably all right now, he figured. Because his mother wasn't home yet. Her doctor's appointment was running late, *as usual,* Alex'd growled when he showed up at the preschool to walk

Petey home. Alex wasn't around either. He'd gone over to Jamey's house, even though he wasn't supposed to. He was supposed to be here, doing his language arts homework and keeping an eye on his little brother, who was, as no one ever got tired of reminding either one of them, too young to be left alone. But instead he'd dumped his backpack on the kitchen table and run off to Jamey's.

Jamey's house was fun. His mother was really nice, and they had a lot of great toys and computer games like *Morpheus II,* which Jamey had gotten for Christmas and which Alex had badly wanted too but didn't get it, their mother's computer being, as Alex said, "too old and crappy" to make the graphics work. That was probably what they were doing right now, in fact, playing *Morpheus II.* Trying to defeat the Dark Wizard and his poison nerve gas and rescue from his hooded legions the sleeping princess, once and for all.

So Petey, for only the second or third time in his life, was alone in the house. He didn't like it much. He wished Cress was around so they could watch together. One of the reasons Cress was so much fun to watch with was the way she talked back to the screen, like there was some guy hiding in there who she thought was a real dumbbell. She'd say a lot of nasty grown-up sarcastic stuff, stuff that made Alex laugh so hard his face turned red and he even sometimes cried. Petey laughed too, of course, though he wasn't always quite sure why. It was just easy to laugh with Cress. She knew how to joke around. She was always calling him Peter Peter Pumpkin Eater and blowing the hair back off his forehead like the Big Bad Wolf. And she hardly ever got mean or strict for no reason like his mother did. Even when she yelled at him for peeing in his pajamas that time he got carried away watching *Gulliver's Travels* and forgot to go to the bathroom, he could tell she was sorry right away. She'd tried to make up with him by letting him drink chocolate milk, and then when he spilled some on the table she was still very nice, gave him a big bowl of ice cream which he happily ate, even though it was strawberry, which wasn't one of his favorite flavors, and icy on top from being left too long in the freezer. Sometimes his mother, when she got mad, just shut the door to her room and lay down on the bed.

Maybe that was where she was right now: in her room, lying down. But Alex had already checked when they came home, and she wasn't. She was still at the doctor's. He had the house to himself. So he lifted the remote control and pushed the red button again with his thumb.

Only nothing happened.

Maybe the red button was broken, he thought. He tried the others, the numbers, then the ones with letters on them, pushing each button separately and, when that didn't work, several at once. Nothing. No matter what he did, he could not coax Batman out of his dark cave behind the screen.

Suddenly everything was wrong. Life wasn't working the way it was supposed to, but some other, messed-up way that all the numbers and letters and remote controls in the world could not put right. This must be how Alex felt, Petey thought, when he went stomping around the house saying how everything sucked and wasn't fair. It *wasn't* fair. Like now it was four-oh-seven, and *Batman* would be over, he knew, at four-two-eight. Then a commercial would come on, for Lucky Charms or Count Chocula or one of the other really good breakfast cereals his mother refused to buy at the market, which was also unfair, now that he thought about it, and then another show would follow, either *Power Rangers* or *Gargoyles,* he forgot which, and then, at five-oh-oh, like an alarm clock going off, or a door slamming shut on the afternoon's brightness and magic, there'd be the news. The most unfair thing of all!

Now it was four-oh-nine. Petey was proud of his ability to read the time; it was one of those things he'd learned early because he was good with numbers—he could count to fourteen without any mistakes, sometimes higher. His mother said he was a lot better with numbers than Alex had been at his age, and was going to have a great career as a numbers cruncher someday if he didn't get side trapped. She was always saying things that sounded like jokes she didn't think he'd understand. But he did, sort of. He knew that getting side trapped was a bad thing that happened to some people when they got older. It had happened to his father, which was why he lived down in South

America now, Petey supposed, where it was hot and they didn't even speak English. And it had also happened to his mother too. Which was probably why she was so tired and crabby all the time.

Though lately, it was true, she *wasn't* crabby, not crabby at all. Lately she didn't care so much about what they ate, or how often they took baths, or what the teachers had said about what they'd done in school that day, or any of the usual things she worried about. All she seemed to think about was lying down. She did that a lot. Even when she was standing up she sort of looked like she was lying down.

Maybe she was getting sick again, he thought. Lately she seemed to spend whole days in her bathrobe, walking around the house with the cordless phone, leaving messages with people like the doctor, Aunt Suzette, Caitlin's dad . . . she talked to Caitlin's dad most of all. Petey knew, of course, that they were talking about *him:* how he'd stopped napping in the Green Room after lunch, and what to do about that. How he was the only one in his class who didn't sleep at naptime. He'd heard his mom talk about it with his teachers a couple of times, how it was getting to be a problem. She'd taken him to see a doctor about it. Only it wasn't his fault. It wasn't. He tried, but it was just something that was supposed to happen but didn't, like the TV not coming on no matter how hard he pushed the red button.

It was four-one-three. He was going to miss the whole show. And he was beginning to think he might have peed in his pants a little too.

To prevent himself from being able to check, he shut his eyes. As long as he didn't look, there was still a chance he hadn't done it after all, and then his mother wouldn't get mad when she got home and Alex wouldn't make fun of him and call him a stupid dweeb like last time. He wouldn't look at his pants, and he wouldn't look down at the couch either, where it felt, he had to admit, kind of warmer and wetter than it usually did down there. Oh no. He picked up one of the sofa cushions and folded it over his head. He'd just keep his eyes closed and not answer the phone no matter how many times it rang—when had *that* started?—and be asleep when they all came home, because when you were asleep and something bad happened no one could blame you for it.

He counted five rings. Then he heard a click, and his mother's low, raspy voice in the kitchen, which made him think she must have gotten home after all. But no, it was the message machine, saying wait for the beep.

The beep, when it came, sounded slow and tired, as if it were getting worn out from having to take messages all the time. Then his mother's voice came on again, only this time it sounded tiny and far away, like the machine had finally gotten mad at her for making it work so hard and reached out and swallowed her, and now she was trapped—side trapped, he thought—inside. He heard her begging Alex to pick up, pick up the phone, she'd gotten hung up at the doctor's, nobody's fault, nothing to worry about, but she was running an hour or so late, though if the traffic wasn't too bad she'd be home in a few minutes, and meanwhile could he please finish his homework and keep an eye on Petey and also, if he got a chance, would he mind taking the package of boneless chicken breasts out of the freezer, honey, so they could defrost? All the while she was talking, Petey pictured his mother trapped in the back of the machine, unable to get out. And then there was a click, and his mother was gone again, and he dropped the cushion accidentally and when he reached for it his hand brushed against his pants and he felt the wet spot and now he couldn't help it, he started to cry. Where was Mommy? Where was Alex? Where was Batman? He opened his eyes and peeked around the sofa cushion, just for a second. It was four-one-nine. Then, even as he stared at the numbers, they changed again, to four-two-oh. The TV was dark. The only picture it cast was a block of shadow against the opposite wall. Soon, he knew, the room would be dark as well. And he wasn't sure how to turn on the lights.

When next Petey opened his eyes, everything was at once different and the same. He was still alone on the couch, and the TV was still off, but now the lights were on out in the hallway, and his mother was home, and his brother too. He knew, because he heard them yelling at each other in the kitchen. His mother seemed to think that Alex shouldn't have run off to Jamey's and left him, Petey, alone; and

Alex, meanwhile, claimed she had no right to talk, given how she was the one who couldn't even get it together to get home on time. Then he said something else, which Petey couldn't hear. Whatever it was made his mother terribly upset. She didn't yell, but he could hear a weird high trembling sound in her throat when she said how this was turning out to be a really shitty and difficult day for her, and she needed him to understand that, and could she please get through just this one fucking night without a major hassle because she had a lot on her plate just now. That was the expression she used. A lot on her plate. Something to do with dinner, he supposed. After that he didn't know what happened, but the house became very quiet again.

It did not seem like such a great time to show himself, really, or to complain about his problems with the television.

And then a second later he heard the front door open. He figured it must be Alex storming away as usual in the middle of an argument. But no, Alex was still in the kitchen, trying to apologize to their mother for hurting her feelings yet again. Also, the sound, he realized, was not of someone going out the door, but someone coming *in.*

And then someone called out, Hello?

And then he felt this sort of big, soft pressure in his head, one he'd felt before, he was sure of it, at odd moments of day and night, ever since he could remember. Sometimes it was there just for a second and then flew off, the way the seagulls used to do when he and Alex would chase them over the flats last summer—though he was not sure they'd done so for the same reasons—at Cape Cod. But this time was different. This time, before the voice could get away, he rushed right out of the darkness and into its waiting arms.

"Daddy!" he cried.

And so it was.

Later, miraculously enough, they were all still there. Alex, his father, his mother, Sueno—just sitting around the dinner table like it was the most natural thing in the world, eating some leftover chicken curry his mother had taken out of the freezer, and a big, colorful salad with lettuce and red onions and clementines and black olives and a couple of other things from the bottom drawer of the fridge, the one reserved for all the foods his mother liked and Petey and Alex didn't. Oh, and Dr Pepper for the boys. If there was any doubt about this dinner being a special event, the presence of Dr Pepper on the table settled it; his mother hardly ever bought the stuff anymore because of how it rotted out your teeth. Tonight, however, she let them have as much as they wanted. And there was a lot. Because the grown-ups weren't even drinking it. His mother was drinking milk, which she claimed to have developed a taste for, and his father and Sueno were drinking the red wine his father had brought with him from Chile—which was just as good as the wine from France, he said, and a much better value. He had plenty to say about wines, his father did, about wines and values. He even offered some to Petey, but Petey shook his head no, he had no interest in wine, and besides, he didn't want to upset his mother again. In all truth he'd have preferred to be down on the floor by now, playing with the action figure his father, wondrously, had known to bring him for a present—had the two of them ever discussed action figures on the phone?—along with the set of maracas from Sueno, which he already knew about from music class at preschool and did not particularly care for, though of course he told her he did. Alex, he knew, didn't like either one of his presents; the T-shirt was way too small on him and the hammock, which looked like a huge, droopy spiderweb of colored string, seemed to defeat him completely. Moreover, Petey knew from long exposure to his brother's radioactive moods and preferences that Alex *hated* chicken—he called it "dead bird"—in any of its various forms of presentation, and was bound to explode at any moment just from the presence of that goopy yellow drumstick on his plate.

But here was another miracle: Alex didn't say a word. He didn't whine, he didn't complain, he didn't threaten to call Children's Protective Services, or say he was going on a hunger strike; he didn't even shove back his chair in the middle of dinner to fix himself an instant burrito in the microwave. He just sat there in a slouch, not eating, listening with a very calm expression on his face while the grown-ups talked in their odd, grown-up way.

Actually, it was their father who did most of the talking. When he ran out of things to say about the wine, he started in on the political situation in Chile. This, he explained patiently to Petey, had to do with who ran the country and how they did it. Like who were the good people and who were the bad people and what kind of laws kept them separate from each other. The political situation was really unfortunate down there, he said. Petey was pretty sure unfortunate meant sad, but from the way his father's eyes lit up and a sort of animated energy came into his voice, it could have meant the opposite. There was something confusing about his father and the things he said, but maybe it was just that Petey wasn't used to him. It had been a long time. His father was a lot taller and skinnier and more wrinkled in the face than Petey remembered, like the sun down there was drying him up. He had shaved off his beard, too, so his jaw looked all pointy and white, and a tiny bit soft in the center. Compared to Batman, his father, Petey thought, did not have a very strong chin.

Petey was feeling a little like a superhero himself, all of a sudden, with this new X-ray vision of his. For instance, he was pretty sure he could see silver glowing at the back of his father's teeth, like he'd swallowed treasure. He could also see, though maybe he was imagining it, his father's skull shining right through his hair. Strange: he'd seen plenty of bald men before, and plenty of men with full heads of hair, but he did not recall seeing anyone who was both so hairy and so bald at the same time.

"How come Daddy's not eating?" he asked his mother, when his father had finally stopped talking.

"I don't know," his mother said. She sounded distracted, and not just by his question. She had the look of someone listening to a radio. "Why don't you ask him?"

But before he could ask, his father cleared his throat and smiled. "Daddy's a vegetarian, sweetpea. Do you know what that means?"

"Uh-uh."

His father looked at his mother, raising his eyebrows like he was disappointed in her for not teaching the boy these things. "It means," he explained, "that Daddy doesn't believe in stuffing poor little chickens and moo-cows with potentially toxic chemicals and growth hormones and then, once they get really fat, cutting their throats. Daddy prefers to live on rice and beans and fruit. Natural things. From the earth."

"As I recall," his mother said, smiling, "Daddy was also partial to that great natural substance Häagen-Dazs."

"Ah, *sí,*" Sueno said. "Rum raisin."

His father laughed. "Better watch it, guys," he said, winking at Petey and Alex. "They're ganging up."

Sueno was actually kind of nice. She was dark and short and young and pretty, a lot younger and prettier, really, than Petey's mother. She had dark, smooth fingers and great big black hair that fell down her back in a wave, and around her neck she wore a skinny silver necklace with blue rectangular stones that jiggled every time she laughed. The only problem where Sueno was concerned was that she had a little bit of a mustache, which Petey wasn't sure whether to mention or not. He kept sneaking looks at her when she wasn't looking, to make sure he wasn't imagining it. Nope. It was there. But it didn't seem to bother anyone else, so he tried to forget about it and just go ahead and like her.

Sueno seemed to laugh a lot, he noticed, for no particular reason. This too made her different from his mother. His mother needed a reason, a very good reason, usually one having to do with Petey himself, something he'd said or done—or sometimes when he was just lying there in bed in the morning, pretending to sleep—to laugh. But Sueno laughed all the time. Even when she wasn't laughing she would smile in a sad, bright way that was just as nice. Her mouth was like a little piano. The lips were wide and dark and full, the teeth were white as keys, and every time she smiled it came out like a song.

She seemed to smile especially at Petey. Possibly his father had told her that he was a boy who liked to stare and be smiled at. They were good friends so they probably talked about everything, he thought. Even him.

"No wine?" his father asked his mother, cocking an eyebrow. "I brought it for you, you know."

"Then why are you drinking so much of it?"

"Someone has to, once it's open. It won't keep."

"How altruistic of you," his mother said. "And here I thought you might be nervous."

"Me?"

"Oh, Leon. Don't playact with me. You always drink when you're nervous."

"Do I?" His father looked amazed. "Now that you mention it, I *was* a little nervous, granted, back there at the front door. But now, no. Now, sitting here at this table, surrounded by the people I love most in this world, I'm completely at peace."

"How wonderful for you," his mother said quietly. She was obviously trying to be nice too. She did seem a little sad that night, a little tired and not-there. She had both hands on her stomach; it was like she was feeling around for a bone or something she had swallowed by mistake.

"Hey, c'mon," he said. "Of course I'm nervous. Don't tell me you've gone and lost your sense of humor too?"

"What do you mean, too? What else have I lost?"

"Nothing. Sheesh, Bonnie, relax. No one's lost anything."

"Sorry," she said, her eyes wrinkling up at the corners. "I seem to be having a bad day."

"Well, you're not the only one," his father said at once, to make her feel better, Petey supposed. "You wouldn't believe the flight we had in that shitty third-rate jet. Then we get to the hotel, and naturally they've lost our reservation, and the central heating's blasting all over our place and you know what that does to my allergies. Turns out I left my medication back at the house. So just trying to *breathe* since we got in has been this major reclamation proje—" Abruptly, his father stopped, as if he'd just realized that the story of his bad day wasn't going over all that well, though Petey for one was enjoying it tremendously. "Hey," he said, looking down the table at Petey, "how you doing over there, sweetpea?"

"Good."

"I love you like crazy, you know."

"Uh-huh."

"I have this big framed picture of you and your brother," now he was looking at Alex, everyone was always looking at Alex, "right over my desk. This one from last year where you're hiking on the beach. Where was that, Uncle Joe's?"

"Cape Cod," Petey offered, when Alex did not reply. Perhaps if he was very helpful he would regain his father's attention. "We went there."

"Sure, Cape Cod." His father's eyes had softened, gone inward and fuzzy at their dark centers; he was not looking at any of them now. "It's funny. Sometimes, when I'm at my desk, and I'm right in the middle of writing something, I'll lean back and close my eyes for a second, and I'll picture you two guys, your life up here, what you're doing right at that moment. For us, you know, everything's reversed—when it's summer here it's winter there, and when it's winter there it's summer here. Did you know that?"

"Uh-huh," Petey said. "And when it's dark here it's light there."

His father smiled. "Not exactly, sweetpea, no. It's only the seasons that are reversed. Not the days and nights."

"Why?"

"I have no idea. I guess it has to do with the angle of the sun."

"Uh-huh."

"But sometimes, say on a day it's really hot, what I'll do is I'll think of you guys up here in your heavy sweaters and jackets, playing in the snow. It makes me feel cooler somehow. Know what I mean?"

Petey nodded carefully. He didn't exactly know, but he thought maybe he sort of knew what his father meant. Anyway, he didn't want to give the wrong answer, or do anything to mess up this serious conversation his father had embarked upon.

"When you're older, you guys'll understand better. What it's like. What it's all about. How you can have two different worlds juggling around in your head at the same time. The past, the present. Memories. Repetitions. It all gets pretty confusing, let me tell you."

"Why?" Petey asked. Alex was just sitting there.

"I don't know. I guess because you learn everything you learn in life by making mistakes. And usually it's too late to go back and correct them."

Petey's mother cleared her throat pleasantly. "Mistakes?"

"I was speaking generally."

"Ah."

His mother got up to rinse off the dishes. Sueno offered to help, but his mother said no right away, as if she were mad at Sueno now too for some reason. So poor Sueno sat there folding and refolding the napkin on her lap as if she were making something with it. She wasn't smiling at anyone now.

Meanwhile his father had reached down into his leather rucksack, taken out a thick black notebook stuffed with papers, and set it on his lap. Petey had seen it before, on previous visits. His father always had it with him. Three red rubber bands held the pages together. Sometimes right in the middle of an activity—a trip to the zoo, or the aquarium, or out in the left-field bleachers at Fenway Park—his father would pull off the rubber bands one by one, open the notebook, unscrew his fountain pen, and start to write things down, no doubt some terribly grown-up and important idea he had only just thought of. The black notebook was bursting with them.

"Well, well," his mother said, settling back into her seat. "The journal lives."

His father shrugged. "Someone has to keep a record."

"For God's sake, why?"

"Because," he said, "it runs through your fingers if you don't."

"Oh, Leon," his mother said, with a mournful smile.

"Please don't start with the 'Oh, Leons.' Not now. Pretty much the last thing in the world I'm looking for is another of your 'Oh, Leons.' "

"Fine," his mother said. "Forget it."

"Oh Leon, what?" he said.

"No, no. You're right," she said. "Not now. Let's change the subject."

"C'mon, c'mon," his father persisted. "Oh Leon, what?"

"Don't you see? All that psychoanalysis, all that journal writing, all those heavy insights and dreams you just had to get out of bed in the middle of the night to write down—" She looked at Sueno. "He still does that?"

Sueno smiled her sad, willing smile. "Of course."

"Oh Leon, *what,* for chrissakes?"

"Can I be excused?" Alex asked. "I've got social studies homework."

"No," their mother said, "I want you to hear this."

"You're just going to fight. I've seen it before. I don't want to watch."

"Don't be silly. We're not going to fight, are we, Leon? We're just catching up like old friends."

"If the boy wants to be excused, let him be excused," Petey's father said. It sounded wonderfully reasonable, the way he said it. So reasonable that Petey thought *he* should ask to be excused too. But where would he go?

"What are you, a parent now?" his mother asked. "This is my house. I'll excuse him when I'm good and ready."

Alex pushed out of his chair. "I'm going to Jamey's," he said. "You can't stop me."

"What about your homework?"

"Don't got any."

The door slammed behind him. Petey knew, of course, that this was a lie. Alex had a really strict math teacher, Mrs. Kabakow, whom he always complained about because she gave him homework every single night. But he knew better than to try and say anything at a time like this.

"What's with him?" Petey's father asked in a low voice, once the glass window in the door had stopped rattling. People always talked about Alex in low voices, Petey had observed. Alex was like one of the math problems Mrs. Kabakow would send home; you had to spend half the evening bent over the table, scribbling things and erasing them, before you figured it out. Only with Alex no one ever seemed to come up with the right answer. "The kid seems, you know . . . troubled."

His mother's eyebrows flared, and her mouth, the way it often did when the subject of Alex came up, went pinched. "You're supposed to be a writer," she said. "Can't you find a better word? I really hate that word."

"He was always intense. Remember? Even as an infant he howled and howled. It was like we could never satisfy him."

"Of course the divorce didn't exactly help."

Petey's father nodded. "And the shrink? What does he say?"

"Please," she said, glancing impatiently at Petey, "don't let's talk about this now."

"I'm just—" Right then Sueno leaned forward and whispered something in his father's ear. "Okay, okay," his father announced loudly. "We'll talk about it later." He nodded toward Petey. *"Çelui-çi? Encore un rêve?"*

His mother looked at him again. Her eyes were full of tears. They always were, he recalled now, whenever his parents began to speak to each other in French. *"Toujours,"* she said.

"*Formidable.* Well, that's something." He scratched his chin thoughtfully. "So?" he asked. "What were you going to say before?"

"It doesn't matter," she said wearily, scraping some wax on the table with her thumb. "That's all I was going to say."

"What doesn't matter?"

"Your journal. The way you try to capture everything that happens to you on paper. You really think you can stop it from running through your fingers anyway?"

"Of course not," his father said. He looked relieved, as if he'd been afraid she would say something much worse. "Which is why the journal's so important. Life goes fast, so I want double portions of everything. The event and its contemplation both."

"You were never any good at math, were you," she said. "I know you, Leon. You'll spend half of tomorrow scribbling away in that thing, trying to catch up on today. You wind up with half as much, not twice."

"And you?" Petey's father asked. "Who are you to talk? What have *you* been doing all this time? Have you found a new job? A new man? A new apartment? Christ, look at this place. It's been three years since we signed the papers, Bonnie. Have you even finished that crummy dissertation yet?"

She winced. Her lower lip began to swell. "I've given it up."

"Again?"

She nodded, silent. Her palms ran over her belly.

"How long've you been carrying that great big nineteenth-century chip on your shoulder, anyway? Let me see if I remember this right. According to you, Thoreau's a jerk, your dad was a jerk, I'm a jerk, everyone's a jerk but you. You're the last pure spirit in America," he said. "You're your own little hut in the woods. Also you're getting fat—"

"She's not fat," Petey declared hotly. Though in fact she *was* getting a little fat, he thought, even Alex said so. "She's not."

"Excuse me, Petey, you're absolutely right. Your mother is a lovely, big-boned, full-figured woman, and it was wrong of me to imply anything different. My only point," his father went on in a more agreeable voice, "is you're not exactly a poster girl for the unexamined life yourself. What gives you the right to lecture me?"

"This," she said. Her voice was trembling and pinched. She waved her arm around the table, finally bringing it to rest around Petey's own shoulders. He squirmed a little to push it off. "This gives me the right. Because *we*'re what ran through your fingers. *Us.* And nothing you write in that fucking notebook is going to bring us back."

He was quiet for a moment. Sueno wiped her mouth with her napkin again, even though she hadn't eaten anything that Petey had seen in several minutes.

"What makes you think I want you back?" he asked coldly.

"Honestly, Leon. I don't care what you want."

"I came because I wanted Sueno to meet everyone. You guys, my parents, my sister. That's all."

"Okay, fine. I've met her. She's a lovely girl." His mother turned to Sueno and said, "You're a lovely girl. Really. You're pretty, you're modest, you've got phenomenal posture, and no doubt underneath all those good Catholic manners is a very shrewd, intelligent brain. Plus I assume from all that lapis around your neck you're also loaded—"

"Now now," his father said, "I knew you were going to start with that."

"—but even if you're not," she went on, "even if you're poor as dirt and twice as ignorant, believe me, you could do better. On the other hand, what the hell. He's a sweet enough guy, he'll never hit you, and he isn't bad in bed. You could also do worse."

"Thank you," said Petey's father. "That's an inspiring speech. Should I go ahead and invite you to the wedding? You can give the toast."

"Ai!" Sueno said. For the first time she looked really angry. "You promised."

"Yeah, well, what difference does it make? I was going to tell her anyway, sooner or later." His father turned to Bonnie. "I'd like to have the boys at the wedding. Don't worry, I'll pay for the tickets. We're thinking Labor Day, unless it's some Catholic holiday or something. But I want them there. I want to be part of their lives from now on. No more missed occasions."

Petey watched his mother's nose turn pink, an indication that tears were either coming or going, or, as in this case, heading in both directions at once. "We'll have to see," she said.

"What does *that* mean?"

"It means we'll have to talk about it. There may be something going on up here too, around the same time."

"Like what? What could possibly be more important than their father's wedding?"

Sueno put her long hand on his arm.

"We must go," she said to Petey's mother. "You have been very kind."

"No, I haven't. But it's kind of you to say."

They shook hands. It was very strange; Petey had never seen women shaking hands before. Probably they hadn't either, and that was why they weren't so good at it. They didn't really shake the way men do, but just sort of clutched loosely on to each other's wrist and held on for a second, looking kind of thoughtful and sad. He was tempted to show them the right way. He knew just how to do it.

"You must please say good-bye to your son for me," Sueno said. "I liked him very much. He has such a proud, handsome face."

"And Pedro," she said, turning to Petey, "what about you? You are such a little grown-up."

Petey nodded tentatively.

"God knows what you think of us, eh?"

She swooped down, as if determined to solve this mystery for herself, coming so close to the boy that he could feel her breath on his face fogging up his eyes. The stones around her neck clicked together, then slid apart, then clicked together again, making a sound like those maracas she'd given him earlier—for which he had, he hoped now, been polite enough in thanking her. Maybe he'd play with them after all. Because he liked Sueno. It was true. He hadn't realized it until now, when she was leaving, but he liked her a lot. He had completely forgotten about the mustache. With her standing so close he could see it there clearly, of course, but it did not look at all bad, or get in the way of her shining face, or the two dark curls that jounced and swung against her honey-colored neck, or the sweet, rising smell that came off her skin, like almonds or coconuts or some other agreeable component you might find mixed inside a cake.

She was going to kiss him, he realized. It gave him a strange feeling, part horror, part something else. She was going to kiss him. At the very least she was going to smooth back the hair off his forehead, the way his mother did all the time whether he wanted her to or not, and say some more nice things to him.

But though he leaned forward, and even closed his eyes for a second to allow her to do so, Sueno never did kiss him. Nor did she say something nice. She simply reached for his hand and gave it a brief shake, and then she stepped aside, and his father's big pointy face and his lit-up eyes were coming toward him, and all at once Petey was caught in a hug so powerful he could hardly breathe. And then just when he'd begun to relax and settle into *that,* he was let go of again. It was hard to know how to react. But then the whole day had been full of mysterious comings and goings, things that didn't happen when they were supposed to and things that did when they weren't.

Soon it would be bedtime. The day was over. It had run right through his fingers, just as his father had said. And now it was gone.

Later, much later—probably because with all the excitement of the visit he'd forgotten to ask his mother for her usual night magic—he had a terrible dream. He dreamed his mother was in bed with him. Her arms and her legs were draped around his waist and she was hairy like a spider, and she was squeezing him hard, so hard it was hard to breathe.

Then he opened his eyes and saw his mother. She *was* in bed with him. Only, and here was the part he did not understand, *he* seemed to be the one who was squeezing *her.*

22

Transparency

SHE DID NOT take one of her last three pills before getting into bed. Whether this was act or nonact, superstition or sacrifice, she didn't know. Sorting it out at this point would burn too much valuable energy. Why try? All she knew was that this thing she wanted so badly, she could not have.

That was the deal, she thought. Give up one, get the other. Trade in the dream.

It was 12:54.

Tomorrow, she thought. The word was a metal pole sunk into the earth. Upon it, the small, dangling toy that was her fate silently swung.

Tomorrow she must be clear-eyed and cool, impervious to distractions. Leon of course was a distraction. Alex—despite the fact that it was a school night, he'd chosen to sleep at Jamey's house, and she'd chosen to allow him—was a distraction. Petey too, his blatant happiness that evening, his chronically needy, fitful desperation to please. The three dozen unmarked essays in the plastic shopping bag below her desk, those as well. The only thing that mattered was tomorrow, her return trip to the hospital and the tests that awaited her when she arrived.

One twenty-three.

She threw off the covers and wandered the cold flat like a ghost. Outside she saw a trickle of snow. How ridiculous, the first day of

April. Nature just refused to grow up, she thought. It was still out there fucking around, playing pranks.

Two o'clock.

Without the drug she would never sleep. She saw that now. Even if she could, she was not about to let herself. She had slept too much already.

Two-thirteen.

Tomorrow was padding toward her on its big black feet. There was nowhere to go, no one to call. Anyway, self-reliance was the thing now. Perhaps if she brazened it out, stared tomorrow in the face, refused to flinch or show fear, then it would slink away, as Leon had. His appearance that evening, looking back on it, was more symptom than cause. Though perhaps it was both.

Labor Day, she thought, doing the math in her head. Yes, it would come around then. One really did need to hold on to one's sense of humor.

In the kitchen, she made a pot of Sleepytime tea and brought it over to the table, inhaling the sweet, enhanced steam in the darkness. Rosehips, hibiscus, blackberry leaves, chamomile flowers. The world was a garden, durable and voluptuous, a garden of earthly delights. Just breathe it in.

The numbers on the clock were getting comical at this point. She saw no point in trying to follow them any longer.

There was, she had to concede, a certain grim familiarity to the scene. Just sitting at the table at this bleary blue hour, poking idly at the bread crumbs and water rings left over for dinner, seemed an occasion for nostalgia. She tried to connect the dots into squares and triangles, spiraling chains, infinity's toppled figure eights. The radiator ticked and bucked. The fridge rumbled in the corner. Wasn't this where she'd come in? It did not seem possible that her interval away could have been so short.

The hell with it.

Fishing the bottle angrily from her shoulder bag, she hurried down the hallway. Three pills left. With every step they presented themselves, rattling in her hand like dice.

In the bathroom she laid them out along the sink, switched on the light over the medicine chest, and drew a glass of water from the tap. It emerged in a dense, milky cloud. Clutching her robe to her neck, she watched the water settle in the glass, changing properties with maddening slowness, as if unfolding in biblical time—the sediment drifting for a while, then falling gradually, as if reluctantly, to the bottom, in a state of cushioned sleep. The next thing she knew the water was transparent.

Well, she told herself, if you're hoping for purity, you'd better learn patience.

She cradled the pills thoughtfully in her palm. As if in testimony to their benignity, the bags under her eyes, she observed in the mirror above the sink, were gone. Or were they? Perhaps they had only been displaced, like everything else, to her hips and rear. Because there was no Wite-Out for experience, no magic eraser. This was what you learned in that tedious and demanding middle school called adulthood. It all stayed with you: every fat cell, every false start, every subtle betrayal and discarded husband. Only the forms they assumed might take you by surprise—like Alex in his new body, or Leon with his new wife, or, to take an even more immediate and depressing example, this reflection of hers in the bathroom mirror, this floating gaze, this hawkish and irregular nose, this doughy, pallid head with its top-heavy ziggurat of curls. Was this really her? Even if it was, it was only, she knew, a reversed image, an inversion, like the climate in South America. It had something to do with the twinned hemispheres of the brain. Reflected things looked right and at the same time subtly wrong; a distance remained. So what she saw in the mirror was not herself but someone else. Some*thing* else. Though it was her too of course.

She picked up the glass of water. No, it was not in fact transparent after all. The fluorides were invisible, true, but if you looked closely you could see tiny drifting particles and spores, traces of carbon or lead or whatever they were, these random impurities that crept into even the simplest things. At bottom, the water was a compromise, a messy admixture of the natural and the synthetic, the pure and the profane. For all she knew the chemistry involved in this one glass of water posed a greater threat to her baby than all the drugs in the world. In which case she might as well go ahead and take the pills tonight. Take it all—the pills, the water, take every damned thing she could get her hands on.

But she poured them out into the toilet instead. All three pills, and the water too. And watched them whirl away.

Afterward, she tiptoed into the boys' room and lay rigid beside Petey on the bottom bunk. It was as if he'd been expecting her. He reached for her at once, and with a certain intuitive male confidence—some latent instinct of possession, of night-knowledge—twined himself around her torso, burying his sharp face in the spongy, comforting cellulite of her upper arm. She tried to accommodate him as best she could. She had nowhere else to go. Enfolded by his skinny tremoring limbs, she remained there, blinking back the darkness, waiting for morning's big recycling trucks to come haul it away.

23

A Trail in the Snow

AND IAN OGELVIE? Had anyone been sufficiently invested in the subject to ask for an account of his night's activities, he'd have been hard-pressed to comply. He did remember, though in a muffled, distant way, ducking out of Barbara's opening reception at the Summer Street Gallery around seven o'clock. This would have been perfectly acceptable, of course, had it not started at six-thirty, and had he not promised his sister that on what was arguably the most important night of her career, he'd stay and support her to the very end. That had been his intention. Hang out, look at the art, perhaps meet some new, attractive, successful people who would be fascinated by his casual replies to their questions about the work he did—so different, so much more urgent and substantial in some ways than their own—followed by a late dinner at some pricey Newbury Street bistro afterward with Barbara, her brilliant and effusive new dealer, Yves, and a few carefully selected insiders. And then afterward, if he was feeling up to it, and he suspected he would, he'd make a bold dash over to the hospital, to try to cross paths with Marisa Chu in a sexually open-ended way before she went home.

What he hadn't counted on were all the variables. First, the fact that if his throat pain, body temperature, and general light-headedness were any indication, he appeared to be coming down with Barbara's flu. Second, the precipitous, perhaps causative drop in the quality and duration of his recent sleep. Third, his continuing metabolic difficulties when it came to assimilating alcohol. Fourth, the narrow, crowded, smoke-thronged room and its various attendant breathing issues. And fifth, fifth was something, or someone rather, he chanced to glimpse in profile across the wine-and-cheese table about ten minutes to seven, as he stood there with his third glass of tepid Chardonnay, fighting for a cracker, trying to hold up his end of a series of boring and demoralizing and oft-aborted conversations with Barbara's friends.

"Hey, you. Stop hiding and kiss me already."

Barbara. She had come up from behind, wearing the padded black silk blouse she always wore at openings, and proceeded to kiss him noisily and muss his hair, as she always did at openings. As with many introverts, the anxiety of attention turned her giddy and loud. Ian forgave her for it. Openings were stressful events; it wasn't Barbara's fault if she manifested her tension in more physical and spontaneous ways than he did. And yet the evening was going well, he could see it in her shining eyes and flushed, busy face; his sister was excited and relieved and feeling vaguely sentimental about all these dear, wonderful people who had come to celebrate with her. "I better not," he said. "I'm not feeling too well."

"What's the matter?" she asked. "Don't like the show?"

"The show? The show's fantastic. Really. First rate."

"Never mind," she said quickly, her reflexive response to any compliment on her work. "Talk to Mom? She called earlier. They were going to fly in but there's some freak blizzard in the Midwest."

"Thank God," he said.

"What?"

"That they didn't take a chance. With the weather, I mean," he added, looking over her pillowy shoulder. It couldn't be the person over there he had thought it was.

"Are you all right, Eeny? Your eyes look sort of glazed."

"Sure, sure." What had they been talking about? Oh right, the blizzard. "You know, we see a lot of air-traffic types at the clinic. It's pretty scary, the shape these guys're in. Talk about heavy meds."

Barbara observed him in silence for a moment. "You're quite the little gloom bird these days, aren't you?"

He nodded absently.

"What?" she asked, craning her neck to follow his gaze. "What are you staring at?"

"Please tell me I'm hallucinating," he said, "and that person by the grapes isn't who I think it is."

"Who, Wendy?"

Wendy. Wendy Lesher. Big Long-Range Mistake Wendy Lesher.

"Oh. Well, I guess she's on the mailing list," Barbara said. "What, is this awkward for you?"

"Awkward?"

"She's never come to an opening before," Barbara said, a bit guiltily. She was beginning to look around the room for a place to go. "I didn't think it would be a problem."

"She must be a big fan of your work. To come all the way from Africa."

"Africa?" Barbara looked blank for a moment.

"That huge jungly place across the ocean? With all the lions and giraffes?"

"You don't know, then?" Barbara's mouth took on a thoughtful pucker, the kind, he thought, that comes from holding inside it some fresh sour wedge of hurtful information. "She's been back for over a year."

"Oh."

"I'm sorry, Eeny. I thought you knew."

"You know, I really don't feel so hot," Ian said.

"She's got this great job. Runs a huge HMO down in Providence. You've probably seen their signs on the T."

"Feel my forehead, would you? I think I'm getting a fever."

"Could be," she said, after a patronizing little kiss on his brow. I guess I should have said something about Wendy. But we've both been so busy. And it's not like you just broke up or anything. You've moved on, right? You're a hotshot at work, you've got this Asian girl you're seeing—"

"I wouldn't say seeing, exactly."

"She does look happy, though, doesn't she? Wendy, I mean."

"She's put on weight," he observed. "Look how big her hips are, how tubby she's gotten around the middle. Hell, she almost looks—"

"Here you are!" A man with black glasses was draping his arm around Barbara's shoulder in a studied, proprietary way. "I have been searching for you everywhere."

"Just talking to my bro here," Barbara said, smiling prettily.

"Bro? Or beau?"

"Gotta go," Ian said.

"Ian's not feeling well. What do you need, sweetie?" Barbara reached for her purse. "Advil? Tylenol? Valium? I've got three different painkillers here."

"I'll try a couple of each."

"By the way, did you meet Yves yet? My dealer?"

"No."

The man was almost preposterously handsome, tall and slender, with a square, chiseled head and thick white hair cut very close to the scalp. He looked like a Roman senator, Ian thought. Luckily, he had just enough wine in his glass to wash down all six pills.

"Ah, the little brother. The, how do you call it? Couch potato."

"The what?" Ian said.

"Your sister is fantastic. I love this woman. Her work, it's so perfectly contained. It excites me to the highest praise."

"She's always been a high achiever," Ian agreed. "Our parents pushed us pretty hard."

"May I tell you something?" The man wore dark glasses as round and tiny, as perfect, really, as dimes. His skin gave off a delicate musk. He leaned very close to Ian's face and confided in a whisper, "We are selling out."

Barbara by now had moved off to greet some friends. Ian, in a sort of trance, heard the conversations gurgling up around him . . . *my work my show my gallery my grant my* . . .

"You mean the show," Ian said. "The show is selling out."

The dealer nodded. "Boston, I am sick of it. A smug, provincial city. In six months my gallery in Chelsea will open. Then Brussels. Your sister will do well in Europe."

"I'm sure she will."

"Sometimes this is all it takes. One night. You touch the world just so, and it opens its legs for you, like a woman. No objection."

Ian nodded foggily. In the man's black glasses he saw, as if in slow motion, the crackers on the table crumble and split, the seedless grapes, scrubbed diligently for pesticides, fall off their stems, the wedge of Brie melting down, shedding its white, ammoniacal skin. He saw Barbara over in the corner, accepting vaporous kisses and compliments. He saw Wendy Lesher, all alone, her honey-colored hair swept up in a bun, turning to read the text on the white card beside *Invisible Environment #5,* looking gloriously and undeniably beautiful in her baggy yellow-lavender dashiki, and also gloriously and undeniably—you could see it in the high-shouldered, self-correcting carriage, and the slow, pendulous stoop of her belly—pregnant. And he saw himself too, Ian Ogelvie, holding his empty plastic cup (running a finger by habit over the ridged letters embossed along the bottom), wondering if any of this was really happening, or was it only some miasmic, dolorous reverie that went with the flu. What difference did it make? The facts were on the ground. He had lost his love, his apartment, and his funding. And his integrity as a researcher: if his current project did not succeed, that would be gone too. Gambled away. How would he ever win it all back?

"Excuse me," he said. "I need to go do something."

He heard himself explain, not all that coherently, about this patient he had to check on right away, an emergency, in fact, about an hour away out of town, a place called East Lowell. And then he watched a shadow flash across the man's black glasses—inside or outside, he couldn't tell—and disappear.

The evening traffic was slow, the sky hazy and moist with some obscure night vapor. In the borrowed Jetta he wound his way along Massachusetts Avenue, through Boston, through Cambridge and its slanting squares, into the busy roads and snaking waterways of

Arlington and Medford. His head thrummed. He could feel the city's stubborn gravity tugging at him from behind, trying to restrain him. But he was too far gone. Soon he'd come to the on-ramp for Route 93, and his foot was mashing down the gas pedal, and after a brief hesitation the motor surged with a roar, and he was free.

For a while he drifted through a flat, featureless zone of suburban towns, the yards growing larger with every mile, the woods greedier, more punitive, swallowing greater and greater portions of sky. A fine salt spray was in the breeze. The ocean, he thought. He couldn't see it, but he could feel it tossing behind him, massive and impersonal, aching to rise. And everything he passed, the billboards and car dealerships and gas stations and cheap motels, and the tawdry illuminations of the food franchises, the bright, brittle chains that bound the towns together—they all seemed, in their tireless industries, both part of and response to that unseen ocean. He drove past a drive-in theater, the great empty bowl of the screen looming above the fields. The concession stand was dark, the teeter-totter askew; the speaker poles spread like headstones, stark and stoic in the macadam lot. And then beyond that the towns fell away, and there was only darkness, and the fizzy halos of the sodium lamps, the sudden flares of the passing cars.

He followed the signs. At last he found the right exit and circled down the off-ramp to see, burning dully through a frozen mist, the red clustered lights of East Lowell. From a distance they were beautiful, like all city lights. Nothing like the terror of vacancy and darkness, he thought, to incite our best work, summon our most intricate, ingenious technologies. Did the whole human project come down to this: this ongoing business of holding off night?

Up close, however, East Lowell was not beautiful. Up close it was a remarkably homely, leaden place, the buildings rust-colored and asprawl, like invalids in a long-term-care ward. About the streets there was an air of failed invasion. Trampled newspapers lay strewn in the gutters. The parking lots were vacant, the meters' arrows frozen in red. Shards of glass glittered wanly under the vapor lamps. Only in the industrial zone was any movement to be seen, cars trickling into and out of the lots, small flames—they looked like dragon's breath—rising over the plumed silhouettes of the smokestacks.

Downtown, looming beyond the shuttered storefronts, the cathedral's rose window was dark, a closed eye.

Though it would be April in a few hours, it did not strike Ian as particularly surprising or depressing when a light snow began to fall, drifting like confetti over the trash bags on the curb. The flakes looked gay and decorative and at the same time transient, superficial; they would be gone the next day. Squinting, he tried to read the unfamiliar signs through the clumsy falling flakes, looking for one that corresponded to the address he'd scrawled hastily on a piece of scrap paper down in the warden's office at Walpole. Part of him hoped he never found it. Should he fail to find it, his life, he reasoned, could go on just as it was, which for all its multiple imperfections seemed better to him even now than the great shapeless mass of all it wasn't. But change too was natural, Ian thought. To hold off change by artificial means involved denial and repression: two psychic felonies he was determined to commit no longer. He remembered considering this issue with great clarity and detachment as he circled the smoldering maze of East Lowell.

And then against all odds he actually *did* find the place. Parked at the curb. Tiptoed in his good leather shoes over some runny, snow-dusted dog turds laid out like a Rorschach blot in the middle of the sidewalk. Climbed the four steps to the porch. Knocked and knocked on the front door. And after that—

After that he could not quite account for at the moment. After that his memory turned blurry and congested, as if despite all the pills he had swallowed—or because of them—his frontal lobe had caught a distressing virus. Whatever had happened after that, he would have to come back to later, when he was feeling a little better about himself—make that a *lot* better about himself—than he was feeling right now.

Accounting for the past several minutes, on the other hand, posed no problem at all. They had been spent right here in Jamaica Plain, in the cramped, elliptical lobby of Marisa Chu's apartment building, in approximately this same position: his head lolling against the wall, his thumb depressing the buzzer of apartment 3E, playing a weary on-and-off electrical dirge as the blood dripped down from his throbbing nose, over the torso of his best V-neck sweater, and onto the floor. The floor had been pretty colorful to begin with, what with all the green-and-red Chinese take-out menus, yellowed cigarette butts, rancid blue candy wrappers, pink desiccated moons of bubble gum, and the rainbow assortment of discarded crack vials that were everywhere underfoot—but now, with the dappled, blotchy addition of his blood and the sallow glow of the overhead light, it began to take on a kind of lurid beauty, like some wild, alarmingly expressive work of abstract art.

One nice thing about being a psychiatrist, Ian reflected, was how little daily contact one had with actual human plasma, particularly one's own. Could you die of a bloody nose? He wouldn't have minded, really. For one thing, it would be a relief to have the night over with, to lay the whole subject of his future to eternal rest. There would also be the subsidiary pleasure of everyone coming to the funeral and feeling bottomlessly horrible about themselves for not treating him much, much better while he was still alive. He pictured Howard Heflin, in one of his bow ties and hand-tailored suits, delivering a warm, magisterial eulogy. And Wendy Lesher, wailing and distraught in her Zulu maternity dress. And, somewhere in the back row, weeping discreetly into a handkerchief, would be Marisa Chu. She wore black most of the time anyway, like the people at Barbara's opening; it was as if they were already in rehearsal for such an event.

Why didn't she answer? Did he have the right apartment? It said "Chu" on the mailbox, but no doubt it was a common enough Asian-American name. He was not sure how long he'd been waiting there, exactly. To know that he would have to consult his watch, which it so happened he was no longer wearing, having donated it somewhere along the bumpy, demoralizing course of the evening to his new charitable cause: the East Lowell Foundation for Violent and Larcenous Youth. But by making a tally of the blood drops from his nose, then multiplying that number by the seconds between drops, then dividing this number by sixty, he was able to arrive at what seemed a reasonable estimate of nine minutes. To allow for time lost to calculations, he added, at the end, two more.

So: eleven minutes. Or ten, or twelve. Why this passion for accuracy? What in the world was the difference? The real mathematics, the frail geometry of the heart, remained beyond his reach.

Outside the buses rumbled past, the delivery trucks, the dogged plows with their revolving yellow lights.

Someday, Ian thought calmly, he would be an old, wizened retiree in a madras shirt, shuffling barefoot around a ranch house in Santa Fe. The place would be full of cacti, representational paintings, towheaded grandchildren on swerving trikes. In the mornings he'd go into his study, close the door, and sit down at his desk to compose the long, complex story of his life. He would share it all with them: the good, the bad, the not so good, the not so bad, the incredibly good, the incredibly bad. This chapter here, the one he was bleeding through like so much red ink at this very moment, would be a pivotal one indeed. This would be the chapter where all the contentious factions of bad and good threw up their arms and came together in a soundless truce.

He knew just what he was going to call it too. *Time Lost to Calculations.*

"Who is it?" someone—Marisa—called querulously through the roaring intercom.

"It's Ian," he said. His voice cracked on the word, as if his own name were encased in a hard shell. "Can I come up?"

There was no immediate answer. It occurred to him that without in any way intending to he had, just by pressing her buzzer at this late hour, delivered an ultimatum of sorts. Declared himself. And this time it wasn't a dream. This time there would be actual consequences in the living world. Whatever *that* was.

"Oh for God's sake," she said.

It was difficult, even for someone with half a dozen years of advanced clinical training, to read into these four words much in the way of promising latent content. Nonetheless he was now fully invested in the notion of a fateful encounter, a turning. So he persevered. "Please," he said. "Just for a minute."

The pause that followed seemed to go on for weeks. But then behind him came the click of a lock—like a membrane being punctured—and then, a moment later, as if causes and effects had become as confused out here in the world as they were in his head, there followed the soft indeterminate hum of the buzzer.

He was headed up.

Marisa Chu stood at the top of the landing with her arms folded like a short, gray-eyed sentinel. She wore a two-toned cotton nightshirt that fell halfway down her thighs, and her usual white Kabuki mask of implacable calm. "Jesus," she said, "what's with you?"

"Apologies in advance. Won't stay long. Spur of the moment. In the neighborhood. Sorry to disturb." All his carefully rehearsed sentences came tumbling like clowns from the little Volkswagen in his mouth.

"Are you bleeding? Your nose looks like it's bleeding."

"It's not as bad as it looks," he said. "Or wait, maybe it is."

"I better get some tissues."

"Bravo. Down to business. Here you are in your nightshirt, feeling baffled and/or annoyed. Let's stop the bleeding, you say to yourself. First things first."

"You haven't been drinking again? It doesn't suit you, you know."

"Tell me about it."

"But you seem to keep drinking anyway."

"Well," he said, "I'm trying to get better at it."

"Poor Ian. Maybe you should just give up."

"Oh no." He shook his head gravely. "Patience. Discipline. Focus. Slow, incremental improvements. That's my methodology. Too late to change now."

"I see." She was breathing hard, as if she were the one who'd trekked up three flights of stairs, not him. Her pale cheeks were mottled; from passion or irritation, he couldn't tell. Perhaps she had been scrubbing her face, readying herself for bed. For dreams. Who knew what faces appeared to her in the night? "Well," she said, "you'll have to wait here. You can't come in."

He heard some sort of low, moody jazz playing inside the apartment. He tried to peer around her head but the door behind her was open only a crack. "Company?"

"I'm going to take that as a rhetorical question, Ian."

"Okay. Though I have to tell you, I have no idea what that means."

"Basically it means mind your own business."

"Fair enough." He coughed into his blood-streaked hand. "The reason I'm here, though, I mean the real reason, is to say something. Something important."

"Can't it wait till tomorrow? It's freezing out here. And what in the world happened to your nose?"

"My nose is not the issue. Though if you had twenty or thirty Kleenex handy that would be great."

"God." She looked him over closely. Some clear fluid of tolerance or affection was in her eyes, mixed with one or two cc's of alarm. "Is that real blood?"

"I'm afraid so."

"Wait here."

She disappeared into the apartment, closing the door behind her. Ian didn't mind; it gave him the opportunity to lean against something, and thereby prevent himself from falling down. He could feel the ridged circle of the peephole impressing itself upon his forehead like the outline of a third eye. He tried to see through it to the dark interior of the apartment. But peepholes are one-way mechanisms; all he could make out was a bulbous, distorted version of his own features.

At last Marisa returned, wearing black Chinese slippers and carrying bunched in one hand an enormous wad of toilet paper. "I'm out of tissues. Try pressing this to your nose. I ran it under cold water."

"Thanks." He arched his head back. The cold paper was a pleasant shock.

"You should go home and lie down," Marisa said. "You look like you've about had it."

"Agreed. First, though, we need to talk."

She took a breath. "I don't want to hurt you, Ian."

"Good. We're agreed there too. I don't want you to hurt me either."

"I think you're a really nice, intelligent person. I respect your mind. I enjoy talking to you. I'm delighted we work on the same project. Can't we leave it at that?"

"No."

"Why not?"

"I don't know. It's hard to explain. But I'd like to make love to you now if you don't mind. It's relatively important."

"Not now," she said.

"I've had a really bad week," he said. "One for the books. Tonight would be best."

"No."

"Okay, fine," he said. He examined the toilet paper for blood. "They rejected my grant application, you know."

"I know."

"Not even a revise-and-resubmit. Not even the usual bullshit apology for how difficult it was to select among so many highly qualified applicants this year. A flat-out no."

"Those are the worst," she agreed.

"I thought I was past the point of getting crushed by rejection, but guess what? It turns out I'm not."

She nodded coolly. "No one ever quite gets past that point, I don't think."

"True. A little patronizing, but true. A little knowing, a little distanced and condescending. But true." He peered around the toilet paper to see her face. "I take it you got one."

She frowned. "I'm not into this whole competitive trip, Ian. It's demeaning."

"Balls," he said. "That's what competitive people always say. They aren't into being competitive. But here's the thing: if competitive people aren't into being competitive, then who is?"

"You still haven't told me why your nose is bleeding," she said evenly.

"I'm aware of that. I'm trying to cultivate a little mystery here. Enjoy knowing something for a change that you don't."

"It's one in the morning," she said. "How long do you expect me to stand here asking?"

It was not a nightshirt she was wearing, he realized, but a dress shirt, an oversize, fitted blue oxford with a white collar. Or possibly a *proper*-size shirt, if the person who bought it happened to be a good deal taller and heavier than she was.

The damp toilet paper had begun to fall apart in his hand.

"I went up to East Lowell," he began, "to see a guy named Eddie."

"Who?"

And so he went ahead and recounted the story of his trip. The little rowhouse across from the railroad tracks. The trains going by, stooped and shadowy, dragging their endless, clattering cargo. The woman who opened the door, Eddie's mother, maybe his wife. Her pained, suspicious face. Her graying nimbus of hair. Nothing would surprise this woman, from the looks of her. Life was a succession of visits from white folks with clipboards. Case workers, parole officers, church people. What was one more? Besides, this was only a routine follow-up, he'd taken care to explain that. A mere procedural review. His tone was serious but bland, unthreatening, neutral as Switzerland. Just a hospital technocrat performing a tedious home visit. A half hour of your time.

Finally, whether because she'd chosen to believe him or because she'd chosen not to weary herself in this particular way any longer, she'd held the screen open for him, none too widely, and pointed down the hall. He'd gone past the kitchen, which smelled of bacon and rice, and into a small paneled den at the back of the house. And there, looking rather regal on a high, unfolded La-Z-Boy, wearing vinyl name-brand sweat clothes and expensive sneakers, his thin, stuporous, sunken-eyed face blue lit by one of the biggest and loudest television sets Ian had ever seen, was Eddie Lincoln.

"Yo," the man had said, congenial in the face of intrusion. "Do I know you?"

"Mr. Lincoln, my name is Ogelvie. Ian Ogelvie. I'm from Boston General."

"Uh-huh." Eddie nodded knowingly. A commercial for Ebinox filled the enormous screen.

"I'm here to ask you a few questions. Would you mind? About the study you participated in."

"Uh-huh."

"You know the study I'm talking about?"

"Uh-huh."

"You were given a certain experimental compound over a period of several weeks. It affected your sleep mechanisms. It may have caused some irregularities."

"Uh-huh." Eddie appeared to think for a moment. "Boston General. What's that, a hospital?"

"Exactly," Ian said. "We were the ones who designed the study you participated in at Walpole. So it's our job to follow up. Of course it's all very routine. Just covering the bases, so to speak."

"Hell," Eddie said, "I been expecting you."

"You have?"

"Uh-huh. I seen you before, with Erway. In the joint. You one of his croakers."

"I'm not sure what a cr—"

"Sshh. Siddown. I want to see this."

Ian perched himself temporarily on the arm of the second La-Z-Boy, relieved among other things to set down the heavy video camera in its cumbersome case. He felt hoarse, light-headed, feverish; his nose was now completely fogged in, closed to air traffic. He unzipped his jacket. An overworked space heater leered red-mouthed in the corner. Eddie Lincoln was lost in some stupid cop show. Ian studied the Jamaica posters on the opposite wall for what seemed a ridiculously long time, then cleared his throat. "If I could just have a few minutes of your time."

Eddie, rapt, lifted one hand to shush him. The fingers trembled.

There was nothing to do then but pretend interest in the events on-screen. A tall, good-looking detective was handcuffing a ratty-looking drug dealer in a weed-strewn lot. There was some tough, acerbic banter. Then they all wound up downtown, where a couple of fast-talking lawyers got involved, and there was a lineup that proved inconclusive, followed by a run-in with the station's supervising officer, who seemed stern but fair, and then a thrilling, roan-haired woman, also a police officer, it turned out, whispered something mildly risque to the handsome detective about what she would do to him after dinner that night, and then the next commercial came on. Detrol tablets.

"You watch this every week?" Ian asked.

"Week?" Giggling and coughing, Eddie brought a small bottle to his mouth and drank. "Man, every *night.*"

He offered the bottle to Ian. It shook with his hand, spilling two drops of red on the off-white carpet. "You want?"

Ian hazarded a small sip. Whatever was in the bottle tasted syrupy and rich. When he swallowed, the very tissues of his throat seemed to loosen, to swell.

"NyQuil?" He inspected the bottle. "I thought this was for colds."

"I'm cold," Eddie said. "Feel my fingers."

Ian felt the man's fingers. They were cold. Ian come to think of it was pretty cold himself.

"Go ahead," Eddie said with a generous wave. "Plenty more where that's from."

"Thanks." Ian took another sip. "I just have this short list of questions," he said.

"Sshh. After the show."

They watched the next segment in silence, passing the bottle between them. From time to time Eddie coughed, or chuckled appreciatively, or clenched his fists, acutely responsive to all of the show's varied manipulations. He was a man who submitted himself to things. An admirable trait, Ian thought, but a dangerous one. Still, Eddie, though he'd obviously had some bad breaks in his life, seemed all in all a pretty good guy to hang out and watch TV with, if you could stand all the giggling and coughing and long intervals of silence that entailed. Why didn't he have more friends? Ian wondered. It was pleasant, just sitting there in the dark, a couple of regular guys on La-Z-Boys, knocking back the NyQuil and watching some tube. Snowflakes ticked against the windows. The space heater roared like a dragon. He felt so strange, so logy. Strictly for prophylactic purposes, he took one last gulp of the NyQuil. Odd, but the bottle was now empty.

"About the study," Ian said, when the show was over. "I have one or two questions."

"Uh-huh." Eddie nodded sleepily, wiggling in his chair.

"Well, to begin with," Ian, glancing down at his list of questions, found it difficult to read for some reason, "what did you think about it?"

"Think?"

"What I mean is, did you feel properly briefed beforehand? Did it seem to you that the study was conducted professionally?"

Eddie blinked at him. Now that the colors on the screen had changed from police show–dark to sitcom-bright, his eyes were revealed as the sullen, monstrously red-lidded orbs they were. His skin, Ian saw, was yellow, his bones scooped from his face as if by claws. His chest was so concave it was practically inside out. "I don't follow you, man."

"I'm just trying to clarify," Ian said, "that you knew what you were getting into before you signed up."

"Knew what?"

"Well, that you were told about the dosages you would receive, for example. About possible side effects and so on."

"Side effects?"

"Hallucinations. Nightmares. Panic attacks."

"Yeah, yeah. I get those all the time."

"What I'm asking is whether the study made them worse."

"Who wants to know?"

"I do," Ian said. "That's why I'm here. For example, once it was under way, was there ever a time you felt you wanted to come off the drug but were not allowed to do so?"

"What you fucking talking about, man?"

Ian started again. "I'm just trying to establish if—"

"Hey," Eddie said, "I got no words with Erway. Erway's cool. What you want to fuck him for?"

"I don't want to do anything to Erway," Ian explained. "I'm simply trying to establish that the study you took part in was conducted along proper lines. If any corners were cut, it would mean the results, for one thing, are unreliable. There would be an issue of medical malfeasance. You might even be entitled to compensation."

Eddie's face took on a new, canny light. "You trying to bribe me, right?"

"No, no. I'll explain—"

"I can tell right away with croakers. I been in and out of joints my whole life. I know which ones are solid and which ones ain't. Erway's solid. But you. I don't know about you, man. You're one corrupt motherfucker."

"I'm on your side, Eddie."

"The hell you are."

"I'm just trying to get some things straight for the record. If I can just plug this camera in somewhere . . ."

"Uh-uh. Put that thing away."

"Listen, it's only a video camera. I need it to get your statement down for the—"

"I *been* videotaped, all right? You want to see pictures of my pretty ass, go talk to Erway. I ain't sitting still for it no more. You got no right." The man's face looked not angry now but stricken, powerless. His eyes were full of tears. As if, Ian thought, even here, in his own shitty little underheated house, he did not quite expect his will to prevail.

"Okay," Ian said. "Okay, Eddie. Look, I understand."

"Fuck you."

"No, no. You're right." He began to pack the unwieldy video camera into the molded slots of its carrying case. "I'm going."

"Yeah," Eddie said, gaining confidence now. "Get the hell out, man. I don't like your face."

He was consumed then by another coughing fit. It lasted the entire length of a Claritin commercial. Ian reached into his coat pocket and found some samples he had brought with him, gifts from the sales reps. He left a couple of foil sachets on the arm of the La-Z-Boy.

"What's this here?" Eddie, red faced, held up one of the sachets.

"Just multivitamins. To help build up your resistance."

"You trying to poison me, right?"

"Don't be ridiculous," Ian said. "They're vitamins, okay? Your system is run down. Abused. That's partly why you're coughing so much."

"I seen you, man. In the joint. I know who you are. You're trying to fuck with my head."

"I'm not trying to fuck with you!" Ian yelled. "I'm trying to help you, you moron! Don't you see that?"

Eddie nodded coolly.

"I see you better take your ass out of here, man. Right now."

It was no use. Ian picked up his video camera by the handle and carried it down the hallway. His journey took him through the kitchen, past the cold, opaque stare of Eddie's motherlike wife, or wifelike mother, who sat at the Formica table knitting a bloodred scarf. Beside her was a boy of five or six, lost in a Game Boy. As Ian opened the door to let himself out, the boy looked up and smiled, his fingers pausing at the controls, as if an intriguing new development had scrolled across the screen. All the while Eddie was muttering behind him, ". . . most evil croaker I ever saw."

"Well," Marisa said, "what did you expect?"

"I thought he'd want help."

"From *you*?"

"Here's my theory. He wasn't *allowed* to talk. Maybe they threatened him before he left. Made him sign some sort of gag clause."

"Who, Erway?"

"Or Heflin."

"Howard?" A small irritation flickered across Marisa's pupils. "You give him too much credit. The man can't even make out a simple flow chart." She pointed toward the swollen mass at the center of Ian's face. "So what happened? He punched you out?"

"Eddie? You must be kidding. He doesn't even have the strength to brush his own teeth. No," Ian said, "this was my own fault. There were some kids sitting on my car when I got out of Eddie's. Just playing around. But I was in a pretty down mood by then. Also it's not my car; it's my sister's, and I felt responsible for it. So I asked them to move. Told them, actually. I figured, tough but firm—that's how you handle late adolescents. Two of them, the nicer two, got off right away, but this one guy, I think he may've been on something, crack, or angel dust; anyway, he pulls a power trip. Gets up in my face, starts huffing and puffing how I'm disrespecting him. I told him to stop acting like such a baby. Then I recommended he get, you know, some counseling, to deal with all his drug and aggression problems. He took exception to that, boy."

"Have you lost your mind?"

"Not at all," Ian said. "If we'd been sitting in my office I'd have said the same thing. But we were out on the street. In the snow. So he took my watch off my hands. The Sony too. Then he arranged for me to meet his good friend the sidewalk. And there you have it."

"You're lucky," Marisa said. "You could have gotten hurt a lot worse."

Ian nodded abstractly. It seemed possible to him that he had been lucky in some ways, though they were difficult to identify.

"Did you call the police?"

"What on earth for?"

"You were robbed and assaulted," Marisa said. "For most people that's reason enough."

"You've got to look at the environment," Ian argued. "Economically depressed. Prevailing attitudes of hopelessness and rage. Add in developmental factors like lousy impulse control, maybe some attention deficit issues at school. . . . My feeling is, let's try fifty milligrams of Zoloft plus a short-term course of family therapy. Then we'll decide."

Marisa's mouth formed a glum line. "Poor Ian."

"Yes, poor Ian. Whatever became of him? He had such promise."

"So what now?"

"Good question. Any thoughts? I'm sort of at the no-idea-in-the-world stage myself."

"You can't go up against Howard, you know. Not on ethics. He's the golden calf."

"I realize that," Ian said.

"For all you know this Eddie person's experiencing an adverse reaction to something else. He's a regular user; he'd probably test positive for half a dozen controlled substances."

"I realize that."

"Anyway, it's one isolated case," she said. "It's not persuasive. You'd need to run longitudinal studies, gather a lot of data. It would take months."

"I realize that," Ian said.

"Erway won't help you either. He's a fat old lecherous burnout; he's not going to risk his pension on something like this. Besides, I think under all that bluster he really *likes* Howard."

"Everyone likes Howard," Ian agreed. "Even I like Howard."

"So why antagonize him then? At least he believes in what he's doing, which is more than you can say for some people. All you'd do is cause a big mess, and you'd have to leave the project, and then you'd lose your residency for sure. None of the senior staff will risk alienating Howard by taking you on. Not with this merger coming up."

The bleeding, Ian discovered, had stopped. And yet he rather missed it. Let it flow, he thought, let's empty the place out and start again. Something about the trip to East Lowell, perhaps even the otherwise horribly unpleasant experience of getting his nose smashed against the cold snow-strewn asphalt, had cleared out the calcified remains of some stubborn inner blockage. Now his head felt clear. He peered through the window at the end of the hallway. The snow had stopped falling as well. Only a flurry, a gesture. Nothing serious. The business of the streets would not come to a halt. Nothing would change. He scanned the block for his car but was unable to find it. Had he parked on the other side of the building? All he could see from this vantage point was a lone Grand Cherokee straddling the curb with its blinkers on. A dusting of snow obscured the windshield.

He remembered, then, the bottle he had seen on Howard Heflin's desk. Bekarovka. You couldn't get it here. They only sold it in the Czech Republic.

He looked at Marisa. "How did you know that I didn't get my grant?"

Her brow gave birth to a small fissure of uncertainty. "You must have told me," she said.

"I haven't told a soul."

Her dark eyes narrowed. She said nothing.

"Howard sent you to Prague," he said. "Then you come back, and a few months later Malcolm leaves. Why?"

"Things weren't going well," she said, pensive.

"Things on the project, or things between the two of you?"

"I think," she said in a measured tone, "that falls back under the heading of none of your business."

"I feel like an idiot."

"Don't be too quick to understand, Ian. It's more complicated than that."

"I don't care," he said. He paused to conduct a quick internal exam on this subject and found that he had spoken the truth. There was only one way to go after that. "I quit."

"Look, you can't just leave. It would be stupid."

"Good," he said. "I'm tired of being smart. I was never any good at it anyway."

Marisa Chu shook her head. "Can I give you some advice? Never make big decisions like this in the middle of the night. They always turn out wrong."

"Show me the study that proves this. Show me the brain function graphs."

"I don't have to," she said flatly. "I've lived."

"Ah, life. The great teacher. The great communicator. The great steaming pile of horseshit."

She took a short but clearly defined step backward into the apartment. "Go get some sleep. Tomorrow you'll feel better."

"But it *is* tomorrow, don't you see? If you don't go to sleep it's just one long day."

"I'm sorry," she said, "but I find it hard to engage in metaphysics when I'm freezing my ass off in the middle of the hallway."

He watched her biceps unfurl, her hand move toward the doorknob.

"Listen," he said quickly, "here's the plan. First, we march into Heflin's office and resign. Then—" Already Marisa was shaking her head no, which was discouraging, as their joint resignation was the least controversial feature of his entire scheme, but he plunged on. "Then we call a meeting. Present a list of our procedural questions to the staff. Tell them about the special subsets. The cut corners. The ethical brownouts."

"You think they don't know?"

He paused, horrified. "You think they do?"

"Motion sickness? C'mon, Ian, you think anyone working on this project is really interested in motion sickness? When we all know there are tens of millions of people out there who want what we've got?"

"Sheer pacification," he sputtered. "We're playing Disney, don't you see that? Selling trips to the Magic Kingdom. Nirvana on ten dollars a day."

"Where's the harm, if we address a human need?"

"What *don't* humans need?" he cried. "Where does it stop?"

"Why should it stop?"

"Because we're imperfect creatures. That's how we're made."

"That's my point," she maintained stubbornly, her eyebrows skewing into what he'd come to think of as her Radcliffe debating expression. "Where nature leaves off, science fills the gap."

"You want gaps?" he cried. "Look at me. My funding's gone. My nose is smashed. My apartment died in a fire. Tonight who do I bump into but the love of my life, who's supposed to be in Africa stamping out diseases, not running HMO's in Providence, Rhode Island. I've got gaps, Marisa. I've got human needs like you wouldn't believe. Open up your medicine chest, what do you say? Got any FDA-approved nontoxic compounds for those?"

She regarded him evenly.

"You're disappointed about the grant," she said. "It's natural. Anyone would be feeling low right now."

"Low, that's right. Lift me up, Marisa. Give me a boost."

"I'd like to help," she said. "I really would. But—"

"Come with me. Right now. Throw some stuff in a bag and we'll go."

"Go where?"

"Stanford, Austin, Chicago. You name it. We'll be a great team.

You're unbelievably smart and well-connected, and I'm very, very . . ." He could not quite summon it, this thing he very much was.

"We'll talk tomorrow," she said, rather kindly, he thought. "We'll sit down in the cafeteria and talk this whole thing through together."

"Together, right. We'll hang a shingle out in cyberspace. Fear, Anxiety, and Depression Dot Com. Responsible therapy. Very few drugs."

"Let's talk about it tomorrow."

"That's what the Net's for, right? To catch you when you fall."

"I'm going to have to shut this door now, Ian."

"Okay, fine."

"Put some ice on that nose when you get home. It'll keep down the swelling."

"Okay, fine. Get some sleep. Big day coming up. Major changes."

"We'll talk," she said.

"Sure. Only would you just tell me one thing?"

"I'm going to go back to bed now, Ian."

"Just remind me, what kind of car does—"

"For Christ's sake, Ian," boomed a voice he sort of recognized from deep inside the apartment. "Go home. You're keeping everybody up."

24

Third Person

SHE HAD ALWAYS been a reader. Even as a child, brandishing her flashlight like a saber under the tented blankets, books had been her cause and flag, her shield and artillery against night's long, uniform march. Every evening after her bath, face scrubbed and expectant, she would burrow below the covers and reenlist in her own private underground—that shadowy guerrilla camp of rabbit holes, secret gardens, never lands. She'd read until her eyes blurred, and then she'd read some more. To close the book was a betrayal, a surrender to sleep's atomic cloud, which swallowed things indiscriminately and flattened them of interest. She fought it with all her strength. And then the years passed, and her enemies changed, and one day she discovered she could not close her eyes even when she wanted to. And so her troubles had begun.

Now, with the story of her days half over, it seemed to Bonnie that all this time she had not so much been living her life in the first person as reading it to herself in the third. Self-consciousness had spread like a mold. The process was miasmic, perhaps irreversible. Like Don Quixote and Emma Bovary—her spiritual foster parents, she'd begun to feel—every thought and mood, act and nonact, had been infected by other people's vocabularies, other people's dreams. But perhaps that was true of everyone, she thought. Perhaps they all saw themselves as she did, from the outside, as the protagonists of a baggy and meandering novel, encoded inside them at birth like so much invisible ink. At times the story seemed decisively comic, at other times tragic; often it was impossible to identify *what* the tone was, and one was left feeling, as she felt right now, on the verge of some decisive event that would lend the story at last a little shape.

Anyway, the book was not ready to be closed. Not hers. Not yet.

Only the Dodabulax had delivered her, for a while anyway, and set her free. But she had put that aside now.

And here came the withdrawal.

It was like emerging from a movie house in the late afternoon. Suspended between worlds, between two coherent but exclusive modes of perception, her identity at once half shadowed, half illuminated by the onslaught of common light. She felt chilly and ravaged, out of time. Her hands shook. She couldn't eat. Her eyes clicked and jittered in their sockets. The place in life where art left off and science began was no longer clear. Something was missing. She could feel it down in her cells. An absence, a white space. A broken synaptic connection. As if she'd discovered that her left leg, the one she'd always favored, was a phantom limb and would not bear her weight any longer.

Her unhappiness had deserted her. The snug sofa she had made of her grievances was gone. The blue pills had rolled it away, silently and efficiently, like maids with a motel cot. She was on her own.

But she wasn't alone, she reminded herself. There were the boys. And the baby, there was the baby too.

All that night she'd felt movements in her womb, restless but distinct, a rogue foot or fist at war with its constraining sac. The baby was with her still. It seemed almost axiomatic. The worst could not have happened, because she had prepared for the worst too well. All that time lying next to Petey, inhaling the sour-sweet milk of his scalp, the acrid traces of urine on his sheets that all her bleaches and detergents had failed to expunge; all that time in the shower, under the beneficent lather of her aloe–kangaroo paw flower–propylene glycol shampoo; all that time readying the boys for their big Saturday morning excursion to the Science Museum with Daddy, to see the new giant spiders exhibit in the company of all the other Boston-area children of divorce and *their* daddies (though hers seemed unnaturally quiet and self-sufficient this morning, as if too preoccupied with their own apprehensions to add, as they normally did, to hers); all that time driving to the hospital, roaming for a space through the gray hierarchies of the parking structure, riding the elevator (TROUBLE SLEEPING? YOU MAY BE . . .) to the fourth floor, making small talk about the ridiculously mercurial weather with the receptionist in the ultrasound lab; all that time sitting in yet another waiting lounge, leafing through yet another magazine from some bygone month of a bygone year, gawking at yet another young, hipless woman whose hair had been straightened, whose teeth had been whitened, whose lips had been swollen with silicone jelly and eyes been cleansed, in the alchemy of a midtown darkroom of the last lingering residue of shadow—all that time she had spent preparing for the worst. Because the worst liked to catch you by surprise. Like Leon. It was the form of that surprise, not the content, which gave the event its velocity and throw weight, its ashen fallout in her mouth. But she would not be surprised any longer. She had readied herself for the worst. Really, in the end, she thought, compared with most people's, the book of her life had never been particularly fateful or tragic; which meant if there was any logic to be found in either literature or anxiety, the two subject areas—or were they the same one?—over which she had achieved some mastery, then the worst would fail to come.

It was her intention to explain all this to the doctor that morning, both as a means of doubling the strategy's effectiveness and because it was her custom to try and ingratiate herself with medical people, in the hopes that they would treat her to an extra ration from their meager stores of kindness and grace. She wanted not their respect so much as their gentle handling, their compassion. Though she wanted their respect too. But this one was all business.

His name was Preiss. He looked to be a few years younger than Siraj but a few years older than Ogelvie: more or less her own age, in short. He was a compact, trim-waisted, wide-shouldered man. The veins in his wrists were ropy and strong. His blue eyes, unmediated by glasses, shed a quick, ambitious light. In fact he was so hale and good-looking, with those bright blue high-beams of his and the fine, chiseled topography of his head, she found even the waxy baldness of his pate appealing. Possibly Dr. Preiss himself was not so secure on this point, however. As if to compensate for his northern exposure, a fiery-red beard erupted from his jaw and spread with contoured aggressiveness out toward his ears. He didn't smile either, when he bade her enter. He appeared to be complete unto himself, to have no need for surface congeniality. No need, at any rate, to dispense it. Receiving it was another matter. He gave her hand a brief, undemanding shake and waited expectantly for her to say something. She waited too. His freckled scalp gleamed rosily under the lights, as if accustomed to soaking their attentions. His affect, the way he occupied the room, was at once coiled and intense and languidly entitled, like a former squash champion at a private school. Exactly the sort of man who had always interested her least. And now she would spread her legs for him.

At last he instructed her, none too warmly, to climb onto the table and pull up her gown. She hesitated. Unlike her and Siraj, the two of them had no verbal history together, no soft buffers of charm. She wondered if she should insist on a nurse being present. A female touch, to look out for the species' interest. A third person. But she had seen no nurses at the station out in the corridor.

Saturday, she thought. Skeleton crew.

"Well," Preiss said, setting down her chart. "Let's see what's what."

He turned on the machine. This time Bonnie resolved to keep her eyes open. Closing them yesterday had been a mistake she would not repeat. A cowardly act, a jinx. This time she kept the doctor in tight focus, watching him as he watched the monitor. His expression was neutral, benign, impossible to read.

"Siraj tells me you're an academic," he said. His eyes had not flickered from the monitor.

"Sort of."

"A sort of academic." His voice held, or seemed to, the merest accent of mockery. "And what's your sort of field?"

"American literature," she said. "Nineteenth century."

"Ah-ha." Was he even listening? He wore a class ring, she noticed, burnished and expensive. His head remained wondrously still. Up this close, a fine halo of hair-fuzz, the palest of reds, was visible along its sloping plane, like the attenuated atmosphere of a distant planet. He too, she reminded herself, had been a baby once. "Like who?"

"Oh, you know. Emerson, Thoreau, Melville, Whitman. Your basic dead white males."

"Ah-ha."

"Not that they were so bad, as intellectuals go." His indifference made her want to defend them. "They had some interesting ideas."

"Like what?"

For all she knew he was teasing her. But she would answer him seriously. "About breaking free," she said. "About leaving behind old ways of perception. *Walking the walks of dreams,* Whitman says in a poem."

"Any pain down here?"

"No."

"Good," he declared. "And this breaking free. You think such a thing is possible?"

Suddenly, despite his crabbiness, she felt capable of love for him, for all these brilliant, indefatigable, firmly untranscendental young men who strode through the hospital in white coats, carrying people's lives around on their clipboards like so many dangling pens. He had only to speak to her in the right way and she would change her life for good. He had only to say the right words. But he was still watching the monitor.

Was it possible, she wondered, to break free? An image of Florence sprang to mind, wild roses tumbling madly over their ledges, the dim sepia glow of the Madonnas, as they waited, cool and stoic, in their shrouded chapels. Had she been free there? If so, then she never should have left. Perhaps in a sense she never did. Perhaps her life had actually stopped that day, frozen in place, the possibilities trickling away, invisible and unused, like that French-Canadian boy's semen leaking down her legs as she crossed bridge after bridge after bridge. . . .

But no. She had lived, or tried to; she had loved and borne children and attended pointless, interminable meetings in preschool gymnasia, and now she was here, and nothing was left between her and Preiss. No veil, no membrane, no memory. Just the two of them and the droning machine.

She tried to think of something to say to lighten or defuse the tension. But there were only a few words in her head. So she went ahead and said those.

"She's dead, isn't she?"

"I'm sorry."

"It's my fault."

Apparently the doctor's expression, which had been fixed in place for several moments, saw no reason to change now.

"It never felt quite *real,* do you know? Jesus, I was hardly showing. I was only just starting to . . . to . . ."

"You might prefer to be alone right now," he suggested thickly, when it became apparent that she was not going to complete her thought.

"No, thank you."

Oddly, and in defiance of everything she understood about herself, she wasn't crying. What did that mean? She was going to have to begin learning about herself all over again from scratch.

"Should we call someone? Your husband, or—"

"No," she said. "No one."

He nodded. With some deliberation he put a hand on her shoulder, the weight of which she found terrifically annoying. He appeared to be waiting for a signal from her, some word or gesture that would release him. He was good enough at his job not to try to rush her out until she was ready. Though not good enough to conceal how difficult it was for him to stand there this long, not doing anything.

"Go ahead," she said finally. "Explain this to me."

"From the size and appearance of the fetus, my guess is termination occurred about a week ago. Maybe ten days. Without running tests on the tissue it's hard to say precisely."

"What's hard to say precisely?"

"When termination occurred."

"You're saying I've been carrying a dead child in my womb for the past week or ten days. That's the part that's not hard to say."

He looked at her stolidly. By now he had reclaimed his hand from her shoulder and put it in his pocket.

"But I felt something. Just last night I felt something."

He nodded, his eyes crinkling into a sympathetic mask.

"Fuck you," she said. "I did."

"Over the course of a pregnancy," he said, "the body becomes conditioned to responding to internal movements. It's natural to go on responding to them for some time. Even after they've stopped. Until you're made aware of the situation."

She shook her head. She had no idea whether he was speaking in a medical capacity, or a psychological one, or whether he was simply bullshitting her at this point.

"From what I see here," Preiss went on, "my guess is it's a chromosomal accident, dating back to conception. See this thickness of tissue around the neck? That's a clue. And the fingers aren't as far along as we like to see. Probably the fetus wasn't developing in such a way as to be viable." He seemed more comfortable now, talking over the details, relieved of the forced gentility of a moment before. "It would have showed up on the amnio. Nine times out of ten it shows up on the amnio."

"I was scheduled for an amnio next week."

He nodded. "You'd have been faced with a nasty decision then."

She thought she caught him glancing surreptitiously at his watch. He did not seem like such an awful person but perhaps he was. What kind of man bought a class ring? Still, she was not quite ready to let him go.

"Suppose I told you I took something. A drug. An experimental sleep pill. Could that have caused it?"

"Unlikely."

"But possible?"

"What was the drug and when did you take it?"

She told him then about her short, happy affair with Dodabulax. In theory it should have been easier for her to unburden herself to Preiss, a complete stranger, than Siraj, whom she had known and loved all these years, but in practice it wasn't. Nor did it relieve her of guilt to confess her transgressions, if that's what they were. It should have made her feel better but instead it made her feel significantly worse.

"There was nothing on the blood tests," he said when she was through. "I looked over your file. No trace of this drug you mention."

"It's new," she said. "Maybe the guys at the lab didn't pick it up."

"It's possible. But I wouldn't waste your time wondering. These chromosomal accidents occur all the time, especially at your age. If you want to blame someone, blame Mother Nature."

"Mother Nature?" she repeated dumbly. "Mother fucking Nature?"

"Of course," he added, more gently, "this doesn't in any way affect your ability to conceive the next time."

She nodded. He had not found her story outrageous. He had not even found it particularly interesting. But then why should he? Didn't his breath smell of mouthwash, just like hers? Hadn't his teeth been coated that morning with titanium dioxide, his underarms dusted with zirconium trichlorohydrex, his orange juice spiked with tricalcium citrate? The world was made of chemicals. It was only natural to use them. The history of pharmaceuticals was as rich and profuse as the history of pain, of humanity's discomfort with being; their twin fates entwined forever in the logo of snake and staff. Her case was nothing new. In every culture and epoch, in every far-flung corner of the globe, people were ravenous for relief. They'd take anything they could get their hands on. Berries, herbs, mushrooms, the sap of trees, the leaves of plants, the oils and cartilage of ocean fish. Even if it didn't work. As if the taking itself was the cure.

She still hadn't cried. It appeared she wasn't going to.

"So what happens now?" she asked.

"We schedule a D-and-C. Monday, if we can get you in. Tuesday at the latest. Unfortunately it's the weekend. We don't have the staff to do it now."

It was stupid, trivial, a mere by-product of the morning's heartsickness and confusion, but the letters ran together as he said them,

DNC, and made her flash momentarily on that other violation, that other botched shortcut, Watergate. "You mean," she said, "after all this I still need an abortion?"

"It's highly advisable," he said. "Much safer."

"But the baby's dead."

"I meant safer for you."

She considered for a moment. "And if I just skip it? Is there a risk?"

"Sooner or later you'd miscarry on your own. But it could be terribly painful. You could wind up in the emergency room. It depends on the extent of tissue degeneration. Generally we find it's best not to wait, for psychological reasons if nothing else. Most women are more than eager to get it over with anyway. They want to move on."

She nodded.

"Think it over. Consult with Dr. Siraj; he left word with my service for you to call him later. He's very concerned."

"I know."

"You might want to discuss your options with a counselor. We have a very fine clinic upstairs on the sixteenth floor. I could make you an appointment for later this afternoon if you like."

"No, thank you."

Clutching her gown, she began to rise from the table. Preiss moved to help her. Now that she was sitting up, readying herself to leave his jurisdiction, what had been stiff and formal in his manner turned tender, solicitous. Even his bare head gave off a moist and beneficent glow, like a handsome, well-tuned lightbulb. After all was said and done he was part of a service industry, and she a paying customer.

But she waved him off. "Under my own power," she said. "Isn't that the expression? Under my own power."

He watched her reach for her clothes.

"Really, you don't have to stay with me. You've probably got patients lined up out there, waiting."

For a moment he looked puzzled.

"Actually," he said, "you're my only one today." Then, after he'd pulled off his flesh-colored gloves, rolled them into a ball, and discarded them into the metallic hamper, he unscrewed his Pfizer fountain pen and wrote her a prescription.

"In case there's pain," he said.

25

The Hook

HAVING GOTTEN OFF to such an early start, it did not take Ian, as he'd feared, the entire weekend to finish packing up his lab. In fact it took only a few hours. The process was speeded along considerably once he discovered how much of the equipment was affixed, either literally or figuratively, with the hospital's imprint. His computer, his disks, his data journals, his project files, his PET scans and BEAM sheets and CAD/CAM projection models, the Polaroid camera he'd bought at Fretters after two weeks of extensive comparison shopping, the photographs it had yielded, the corkboard that held them, even the imitation brass nameplate that hung on his door and could be of no conceivable use to anyone not named I. Ogelvie—none of these was his to take with him, but belonged instead to the collective entity known as the anxiety team, as spelled out clearly on page xxxii of the staff handbook under "Guidelines for Intellectual Property"—an addendum inserted into the most recent edition of the handbook, he was informed by Joanie, the departmental secretary, at the request of Dr. Heflin.

Naturally, then, the animals weren't his to take either. The spiders, the mice, the fighting fish, the cats, the Chilean degus—for all the flattering attention he had lavished on them, the paternal doting and boasting, the recording of their every landmark achievement, no matter how modest or halting, on celluloid or video, they would remain behind, orphans of the drug storm. Not that he had anyplace to take them even if he could. What was an unemployed sleep researcher to do with a Siamese fighting fish, a Chilean degu? Even in this era of advanced deregulation, he did not think there were many airlines loose enough in their policies as to allow a Chilean degu on the plane.

So there was really very little with which to fill up the half-dozen medical supply cartons he'd salvaged from the Dumpster in the back alley. Books, mostly. His *DSM,* his Jouvet, his Crick, his Hobson, his Havelock Ellis, his *Dynameron.* His dusty volumes of Freud. His framed reprint of Felice Fontana's landmark article, "Convulsive Movements in Sleep of Cats and Dogs," in the original Italian. Several back issues, just beginning to fade, of the journals in which he'd copublished these past four years—*Brain Research, Journal of Pharmacology and Experimental Therapeutics, Neurophysiologie des Etats du Sommeil*—his name sandwiched among three others on the second byline. All were packed up neatly in a box. As were his three framed diplomas. A pair of bike gloves he found under the radiator. Pens, pencils, cough drops, guitar picks, calculators, thumbtacks, nail clippers. A postcard by Tintoretto he had picked up off the floor of a plunging elevator and never returned. The envelope containing his recent one-sided correspondence with the NIMH. The business card handed to him, it seemed years ago now, by Charlie Blaha, executive editor of *Neuropsychopharmacology Now . . .*

He hadn't looked like much of an executive, that night at the Sheraton Plaza last fall. Nor much of an editor either. Egg-shaped and florid, his wide black tie askew, Charlie Blaha had stood by the buffet munching noisily on a plate of popcorn shrimp—courtesy, the suite and shrimp both, of Furst Pharmaceuticals—lifting his gaze every so often to check out the catering babes in their trim white blouses and short black skirts, giving only the most minimal indications of listening as Ian went on detailing so volubly, so earnestly, his proposal for applying expectancy theory to the problem of sleep. Given that placebos were shown to be particularly effective with mild forms of depression, with areas of brain chemistry that adjoined the mechanisms of sleep, it stood to reason, etc. It was still so theoretical at that point, so fuzzy and indeterminate, he should have held his tongue; but like a fool he'd gone on anyway, discussing various forms the treatment might take in facilitating neuron release, the CFR block, the REM stage extension, and so on, until Blaha, picking a bit of tailfin from his teeth, interrupted. *Can you patent a placebo, d'ya think? 'Cause I've got contacts in the field who might be interested. Man, think what this'd do to the big pharma. Fuck them right up the ass!*

At the time the remark had seemed to Ian a non sequitur at best—the by-product of a coarse temperament, an interminable cocktail party, and a huge quantity of expense-account J&B. But now, looking back, he wondered if Charlie Blaha might have been recruiting him for something. A mission. A sort of retribution. Not knowing quite what to expect, he dialed the number on the bottom of the card, only to be transferred to another number at the same office.

"Charlie Blaha? He's gone."

"Do you know when he'll be back?"

"Try never."

"Sorry?"

"Charlie's relocated. Lives in Switzerland now. Basel. They wanted him full time, finally. At the home office."

"Who?"

"Hoffmann-LaRoche. He's been consulting for them for years. Sandoz too."

"I see."

"Oh, we all knew he was going one of these days. Been taking German at the New School for years. Friend of his?"

"We met last fall," Ian said. "At a conference."

"Sure. I get a lot of these calls."

"We were sort of working together. He'd expressed interest in a project I had under way. Asked me to keep him informed."

"Incredible shmoozer, Charlie. No one better at spotting talent. Picking brains. He liked to go out to lunch with smart people, he always said, and listen to them talk. But he must have got tired of listening." The voice on the other end of the line, as if struck by a thought, paused. "This project," he said. "You have funding lined up?"

"Not exactly."

"Look, send me a fax. Let's see what you're up to. It's a funny time—hard to tell what'll break out next. Your name again is?"

Ian put the phone down in its cradle gently, as if laying it to sleep. Time to go, he thought.

He looked around the office. He'd have liked to consecrate the place, leave a mark of occupation, a ring of coal from his own spent campfires. But how? The desk, shorn of its papers, looked weirdly stark and exposed, like a performer without makeup. He could not think what had held him there all these months, what had made him sit still for so long.

He had failed to pin anything down. That would be his legacy. Inconclusiveness. He could not even say with any certainty that it was Howard Heflin's voice he'd heard coming from Marisa's apartment the night before and not someone else's. But maybe there were things one shouldn't try to pin down. Things best left blank. It was a less scientific way of living, a less productive way, possibly a less attractive way. But it was a way, he thought.

He carried his boxes to the door and stacked them beside it. Then, for what was to be the last time, he sat down at his computer. The monitor rose before him, darkly silent, like a formidable opponent in a game of chess. But the face he saw in the sloping screen was his own.

There was a new message from Malcolm Perle. It was night in Kerala already, but Malcolm, he remembered, liked to work at night.

> The only problem is the generators. They're always going on and off. Sometimes you're just waiting around in the dark with your dick in your hand while the insects make hash of you. Not everyone can take it. A couple of Dutchmen just went home. The place got them down. Too hot, too disorganized, not enough to do. Fact is, it's pretty basic practice around here. Lotions. Purges. Wet massage. For an

earache there's a plant in the garden that's shaped like an ear. So simple. A nice, clear, integrated system. The remedies may be two thousand years old but they've got a guy from the Wharton School of Business doing the accounts. And it works. I can't figure out if it works because they believe it works, or if they believe it works because it works. But they believe. And it works.

Last week this NIMH consultant came through, the second one in a month, and offered me a grant. All I'd have to do is study a little Sanskrit, fax in quarterly reports, advise their little subcommittee on "alternative medicine." I said I had to think about it. Told them I had a friend, though, who might be interested. Are you? Fact is, you'd be crazy to come. Sit in the dark playing with ear-shaped plants? No, don't come. It's hot and dirty and the wiring's so primitive you can't run a boombox without batteries. Don't come.

What's up with Marisa? I've sent about fifty e-mails but she never answers. Well, we were never as much of an item as people thought. A little fooling around in the staff lounge was pretty much it. The rest was in people's heads. Not that I'm excusing myself. It was a creepy thing to do. As Gillian and her lawyer keep telling me.

Want to know the real reason I packed it in? Why I flew halfway around the globe to come sweat my ass off in the dark? It wasn't Marisa, or Howard, or even Gillian and my whole fucked-up marriage. It wasn't this project or that project. It was me. It was *me* . . .

Only after the arrangements had been formatted in letters and numbers and printed up on the LaserJet did it begin to dawn on Ian that this was now, and perhaps had always been, the direction of his life. The trip before him felt all at once inevitable, a ticket he had purchased years ago but never made good on. He would make good now. Just sitting in the dark, waiting around to be summoned—for him that would be nothing new. He had been waiting around all along. Waiting for his real life, his real work, to start.

He must have got tired of listening. . . .

His head was clear. Either the Tylenol he'd taken had erased his fever or it had gone away by itself. The distinction seemed of minimal importance.

Bent over the keyboard, he finished typing out his letter of resignation to Howard Heflin, which turned out to be very short, and another letter to Marisa Chu, which turned out to be even shorter. This left only one more letter to write.

He did not know how long he had been at it when the door flung open. "I've been looking for you."

A woman occupied the doorway, lugging an overstuffed knapsack For a moment he almost failed to recognize her. Her color was gone. She wore a boxy black sweater over faded jeans and a weary, intrepid air of preoccupation, as if she'd just returned from a long sea journey where all the food was bad. "You know," she said, "you've completely ruined my life."

"I'm not sure I—"

"I should never have gotten involved in this project. *Never.* All I wanted was to finish the program fast, get my clinical license, and set up shop. But no, I open my big-assed mouth in class one day, and then the next thing I know I'm reporting here to you, and everyone's telling me how valuable I am, how I'm so spunky and direct and whatever, there's just so much I can contribute to the team, and like an idiot I actually believed you. And *now* look at me. Look what I've become."

"I'm sorry. I didn't—"

"I'm a mess! I was here all night! I've been here all night like every night this week! And now half the weekend's gone, and I haven't even showered, and I'm *still* here!" Like an irritated thoroughbred, Emily Firestone shook her handsome mane and snorted breathily through her nose. "The only even potentially good part is Howard promised me coauthor credit on his new article. If I get the data in by tomorrow, which'll take a goddamned miracle. By the way, have you seen him? He was supposed to be in early today."

"He may have been held up," Ian said.

"He's already got a commitment from *The Journal for Research on Biological Rhythms.* And you know about this conference out in San Francisco, late June? He's threatening to take me with him. He says I have this way of asking questions, it keeps him sharp." She sighed faintly. "Just my luck. I was supposed to be getting married that week. What do you think, should I go anyway?"

Ian stared at the woman, half listening. She appeared to be waiting for an answer. She was an intern on a major research project; she saw in him a senior colleague, someone to consult with, to take shape and direction from. He'd been searching for a mentor for so many years; it had never occurred to him to become one. But it was too late now.

"Mark says he doesn't care. The June wedding idea, that was completely mine in the first place. Just this once I wanted us to do the conventional thing. Like in a movie. You know, sunshine, flowers, out by the water someplace, hire some guy with a ponytail to play the cello. Corny, right? But I hate to just *cancel.*"

"There will be other conferences," Ian said.

"That's what Howard says. He's been a peach. He says if I stick with it I could be some kind of hotshot or something."

"Well, Howard's usually right about these things."

"Maybe so." Absently she adjusted one of her bangled bracelets. "But don't think that lets you off the hook. You should have warned me I was being body-snatched. It was your responsibility. Where've you been, anyway? I haven't seen you for days."

"Oh, out and about." He tried to smile.

"What's the deal with your face?" she asked. "It looks all swollen."

"I slipped in the snow."

"No kidding, it snowed?"

"Last night," he said. "It's gone now, I think."

"Jesus, this weather." She shook her head. Whatever happened to global warming, anyway? I could still be using spray deodorant for all the good it's doing."

"You might find the climate more amenable," Ian said, "in Santa Fe."

"Yeah. Santa Fe." She arched an eyebrow thoughtfully. "Well, chances are it's not going anywhere too soon. Which is good, 'cause it looks like neither am I."

"I'm sorry," he said.

"Don't be. I'm not really mad at you."

"I know that."

"Hey, what're these boxes? You switching offices?"

"Yes," he said. "Yes, I am."

"Lucky stiff. You should see the little mouse hole they've got me in. Talk about sensory deprivation."

He nodded toward the monitor. "I was just writing a letter to Howard. I'd be happy to suggest he give you this one."

"Thanks," she said, "but don't bother. Marisa, I mean Dr. Chu? She says I should hold out for a western exposure. You get to see the sunsets over Charlestown. They're supposed to be really spectacular."

"I've heard that too."

"It's the refinery emissions, she said. They enhance the colors."

"I better go ahead and finish this letter."

"Sure thing. Take care, Dr. Ogelvie. I'll see you around the halls."

All the way down to the lobby he was aware of an odd, tumbling lightness in his stomach, as though some vital organ had come unstuck. Was this freedom? he wondered. This falling sensation? This motion sickness? No wonder people were so anxious to find a cure for it, he thought.

The lobby was silent and calm, striped like a flag with morning light. Wheelchairs were clustered by the door. The security guard sat behind his console of screens, blearily unscrewing a thermos. Once in a while a gurney rolled by, pushed by white-coated orderlies, the IV ticking back and forth like a metronome. Ian stuck his foot against the door to prevent the elevator, which was already being resummoned from one of the upper floors, from closing him in again. Then he began to unload his cargo. The boxes were bulky but not heavy. It took only a minute or two to set them down near the exit that led to the street.

The automatic doors were stuck open, as if suspended in the process of a yawn. Three cabs sat idling at the curb. There appeared to be no drivers.

"Heading out?"

And there she stood beside him, clutching her shoulder bag. How long had it been? She looked like a sleeper, he thought, sunken and calm. Her eyes were clear. Her face was pale. She began to button her jacket with her long, ringless fingers.

"I know it sounds lame," he said, "but I was actually going to call you today."

She nodded, expressionless.

"I wrote you a letter instead. Just mailed it, in fact. You should get it in a couple of days."

She looked at him.

"I'm going away. Mainly it's about that. Ms. Chu will be handling my patients for a while."

She just stood there not saying anything. And yet he was glad to have run into her down here, on the ground floor. She was evidence of something, some good service he had performed. She had come to him in pain, and he had relieved it. He had put her to sleep; she in turn had woken him up. The study was over. There would be no more double blindness.

"I looked for you yesterday," she said. "In your office."

"Yesterday was crazy."

She nodded.

"What was it you wanted to talk about?"

"I can't remember," she said. "Isn't that strange? It must have had something to do with the pills."

"The pills." He hesitated, looking down at his boxes. "I should explain about the pills."

"Sure," she agreed. "Only not now, okay?"

There was a quaver in her voice. A note held, or withheld, too long. Her legs seemed unsteady. "Do you need a lift?" he asked.

"Oh damn. I'm afraid so."

"I'll have to get a cab," he said. "I don't have a car."

"I do." She jiggled her keys. The loud, tinkly discordance of their collisions made her wince. "It's out there in the lot. Two-B."

"I don't understand. I thought you said you needed a lift."

She nodded. Her eyes were everywhere. She appeared to have no idea that he had spoken.

"Give me the keys," Ian said. "I'll get it."

So he was the one who drove them home. He piled his boxes into the trunk of her small, unfamiliar Subaru, littered with Cheerios and picture books and tiny crumpled boxes of juice, and together they worked their way through the city's twisting maze, up over the gray-green Charles, where the rangy young crewmen were rowing their boats—facing backward, as they all do, to go forward—and down into Cambridge. The car was silent all the while but for the offer and receipt of directions. Left here, right at the next corner. Go straight. Past the square. The way was written out around them on the cluttered pages of the streets, in arrows and lights and a staggering multitude of signs. Stop. Go. Slow. Yield. He had only to pay attention.

26

The Green Room

SOMETIMES THAT SPRING she'd sit out on the grass with a brown-bag lunch, her face tilted toward the sky. It was the end of term. Reggae floated from the windows. Seagulls wheeled around the chapel spires. Shirtless boys stood skimming Frisbees, lazy and hovering, across the quad, while girls lay back on dorm towels with their oiled shoulders and mirrored shades, soaking in the light. No one could read. The good weather had come waltzing in like a diva at April's end, glittery, imperious, and thrust open the curtains. The days were bright, the air silken and dry as a lady's glove. Petals of apple blossom hung in the breeze. Even the few transient clouds that wandered past looked cottony and thin, timorous as dandelion puffs. You could blow them away with a breath.

Work crews were out pruning the maples, tending the lawns.

Bonnie finished her apple and rose reluctantly to her feet. Now that the academic year was drawing to a close, she found she was almost sorry to see it go. She had grown attached to the campus life, it seemed, even the tenuous, halfway version of it that adjuncting presented. Doubtless there were people who chose to live this way, ad hoc, year to year; people who were comfortable working between institutional polarities, not inside them; people for whom halfway was the whole way, the best way, the true way. Perhaps she was even one of them. It would not have surprised her.

Her grades that semester were turning out to be uncommonly tender. She would reserve all penalties for herself.

These were imposed now, after lunch, when she'd force herself to rise, to trudge across the quad with her lumpy, cumbersome book bag, and ascend the marble stairs of the library. The library, though anemically funded of late, was even more anemically utilized, so it had not been difficult to find a vacant carrel on the top floor of the stacks. To humanize the place, she'd taped up photographs of the boys, along with several postcards—Titian, Caravaggio, Piero della Francesca—from her voluminous reserves. As the afternoon progressed, light would stream in through the window, and the colors on each card would flare up briefly into prominence and then fade again, like passing scenery glimpsed from a train.

Beside her, along the dusty ledge, the husks of two green-bellied flies lay stiff on their backs. A shame, she thought: another few weeks and they might have made it.

Every so often there would be the sound of footfalls through the stacks, the approach of some errant researcher, and this would jolt her out of her work for a moment; but then the sounds would move away, and she'd be left alone again in the maze of words, the sole inhabitant of this dense, twilit city. She had thought in recent weeks to leave these towers behind; now all she wished to do was construct new ones, better or worse, she didn't care, of her own. She would finish the thesis. She would tunnel through to the other side. The knowledge gave her a kind of fighter's peace, a sense of grateful, weary submission. And yet she knew that this too, the intensity of a narrow project, the single-mindedness of it, was a drug, another prescriptive chemical for the system to crave.

Still, she reasoned, systems were fickle. They could be made to crave anything.

Her bed in dreams was thick with lovers. As if the pills still lurked in her blood, enhancing the flow. But of course that was impossible. She was operating under her own powers now. She had *always* been operating under her own powers. Like Dorothy, she had flown to Oz and back on magic slippers and never left the ground.

Regarding recent events she was almost preternaturally cool. Had she been married to someone she would have had to divorce him at once. But she was already divorced. Which meant she had to do nothing. Nothing, or everything. At times there seemed no distinction.

She might get a dog, she thought. The boys would like a dog. But there was no rush.

Two nights after her return from the hospital, she had risen from bed and padded into the bathroom to pee. She did not turn the light on; she was not fully awake; time passed, or didn't, somewhere else. The darkness in the room, at first absolute, was gradually revealed to be relative. Familiar patterns and shapes began to distinguish themselves: the low elliptical tub, the dangling shower curtain, the flat slab of the scale, the tubes and bottles on the vanity, the slim bars of soap in their ceramic dish, eroding from use. . . .

Then the pain arrived, like an envelope through a slot. She ripped it open and found a bill inside, seeking payment for some inconceivable purchase.

She didn't try to push it back. It was too late for that. She let it have its way. The rawness, the definition, were almost welcome. At least now, finally, something would be delivered.

At one point in her delirium she must have cried out, for here was Alex, poking his dark, sleepy, close-cropped head in from the hallway to find his mother lank-haired and shivering on the toilet. "Shut the door," she groaned.

"God, Mom, I was just trying to—"

"Shut the door!" She reached out and slammed it in his face.

How long did it take? A half hour, an hour. Her watch was back in the bedroom. The radiator gurgled and hissed. Her breath came in gasps. She tried not to move, to hold still. There was a considerable effort involved. The task seemed almost intellectual in nature, like pursuing an idea to its source. Odors of grime and disinfectant were rising off the tiles, filtering into her lungs. Always the two together, she thought—the problem and the solution, the itch and the scratch.

On the other side of the door she could hear Alex muttering. Poor baby. He was so used to her crying over *him* he could not believe in any other cause.

Eventually she began to fold up under the pressure, like a sheet of paper. Her head bent toward the floor. The shower curtain hung before her, white, implacable, a movie screen with no movie. She was almost tempted to fall on her knees. She had been waiting for something to believe in, something to propel her forward. Was this it?

It was a little like giving birth after all.

At last the pain began to grow reckless, to get out of control, to become, as pain so often and inevitably does, too much to bear. That was when she freaked. Breathless, frantic, she groped blindly behind her, toward the cabinet over the sink. But she must have groped too hard—the glass shelf, dislodged, lifted off its brackets and clattered against the wall; and then the whole thing came down in a jumble, the shelf, the brackets, various combs and toothbrushes, bottles of Nuprin, Afrin, Bayer, Caladryl, Cefzil, Benadryl—they rained over her head like a judgment.

After that she must have fainted. It was one of those things you understand only after it's over. When she came to she was sneezing so violently it made her whole body shudder. A flame plunged through her and splashed soundlessly into the water.

The pain was gone.

Carefully she tried to stand. Swaying in the darkness, she steadied herself against the sink and pushed down on the toilet lever. The roar of the water made her feel better. She pushed again. Then again. It was a long time before she was satisfied, before enough distance had been achieved between herself and the stringy, shapeless mass she'd glimpsed like a shadow at the bottom of the bowl; a long time waiting for it to whisk away through the pipes, to join the great underground river of chemicals and waste that ran below the houses like a cello line in a string quartet.

Afterward, she washed her face in cold water and patted it dry. She emerged to find Alex asleep on the throw rug, his hands clutched tightly between his legs. He looked like a toppled statue, she thought, handsome and white.

She kneeled at his feet.

Baby, she said, wake up.

It was a Friday afternoon, late in May. She was angled over the desk in the preschool office, writing out a tuition check for the coming month, when Larry Albeit strode in heedlessly chugging the last dregs of a Diet Coke and, in the process, almost knocked the pen out of her hand. "Bonnie!"

"Oh. Hello."

Some weeks had passed since their last meeting, and so she was prepared to find a whole new set of deleterious changes in the man. But once again he'd managed to surprise her. He wore an expensive-looking suit of solid charcoal, fashionably cut, over a crisp cream-colored shirt. His tie was blue silk. Only the knot looked familiarly askew, pulled down a few inches by nervous labor, by the day's ongoing gravity.

"Nice outfit," she said.

"Filene's Basement," he admitted, sheepish. "Couldn't squeeze into the old ones anymore."

"It's very snappy. You must cut quite the figure in the cafeteria."

"Cafeteria?" He crumpled his soda can and let fly toward the trash can.

"The elementary school? Teaching kids about ponds?"

"Yeah, that." He smiled ruefully. "Well, I fully deserve to be teased. And you're entitled more than anyone. You and Kippy. I've behaved unbelievably badly, no question."

"Forget it, Larry. It doesn't matter."

"Of course it does. What could possibly matter more than the way you behave with people?"

"I meant it doesn't matter now."

"To you, you mean."

She nodded. "To me."

"A painful, embarrassing episode for all concerned? Best to move on?"

"Something like that."

His mouth arranged itself into a crooked line. With his patchy new goatee—there was at least as much gray in it as brown—and his additional weight, he managed to look puffy and disheveled even now. The new suit, for all its tailoring, only barely contained him. "I think about you, you know. More than you'd ever believe possible."

"I heard about Kippy," she said quickly, raising the name like a shield. "I'm so sorry."

"Yes. We got your note. Elegantly written, by the way. You have no idea how awful those notes can be. How formal and depressing. But yours was lovely."

"It must be so horrible, having it come back like that. How is she doing?"

"Hanging in. Of course to her it was never really gone." He looked down at the backs of his hands. The nails were cut short. "Naturally the doctors are very hopeful. They've got several new things to try. Plus Kippy's a fighter, they say. Whatever that means."

"You're back at work then?" Bonnie asked. "You must need the benefits."

"Yeah." He was patting his coat pockets, looking for his checkbook. "They've been wonderful down at the office. Nothing like a little cancer in the family to bring out the best in people. Basically we've all agreed to view my recent sabbatical as a stress-related event."

"That seems fair."

"Oh, it is. Very fair. For all I know it's even true." He flipped open the checkbook and began to write, quickly, thoughtlessly. "Now everyone at the firm gets to worry about me, which it turns out they enjoy. I hear the secretaries whispering out in the hall. They're very somber and respectful but there's an excitement there too. I've given them a cause. Something even bigger and more invisible than the law. Of course, the beard doesn't hurt."

"I was about to say how much I like it."

"Kippy says it gives me authority. I look like a man who's emerged from a deep inner struggle, she says, hardened at the core. I don't have the heart to tell her otherwise."

"Maybe it's true."

"Nah," he said, "dream on. Like the song says, I fought the law and the law won."

He ripped out the check and stuck it into the coffee can, right inside hers.

"My sin was hubris," he said. "The oldest one in the book. I thought I was unique."

"Maybe you don't want to be unique," she offered.

"I tried, though, didn't I?" He hadn't seemed to hear her. His eyes were glowing and moist. "I went down pretty far. But guess what I found down there, at the bottom of the sea? What I saw. Little houses and towns of fish. Little fish families obeying little fish laws, sending their little fish kids to little fish preschools."

"People need laws, you told me once."

"That's right. They do. Even when the laws are senseless, which is most of the time. But, hey, what's sensible, right? What we call sensible behavior, *that* isn't sensible. It's just some weird simulation of sensible. No one knows how to live. Not one person. I thought that meant the whole project was invalid but maybe I was wrong. Maybe that's the *appeal.*"

"Your wife is ill," she said. "You have to take care of business. It's as simple as that."

"Yes." He nodded uncertainly. "Yes, of course. You must be right."

But for a moment she too felt infected by uncertainty. She almost lost track of her regrets and resolutions, almost stepped forward to embrace him. Perhaps she really did love this man, she thought, this sloppy, well-intentioned dreamer spilling out of his suit.

"Hi, folks," trilled Mia Montague, wafting by with a tray of graham crackers, orange slices, and milk. "Be with you in a sec."

"Sure thing," Larry said. Once Mia had passed from view, he put his hands into his pockets and cleared his throat. "Did I tell you?" His voice held a low note of shyness. "It looks like we're getting another kid after all."

She did not understand, but nodded as if she did.

"We've got our eye on one of those Chinese girls. Internet adoption. That's how they're being done now. They're trying to hurry it through." Eyes averted, he hurried on. "Then in July, if Kippy's doctors say it's okay, we'll fly to France for a couple of months. Ginny Stern put us on to this farmhouse in Normandy. Doesn't get dark until midnight. You live like a farmer, dawn to dusk. I see myself drinking Muscadet out in the garden, while Kippy rests and the girls go cartwheeling across the lawn."

"It sounds," Bonnie said, "like a very attainable vision."

"Hopefully." He hesitated; his eyes turned grave. "Kippy, she, um, told me what you wrote. About the baby."

"Oh." She put away her checkbook and zipped her purse.

"Jesus." His hand had begun to play around in his new beard. "It's hard to know what to say, Bonnie. A thing like this. I mean, boy, some pair, eh?"

It was not entirely clear which pair he was referring to. But she was content to take his statement philosophically.

"Have they written you, by the way? Those guys down at the hospital?"

"I got a letter," she said.

"Me too."

There was a short, measuring pause. They might have been two students discussing grades.

"A placebo," she said.

"What?"

"That's all it was. A sugar pill. A fucking M&M."

"You're joking."

"There were two groups. An experimental group and a control group. He explained the whole thing in his letter. It's what they call a double-blind experiment. No one's supposed to know who gets what. But in my case he cheated. He wanted to use me for a paper, he said. He was pressed for time, needed a fast result. So he took a little shortcut. He felt pretty bad about that."

"But you responded to the drug," Larry said. "The same way I did."

"He explained that too. There's a hormone called prolactin. The body releases it when you sleep. But also when you're pregnant, it turns out. So that might account for it. Or else," she said, "I'm just wildly suggestible. According to him it happens a lot. You have that one really great night, and then you just sort of coast." She smiled vaguely. "How do you like that? I couldn't even manage to donate myself to science right."

"You could sue," Larry pointed out.

"Good Lord, why?"

"You said it yourself: the guy violated the rules of his own study. Who knows what other rules got bent? I'd like to see some documentation on who was behind the whole thing. You've got pharmaceutical companies out there running studies on their own products. Classic conflict of interest. These unapproved substances they're bringing over from Eastern Europe—*way* under the counter, that stuff. There are even rumors of CIA involvement."

"Oh please, they've been saying that since the sixties. Besides," she said, "what in the world would we sue for?"

"The usual. Unnecessary pain and suffering. And that's just for starters."

She shook her head to get it clear.

"Who knows what's necessary," she said, "and what isn't?"

"What does *that* mean?"

But before she could say anything else, here came Mia Montague again, like a cheerful apparition, carrying an empty snack tray and her usual sweet-and-helpful air of manic efficiency. "Looking for your children?" she trilled.

Bonnie nodded. Had Mia been listening beyond the door? Did she know about the two of them? Did everyone? This must be why people have affairs, she thought. To elevate in their own minds the role they play in other people's imaginations. To feel part of a plot.

"They're in the gym. The kids in the Green Room are putting on a performance."

"Performance?" Bonnie asked.

"Oh now, shame on you. We sent home a flyer last week."

"I must have misplaced it somewhere."

"Me too," said Larry.

"Well, then," Mia said. "Come see."

*   *   *

So they filed one by one down the narrow corridor. Brownies were baking in the cooperative kitchen. The smell of chocolate followed them past the blue nap-mats, past the water tables and portable sandboxes, the construction-paper galaxies and erasable-marker rainbows, to the gym. Parents stood clustered by the open door. Bonnie recognized Ginny Stern and Alice Orkin, tilting forward, their faces lit with expectancy. Inside, the children had begun to sing.

She rose up on her tiptoes, trying to see.

"What are they doing?" Larry whispered, craning his neck beside her.

"I'm not sure."

"I hate being this far back. Follow me. I'll push us through."

"You go ahead," she said. "I'll be there in a minute."

"You sure?"

Hungrily he pressed in toward the center without waiting for an answer. His coat brushed the wall, knocking two paper stars to the floor. She bent down to get them. When she rose, Larry, as if swallowed by a whale, had disappeared. She looked around. The brownies were on their way; the performance was almost over. A voice that might have been Petey's emerged from the gym, piping and clear, bearing a message of some sort. She leaned forward, with the other late arrivals, to receive it.

ROBERT COHEN is the author of two previous novels, *The Organ Builder* and *The Here and Now.* His short fiction has appeared in *Harper's, GQ, Paris Review, Ploughshares,* and other publications. He is the winner of a Lila Wallace–Reader's Digest Writers Award, a Pushcart Prize, and the Ribalow Prize. He teaches at Middlebury College in Vermont, where he lives with his wife and sons.